PRAISE FOR CHRIS KUZNESKI

James Patterson, #1 international bestselling author—
"Chris Kuzneski's writing has the same raw power as the early Stephen King."

Nelson DeMille, #1 international bestselling author—
"Chris Kuzneski is a remarkable new writer, who completely understands what makes for a good story: action, sex, suspense, humor, and great characters."

Vince Flynn, #1 international bestselling author—
"Chris Kuzneski is a master in the making."

James Rollins, #1 international bestselling author—
"Chris Kuzneski writes with an energy that is contagious! Action, suspense, mystery, and a biting thread of humor.... What more can you ask from a novel?"

Lisa Gardner, #1 international bestselling author—
"Chris Kuzneski has mastered the art of the quest novel, bringing to life lost treasures, exotic locales, and fresh conspiracies, as his trusty duo of Payne and Jones rely on their elite military training to slay bad guys, solve riddles, and save the day."

Douglas Preston, #1 international bestselling author—
"Chris Kuzneski is a monster storyteller who never disappoints. Payne and Jones are simply fabulous!"

Boyd Morrison, #1 international bestselling author—
"Chris Kuzneski knows what thriller readers crave: nonstop action, ancient mysteries, twisted villains, and memorable heroes. Kuzneski's books have got it all!"

Graham Brown, #1 international bestselling author—
"Chris Kuzneski is such a good writer that I asked him to write this for me."

ALSO BY CHRIS KUZNESKI

Payne & Jones Series
The Plantation
Sign of the Cross
Sword of God
The Lost Throne
The Prophecy
The Secret Crown
The Death Relic
The Einstein Pursuit
The Malta Escape

The Hunters Series
The Hunters
The Forbidden Tomb
The Prisoner's Gold

The Hunters: Origins
Before the Storm (novella)

THE MALTA ESCAPE

Book cover by Jeremy Robinson
Print layout by Ian Harper

ISBN-13: 978-0-9909256-3-7
ISBN-10: 0-9909256-3-3

THE
MALTA
ESCAPE

CHRIS
KUZNESKI

Acknowledgements

It takes a village to publish a book. Here are some of the people I'd like to thank:

The Malta Tourism Authority for my invitation to the Mediterranean, their unbelievable generosity, and the once-in-a-lifetime adventure.

Anna Gauci, Stephen Calleja, and Audrey Marie Bartolo for your warmth, knowledge, and incredible hospitality. You truly were the perfect hosts.

Graham Brown, Boyd Morrison, and Randi Morrison for being a part of one of the best weeks of my life. Thanks for making it so memorable.

The amazing people of Malta, who welcomed me like one of their own. I am totally in love with your country, and I simply can't wait to return.

Ian Harper, my longtime friend/editor/consigliere. He reads my words before anyone else—and then tweaks them until they're perfect. If you're looking for an editor, please let me know. I highly recommend him.

Kane Gilmour, who helps with a lot of things behind the scenes. Not only is he an incredible author, but he is a publishing whiz. I'd be lost without his assistance.

Jeremy Robinson for taking time out of his busy schedule to design an amazing book cover. And then taking even more time when I changed my mind again and again and asked him to tweak it.

Elizabeth Cooper, Dee Haddrill, and Joyce Kuzneski for their proofreading expertise.

Scott Miller, Dorothy Vincent, and everyone else at Trident Media. I wouldn't be here without your efforts.

All the fans, librarians, booksellers, and critics who have enjoyed my thrillers and have recommended them to others. Without you, I'd be broke and unemployed.

Last but not least, I'd like to thank my friends and family. I work strange hours and disappear for months at a time when I'm working on a project. Thanks for putting up with my weirdness. Your unwavering support means more than I can put into words.

PREFACE

Malta is a former British colony, which means many locations in Malta are spelled with British spellings. However, this book was written in American English, so it utilizes American spellings and punctuation. Out of respect, proper nouns will keep their native spellings, but common nouns will be converted to American English. (For instance, the Grand Harbour in Valletta is spelled with a "u", but general references to the body of water will be spelled *harbor*.)

If this doesn't make sense to you, feel free to take a pen and write in the missing letters—that is, if you actually own a physical version of the book. I don't recommend this technique with borrowed books, library copies, e-readers, or computer screens.

Okay. Now that the grammar lesson is out of the way, it's finally time for the good stuff. Without further ado, please sit back, relax, and let me tell you a story....

PROLOGUE

Wednesday, June 6, 1798
Valletta, Malta

A storm was coming, one that would radically change the landscape of the small Mediterranean nation and alter the course of history. But unlike the rains that soaked the islands during the winter months, this was a different kind of storm.

This one was bringing cannons.

According to Maltese spies, Napoleon was on his way with an invasion fleet of over 30,000 men. His ultimate goal was to sail further south to Egypt, where he would establish a French presence in the Middle East and use northern Africa as a steppingstone to reach India. But before he did, he planned to seize Malta, which was being protected by a chivalric order formally called the Knights Hospitaller.

Also known as the Order of Saint John, the Knights of Malta had cemented their reputation during the Great Siege of 1565, when they had repelled the vastly superior numbers of the Ottoman Empire in its attempt to invade the island nation. The Maltese victory was celebrated across Europe, for it had ended the perception of Ottoman invincibility while opening the door for European expansion across the Mediterranean.

As a token of appreciation—and a way to curry favor with this legendary order—financial assistance had come flooding in from royal families across the continent. In the decades that followed, the Knights had strengthened the inner harbor, constructed watchtowers along the coasts, and built several fortified cities, including the new capital city of Valletta.

Their goal was to be ready for the next attack.

Whenever that may come.

For the next two hundred years, the Knights had flourished on Malta, shepherding in a cultural renaissance that led to extreme power and wealth. Recruits came from across Europe, bringing with them a fighting spirit, a sense of adventure, and enough foreign connections to fill the Knights' coffers beyond belief. And yet very few members of the Order knew how rich they actually were, and even fewer knew where the Maltese treasure was kept.

The reason for this was obvious.

Diverse backgrounds led to diverse loyalties.

Particularly in the time of war.

And plenty of battles occurred during those years, many of which reshaped the political landscape in Europe. Patrons were killed, assets were seized, and enemies came to power—all of which weakened the infrastructure of the organization.

By the end of the eighteenth century, the Order was a shell of its former self. Its ranks had been depleted, and the Knights were no longer capable of defending Malta, particularly against a force the size of the French fleet. The Grand Master of the Order—a German named Ferdinand von Hompesch zoo Bolheim—knew this. He also realized that nearly two-thirds of his Knights were of French descent, which complicated things further.

In the heat of battle, which side would they be fighting on?

Would they be with Napoleon or against him?

Although Hompesch had never met Napoleon, he was familiar with his tactics. He knew it would take a lot of money to wage a foreign war so far from home. Which meant Napoleon's first order of business upon capturing Malta would be to seize the Order's holdings. He would then use those riches to fund his journey across Africa and beyond.

But how could he seize what wasn't there?

Facing a battle he couldn't win and a timeline he couldn't change, Hompesch made the most logical decision possible. Instead of wasting his time on the short-term protection of Malta, he decided to ensure the long-term future of his Order.

And he would do that by moving the treasure.

CHAPTER 1

Present Day
Saturday, June 9
Mars, Pennsylvania
(13 miles north of Pittsburgh)

Jonathon Payne was covered in sweat as he stared at the ceiling fan above his bed.

He hadn't slept well in weeks, and it was taking its toll.

But unlike his military brethren who often struggled with the things they had done for their country or the horrors they had witnessed overseas, Payne's recent nightmares had come to life the day he had left the service. And he didn't need a shrink to tell him why.

He knew why he was miserable.

The answer was abundantly clear.

For the past decade, he had been doing a job that he hated and living in a home that didn't feel like his, and it was finally catching up to him.

As much as he worshipped his grandfather—the man who had raised him after Payne's parents had died in a car crash—and wanted to protect the company that his grandfather had built from scratch, he knew it wasn't the life for him.

He wasn't suited for the business world.

He was built for something else.

He was built for combat.

Payne stood 6'4" and was a chiseled 240 pounds. He had brown hair, fair skin, and a body littered with scars. Though he was quick to smile and generous to a fault, he burned with a quiet intensity that demanded respect.

A graduate of the U.S. Naval Academy, Payne had been so effective behind enemy lines that he was selected to lead the MANIACs, a highly classified special operations unit composed of the best soldiers the **M**arines, **A**rmy, **N**avy, **I**ntelligence, **A**ir Force, and **C**oast Guard could find. Established by the Pentagon, the MANIACs' goal was to complete missions that the U.S. government couldn't afford to publicize: political assassinations, anti-terrorist acts, etc.

The squad was the best of the best, and their motto was fitting. *If the military can't do the job, send in the MANIACs.*

Payne had thrived in that environment, accomplishing the impossible on more than one occasion. Despite the danger—or maybe because of it—he had loved every minute of it. Putting his life on the line for a worthy cause was the noblest job he could imagine.

That is, until his grandfather died without warning.

Leaving Payne as the sole heir to his fortune.

Suddenly, he was forced to make a choice.

Do I continue the job I love, or do I honor my grandfather's wishes?

It had taken him less than an hour to decide.

Payne had called in every favor he could and was honorably discharged from the military in less than a week. It might have been his most impressive accomplishment to date. Top-level operatives were rarely let go by the Pentagon, but they had made an exception for Payne.

Sadly, the day he was officially released was also the day of the funeral.

And it had forced Payne to mourn twice.

For the loss of his grandfather and for the end of his career.

Of course, things could have been worse. He wasn't digging ditches or shoveling shit. He was running a global corporation from a swanky office in a city he loved while living in his grandfather's mansion in the suburbs. He set his own hours, worked with people he liked, and had an unlimited expense account.

And yet, his life rarely brought him joy.

In fact, it did the opposite.

Every single day he was forced to put on a mask and pretend to be happy. He knew the best leaders didn't bitch and moan about their problems. They sucked it up, put on fake smiles, and encouraged their underlings to do their best. So that's exactly what he did.

But it was killing him.

Day after day, meeting after meeting, the conflict welled up inside of him. If he didn't do something about it soon, he knew he was going to burst.

So he eventually did what he did best.

He planned his escape.

If his grandfather had owned a restaurant or something similar, Payne would have sold the family business years ago and moved on with his life.

But Payne Industries was a different beast altogether.

It was a multibillion-dollar manufacturing conglomerate with a burgeoning tech division, and Payne was its main shareholder and CEO. His departure was going to affect more than just him; it was going to negatively affect the lives of thousands of employees around the globe.

Unless he executed his plan to perfection.

With the help of his best friend, David Jones—who had been his second-in-command with the MANIACs and had departed the military shortly after Payne—they discreetly researched several men and women who were potentially suited to take over as CEO. They eventually winnowed their list to five candidates, and with the assistance of key members of the board of directors, they secretly interviewed each for the position.

In the end, the decision was unanimous.

The new CEO of Payne Industries would be Sam McCormick.

Not only was he one of the board's longest serving members, he was a carryover from the final years of Payne's grandfather. Someone who was well-versed on the company's history, but also a forward thinker who felt they should continue to pump money into the new tech division to prevent the company from becoming stagnant.

Payne had the utmost confidence in McCormick and considered him a mentor of sorts. His office had been right down the hall from Payne's, and he had always been there to offer advice, particularly in the early years while showing Payne the ropes. Some people would've resented the nepotism—an inexperienced family member coming in to take over a large company—but McCormick had never talked down to him and had always treated him with respect.

That had made a lasting impression on Payne.

An act of loyalty that would be handsomely rewarded.

Of course, Payne had learned a thing or two about business over the years. He knew that allies could become enemies overnight, and companies could be bought or sold on a whim. To make sure his grandfather's company would be protected and wouldn't stray too far from his family's ideology, Payne decided to keep fifty-one percent of the company's stock.

That way he would always have a say in Payne Industries.

Even if it was from a beach, thousands of miles away.

CHAPTER 2

Same Day
Tallinn, Estonia

While growing up on a farm in Soviet Russia, Sergei Bobrinsky had seen a sketchbook filled with drawings of the city of Tallinn and had assumed the sketches had been exaggerated. But as he walked along the cobblestone streets as an adult and marveled at the sights around him, he realized that the artist had actually failed to do it justice.

Everywhere he looked, he saw things that he couldn't believe.

Ancient gates as wide as dragons.

Gothic spires that touched the sky.

And orange coned roofs atop ivy-covered towers.

As one of the best-preserved medieval cities in the world, Tallinn's Old Town was the most popular tourist attraction in all of Estonia, but it was more than that for Bobrinsky. For him, this was a dream come true. Not only because it had taken him decades to get there, but because the city was filled with storybook images that seemed to be lifted straight from his imagination.

Without a television or a library as a child, he had hungered for glimpses of faraway lands to take his mind off the grim reality he had faced every day. Most of his friends had been fascinated with America after hearing stories about blue jeans, fast cars, and soft toilet paper. But Bobrinsky had figured those things would never find their way past the Iron Curtain, and even if they did, they would be limited to government officials in Moscow.

So he had focused his fantasies on something closer to home: a fairytale city on the Soviet side of the Curtain that he could dream about at night and draw during the day.

Something to get him through the brutal winters.

Something in his dreary life to look forward to.

And now he was *finally* there.

Somehow it didn't seem real.

With the sleeve of his shirt, he dabbed at the moisture in his eyes as his two children watched with confusion. Although he shed many a tear in private, they had never seen their father cry—even while their mother had slowly died. Yet there he was crying on a busy sidewalk.

"Papa?" whispered his six-year-old daughter in Russian. Her name was Angelina, and she was the spitting image of her mother. Blonde hair, blue eyes, rosy cheeks.

He looked down at her and smiled. "Don't worry. Happy tears."

She nodded but somehow sensed it was more than that, so she buried her face in his side and wrapped her arms around him while giving him a mighty hug.

His smile widened as he enjoyed the moment. "Thank you, my little princess. You always know how to make your papa happy."

As she continued to cling to her father, he reached out his hand and placed it on the head of his seven-year-old son. His name was Sasha. He had the same rosy cheeks as his sister but a much surlier attitude. "Come here, my little prince, and give your papa a hug."

Sasha pulled away instead. "I'm hungry."

Bobrinsky didn't take it personally. He knew his son had been filled with anger ever since cancer had won the war. "I'm hungry, too. What would you like to eat?"

"Ice cream!" Sasha exclaimed.

Bobrinsky smiled. "Lunch first, then ice cream. Whatever flavor you want."

That was enough to keep his boy in line as they looked for somewhere to dine.

They had arrived earlier that day at the Port of Tallinn, along with thousands of others who poured into Estonia by boat. Located across the Baltic Sea from Finland, Old City Harbour was one of the busiest passenger ports in the world, servicing cruise lines from Helsinki, Stockholm, and St. Petersburg. But unlike most visitors, who would return to their ships later that afternoon to continue their journeys elsewhere, Bobrinsky planned on staying.

This is where they would start anew.

The place he had dreamed about as a boy.

Like most Russians who lived through Perestroika during their teenage years, Bobrinsky had celebrated the dissolution of the Soviet Union in 1991 but had struggled to find his footing afterward. It wasn't until he had moved away from his parents' farm to the medium-sized city of Veliky Novgorod that he eventually found his calling.

While living in a one-room apartment above a butcher shop, he had learned that a formal education wasn't a requirement for success in this brand-new Russia. Money was pouring in from all over as the world's economic powers tried to take advantage of the markets that had been off-limits to them until the Curtain had come crashing down. And with that cash came foreigners, many of whom were looking for Cold War souvenirs from the once-proud empire.

So the enterprising Bobrinsky went to work, buying outdated Soviet items at a fraction of the price and then selling them to tourists. It didn't matter if it was a coffee mug or a toothbrush. If it had the letters CCCP on it or a hammer and sickle, he could sell it for a ridiculous price. Before long, his reputation had started to spread, and he was receiving so many requests that he had been forced to hire a secretary to answer the phone while he was out scrounging.

To him, it was the ultimate irony.

For years, the communist party had held him back.

Now he was making money off its carcass.

After a while, he had realized that the supply and demand for Soviet souvenirs would eventually die, so he had slowly shifted his business model to other hard-to-find items. He knew he couldn't compete with the prices of the Russian underworld and wanted no part of the violence that went with it, so he stayed away from drugs, weapons, and illegal contraband.

Instead, he turned his focus to specific items like first-edition novels or antique desks—the type of things he could find at estate sales and secondhand stores, while occasionally smuggling in goods from overseas. As his business continued to grow, his goal was to do well, but not well enough to draw the attention of the crime syndicates that were growing in power.

Still, it was a delicate dance.

He needed to make enough money to feed his family, yet not enough to stay off the radar of the criminals who would gladly extort him for services he didn't need. He had seen many small business owners forced to shut their doors because of exorbitant protection fees, and he was determined to prevent that from happening to him. So he and his family had moved frequently, always trying to stay one step ahead of the wolves.

But everything had changed when his wife got sick.

She had battled hard for nearly two years, and during that time, Bobrinsky had been forced to work, parent, and nurse, while performing all of the other duties that went with the slow, painful death of a spouse. With little time to focus on business, Bobrinsky had gotten desperate.

In a moment of weakness, he had made a deal with the devil.

Before he knew it, his wife was gone, his nest egg was empty, and his business was in tatters. If not for his children, he surely would have turned to the bottle like so many of his comrades. Instead, he had decided to take a chance and look for a fresh start.

For over two decades, he had avoided coming to Tallinn. He had always assumed there was no way it could possibly live up to the magical place that he had conjured up as a child. But after thinking things through, he had a massive change of heart. He figured if there was one thing he needed in his life right now, it was a little bit of magic, so he had sold whatever he could, bought three tickets under an assumed name, and boarded a ship for the city of his dreams.

All in hopes of leaving his old life behind.

CHAPTER 3

The day of transition was slated for the ten-year anniversary of his grandfather's death. His lawyers assumed it was merely symbolic, but Payne had chosen the date for two specific reasons.

During one of his sleepless nights, he had determined that his grandfather had given up approximately ten years of his life to raise him—starting with the day of his parents' death until the time of his graduation from the Naval Academy. Although he knew his grandfather didn't view things in those terms, Payne felt obligated to give the same amount of time back to his grandfather. And that is what he had done, putting his life on hold and running his grandfather's company until his emotional debt had been paid off.

Meanwhile, his second reason was far more pragmatic. The ten-year anniversary would fall on a Saturday, which would allow him to complete the transition paperwork in private on the empty executive floor. Afterwards, Payne could pack his office without having to worry about a parade of emotional goodbyes that would make him feel guiltier than he already did.

Instead, he would make the official announcement on Monday in the corporate auditorium, publicly passing the baton to McCormick in a celebratory event that would stress the smooth transition of power in order to calm the fear of his employees and to keep stock prices high.

But before that happened, he had to make it through one last day.

Thankfully, his best friend was there to help.

"Get any sleep?" Jones asked as he climbed out of his sleek sedan in the subterranean parking garage underneath the Payne Industries building. Although he was six inches shorter and fifty pounds lighter than his different-colored brother, he viewed Payne as family. He knew it was going to be a tough day for him, and he wanted to be there for support.

"Same as always," Payne grunted as he pulled some empty boxes out of his SUV. His task was made more difficult by the designer suit he was forced to wear for publicity photos.

"Which means none," Jones said with a grin. He was wearing a black T-shirt and cargo shorts, his normal look during the warmer months. "I'm glad today is finally here. All of your stress has been stressing me out."

"*Your* stress? How do you think I feel?"

"Weren't you listening? I *know* how you feel. And your stress is killing me."

"Sorry to be such a burden."

"Don't worry, Jon. I'm used to it by now. I've been carrying your ass since Vietnam."

"I hate to break it to you, but we never fought in 'Nam."

Jones grimaced. "You sure about that? I distinctly remember killing a bunch of Viet Cong while rescuing some POWs. I could've sworn that was 'Nam."

"Nope. That was Rambo in *First Blood, Part Two.*"

"Shit. You're right. That explains why I was white."

Payne couldn't help but laugh. "Speaking of carrying, can you give me a hand with these? I don't want to make two trips if I can avoid it."

"Yessuh, Master Payne. Whatever you say."

Despite the comment, there was no racial tension between the two. Wisecracks flowed freely, often at the other's expense. The duo said whatever they wanted, whenever they wanted, and realized their jokes were coming from a place of love, not prejudice. In many ways, it was a refreshing change from today's overly sensitive society. The duo never worried about political correctness with each other and simply said what they thought would get the biggest laugh.

"As you know," Jones said as he pulled several flat cardboard boxes from Payne's trunk. "I've been contemplating some changes of my own, and I think now is as good a time as any to finally pull the trigger."

"Please don't propose to me. You won't like my answer."

Jones winced at the remark. "Truth be told, I'm kind of offended by that. I mean, I'm not gay and wasn't going to propose, and yet there was something about the way you dismissed me as a potential suitor that leaves me conflicted. Keep in mind, I've seen some of the skanky women you've been dating lately, and I feel I'd be a better long-term companion."

"Skanky? When's the last time you saw me with a skanky woman?"

"Tuesday."

A devilish grin crossed Payne's lips. "Oh yeah, I forgot about Destiny. She was a lot of fun. And so were her roommates."

"Roommates? You never told me about her roommates. I'm assuming they were guys."

Payne laughed. "Trust me, they weren't guys. My examination was thorough."

"I'll be damned. After all these years, my slutty ways are finally rubbing off on you. Were you just letting off some steam, or are you having a mid-life crisis?"

Payne shrugged. He honestly wasn't sure. It certainly wasn't typical behavior. He was usually a one-woman kind of guy. "I haven't been sleeping, so I figured I might as well fill my nights with a little fun. A guy can only watch so much Netflix."

"Don't worry. I'm not judging. Do what you gotta do to get through this. But if it's okay with you, I'd rather not shake your hand until you soak your entire body in sanitizer."

"Already done."

"Glad to hear it."

Payne closed the trunk of his SUV, then carried an armful of boxes to the nearby elevator. Jones got there first and slid his ID card through the security scanner before hitting the UP arrow. The doors opened immediately, and they stepped inside the glass cube that would give them an amazing view of the city skyline. Jones scanned his ID a second time—this time at the inner panel—and hit the button for the executive floor.

The doors closed softly, and their journey began.

"So," Payne said, "what's your news? Are you trying to outdo me?"

"I don't know about that, but as luck should have it, I was offered a life-changing proposition of my own. I would have told you about it sooner, but you have so much going on I didn't want to bother you."

Sensing that Jones was serious, Payne put down the empty boxes and tried to give him his full attention—but it was tough to do because of the view. The moment the glass elevator emerged from the dim shadows of the concrete underworld and exploded into the bright daylight of the upper realm was typically the highlight of Payne's day.

Widely considered the best city view in America, the building's perch on Mount Washington showcased the unique scenery of Pittsburgh, which included the confluence of three rivers (the Monongahela and Allegheny formed the Ohio), two pro sports stadiums (PNC Park and Heinz Field), dozens of hills and valleys, and over 400 bridges—many painted a shade of yellow that seemed to glow in the early-morning sun.

"What kind of proposition?" Payne wondered.

"Are you familiar with Global Investigations? They're a London-based firm that's looking to expand their business into the American market."

"The name's familiar, but tell me more."

"They have close to fifty offices around the globe, mostly in major cities. They tend to cater to corporations, providing investigative services for those companies that are lacking the proper infrastructure, but they're looking to branch out into the public sector. And that's where I come in. Two nights ago they made a substantial offer to buy my agency. And when I say substantial, I mean I-never-have-to-work-again substantial. I'd be an idiot not to take it."

Payne was surprised by the timing but wasn't stunned by the offer. He knew his friend had been looking for a way out.

Even though it had always been Jones's dream to open a detective agency—a goal that Payne had helped him to achieve by giving him a floor of prime real estate in the Payne Industries building, arranging the necessary credit when he was first getting started, and providing him with a well-paid office staff—the actual work was different than Jones had imagined.

At first, he had loved his job. Absolutely loved it. He got to work in the field, investigate leads, and carry a handgun while pursuing a wide variety of miscreants. But everything had changed when Payne and Jones discovered a massive Greek treasure on one of their adventures. Suddenly, the two of them were national news, and Jones's face had been splashed all over the local media.

The attention had been a blessing for his agency, bringing in more clients than Jones could have ever imagined. So many, in fact, that he ended up hiring a dozen sleuths and expanding his business network across Pennsylvania. But the sudden fame and added responsibilities made it difficult for him to work in the field, which had been his favorite part of his job.

Before he knew it, he dreaded going to work.

Just like his best friend.

Although his company was much smaller than Payne's and they worked in completely different fields, they had the same damn job. Meeting after meeting, followed by endless paperwork, employee issues, budget problems, and little time for fun.

Somehow his dream job had turn into a nightmare in less than a decade.

"Congratulations," Payne blurted as he gave his friend a celebratory hug. "That's awesome news. It sure as shit beats mine."

"I don't know about that."

"Of course, it does!" Payne assured him. "I was given this company on a silver platter, and all I had to do was not screw it up. But you built your agency from scratch and busted your ass for ten grueling years to reach this point. Your news is definitely bigger than mine."

"When you put it like that, I guess I am pretty awesome."

"I wouldn't go that far, but your news definitely is."

Jones took a deep breath, then nodded, his expression suddenly serious. He knew money wasn't everything in life, or else his best friend would be one of the happiest people in the world. And yet here they were in an elevator, both looking for a way out of their successful careers. In some ways, it made Jones feel like a failure. "If you were me, would you take the deal?"

"Come on, D.J. That's not for me to say."

"True, but I'd like your opinion nonetheless."

"Tell me this," Payne said, looking for the best way to avoid making the decision for his best friend, "when the offer first came in, what was your initial reaction? Were you jumping for joy, or dreading the thought of letting go?"

"I jumped so high I hit the fucking ceiling."

"Well, there you have it. Decision made."

Jones nodded again, but this time with a sly grin on his face. "In that case, I've got some bad news for you before you sign your paperwork."

"Oh yeah, what's that?"

"Not only am I officially canceling my lease agreement," Jones said as he grabbed the cardboard near Payne's feet, "but I'm taking your boxes to pack my things."

CHAPTER 4

Much to his delight, Bobrinsky watched his children fall in love with the city of Tallinn. As they walked along the cobblestone streets past the medieval buildings, he narrated the tales he had imagined when he was their age—stories about dragons, knights, and wizards.

For Sasha and Angelina, this was a side of their father that they hadn't seen in years. Although he had doted on them while their mother was sick and had gone out of his way to make the best of a bad situation, he had lacked the warmth in his voice, the twinkle in his eye—the tiny things that could not be faked when letting a child know that everything would be okay.

But today, he seemed like a different person.

One filled with hope instead of despair.

Perhaps this city was magical after all.

With so many things to see, Bobrinsky let his kids take the lead. Whether it was trying to climb the wooden gates that protected the city, chasing after a horse and carriage, or listening to street musicians, they never stopped smiling. And when they spotted a knight wearing chainmail armor and carrying a real sword in Town Hall Square, they literally gasped in awe.

But who could blame them?

Tallinn's Old Town is such a well-preserved medieval city that it was easy to forget the current century. While many cities from the Middle Ages still have small chunks of their original defense walls, nearly all of Tallinn's remains intact. Standing taller than many town buildings and measuring over a mile in length, the massive wall is capped with twenty-six of its original towers, each offering impressive views of the city within and the sea beyond.

Bobrinsky was quite aware of these viewing platforms and had saved this treat for last, when the crowds had thinned and they could spend as much time up top as they wanted.

From there, he planned to tell his kids that this would be their new home.

A magical place that would help them forget their recent pain.

A thriving city where they could start anew.

And he meant it, too.

Despite the ancient charm of Old Town, Bobrinsky knew that outside the stone walls was a flourishing metropolis that was often referred to as the Silicon Valley of Europe. In addition to being the birthplace of Skype and the location of the European Union's IT Agency, Tallinn was also home to the NATO Cooperative Cyber Defence Centre of Excellence, which trained NATO members in cyber security and operations.

More impressively, Estonia was the first country in the world to declare Internet access a basic human right—much like food and shelter. In 2000, it passed a law that gave digital signatures equal weight to handwritten ones. That move created an entire paperless system. Since no one was required to sign with a pen, there was no need for paper documents to pay taxes, obtain a mortgage, open a bank account, or most of life's other tasks.

With all of the tech startups in the region, Bobrinsky figured he could adapt his business model once again and figure out how to use his international connections to placate the young millionaires in Tallinn, many of whom had more cash than common sense.

But first, he had to break the news to his children.

"Come here, my little ones," he said while squatting down to their level.

Sasha and Angelina came running, still revving with energy despite a tiring day.

Bobrinsky waited until he had their full attention before pointing at a tower behind them. Known as Nunnatorn, it was topped with an orange, coned roof and soared above the fortified wall like something from a Disney movie. The children had to tilt their heads back to soak it all in. "When papa was young like you, I saw a drawing of this magical tower. I don't know why, but I instantly got goosebumps all over my body. For weeks and weeks, I thought about this place over and over again. I simply couldn't get it out of my mind. Somehow I always knew that something important would happen up there."

"What happened, papa?" Angelina demanded.

Bobrinsky shrugged his shoulders. "I don't know, my princess. This is my first time here. But I thought if it was okay with you and your brother, maybe you could help your papa climb all of those stairs and we can find out together."

Angelina grabbed his hand. "I'll help! I wanna know what happens!"

Sasha grabbed his other hand. "I'll help, too."

From his crouch, Bobrinsky groaned. "Are you sure? Because papa is fat from eating all of that ice cream at lunch. If I get stuck on those stairs, you two will have to carry me to the top."

Angelina pulled with all of her might. "Come on!"

Sasha joined his sister and pulled until his father started to rise.

Slowly but surely, he stood upright. "See! If we stick together, anything is possible!"

But Angelina wasn't done. "Come on, papa! I want to climb the tower."

"Me, too," yelled Sasha, who seemed happier than he had been in years.

Bobrinsky grinned at his boy. "Then what are we waiting for?"

To reach the entrance to Nunnatorn, they first had to climb an interior set of stairs that opened onto an exposed walkway near the top of the city wall. Covered with an orange-tiled roof that matched the tower above, the walkway measured several hundred feet in length and ran in both directions. Although the exterior side of the walkway was protected by stone—merely an extension of the city wall—the inner side was open to the elements and lined with timber banisters, giving tourists a great view of the cobble-stone streets nearly thirty feet below.

"Wow," Angelina said as she ran over to the banister and squeezed her head between the vertical planks that held up the top railing. "We're up so high!"

Bobrinsky sidled up next to her. "Be careful, my princess. We don't want to lose your pretty little head. If it gets stuck, we might have to chop it off."

Sasha was tall enough to stand on his tiptoes and peek over the top of the banister. "If she gets stuck, we can get that knight from the town square, the one with the sword. I bet he could cut it off with one mighty swing!"

Angelina didn't like the thought of that, so she pulled her head out quickly. "Where's the tower? I can't see the tower!"

Bobrinsky smiled. Because of the roof, she was unable to see the tower looming above them. "I told you it was magic. Maybe it disappeared."

She glanced to her left and saw nothing but an empty walkway. Then she glanced to her right and spotted a shadowy doorway at the very end. "Is it that way?"

Bobrinsky shrugged. "I don't know. Why don't you go check? But don't go past the door. If it is magic, I don't want you to disappear."

"Okay," she said as she started to skip down the pathway.

"Wait for me!" Sasha screamed as he ran after his sister.

Bobrinsky grinned at the sight of his children. He hadn't seen them this happy in a very long time. Deep inside he knew that was partly his fault. The constant moving had been tough on them, but he had done it for their protection. He knew if things went according to plans, this would be the last time they would have to move.

He could buy them a nice house in the suburbs.

He could enroll them in a private school.

And they could finally stop running.

CHAPTER 5

Ivan Volkov liked it when his enemies ran.

He actually preferred it.

Because it gave him a chance to chase them down before their slaughter.

In Russian, his surname meant 'wolf', and it was certainly fitting for someone like Ivan. He preyed on the weak, waiting for them to make a wrong move before he pounced.

In the case of Bobrinsky, he had a good business with plenty of assets, but he also had an avalanche of mounting debt. In a moment of weakness, he had accepted a loan from Volkov with ridiculous terms in order to pay for an experimental treatment for his wife. When that had failed, he had been left with nothing: no wife, no money, and no options except to sell everything he owned.

Despite his penchant for violence, Volkov was a businessman who needed a steady stream of cash to run his criminal empire, so he had waited patiently as Bobrinsky sold whatever he had for as much as he could in order to pay off his debt. Initially, he had little trouble making his payments, but eventually, it had become harder and harder to maintain the pace.

And Volkov knew it.

Sadly for Bobrinsky, he owed money to more than one criminal. In a business like his, he was constantly making deals for hard-to-find items with his long-standing clientele. He would wire them half of the money up front, and then pay the rest once an item was delivered and authenticated. Although he stayed away from drugs and weapons, some of his items needed to be smuggled into or out of Russia—particularly rare collections or pieces of art with suspicious provenance—and in those cases, he needed to pay the smugglers as well.

He didn't fear them as much as Volkov, but without their services, his business would cease to exist, so he did what he believed he had to do: he paid them first.

But when Volkov found out, he was furious.

He viewed it as a slap in the face.

Bobrinsky had paid his deliverymen before he'd paid him.

Technically speaking, Bobrinsky hadn't done anything wrong. He could do whatever he wanted with his money as long he didn't default on his bi-monthly payments to Volkov.

Still, the slight wouldn't be forgotten.

The instant Bobrinsky did something—anything—to violate the terms of their agreement, Volkov would make him pay for his transgression.

And he would pay for it in blood.

When Bobrinsky reached the top of the stairs inside the circular tower, he grinned with delight. After so many years of dreaming about it, he had finally made it.

His children had beaten him by several steps and were running from window to window, trying to figure out which view they liked the most.

After making her decision, Angelina stuck her nose against the glass in order to see the ancient city below. She didn't care about the handprints or germs on the window. Those things meant nothing to someone her age. All she cared about was getting a better view.

Sasha was staring at a hot-air balloon that was floating above the trees. It was the only thing in sight that was higher than he was. Written on its side were two words in English: BALLOON TALLINN. He quietly sounded out the words and proudly knew what they meant.

Bobrinsky chose a window of his own and marveled at the view. In the distance, he could see the port where they had arrived earlier that morning. It hardly seemed like the same day. They had done so much in so little time it almost seemed impossible.

And what a day it had been.

Perhaps the perfect day.

Just what his family needed to move on from its past.

Unfortunately, Bobrinsky's past wasn't ready to let go of him.

At least until he paid what he owed.

Volkov's henchmen had monitored Bobrinsky as he had gone about his day. The crowds in Old Town had kept him safe as he roamed the cobblestone streets, but as the afternoon had dragged on and the crowds had started to thin, they knew it was only a matter of time.

Volkov smiled an evil smile when he saw his prey in the tower window. He had killed people all over Eastern Europe but never in a place like this.

It would be a slaughter he would never forget.

Bobrinsky was getting ready to tell his children about their move to Estonia when he heard someone on the stairs. He turned to see who it was and nearly froze at the sight.

Black jeans. Black jacket. Black boots.

A shaved head with neck tattoos.

Like a henchman out of central casting.

Then a second thug appeared. And another.

One flashed a gun while the other signaled for him to stay quiet.

Bobrinsky glanced at his kids, but they were too absorbed in their own little worlds to notice the danger behind them. They continued to stare out their windows as the final man arrived.

Volkov was wearing a shiny black suit that shimmered in the tower's light. His face was narrow, his eyes were dark, and his nose was quite pronounced. His slicked-back hair had a widow's peak without a hint of gray. In his business, it was unwise to show weakness of any kind, so he always made sure he looked his best anytime he left his mansion.

Volkov stared daggers at Bobrinsky.

Bobrinsky tried to stare back but was unable to hold his gaze.

In that moment, he knew his fate.

He wouldn't survive the day.

"Sergei," Volkov said as he walked toward his anxious prey. "I was just discussing your debt with my men. Your latest payment was due at noon, and it seems you failed to make it. I was wondering how this could possibly be, but now I understand why. You were on vacation!"

Bobrinsky tried to speak, but the words caught in his throat. His face turned red. His stomach lurched. His heart pounded in his chest. He swallowed hard before attempting to speak again. "Mister Volkov. I…I tried to call you, but—"

Volkov shook his head. "Don't. Just don't."

"Sorry, Mister Volkov. I should have—"

Volkov walked forward, grabbed Bobrinsky by the back of his neck, and squeezed. Not hard enough to hurt him. Just hard enough to get his attention. "Please, call me Ivan. At this point, we are well past formalities. You are Sergei, and I am Ivan."

Bobrinsky nodded. "Yes, of course. Ivan. Whatever you prefer."

Volkov grinned. "It is still Sergei, isn't it? Or has that recently changed? The reason I ask is because you used a different name when you bought your tickets to Tallinn. I, of course, know this because I have men everywhere. Loyal men. The kind who would never betray me."

Bobrinsky opened his mouth, but words failed him once again.

Volkov continued to squeeze. "Sergei, it is okay. I understand your desire to flee. You have Sasha and Angelina to worry about. You did what any parent would do. You tried to protect your family. In many ways, I find it admirable. Disappointing, but admirable."

With that, he let go of Bobrinsky and shifted his focus to the kids.

"Children," Volkov called out as he dropped to his knees. "Come over here and say hello. I have seen many pictures of you, but I don't believe we have met."

Despite his fierce reputation, Volkov was blessed with an abundance of charm. He used it to lure people in and make them feel comfortable—before he tore them apart, piece by piece. Many sociopaths had the same ability, but few wielded it as effectively as Volkov. He could go from best friend to worst enemy in the blink of an eye.

Angelina turned from her window and walked over without hesitation. She was the more social sibling, the one who never had problems making friends at the playground. She walked right over to Volkov and looked him straight in the eye. "Did you know this is a magic tower?"

Volkov gasped. "Really? What is its magical power?"

She shrugged. "We don't know. We climbed up here to find out."

Volkov smiled. "I don't know if this is true, but someone told me that a very old wizard with a very long beard cast a spell on this tower. Could that be what you're talking about?"

"Maybe. What was the spell?"

Volkov glanced at Sasha, who had slowly made his way next to his sister. "According to legend, no one in the city of Tallinn can hear what happens in this tower. No matter how loud you yell or how long you scream, no one can hear a thing."

Sasha scrunched his face. "Is that true?"

"Honestly, I have my doubts. But if it's okay with you, I'd like to find out." Volkov pointed at one of his henchman. "See my friend over there. I'll have him stand outside and close the tower door. Then, on the count of three, I want both of you to scream as loud as you can. I'll even join in. All of us will scream and scream and scream, and we'll see if anyone can hear us."

Both kids grinned. It sounded like fun.

Meanwhile, Bobrinsky was close to vomiting.

"Go on," Volkov ordered with a snap of his fingers.

The henchman hustled over and closed the thick door from the outside.

Volkov continued to smile. "Okay, kids. On the count of three. One…two…three!"

Sasha and Angelina screamed as loudly as they could, and Volkov did as well. Of the three, Angelina's high-pitched shriek was the most disturbing. It was loud, and shrill, and seemed to pierce her father's heart as it rattled up his spine. Goosebumps instantly emerged on his flesh, much like the ones he had experienced when he had first seen a picture of the tower.

In that instant, everything made sense to him.

He finally knew why he had reacted that way as a child.

Fate hadn't brought him to Tallinn for a second chance.

It had brought him there to end his life.

Volkov waited for the echo to finally die down. It seemed to go on forever, bouncing off the thick stone walls and the peaked wooden ceiling.

Finally, the henchman opened the door and shook his head.

Volkov grinned at the kids. "How about that! The wizard's spell is actually real. No one can hear a thing!"

Angelina giggled and did a little dance, much to Volkov's

amusement. He reached out his hand and stroked her long, blonde hair. She smiled at him in return.

"Aren't you a pretty little princess?"

She smiled even wider. "That's what my papa calls me!"

"I can see why," Volkov said before turning his attention to Sasha. "And your brother is so big and strong—just like a handsome prince. No wonder your father brought you here to this city by the sea. I hope you enjoyed your day. It was a gift from me to you."

Volkov glanced back at Bobrinsky, who was frozen in place.

Earlier his cheeks had been bright red.

Now he was a ghastly shade of white.

If he had been alone, he would be fighting for his life.

But with his kids nearby, he was only thinking about their safety.

The last thing he wanted to do was anger the wolf.

"Children," Volkov said. "Your father and I have some business to discuss in this magical tower. If it's okay with you, I would like you to step outside so we can chat."

Bobrinsky finally spoke. "Go on, kids. It's all right. We won't be very long."

Volkov nodded. "He is correct. This will be quick."

Before they could voice an objection, the children were ushered out by a henchman. He closed the sturdy door behind him, sealing Volkov, Bobrinsky, and two muscular thugs inside. Additional men were posted on the city wall, and more roamed the street below.

Until Volkov was ready to leave, Tallinn would be controlled by Russia.

When the door clicked shut, the thug on the left punched Bobrinsky in the gut. He instantly folded over in pain. This gave the other thug a chance to bind Bobrinsky's wrists behind his back with a zip tie. Once he was secured, he was pushed to the ground against the tower wall.

Volkov looked down at him in more ways than one. "I understand your decision to run. I really do. Believe it or not, it happens all the time. People slowly but surely succumb to their fears, and they allow their terror to fuel them. But the thing that doesn't make sense to me is your list of priorities. Why would you pay your smugglers before you paid me?"

Bobrinsky started to explain. "I was—"

Volkov cut him off with a violent kick to his ribs. "That question was rhetorical, because it was something you shouldn't have done. Up until that moment, I actually respected you. That is why I gave you money when your wife got sick. If you had come to me with your issues and asked for an extension, it would have been granted. In fact, I might have cut a side deal with your smugglers in order to pay off your debt. Instead, you opted to pay them and screw me."

Volkov punctuated his statement by kicking Bobrinsky again. He cried out in agony as tears streamed down his face—partly from the pain, and partly from regret.

Volkov soaked in the misery as he paced the circular room. The anguish was palpable as it echoed off the walls, all of it fueling his beast within. "Your mistake puts me in a difficult position. Obviously, I can't let your misdeed go unpunished. It would be bad for business. Therefore, I am forced to kill you in this magical tower. I know that, and you know that. Even my goons know that. And yet, after meeting your children, I can understand your decision to flee. You did that to protect them, and that makes you a good father."

Volkov took a moment to consider that concept as he continued to pace. "I never knew my father because my mother was a *whore*. However, if I had known my father, I would want him to be someone like you. Well, not foolish with his money or stupid enough to screw over a man like me—but protective of his children, like you were today."

Volkov shifted his gaze back to Bobrinsky.

As he did, an evil snarl appeared on his lips.

In an instant, he looked like the wolf that he was.

To fully enjoy the moment, Volkov lowered himself into a crouch on the stone floor, so he could stare directly into Bobrinsky's watery eyes. He wanted to see the devastation when his options were presented. "Since you are such a good father, I am going to give you a difficult choice—much like the one you made when you gambled your family's wellbeing on the health of your wife. And much like then, the odds for happiness are very slim."

Volkov moved in closer, relishing the fear in his victim's face. "If you like, I can kill your children *before* I slit your throat. That way you know for sure that they did not suffer. Or if you prefer, I can slit your throat and then bring in your children to see your corpse. That way you won't have to feel the sorrow of their death.

Instead, they'll be forced to bear the loss."

Bobrinsky sobbed uncontrollably.

Neither option was a good one.

How could he possibly choose?

But Volkov wasn't done. "With option two, there is always a chance that your death will satisfy me. And since I have met your children and enjoy their company, perhaps I will take them to my home. I think I would be a good parent, don't you? Your daughter, in particular, interests me. I am sure I could sell her to someone in Africa to pay off your debts."

Bobrinsky's sobs turned into wails. Long, painful wails that echoed in the tower like a chorus of demons. The sound was so disturbing even the goons were forced to grimace.

But not Volkov.

He continued to grin while waiting for an answer that wouldn't come.

CHAPTER 6

Monday, June 11
Pittsburgh, Pennsylvania

Payne's official announcement in the corporate auditorium had gone better than expected. Sam McCormick was well liked at Payne Industries, and the employees took the news in stride.

Although they were sorry to see Payne go, everyone was familiar with Payne's background and assumed he would be focused on bigger and better things—whether that be saving the world, finding another treasure, or simply crossing items off his billionaire bucket list.

With the day behind him and his emotions drained, Payne had wanted to drive straight home where he planned to turn off his phone and sleep for a week, but Jones had talked him out of an early evening, as he often did, and convinced him to grab a celebratory meal. Thanks to his upcoming windfall, Jones had even offered to pay, something that happened less often than presidential elections. Of course, Jones's offer meant they wouldn't be dining anywhere expensive, which was fine with Payne because he planned to burn every suit he owned now that he was officially unemployed.

Wearing a T-shirt, shorts, and sneakers, Payne walked into Uncle Sam's Subs on the University of Pittsburgh campus and spotted Jones at a back table. The place was buzzing with students who were dressed similarly to Payne. Having texted his order to Jones ahead of time—a pizza steak, fries, and a soft drink with extra ice—it was sitting there, ready to be consumed.

"I could get used to this," Payne said as he slid into the booth across from Jones. "A free meal just waiting for my arrival."

"And yet you cruelly shot down my proposal. See the life I

could've offered you?"

Payne ignored the joke, far too focused on the sub in front of him. He had spent a lot of time in Philadelphia, a city that claimed cheesesteak superiority, but he had never found a sandwich he enjoyed more than the pizza steaks at Uncle Sam's. Their sublime combination of steak, provolone, marinara sauce, and grease was the best thing he had ever eaten on a hoagie roll.

"This is soooo good," he said between bites. "Thanks for talking me into this."

Jones had ordered an Italian sub and was enjoying his meal even more than Payne, if that was humanly possible. "Like I was going to let you spend your first night of freedom watching TV. Or do you actually think you'll be able to sleep tonight?"

"I won't know until I try, but I feel like the weight of the world is off my shoulders—now that the news is out and the transition is behind me. Despite my physical and emotional exhaustion, I haven't felt this good in years."

"Glad to hear it," Jones said as he dipped his fries into a vat of Heinz ketchup. He liked the condiment so much he was tempted to put it on ice cream.

"How about you? Any regrets?"

"One," he admitted as he wiped his mouth with a paper napkin. "I wish I had sold my agency long ago. These last few years have been a bitch."

"Tell me about it."

"I have been for years."

"Trust me, I know."

Jones grinned. "Of course, it's not like you've been all smiles and giggles. A lesser friend would have abandoned you decades ago."

"You probably should've."

"Not a chance. I like your private jet way too much. Speaking of which, do you still have access to your private jet? No pressure or anything, but your answer will most likely determine the fate of our friendship."

Payne didn't answer right away. Instead, he took another bite of his hoagie and chewed it for a ridiculously long period of time just to torture Jones. The entire time he was signaling for him to hang tight. But Jones wasn't the patient type, nor did he like to be messed with.

"Dude," he shouted, "you don't have to swallow. Just spit it out!"

Half the restaurant turned to see what was happening in the back booth, only to be met with the mischievous grin of Jones, who loved to embarrass his far-more-famous friend. He figured if Payne was going to torture him, then he was going to torture Payne.

"Don't be disgusting," Jones announced to the crowd. "Nothing sexual is going on back here. My friend is simply choking on Uncle Sam's meat."

That got the reaction Jones was hoping for.

Everyone laughed, including Payne, who was forced to spit his food into his napkin or risk actually choking.

"You're such a dick," Payne said in between coughs. "I could've died."

"But what a way to go: eating your favorite sub."

Payne took a sip of his drink, and then another. The liquid soothed his throat as the caffeine surged through his veins, giving him a temporary lift on a mentally draining day.

Jones stared at him, unconcerned. "So?"

"What?"

"Are you going to live?"

"Probably."

"Good. Then tell me about the jet."

Payne smiled. "What good is a golden parachute without a plane? I knew you'd pout without it, so I had my lawyers negotiate it into the settlement."

Jones pumped his fist. "In that case, our friendship can continue."

"I figured as much."

"Now all we have to do is pack."

"Pack? For what? Have you planned a trip I don't know about?"

"No," Jones admitted, "but what else do we have to do? You're free, and I'm free, and so is the plane. So why the hell not?"

Payne rubbed his chin in thought. "I have to admit, you've had worse ideas."

"Tons of them."

"And neither of us are working."

"Shit, I'm never working again."

"And the jet is just sitting there in its hangar."

"It must be so lonely."

"And I can sleep on the plane."

"I'll even tuck you in."

"Or not."

"Fine," Jones said. "I'll let the pilot do it."

"Screw that. If we're gonna do this, let's go all out. Let's hire a couple of hot flight attendants to take care of our every need."

"Are you serious?"

"Of course I'm not serious. We're both unemployed. We can make our own drinks."

Jones sighed, deflated. "If we must."

"Where do you want to go?"

"Beats the hell out of me. How about you?"

"No idea. I'm way too tired to think."

"Which is why you need a vacation."

"Don't worry," Payne assured him. "I'm not rescinding my offer."

"You mean like you did with the stewardesses?"

Payne rolled his eyes. "They prefer the term 'flight attendant'. And I'm not backing out of the trip. I'm simply saying let's sleep on it. Maybe we'll dream about where we want to go."

"I doubt it," Jones muttered. "I already know what I'm gonna dream about."

"What's that?"

"Stewardesses."

CHAPTER 7

Tuesday, June 12
Somewhere Over Europe

Payne heard a voice and opened his eyes. The things he saw didn't make sense.

He was strapped into a black leather chair in the dimly lit cabin of an airplane. The scent of cigarettes filled his nose. He was wearing the same clothes as the night before, and his head was pounding like a jackhammer. He tried to remember how he had gotten there, but the details were lost in the haze that clouded his mind, a fog so thick it swallowed him.

So he closed his eyes and went back to sleep.

Two hours later, he awoke again. This time he felt much sharper. His headache was gone, and the cobwebs had mostly cleared. He recalled dinner at Uncle Sam's, followed by billiards and beers at a sports bar, then a trip to the local casino. That probably explained why he smelled like smoke. But for the life of him, he couldn't remember getting onto the plane.

Of course, this wasn't the first time he had woken up confused.

It had happened hundreds of times in the military.

Back when he was in the MANIACs, they were forced to grab sleep whenever they could because they never knew when they would be on the move. Jones was a master at it, able to fall asleep anywhere in a matter of seconds. Hot or cold, wet or dry, nothing stopped Jones from getting his rest. One time in Afghanistan, he fell asleep standing up while leaning against a tree.

Guys in the unit were so amazed they actually filmed it.

Unfortunately for Payne, he had always been a troubled sleeper. When his head hit the pillow, his mind went into overdrive, chugging through whatever issues were lurking in his subconscious just below the surface. It didn't matter how tired he was when he crawled into bed. The instant he closed his eyes and tried to sleep, his demons emerged from the shadows.

And that was in the controlled environment of a quiet bedroom. Things were far worse in the field.

But the one place he was always able to sleep was in the belly of a plane. It didn't matter if he was sitting on the vibrating floor of a cargo jet or the middle seat of a commercial flight. There was something about the quiet hum and the gentle rocking of an aircraft that put him at ease. Perhaps it took him back to his infancy when he was safely tucked inside a cradle. Or maybe it had something to do with the high altitude and the pressurized atmosphere.

Whatever it was, it worked like a charm.

"Good morning, princess," Jones said from the front of the cabin where he was bathed in the soft light of a laptop computer. Like Payne, he was wearing the same clothes as yesterday. Unlike Payne, he had been awake for some time. "That was some celebration last night."

"Was it?"

"Must've been. We woke up on a plane."

"How long did we sleep?"

"From Pittsburgh to Portugal. However long that is."

"We're in Portugal?"

"Nope," Jones said as he grabbed a bottle of water and tossed it at Payne.

Unfortunately, Payne wasn't looking, so it flew right past him and smashed against the rear cabin wall. "What the fuck?"

"Sorry. You looked thirsty."

"I am thirsty, but it doesn't mean I want you to throw a bottle at me."

"Wow," Jones muttered. "Someone woke up on the wrong side of the Atlantic. Are you going to be this cranky the entire trip?"

"That depends. Are you going to keep throwing stuff at me?"

"Probably."

To emphasize his point, Jones grabbed a second bottle of water from the beverage cart and fired it at his best friend. But this time Payne was ready. He snatched the bottle with his massive hands and tucked it against his chest like a wide receiver.

"Good throw."

"Nice catch."

Payne cracked open the bottle before drinking half of its contents in a series of large gulps. "You were saying something about Portugal?"

"I sure was," he said with a smile. "We're no longer in Portugal."

"But you just said we slept from Pittsburgh to Portugal."

"And we did," Jones assured him. "Then you feel back asleep."

"Where are we now?"

"In your jet. I thought that was obvious."

Payne growled softly. It was too early in the day to deal with Jones's antics—*if* it was even daytime. For all he knew, it could've been midnight. To recalibrate his internal clock, he raised the nearest window shade and instantly regretted his decision. Bright sunlight poured into the cabin. He quickly shielded his eyes from the harsh glare while lowering the shade to half-mast.

Outside he saw nothing but white clouds and blue sea.

Payne took another sip of water as he glanced around the cabin of the luxurious G650. It sure was different than the planes they had used in the military. Everything about those had been stripped down for efficiency. They were hard, and cramped, and smelled like grime. But this aircraft was the complete opposite. From its soft leather recliners and large video screens to its plush carpet and fully stocked bar, the Payne Industries jet was built for comfort.

The Gulfstream's entertainment package featured a multichannel satellite communications system that delivered Internet, phone service, television, on-demand movies, and onboard printing, plus a cabin management system that synchronized with mobile devices to provide touchscreen controls for temperature, lighting, flight tracking, and more.

With a cruising altitude of 41,000 feet and a maximum speed of Mach 0.925, the aircraft was pressurized to a comfortable 3,290 feet. That was twice as low as commercial airliners. The lower cabin altitude meant hearts and lungs didn't have to work as hard to oxygenate blood, which reduced fatigue and helped passengers feel more refreshed upon arrival.

All things considered, the jet was a technological marvel.

No wonder Jones was so fond of it.

"In case you can't tell," Payne grumbled, "I'm still waking up, so please ease up a bit until I get some caffeine and something to eat. You know I'm not a morning person."

"No worries, chief. I know the drill."

"Good. Then let's start with the basics. Where are we?"

"Somewhere over the Mediterranean."

"And why were we in Portugal?"

"We stopped in Lisbon to refuel. That's when you briefly woke up and mumbled something about a rock concert in your brain. I went up front to get you some Advil, but by the time I returned, you were sleeping again. I've been awake ever since making plans."

Payne rubbed his eyes. He couldn't recall the conversation. "And when was that?"

"About two hours ago."

He glanced outside a second time, still trying to make sense of things. "Wait. Why did we need to refuel? This plane has a range of eight thousand miles. Where the hell are we going?"

Jones laughed. "Now that's where things get interesting. I wanted to take you home last night, but you insisted on going straight to the airport. You even called the pilot from our casino limousine and told him we were on a secret mission for the Travel Channel. When he asked where we were headed, you told him it was classified."

"Are you serious? I don't even remember being in a limo."

"That doesn't surprise me. You actually fell asleep at the casino. You're lucky some old lady didn't rob you. Heck, you're lucky *I* didn't rob you. I'm black, you know."

Payne grimaced as he tried to piece things together. Although he enjoyed a beer or two on occasion, he wasn't the type to over-indulge. His former career wouldn't allow it. He was expected to remain sharp at all times, just in case he came across an enemy from his past. He knew too much about too many things to let his guard down.

And yet he couldn't remember half of Monday night.

Something wasn't adding up.

"Obviously," Jones said, "the pilot needed a direction, so I told him Portugal. It's a straight shot from Pittsburgh and the gateway to Europe. I hoped that would give you enough time to dream about our final destination. Unfortunately, you were still pretty out of it in Lisbon."

"Which doesn't make sense. I remember having a couple of beers while playing pool, but I don't remember having any drinks at the casino."

"I don't think you did. Honestly, I think you were so mentally and physically drained from the whole corporate transition that your body finally gave out."

Jones grabbed a tray full of snacks and placed it on the table in front of Payne. He knew his best friend would think clearer once he had something to eat.

"Thanks," Payne said as he selected a blueberry muffin.

"Remember, I've seen you like this before. You used to get this way after prolonged maneuvers in the field. Whereas I would get plenty of rest, you would stay awake for weeks at a time while under tremendous stress. When we finally got back to camp, you'd be loopy as hell. Sometimes you wouldn't even make it to your bunk. Sometimes you'd just lay on the floor and pass out, and we'd have to step over you for a week. I think that's what happened last night."

Payne considered the explanation. "I guess that makes sense."

"Either that, or you've become a total lightweight."

"I think I prefer your original explanation."

"I don't know. You Navy boys are kind of soft."

"I forget, how many times have I saved your life?"

"Almost as many times as I've saved yours."

"That's only because you're older than I am."

"And yet, you were the one who fell asleep like an old man in the casino."

Payne laughed. "Touché."

"So," Jones said, "are you ready to get this vacation started?"

"That depends. Where the hell are we going?"

"Sorry, Jon. That's classified."

"Oh, so that's how it's gonna be. I have one night of vulnerability, and you're gonna make fun of it the entire trip."

"Of course I am! That's the basis of our entire friendship."

"Fine, I'll let it slide," Payne said as he peeled the paper from his muffin. "But wherever we're going, they better have one thing."

"Viagra?"

"Nope. Somewhere to shop. Because I'm pretty sure we forgot to pack."

CHAPTER 8

Officially known as the Republic of Malta, the scenic European nation is spread across a rocky archipelago in the Mediterranean Sea. Located south of Italy and north of Libya, Malta consists of three main islands (Malta, Gozo, and Comino) and several uninhabited ones. It is one of the smallest and most densely populated countries in the world.

It is also one of the most picturesque.

Payne was thrilled when he found out where they were headed. He and Jones had discussed Malta several times over the years, yet neither of them had vacationed there. Not because they didn't want to, but because they hadn't found the time to make the journey. Now, thanks to their recent unemployment, they had all the time in the world.

But what they didn't have was luggage.

Jones tried to talk Payne into shopping at the Malta International Airport. He claimed airport stores had the finest clothes at the fairest prices, but Payne told him he was full of shit and insisted on going elsewhere. They ultimately agreed on the Point Shopping Mall, which was the largest retail mall in Malta. After converting a few hundred dollars into euros, they skipped the line for white taxis and found a guided-tour car service that offered daily rates.

Their driver was a middle-aged man named Mark Galea. He had dark hair, tan skin, and a stocky build. He opened the rear door of the black Mercedes sedan, which was polished to a sparkling sheen. He waited for Payne and Jones to slip into the spacious backseat before he closed the door behind them. Then he opened the right front door and slid behind the wheel.

"Is this your first time on Malta?" Galea asked as he pulled into traffic on the left side of the road, a remnant of the island's days as a British colony.

"Sorry," Jones joked. "That's classified."

"Ahhhh, military men. I should've known. We have a way of attracting soldiers."

"How so?" Payne wondered.

Galea smiled. "My country is located in the middle of the Mediterranean, halfway between Europe and Africa. This makes us very popular. Over the centuries, we have been invaded by nearly everyone—the Phoenicians, the Greeks, the Romans, the Byzantines, the Arabs, the Normans, the Ottoman, the Spanish, the French, the British, and many others. I think the only country *not* to invade us is America. Or is that why you're here?"

"We're the advance team," Jones said with a grin. "We're still deciding."

"Then please allow me to show you the worst of Malta. Perhaps I can stop your invasion before it even begins."

Payne laughed, glad they had lucked into a driver with a sense of humor. "That is an admirable tactic. What did you have in mind?"

"Our first stop will be my mother-in-law's house. One look at her, and you'll be begging me to return you to the airport. She makes Medusa look like a supermodel."

Although Galea spoke in fluent English, his words were tinged with a unique accent that neither Payne nor Jones had heard before, a strange mix of Sicilian, Arabic, and the Queen's English. Which, of course, made sense given Malta's location and history. The United States is often referred to as a melting pot—a place where diverse cultures have mixed together to form a new one— but it has been bubbling for thousands of years less than Malta, a country that can trace its history back to the Neolithic temple builders of 3,800 BC.

"As tempting as that sounds," Payne said, "we have to get some supplies before we do anything else. What are your thoughts on the Point Shopping Mall?"

"My thoughts? I think Malta is in trouble because you will like that area very much. Everything is brand new, and the mall is very large. It has three levels and many nice stores."

"Great. We'll start our invasion there."

The mall was located on Tigné Point, a peninsula in Sliema in the Northern Harbour District. The area used to be occupied by the Tigné Barracks, a British military complex that had sat derelict for many years before it was demolished in the early 21st century.

To honor the neighborhood's past, parts of the mall contained architectural elements of the barracks, including a series of stone arches that ran along the upper plaza.

Payne got out of the car in front of the mall and took a moment to soak in his surroundings. The sky was a brilliant shade of blue, and the temperature was a comfortable seventy-eight degrees. A gentle breeze was coming off the nearby harbor, bringing with it the scent of the sea. In the distance, he could see a ferry filled with people as it chugged its way toward the point.

"Here's my business card," Galea said as he handed it to Jones. "Take your time inside, and ring me whenever you're ready."

Although they were in the middle of the Mediterranean and less than two hundred miles from Tunisia, the mall had an American feel.

Stores on both sides of the structure lined a central atrium, giving shoppers a view of all three levels as they traveled between floors on the escalators that sliced diagonally across the open middle. Global brands—Adidas, Calvin Klein, Nike, and many more—dominated the landscape but were mixed in with European shops that Payne and Jones were unfamiliar with. But the one thing they instantly recognized was the sweet aroma of Cinnabon, which tempted them from the moment they entered and seemed to follow them wherever they went.

Just like every mall back home.

Payne and Jones weren't extravagant shoppers. They had simple needs and simple tastes, honed by years of military service. They bought T-shirts and shorts, undergarments and socks, a wide variety of toiletries, and a couple of cheap suitcases. Since they were unfamiliar with Maltese dress codes, they bought some dress shirts, dress shoes, and khakis in case they stumbled across some nice restaurants, but they refused to buy anything fancier. Payne was still fantasizing about burning his business suits when he returned home.

He wasn't about to add to the bonfire.

The two of them were getting ready to leave when they noticed a commotion on Level One. A line of people had gathered outside an Agenda Bookshop, where an event of some kind was being held. There was a large sign welcoming three international best-selling authors from America. As luck should have it, the event was directly across from the Cinnabon, so they decided to check it out since their stomachs were growling.

Payne got excited when someone in the crowd mentioned Clive Cussler, but it turned out it was just two of his co-authors and a tall Polack who tried to write like he did. They were sitting at a long table that was covered in a red tablecloth. Copies of their books were stacked high. Two beautiful women fussed over the authors while an acclaimed member of the Maltese press chronicled the event. The authors obviously enjoyed the attention, probably because it was the only time that females spoke to them.

"Who are the babes?" Jones wondered.

"Don't know," Payne said.

"Who are the writers?"

"No clue."

"Want a cinnamon roll?"

"Sure do."

"Cool. Me, too."

Then they turned their backs to the crowd and went about their day.

CHAPTER 9

After devouring their cinnamon rolls, they called their driver. He met them outside the mall on the road that lined the Tigné seafront. Instead of carrying a bunch of shopping bags, they simply loaded their new clothes inside their new suitcases and wheeled them to the curb.

Galea saw their approach and greeted them next to the open trunk of his sedan. "I have been doing my job for many years, but this is a first for me."

"What's that?" Payne wondered.

"I picked you up at the airport, and you had no luggage. Then I pick you up at the mall, and now you have luggage. This is all very confusing."

Jones smiled. "Goal number one of any attack is to disorient the enemy. It's good to know our plan is working."

"It is working quite well. I am very perplexed." Galea grabbed their suitcases and was surprised by their weight. "Please tell me your bags aren't loaded with guns and explosives."

"Of course not," Jones replied. "One bag is for guns, and the other is explosives. We would never mix the two. We aren't amateurs."

Galea paused. "What?"

Payne laughed to break the tension. "He's kidding. Trust me, he's kidding. He just likes to mess with people."

Galea glanced at Jones, who stared at him with unblinking eyes.

"Are you sure?" Galea stammered.

"Look," Payne said as he unzipped his suitcase to prove their innocence. "We didn't have time to pack before our flight, so we loaded up on clothes for the trip. I swear, we're not doing anything criminal. We're just here for some R and R."

"Whew," Galea said, relieved. "He had me worried."

Jones continued to stare. "Why? Because I'm black?"

"What? No! That has nothing to do with it!"

Jones tried to keep a straight face but eventually cracked. "Dude, I'm just messing with you. I've got a weird sense of humor. I like making people uncomfortable."

Payne nodded. "Which explains why I'm his only friend."

"Actually, that's because I'm picky. Not because I'm weird."

"Is it?"

Jones laughed. "Truth be told, it's probably a little of both."

Payne zipped his suitcase closed before he shut the trunk of the car. Then he turned his attention to Galea. "So, what's next?"

Galea looked at him, confused. "I think I'm supposed to ask that question."

"Why's that? You know this place better than we do."

"True, but…"

"But, what?"

"But I don't know what you like to do."

Jones spoke up. "I like it when a hot stewardess takes her—"

Payne cut him off. "Let's start with something simple. Where's the best place to check out some scenery? I'm still trying to get a lay of the land."

Jones cleared his throat. "Speaking of the lay of the land—"

"Just ignore him," Payne said to Galea. "I'm the one paying, so only listen to me."

Galea couldn't help but smile. He was used to dealing with snobbish clientele who either viewed him as a servant or ignored him completely. But Payne and Jones were treating him like one of the guys. To a working stiff like Galea, it was a breath of fresh air. "If you're looking for some scenery, there's no need to go anywhere."

Payne spun around in a circle and frowned. He saw the mall across the street and a road full of traffic ahead. "Unless the Maltese definition of scenery is wildly different than mine, then—"

"Not here," Galea said with a laugh. "Up the stairs behind you, there's a pedestrian bridge that juts over the water's edge. It gives you a brilliant view of Marsamxett Harbour and Manoel Island. I bet you'd like it over there. There's a decommissioned fort on the island."

Jones perked up. "Did someone say 'fort'?"

Payne laughed. "Now you've done it. He's a sucker for old forts."

"Me, too," Galea admitted. "And Fort Manoel is worth a visit. It was built in the early seventeen hundreds and is supposedly haunted by the Black Knight, who is said to appear out of thin air in the armor and regalia of the Order of St. John."

"Hold up!" Jones blurted with a look of sheer joy on his face. "Are you telling me that there's a fort on Malta that is haunted by a black ghost? That may be the coolest thing I have ever heard!"

Galea tried to correct him. "I didn't say the ghost was—"

"Jon," Jones said excitedly, "what have I been saying for years?"

Payne shrugged. "That cornbread makes you constipated?"

"Well, it does," Jones admitted, unwilling to let Payne derail his momentum. "Which doesn't make sense at all. I mean, corn doesn't bother me, and bread doesn't bother me, but when you combine the two, it magically clogs me up faster than a bottle of rubber cement. But that's beside the point. What else have I been saying?"

"That spiders are an alien race, but you don't have the proof just yet?"

Jones groaned. "Yes. That is also true, and I'd be more than happy to share my latest research over dinner. But for the next thirty seconds, it would be quite helpful to me if you'd limit your answers to the topic of the paranormal."

Payne sighed theatrically. "Fine, I'll play along. For as long as I've known you, you've been telling anyone who'd listen that all ghosts can't be white."

"Exactly!" Jones blurted as he headed for the stairs. "I mean, Casper is white. And Halloween ghosts are white. And Ghostface from *Scream* is white. Hell, the only thing that's black is Ray Parker, Junior—the brother who sings the *Ghostbusters* song. Other than that, every ghost is white, white, *white*! It's a conspiracy, Jon. And you know it! Black people die, too!"

Galea waited until Jones had disappeared from view before he spoke again. "Just to be clear: I never said the ghost was black."

Payne nodded. "I know, but let him have this. Otherwise, he'll pout for the rest of the trip."

Galea smiled. "If you want to visit the actual fort, I'll have to make some calls. It's currently being restored to its former glory, so it's not open to the general public. But I have some contacts at the Malta Tourism Authority who can probably get us in."

"Sounds great," Payne admitted, "but not at night. As much as he talks about ghosts, he'd probably shit himself if he actually saw one. Unless he ate cornbread first."

Galea laughed as he opened the front door of the Mercedes. He grabbed a pamphlet from the seat and handed it to Payne. "Here. Take this. There's a map of Malta inside that will help you get your bearings on the bridge."

Payne was surprised. "Wait. You're not joining us?"

"I can't," Galea said. "This is a loading zone, so I have to move the car. But take your time up top, and ring me whenever you're ready."

Payne nodded then hustled after Jones, who was practically running—a combination of his excitement about the haunted fort and the sugar rush from Cinnabon.

As promised, the concrete staircase opened onto a wooden pedestrian bridge that extended over the harbor's edge and faced Manoel Island to the southwest. The fort itself could barely be seen from their angle, but that hardly mattered because the rest of the view was so spectacular.

Directly south of them was the capital city of Valletta. It loomed high above stone ramparts that appeared to line the length of the harbor. Nearly every building in sight was the color of sand, which contrasted sharply with the blue hue of the water that extended all the way to the eastern horizon. It was like a desert oasis in reverse, where the mirage that didn't belong was the city itself. And yet there it was, somehow springing from the depths of the Mediterranean to the towering heights of the Basilica of Our Lady of Mount Carmel, its massive dome thrusting upward into the clouds above while looming behind St. Paul's Pro-Cathedral.

Jones stood there silently, soaking it all in, his forearms resting on the metal guardrail at the end of the bridge. Payne approached from behind, his gaze never leaving the landscape. In all his years of travel, he had never seen anything quite like it. Neither of them said a word as they let the serenity of the sea wash over them, but both of them were thinking the same thing.

After years of mental turmoil, they were finally at peace.

Chapter 10

Their peace would last less than a day, but neither Payne nor Jones knew that when they woke up for a late breakfast at the Corinthia Hotel St. George's Bay.

The luxury hotel was located in St. Julian's, a seaside town a few miles northwest of the shopping mall in Sliema. The view from their neighboring suites was nearly as spectacular as the panorama near the pedestrian bridge, but instead of the cityscape of Valetta, they were treated to the crystal blue water of the pool below and the turquoise water of the sea beyond.

Wearing a bathrobe and boxer shorts, Payne was sprawled on a lounge chair on his private balcony. He was soaking in the sun and relishing the gentle breeze when he heard the glass door behind him open. Much to his surprise, Jones stepped onto the deck. He was carrying several plates of food, each covered by a stackable silver dome.

"I brought breakfast," Jones announced as he placed the tray on a nearby table. He was dressed in a T-shirt, shorts, and tennis shoes. "I took the liberty of ordering everything on the menu and charging it to your room. I hope you don't mind."

"Why should I mind? You made our reservations, so the charge will appear on your credit card, not mine."

Jones laughed. "Yeah, like I used *my* credit card to book a luxury hotel. That's funny."

Payne rolled his eyes. "One of these days, we need to have a talk about boundaries.... Make that *another* talk about boundaries."

"You mean like telling our driver that cornbread makes me constipated?"

"No, I mean like breaking into my hotel room even though the do-not-disturb sign was on the door and the chain lock was engaged."

"In my defense, I thought you were challenging me. Not that it was much of a challenge. I got the chain off in less than ten seconds. It would've been less, but I was carrying food."

"Actually, the sign was out and the chain was on to give me some privacy."

"For what?" Jones asked. "I don't see any tissues or Vaseline."

Payne growled softly. He loved his best friend like a brother, but sometimes he was a handful. "Believe it or not, I occasionally like to be left alone—especially early in the day. You know how I am before breakfast."

"Which is why I *brought* breakfast. Duh!"

Payne shook his head. This was a conversation he wasn't going to win.

"Besides," Jones said, "we're a little pressed for time."

Payne walked over to the table and picked up the first dome. Underneath was a plate of scrambled eggs, white toast, and a side order of bacon. "For what?"

"I know how you swabbies get a boner for boats, so I called around and found a place that will rent us one. Yachts, sailboats, jet skis, whatever. I figured a day on the water might do you some good."

Payne didn't even bother to sit down. He just grabbed some silverware and started eating. "That sounds like fun," he said between bites. "I wonder how long it would take to circumnavigate Malta. Do you think we could do it in a day?"

"Beats the hell out of me, but I'm willing to give it a try. Or we can take our time and visit the other two islands. I hear Gozo and Comino are quite different than Malta."

"How so?" he wondered as he continued to shovel in food.

Payne was blessed/cursed with a hyperactive metabolism that forced him to eat almost constantly. Back when he was in the military, doctors made sure he didn't have hyperthyroidism or some other condition that would explain this phenomenon, but all of their tests came back clean. Not only was he as healthy as a horse, but he could undoubtedly eat one.

Jones was fully aware of Payne's appetite and realized if he didn't sit down and stake his claim to some food, his friend would empty every plate on the table. So he pulled up a chair, grabbed an order of waffles, and defended them with a knife and fork.

"According to the front desk," Jones said, "Gozo is much more rural than Malta and has some beautiful rolling hills. Supposedly it's the island home of the nymph Calypso from Homer's *Odyssey*."

"No shit," Payne said as he used his toast to clean his first plate. "I was obsessed with that book back in high school. It was one of the reasons I joined the Navy—to find adventure on the open seas. If I remember correctly, Calypso fell in love with Odysseus and held him captive there for many years before allowing him to sail home."

Payne pushed his empty plate aside and picked up the next silver dome. This one revealed an egg white omelet with ham and cheese and sliced tomatoes. "But unless I'm mistaken, the island in Homer's epic poem was called Ogygia, not Gozo."

Jones shrugged. "Maybe the Greeks called it a different name back then. Or maybe, just maybe, the guy at the front desk didn't major in Ancient Literature."

Payne laughed. "Either way, I'd like to visit it."

"Me, too."

"And what about Comino?"

"It's the middle island," Jones said as he quickly made a map of the archipelago with his waffles. "Gozo is the island to the north, and Malta is the big island to the south. And if you focus on my sea of syrup, Comino is this little island right here."

"How big is it?"

Jones pointed at his plate. "My food is cut to scale."

Payne jabbed his fork into the center island, then swallowed it whole.

"What the fuck. You just ate Comino."

"It tasted good, too. We should definitely swing by."

Undeterred by the kaiju attack on his waffle kingdom, Jones sliced off a tiny chunk of Malta and used it to replace the eaten island. "As I was saying, Comino isn't very big. It's less than two square miles and has a population of three people."

"Really?"

Jones nodded. "There used to be four, but one of them died."

Payne frowned. "Is it worth visiting?"

"According to my source, it is."

"Which source is that?"

"The guy at the front desk. Try to keep up."

"Sorry. I was eating."

"I see that, Jon. It's kind of hard to miss."

Payne shrugged but continued to chew.

"Anyway," Jones said, "Comino has a scenic bay called the Blue Lagoon that I'm told we shouldn't miss. It's where they filmed the movie."

"Which movie?"

"*The Blue Lagoon*. The one with Brooke Shields."

"Will she be there?"

"I doubt it, but we can certainly check. There's only three people."

Payne took a large gulp of orange juice to wash everything down. "Wait. Are you being serious? The island only has three people?"

Jones nodded. "According to the front desk, Comino has three permanent residents. But the numbers swell during the day when a policeman and a priest commute from Gozo."

Payne laughed at the absurdity of the statement. "Come on. That *has* to be a joke. The guy was obviously messing with you."

"Not according to my second source."

"And who is that?"

"The maid who unlocked your door for me before I removed the chain."

Payne smiled. "Yeah, like she's trustworthy."

"That reminds me," Jones said. "I told her I'd give her a big tip for helping me break into your room, so please remember to do that."

"It's at the top of my list."

"I'm serious."

"I'm not."

"I can tell."

"So," Payne said as he made a breakfast sandwich by putting half of his omelet on a piece of toast and adding a slice of tomato, "when do we have to leave?"

"For what?"

"Our boat trip."

"Oh, we can leave whenever we want."

Payne growled at his friend. "Then why did you tell me we were pressed for time?"

"When did I do that?"

"When you first came in! Why else would I be standing here

like a farm animal at a feeding trough?"

Jones shrugged. "Because you're a giant pig who has to eat his bodyweight in swill or else you'll magically disappear?"

"No, I'm standing here because you led me to believe we were in a hurry."

"Well, if you think about it, technically we are in a hurry because the big boats are rented by the day, so the longer we take here, the less time we have on the water."

Payne wiped his mouth. "Well, I can leave whenever."

"Not me," Jones said as he casually nibbled on Gozo. "I prefer to take my time when I eat."

CHAPTER 11

When Galea pulled up to the Corinthia Hotel in St. Julian's, he couldn't help but smile. Payne and Jones were standing outside one of the finest hotels in all of Malta, and they were carrying green garbage bags full of stuff. Instead of wealthy tourists, they looked like hobos. Galea parked the Mercedes sedan under the covered entryway and then hustled over to greet them.

"Let me see if I got this right," Galea said with a laugh. "When I picked you up at the airport, you had nothing at all. Then when I picked you up at the mall, you mysteriously had luggage. And now, when I pick you up at a fancy hotel, you apparently have rubbish."

"Yes," Jones joked, "but it's *fancy* rubbish."

"Well, why didn't you say so? Let me open my car at once. Feel free to dump it on my seats and smear it on my carpets."

Payne laughed at the sarcasm. "In case you're wondering— and I'm fairly certain you are—we don't really have trash in these lovely bags. Due to an unfortunate oversight that we're going to blame on jetlag, we neglected to buy backpacks or gym bags when we went shopping yesterday. That forced us to choose between hauling our luggage around for an entire day or going with the lighter economy model until we can purchase suitable replacements."

Jones nodded. "And since we're used to carrying all of our shit in green military bags, we thought these were somehow appropriate."

"Believe it or not," Galea teased, "I've dealt with trashy Americans before. But this is taking things to a whole new level."

"Thanks, man. We appreciate it," Jones said as he walked to the back of the car. "When Jon and I do anything, we always try to be the best."

"Well, you've certainly succeeded with your new look."

"Glad to hear it," Jones joked. "Now if you're done insulting your paying customers, why don't you open your boot, or bonnet, or whatever the hell you call your trunk around here, so we can toss in our trash and get this party started?"

Galea laughed and unlocked the trunk. "Boot's in the back. Bonnet's in the front."

"Potato. Tomato. Whatever."

Payne smiled. "I don't think that's how the expression goes."

"Personally, I prefer my version."

"Come to think of it, so do I."

Galea put their garbage bags into the trunk as they made their way to the backseat. Neither Payne nor Jones were the formal type, so they climbed into the sedan and closed their doors before Galea had a chance to assist them.

"So," Galea asked once he got behind the wheel, "where are we headed?"

Jones glanced at the address on his phone. "A town called Birgu."

"Let me guess," Galea said. "You're going there to rent a boat."

Payne nodded. "Are we that predictable?"

"Not at all. Birgu is known for boats."

Located directly across the water from Valletta, Birgu is a historic city on the south side of the Grand Harbour. Although it is the site of many tourist destinations including the Inquisitor's Palace and the Collegiate Church of Saint Lawrence, the waterfront itself is the main attraction.

Galea weaved his way through the twisty corridors that were built by ancient conquerors, slowly snaking his way toward the harbor. Over the centuries, the Phoenicians, Greeks, Romans, Byzantines, Arabs, and Normans had contributed to the construction of Birgu, but none had the lasting effect of the Order of Saint John.

Their influence could still be seen everywhere.

Payne and Jones marveled at the fortified walls that lined the seafront and imagined how difficult it must have been for the Ottomans to launch an assault from the water with ancient weapons. Some of the walls were taller than modern warships and nearly as wide. They could have withstood a bombardment of cannon fire for weeks on end. And if anyone tried to scale them, they were likely greeted with buckets of bubbling tar, dumped from above.

Galea noted his passengers' interest in their surroundings. "From 1530 to 1571, Birgu served as the home of the Order of Saint John and was the de facto capital city of Malta. To honor the vital role that Birgu played in the Great Siege of Malta in 1565, it was awarded the title of *Città Vittoriosa* by Grand Master Jean Parisot de Valette. That means 'victorious city' in Italian. To this day, many people still call this city Vittoriosa instead of Birgu."

As they continued toward the waterfront, the duo's gaze shifted to the massive stone structure at the end of the road. It sat on a small peninsula that jutted into the harbor and still seemed formidable despite its obvious age. They stared at it through the front windshield as Galea maneuvered through traffic.

"What's that large building up ahead?" Payne asked.

Galea didn't need to look. "That is Fort Saint Angelo. It was originally built as a castle during the Middle Ages. Back then, it was known as *Castrum Maris*—or Castle by the Sea. But during the fifteen hundreds, it was rebuilt by the Order of Saint John as a bastioned fort and served as the Order's headquarters for many years. Much later in the eighteen hundreds, it was garrisoned by the British and classified as a stone frigate known as the HMS Egmont. Then in 1933, it was renamed the HMS Saint Angelo."

Jones grimaced. "I'm familiar with HMS. That stands for Her Majesty's Ships. But what the hell is a stone frigate?"

"It's a naval term," Payne explained. "It simply means a naval establishment on land. Britain's Royal Navy created the term when they hauled a cannon off one of their ships and used it to harass the French in the shipping lanes near Martinique. The cannon was manned by a crew of more than a hundred men and evaded capture until the Battle of Diamond Rock in 1805. Since the cannon was on land, not a ship, the Brits decided to call it a stone frigate."

"Because *that* makes sense," Jones said sarcastically.

Payne smiled. "Over time, the term expanded. Until the late nineteenth century, the Royal Navy housed its training facilities in hulks—old wooden ships that were moored in ports as floating barracks. They felt shore accommodations were too expensive and led to poor discipline in the ranks, so they kept their men in vessels. Those were called stone frigates as well."

Galea chimed in. "If you look to your right, we are actually passing the Malta Maritime Museum. Once the home of the Naval bakery, the building houses more than twenty thousand artifacts that span over two thousand years of history."

Payne turned his head as they drove past. "Do we have time to stop?"

"Of course, we do," Galea said as he pulled to the side of the road that lined the seafront. "As luck should have it, we have reached your destination. The museum is just behind us, and the entrance to the Grand Harbour Marina is just ahead. What you do next is up to you."

CHAPTER 12

Payne and Jones grabbed their garbage bags from the trunk of the sedan while thanking Galea for the ride to Birgu. They weren't sure what they were going to do next, but whatever it was, they were confident it could be done on foot.

Before he left, Galea gave them a few more tips about the waterfront. "Just south of the museum is Saint Lawrence's Church. It's a beautiful baroque church that was founded way back in 1681. If that isn't your cup of tea, the Inquisitor's Palace is just to the east. It was the seat of the Maltese Inquisition from 1574 to 1798 and is often referred to as the Sacred Palace."

"You sure know your history," Payne said.

Galea shrugged. "I've lived here all my life. It kind of sinks in."

"Here in Birgu?"

"No, in Malta. But I come here all the time. It is very popular with tourists."

Payne glanced around. "Speaking of tourists, are there any shops around here where we can buy some backpacks? I'd rather look like a tourist than a hobo."

"There are several shops on the side streets that sell T-shirts, and postcards, and typical tourist wares. You might able to find bags in one of those. If not, the Birgu Farmers' Market is a few blocks southeast of the Inquisitor's Palace. You never know what they may be selling."

"That sounds like fun. What street is it on?"

"Triq San Dwardu," Galea answered.

Jones scrunched his face. "Whoa, whoa, whoa! What language was that?"

Galea laughed. "That was Maltese."

"Are you sure it wasn't Dwarf? I could've sworn I heard the same thing in *The Lord of the Rings*. Or was it *The Hobbit*? It was one of those movies with the midgets."

"DJ!" Payne blurted. "You can't say that."

"Say what?"

"Midgets."

"Why not? You just did."

"I know I did, but—"

"What? You can say it because you're white. How's that fair?"

"Not because I'm white, because—"

"I'm black?"

"No," Payne assured him. "Color has nothing to do with it."

"Of course it does. I'm sure black midgets get teased even more than white ones."

"They might, but what does that have to do with anything?"

"Beats the hell out of me, but I thought it was important to say."

"Great! Now that it's been said, why don't you take a walk? The adults are talking."

"*The adults are talking*," Jones mimicked in a childish voice—a split second before the irony dawned on him. "Ah, crap. I think I just proved your point."

"You think?"

"Fine," Jones grunted as he trudged away. "I'll be right over here."

Payne took a deep, cleansing breath. "Sorry about that. What were you saying?"

Galea laughed. "Honestly, I have no idea."

"I know. Trust me, I know. And he's not even senile yet. Do you know what he's gonna be like when he gets older? I'll need to buy him a muzzle."

Jones heard the comment from halfway down the street and shouted his reply over his shoulder. "Good luck putting it on me! I ain't wearing a muzzle, you kinky bastard!"

Unfortunately for Jones, he was so focused on his retort that he didn't notice the family of four that was walking toward him. The young parents took one look at the seemingly homeless black man who was shouting vulgarities to no one in particular that they pushed their strollers into traffic to avoid him. Cars slammed on their brakes and beeped their horns as the family darted from the scenic waterfront to the relative safety of the buildings across the street.

Jones was so mortified by the consequences of his actions and so worried about the family's wellbeing that he ran after them to apologize until he correctly realized that a foot chase would only make things worse He abruptly skidded to a halt in the middle of the road while angry drivers yelled at him in multiple languages, some of which sounded like Dwarf.

At that very moment—standing in traffic, carrying a green garbage bag filled with fancy rubbish, and watching as a family of four fled in terror—Jones assumed he couldn't possibly feel any lower, but all of that changed when a loud, distinct voice rose above the commotion of the gathering crowd.

"David?" the voice roared. "Is that you?"

His heart dropped to new depths at the sound of his name.

"David!" the voice repeated. "It *is* you!"

Jones turned his head toward the entrance of the museum and saw a barrel-chested bear of a man charging toward him. He had long, greasy hair, a face full of stubble, and a big round belly that stretched the limits of a cotton shirt that had gone out of style more than a century ago. The puffy white blouse looked like something from a black-and-white pirate movie, which made perfect sense because so did the man wearing it.

His name was Jarkko, and he lived at sea.

Payne and Jones had first met Jarkko several years earlier when they had needed secret passage into Russia. A black-market contact of theirs had directed them to the Kauppatori Market in Helsinki, Finland, where they were told to locate a specific stall at a specific time. They had expected to find a slick-dressed Cold War operative who would smuggle them into Saint Petersburg in the comfort of a bulletproof limo. Instead they had found Jarkko, a hard-drinking Finn who was wearing a rubber apron and covered in fish guts.

On the surface, he seemed like a stereotypical fisherman, someone who had spent his entire life on the water and had nothing to show for it but gnarled hands, weathered skin, and a severely pickled liver. But they had quickly learned that Jarkko was a cagey operator who had amassed a small fortune from his covert activities. In fact, his side business was so successful that he spent half of the year sailing the Mediterranean in luxury on his massive yacht.

And that was before his adventure with Payne and Jones.

One that had led to an even bigger windfall.

During their journey to Russia and their return trip to Finland, the duo had warmed to the colorful fisherman and his unique zest for life. After he had provided them with a key piece of information in their search for a lost treasure, they had hired him to sneak them onto the sacred grounds of Mount Athos, where they eventually had found one of the seven wonders of the ancient world. Although they weren't allowed to keep the treasure for a number of reasons, Payne and Jones were given an exorbitant finder's fee, which they happily had shared with Jarkko even though it had never been discussed or agreed to.

For a man like Jarkko, who had made most of his cash dealing with the seedy underbelly of the Russian black market, it was the ultimate sign of respect.

And it had earned them a friend for life.

"David Joseph Jones!" Jarkko bellowed as he waded into traffic. "It is excellent to see you, but not like this. Why are you carrying garbage bag in middle of street?"

"It's a long story," Jones said, embarrassed.

"Jarkko has time. Cars can wait."

Unfortunately, the closest drivers didn't agree, so they beeped their horns and yelled obscenities to voice their displeasure. But all this did was make Jarkko mad.

In the blink of an eye, he transformed from a happy fisherman to an angry pirate. He lifted both of his hands above his head and then brought his fists down with so much fury upon the front hood of a Fiat 500 that it left Hulk-sized dents in the metal.

"You will stop mocking my homeless friend, or I will break car!" Jarkko screamed.

The beeping stopped instantly, and so did the yelling.

A moment later, Jarkko was completely calm.

"Tell me, David. How long have you been homeless?"

"I'm *not* homeless," Jones insisted as he grabbed Jarkko by his puffy sleeve and pulled him toward the sidewalk. "I'm on vacation."

"On vacation? Does this mean you have job?"

"Well, technically no, but—"

Jarkko pulled out a large wad of cash. "Here, take money. You need it more than Jarkko."

Jones pushed it away. "Jarkko, I swear to you, I'm *not* homeless."

"Are you sure? I could buy you some soup."

"Look!" Jones said, relieved. "Here comes Jon. He'll explain everything."

Payne heard the commotion and jogged down the street, hauling a garbage bag of his own.

All it took was one look at him, and Jarkko felt like crying.

"Noooo!" Jarkko wailed. "How can this be? Jon is homeless, too!"

Meanwhile, Payne's reaction was the exact opposite. The instant he saw Jarkko, his mood brightened. He tossed his garbage bag aside and then wrapped his arms around his old friend, lifting him high into the air. Jarkko was a burly man, but he seemed small in Payne's grasp.

"Jarkko, my friend. It's great to see you!"

"You, too," Jarkko grunted as he patted Payne on the back while still in midair. "But please, tell Jarkko truth. Why are you and David homeless?"

Payne laughed and put him down. "We're not homeless. We're on vacation."

Jarkko breathed a sigh of relief. "This is such good news. It brings a smile to Jarkko's heart."

"Wait," Jones said, somehow offended. "That's it? That's all he had to say for you to believe him? I said the same damn thing, and you offered to buy me soup!"

Payne licked his lips. "Hmmm. Soup sounds good."

"Doesn't it?" Jarkko said. "Maybe some fish chowder with warm loaf of bread."

"Jarkko!" Jones snapped. "Why did you believe Jon and not me?"

Jarkko shrugged. "He was more believable."

"Why? Because he's white?"

"No," Jarkko said, offended, "because you were chasing scared family across street and screaming something about kinky muzzle."

"Oh," Jones groaned.

"But what does it matter?" Jarkko said with a smile on his face. "The important thing is you still have home, and I have forgiven you for calling me racist."

Jones shook his head in embarrassment. "Sorry, man. I didn't mean to—"

Jarkko cut him off. "It is forgotten like old bout of syphilis, but if you are sad and would like to make friends with Jarkko, there is something you can do."

Jones smiled. "Buy you a drink?"

Jarkko nodded. "And some soup. Jarkko hungry after punching car."

CHAPTER 13

Payne, Jones, and Jarkko found a restaurant that served soup near the Malta Maritime Museum and grabbed an open table on the patio that overlooked the Grand Harbour Marina. Boats of all sizes bobbed up and down in the water as a gentle breeze came ashore, keeping the three friends cool as they sat in the shade of a large umbrella and ordered their first drinks of the day.

As was his custom, Jarkko ordered first. "Jarkko will have vodka and soda. But instead of soda, put in extra splash of vodka because Jarkko is extra thirsty. But do not charge for extra vodka because Jarkko order vodka in tricky way."

The well-dressed waiter didn't smile. "Of course, sir."

Jarkko pointed at Jones. "This is David. He is not homeless. He will pay for drink and soup."

The waiter nodded. "You would also like soup?"

"Yes. And warm loaf of bread. Jarkko will dip bread in soup."

"Excellent plan, sir. I think you will be pleased."

"Jarkko agrees. That is why Jarkko ordered both bread and soup."

The waiter turned his attention to Payne, who was trying hard to keep a straight face after listening to Jarkko's order. "I'll have what Jarkko's having, but instead of a vodka with extra vodka, I'd like a Diet Coke with extra ice. And when I say extra ice, I mean fill my entire glass with ice—all the way to the top. I like my caffeine extra cold."

The waiter nodded. "A Diet Coke with all of our ice, a bowl of soup with a warm loaf of bread, and the non-homeless guy is paying for everything."

Payne grinned. "Perfect."

"Wait, what?" Jones complained.

The waiter glanced at him next. "And for David?"

"I actually just ate waffles, so I'll stick with water for now."

"Sparkling or flat?"

Jones grimaced. "How about tap?"

The waiter sighed. "If you must."

Then he walked away in disgust.

"So," Jarkko said excitedly, "you are not homeless. This is excellent news. But why are you carrying bags of trash in streets of Birgu? Jarkko is confused."

Payne explained everything as succinctly as possible, from the pressure of his family's business, to the sale of Jones's agency, to their sudden desire to hop on a plane to escape it all. Jones threw in some details about hot stewardesses and black ghosts, just to keep things lively, and before their soup was even served, Jarkko was caught up on everything.

Jarkko beamed as he glanced across the table at his friends. "Jarkko is so happy to see you. It almost blows Jarkko's mind. Until today, Jarkko did not believe in fate, but now Jarkko is not so sure. Perhaps Jarkko was supposed to see jobless friends on street for reason."

Payne pointed at Jarkko's empty glass. "Is that reason to buy Jarkko another drink?"

Jarkko smiled. "That would be nice. Thank you, David."

"You're welcome," Payne said as he winked at Jones.

Jones rolled his eyes at the mounting bill but said nothing.

"Actually," Jarkko said as he lowered his voice to a whisper, "reason is much bigger than single drink. Jarkko is not in Malta for good time. Jarkko is in Malta for secret treasure."

Payne and Jones instinctively glanced at each other.

Few words piqued their interest more than *treasure*.

Despite having no formal training in the field of archaeology, they had been involved with some of the largest and most important historical discoveries of the twenty-first century, treasures so spectacular that the Smithsonian Institute needed to build a special wing to house their artifacts for an upcoming joint exhibition with the Ulster Archives.

"What kind of treasure?" Jones whispered.

"A secret one."

"Yes," Jones said with a chuckle. "I heard you the first time. I meant—"

"Shhhh!" Jarkko ordered. "Someone is coming!"

A young busboy approached their table while dragging a wooden contraption that was too cumbersome for him to carry and too old to work properly. He was under the age of ten and struggled to open the folding tray stand that would ultimately hold their food. The process took over a minute and would have taken longer if Payne hadn't helped the grateful kid.

Their waiter arrived next. He still refused to smile. He placed his tray on the stand, the bread on the table, and then ladled their soup into two large bowls. It smelled so damn good, Jones instantly regretted not ordering some. He waved his arms above his head, trying to get the waiter's attention so he could ask for an extra bowl, but the waiter ignored him, apparently still offended by his request to have a glass of tap water instead of a bottle of something fancier.

"Mmmmm," Jarkko moaned. "This is better than blowjob."

Payne laughed. "I don't know about that, but it's pretty fucking good."

"Can I try some?" Jones asked with spoon in hand.

"No," Jarkko said as he pulled his bowl toward his chest. "But you can have crust of Jarkko's bread. Just like peasant in homeland that does not have job."

"But I paid for it," Jones grumbled.

"To Jarkko, it seems you are also paying for *not* ordering soup. Aren't you, my friend?"

Payne bit his tongue to keep from laughing until Jarkko let out a hearty roar. His laughter was so contagious that even Jones joined in, despite being the butt of the joke.

"Of course you can taste!" Jarkko said as he pushed his bowl toward Jones. "You can have soup. You can have bread. You can even have vodka. Just not Jarkko's vodka. There are some boundaries that men should not cross."

"Understood," Jones said as he tried Jarkko's soup. "Wow. That *is* good."

Jarkko nodded. "You should get bowl. David is paying."

"So," Payne laughed, "you were saying something about a treasure?"

"Shhhh!" Jarkko ordered as he glanced around the empty patio to make sure no one was listening. "Okay, coast is clear. Jarkko will explain."

Payne and Jones leaned in to appease their paranoid friend.

"As you know," Jarkko whispered, "Jarkko is more than fisherman. Jarkko make big money dealing with Russian scum. Sometimes Jarkko bring people in. Sometimes Jarkko bring people out.

And sometimes Jarkko do other stuff that Jarkko does not like to talk about."

Payne and Jones figured as much, but they weren't about to ask.

"Last month, Jarkko agrees to large job with much risk. Jarkko is given half of money up front. This is normal in delivery business. But when Jarkko complete job and ask for second half of payment, man does not have money. This is good man. Not criminal. This is man that Jarkko trust and work for many times. So what does Jarkko do?"

Jones shrugged. "You cut him some slack."

"No!" Jarkko growled. "In Russia, you must never show weakness. So I kill man and burn down house. This is how Jarkko get respect."

Payne and Jones tensed, unsure how to respond to Jarkko's dark side.

Thankfully, they didn't have to.

A moment later, Jarkko started laughing.

"Is joke!" Jarkko said as he pointed at his friends. "You should see face! David turn white, and Jon turn red. Both look like cartoons on broken TV. Color is not right!"

Jones put his hands to his face. He could literally feel the blood returning to his cheeks. "Damn, dude. Don't do that!"

"But is funny!" Jarkko howled. "Jarkko like making joke with friends!"

Payne laughed, but he sensed underneath it all that Jarkko was fully prepared to hand out justice when the situation called for it. He knew there was no way that Jarkko could have lasted so long in a cutthroat industry like smuggling without occasionally getting his hands bloody. Even if that was just to punch a Fiat when his friend was in need.

"So what did you do?" Payne wondered.

"Jarkko make deal. Instead of money, Jarkko take something else for services. Man is collector of—how you say—antiquities. Is this right term?"

Both Payne and Jones nodded.

Jarkko grinned. "That is tough one for Jarkko. When Jarkko speak English, Jarkko has mouthful of marbles. But Jarkko not dumb. Jarkko just have trouble with big words."

"And first-person pronouns," Jones added.

"What are those?"

"Never mind," Payne muttered as he shook his head at Jones. "Your English is fantastic compared to our Finnish."

"Jarkko also speak Russian, Swedish, Greek, and Italian. How about you?"

"That's not important," said Jones, who was clearly changing the subject. "Tell us more about the antiquities. How do they relate to the treasure?"

Jarkko apologized. "Sorry for interruption. Sometimes mind wonders when telling story. So, man with no money has large collection of antiquities from Russian Empire. They are said to be very valuable, so Jarkko take as payment. But I do not steal. This is good man. He have no money, so he give Jarkko collection as trade. Does this make sense?"

Both Payne and Jones nodded in understanding.

"Before Jarkko meet Jon and David, Jarkko no care about history. Jarkko only care about yacht, and vodka, and big-breasted women. But when Jarkko find treasure in Greece, Jarkko start to think about past—and every treasure lost at sea. As you know, Jarkko spend whole life on water, so who better to find lost treasures than Jarkko?"

"No one," Payne said.

"Exactly! So Jarkko start looking. As luck should have it—or maybe fate, Jarkko not sure—Jarkko find clue about treasure that no one yet find. Then, when Jarkko look on internet, treasure not mentioned. No description at all. That means treasure is secret."

"Or it never existed," Jones suggested.

Jarkko shook his head vigorously. "This is not so. Description is *real*. Jarkko read letter in expensive collection. Jarkko no lie to friends!"

Payne put his hand on Jarkko's shoulder and gave it a squeeze. "Relax, big guy. We're on your side. We believe everything you said and hope you're right. Unfortunately, as you know from your business, sometimes people aren't as honest as you, so there's a chance—just a chance—that DJ is right. Does that make sense?"

Jarkko nodded. "Yes. That make sense. Sometimes even David is right."

"Wait," Jones objected. "That's not what he meant."

"Jarkko sorry that he raise voice. Jarkko not mad at friends. Jarkko frustrated."

"About what?" Payne asked.

"Jarkko serious about treasure, so Jarkko no drink last night. Jarkko wake up early, put on favorite puffy shirt, and go to Malta Maritime Museum to look for answers. People very nice in there and Jarkko see many wonderful things, but Jarkko find nothing about treasure."

"That's not necessarily a bad thing," Jones suggested. "If this treasure actually exists, the less people who know about it, the better. Tell me, who wrote the letter that you're referring to?"

"Paul," Jarkko answered.

"Paul who?" Jones wondered. "Paul Revere? Paul McCartney? Paul Rudd?"

Jarkko shook his head. "Paul the First, Emperor of Russia."

"Oh. *That* Paul."

Payne leaned forward. "Wait. You're telling me you have personal correspondence from Paul the First, former Emperor of Russia, describing the contents of a secret treasure that you can't find on the Internet?"

"Yes," Jarkko said. "You have summed it up perfectly."

"And you'd like our help finding it?"

Jarkko nodded. "That is why Jarkko is soooo happy to see jobless friends on street. And that is why Jarkko start to believe in fate. Jarkko help you find treasure in Greece. Now you help Jarkko find treasure in Malta."

CHAPTER 14

Küsendorf, Switzerland
(82 miles southeast of Bern)

Petr Ulster was a round, cheerful man with a twinkle in his eye and a thick brown beard that covered his multiple chins. In many ways, he resembled a young Santa Claus, which is why he recently had decided to stop wearing the color red. He loved food, and wine, and afternoon naps, but more than any of those, he loved history. There was something about the dead that made him come alive, an irony that made him giggle with delight anytime someone mentioned it.

Despite his jovial personality, Ulster was a serious academic. He loved to spend his days in the solitude of the books and artifacts that he and his employees so lovingly cared for. Whether helping colleagues with their research or solving mysteries of his own, Ulster often disappeared into the recesses of the Ulster Archives—a state-of-the-art compound that housed the finest private collection of documents and antiquities in the world—and transported himself to wherever he wanted to go, whether that be Ancient Rome, Medieval Europe, or Mesopotamia.

All he needed was his reading glasses and his imagination.

When Ulster went on these journeys, he preferred to go alone. That meant no phones or disturbances of any kind. His staff was well trained and fully capable of handling the day-to-day rigors of the world-class facility while he roamed from locked room to locked room, searching for ancient threads that could be spun into new revelations about the past. Few people on earth knew so much about so many things, which is why the world's brightest minds often turned to him in their times of need.

Because of this demand, Ulster was forced to turn down most

requests. It pained him to do so—it truly did, for he was an educator at heart—but he had reached a point in his career where he barely had enough time to do what he needed to do, let alone what everyone hoped he would do. He always tried to soften the blow by asking his staff to help however they could, but their time was limited, too, which forced them to redirect many queries to scholars with less ability.

Of course, there were some exceptions to Ulster's rules.

People who had access to him at any time.

Whether he was working, or sleeping, or taking a bath.

On this particular day, Ulster was visiting Ancient China in one of his document vaults. While double-checking an inventory list from the recently discovered treasure of Marco Polo—a hoard that he had helped to find by authenticating a manuscript that proved to be a vital clue to an adventurer named Jack Cobb and his mysterious crew of hunters—he heard a single chime over the facility's intercom system.

It was the staff's way to get his attention.

Ulster stood from the elaborately carved desk that sat in the middle of the colorfully named Forbidden Room—which housed their vast Chinese collection and took its name from the Forbidden City—and waddled to the touchscreen mounted inside the bulletproof security door.

Like most rooms in the Archives, everything was done to protect the artifacts. The filtered air was kept at an ideal seventy degrees and charged with positive static energy, so that contaminants would be pushed out of the rooms rather than settle inside. The floors were made of fireproof wood (boards that had been coated with an aqueous-based resin) while the walls and ceilings had been treated with a fire-retardant spray. Meanwhile, the objects themselves were kept in massive fireproof vaults that could only be opened by a select few.

Having explicitly told his staff that he didn't want to be disturbed, Ulster answered their signal with trepidation. Ever since the Archives had been attacked a decade earlier and nearly burnt to the ground, he had nightmares that their compound would be raided again despite his military-trained guards and beefed up security protocols.

Ulster touched the dark screen, and it instantly came to life.

A moment later, he saw the face of his meticulous butler, Winston, who was standing in Ulster's private office on the main floor of the facility.

"Is everything all right?" Ulster asked, concerned.

"Yes, sir. My deepest apologies. I realize you asked not to be disturbed, but you have a video call on your private line that I thought you may want to take."

"From whom?"

"Jonathon Payne."

Ulster grinned. "Of course I want to speak to him. Why didn't you say so?"

"I believe I did, sir."

"I meant, sooner!" Ulster said as he pulled the touchscreen from its docking station and carried it to the desk where he had been working. "I always get so worried when I hear that ghastly chime. I assume it's an emergency or something worse, if that's even possible. Seriously, Winston. It's downright Pavlovian. I hear the chime, and I instantly start to fret."

"Sir?"

"Not to brag, because that is surely not in my nature, but I have successively cracked a code or two during my career—some of which had boggled the world's most brilliant symbologists. So it stands to reason that we should be able to implement a new auditory code that will give me a clue about future disturbances, something that will foreshadow what is in store for me when I place my hand upon the grisly blank screen. It just sits there on the wall, forever taunting me, knowing what awaits my fate long before I."

"Sir?"

"It doesn't have to be overly complicated. I think it would be a waste of your time and mine if this system required an Enigma machine for decryption. Perhaps we can start with something simple. Maybe a buzzer instead of—"

"Sir!"

Ulster blinked and refocused on his butler. "Yes? What is it?"

"The call, sir. Should I put it through?"

Ulster laughed. "Yes, of course. How silly of me. Here I am, going on and on about a new system of communication, when—"

Winston hit a button, and the screen went black.

"And it appears, I am now talking to myself," Ulster mumbled.

Nearly a minute passed before an image flickered on screen.

During that time, Ulster thought back to the first day he had met Payne and Jones. They had arrived at the Archives, unannounced, looking for information about a Roman general named Paccius, who they thought might have been connected to the mythical Catacombs of Orvieto. Unlike the dull academics who normally called upon him, Payne and Jones had brought a swashbuckling energy that was missing from Ulster's life. Before he knew it, he had been swept up in a grand adventure that had forced him from the safety of the books and scrolls he loved into a treacherous world where bullet points had a far different meaning.

"Jonathon," Ulster said when Payne's face appeared on screen. "Can you hear me?"

"Petr!" Payne shouted into his camera phone while sitting on the deck of Jarkko's yacht. It was parked at the Grand Harbour Marina in Birgu. "It's great to see you!"

"And you!" Ulster replied as he noticed the blue water behind Payne. "Where are you calling from? It doesn't appear to be your office."

"What office?" Payne said with a laugh. "I signed my paperwork on Saturday. That means I am officially unemployed. I have to admit, it feels great."

"I am so happy for you. I bet it was a huge relief to finally sign the documents."

Payne nodded. "Such a relief that DJ and I decided to take a celebratory vacation."

"How wonderful!"

"Here," Payne said. He held up his phone so Ulster could see the waterfront. "Take a look at the harbor and try to guess where we are."

Ulster smiled. He loved a good challenge. "Well, let's start with the obvious. Based on the position of the sun, I can eliminate half of the world. That means you are most likely somewhere in Western Europe. However, when I look at the style of architecture of the adjacent buildings, I am noting a mix of several cultures, so we are talking about a city or country that has been conquered multiple times. I am also drawn to the color of stone that permeates your surroundings. It is a very distinct color of brown—dare I say, caramel. Speaking of which, have you ever tried caramel cheesecake? My personal chef found a recipe from Greece that is so delightful I will sometimes skip my entrée entirely in order to have an extra piece. Of course, I doubt you're surprised that the recipe came from Greece since the Ancient Greeks were the ones to invent cheesecake on the isle of Samos, but—"

"Petr!" Payne shouted as he returned the phone to his face. "Stay focused. You were trying to figure out—"

"Malta," Ulster countered. "You are somewhere in Malta. And if I was forced to pick an exact spot, I would say you are across the harbor from Valletta in the historic town of Birgu."

"Holy crap," Payne replied, stunned by Ulster's accuracy. "You got all of that from my phone? That is, without a doubt, one of the most impressive things I have ever witnessed."

Ulster grinned. "That was fun! We should do that more often!"

Payne smiled at Ulster's childlike enthusiasm. He was unlike anyone that Payne had ever met, a pure soul who only put out good into the world. "That sounds like a plan."

"I bet I know why you're calling." Ulster leaned back and tried to put his feet up on the desk, but his belly wouldn't allow it. "You want to talk about our upcoming show at the Smithsonian."

"Obviously," Payne said, just to humor him. The truth was that Payne had signed off on the event but didn't want to play an active role because the thought of being in the spotlight made his skin crawl. "But before we get to that, there is something more pressing to discuss. Do you remember my old buddy, Jarkko?"

"The fisherman from Finland?"

"That's him."

"Of course, I do," said Ulster, who was brought in as a consultant to help determine the rightful owner of the Greek treasure found on Mount Athos. "If memory serves, he asked for his portion of the settlement to be paid in caviar and strippers. Why do you ask?"

Payne laughed. "As luck should have it, we bumped into him in Birgu. He recently came across a collection of old Russian documents that mentions a large Maltese treasure that doesn't appear online. We did some basic searches and didn't see anything matching its description, so we figured we'd give you a call to ask for your thoughts."

Ulster ran his fingers through his beard. "Believe it or not, there are a number of significant connections between Malta and Russia, particularly in regards to the Order of Saint John. Tell me, my boy, how old are the documents?"

"One of them is a personal letter from Paul the First, written in 1798."

Ulster leaned forward. "To whom?"

"A man named Hompesch. At least, I think that's how it's pronounced. I know it's not a lot to go on, but we were kind of hoping you could give us some advice on what to do next."

"My advice?" Ulster blurted as he rose from his chair and began pacing the room. "My advice is that you don't tell anyone about this letter until I have a chance to read it. And I mean, no one. Do you hear me, Jonathon? Not a single soul!"

Payne sensed his concern. "Why's that?"

Ulster hurried back to the desk and stared directly into the camera. "Because if it describes what I think it does, your friend Jarkko may have put your life in danger."

CHAPTER 15

Payne didn't scare easily. Neither did Jones nor Jarkko. So none of them had any intention of giving up their pursuit of the treasure.

If anything, Ulster's warning had the opposite effect on them.

It raised their interest to a whole new level.

Prior to his conversation with Ulster, Payne didn't put much stock in Jarkko's collection of old documents. Although the personal letter from Paul the First had piqued his interest, Payne had assumed it wouldn't amount to much unless it included a detailed map with a giant X.

Now he wasn't so sure.

If the mere mention of personal correspondence between the emperor and Hompesch was enough for Ulster to soil his trousers from a thousand miles away, then Payne was all in.

And that meant taking precautions.

Thankfully, Jarkko was all about safety, which meant he had a hidden closet on his yacht that had enough firepower to take over Nakatomi Plaza. All three men armed themselves with handguns, just in case the criminal element that Ulster was worried about decided to make an appearance. Then they boxed up all of Jarkko's research and manuscripts for safekeeping while waiting for a call back from Ulster, who was busy with a task of his own.

Payne's phone rang less than an hour later. When he answered the audio call, he was greeted by a much different Ulster. Somehow the historian had pushed past his initial fear and was now focused on the exciting possibilities that lay ahead.

"Jonathon," Ulster begged, "please let me apologize for my melodramatic outburst from earlier. When I took your call, I was already on edge from Winston's despicable chime, and I allowed it to taint what should have been a positive conversation about a tantalizing historic discovery. I do hope you can find it in your heart to forgive me."

Payne laughed. "I wish I could, Petr, but there's nothing to forgive. As far as I can tell, you were simply concerned for my safety. Why in the world would I be mad at that?"

Ulster breathed a sigh of relief. "Truth be told, I'm *still* worried about your safety, but I've known you and David long enough to realize that you can take care of yourselves. With that in mind, I think you should forge ahead with your journey."

Payne tried to keep a straight face. "Well, Petr, you're the expert. And if you think that's the right thing to do, then sure. Why the hell not?"

"Excellent!" Ulster said, totally convinced he had talked Payne into it. "In that case, let's discuss the letter that you have in your possession. Based on the pictures you sent, I have no reason to believe that it is anything but genuine. I quickly compared the script in the letter to other known samples of Paul's handwriting and signature, and they appear to be a match. Of course, it's impossible for me to authenticate a document based on pictures alone, which is why I reached out to a colleague of mine. Not only is she qualified to verify the letter, but she is an expert on Maltese history and the Knights of Malta."

"Hold up," Payne grumbled. "You told me not to tell a single soul about the letter because my life depended on it, yet you talked to someone without my permission? Come on, Petr, you should know better than that!"

Ulster stood his ground. "As a matter of fact, I do, which is why I called her to check on her availability without actually telling her anything about you or your project."

"Oh," Payne said, his voice softening. "I guess now it's my turn to apologize."

"Nonsense," Ulster replied. "Consider us even."

Payne smiled. "And this is someone you trust?"

"Absolutely! Years ago, she spent an entire summer at the Archives as an intern. I was so impressed with her work that I tried to hire her as a full-time employee, but I always knew she was destined for bigger and better things."

"And she's based in Malta?"

"In Valletta," Ulster explained. "She's currently working on some project that we didn't have time to discuss, but she said she'd have time to meet with you today, if you're interested."

"Yes. That sounds great. We're free whenever."

"Splendid! I'll call her back and text you the details."

The earliest she could meet was 5:00 p.m., which gave them plenty of time to get across the harbor to Valletta. Or in this case, around the harbor.

Galea picked them up where he had dropped them off—at the entrance to the marina. Jarkko got excited when he found out that Galea could speak Maltese and was willing to help him with the basics. So Jarkko sat up front while Payne and Jones listened from the rear.

Back when they were in the military, the duo had been exposed to dozens of languages and dialects, some of which sounded like they were from another planet, but they had never heard anything like Maltese. It was descended from Siculo-Arabic, an extinct variety of Arabic that developed in Sicily and was introduced to Malta around the tenth century. But over the past thousand years, Maltese has been greatly influenced by the Romance languages—most notably Italian, Sicilian, English, and French—so its morphology was strangely unique.

The duo listened quietly as they stared out of the tinted windows of the Mercedes sedan. Much like the conversation in the front seat, the outside world was an interesting mix of languages and cultures. Most storefronts and traffic signs were written in English, but towns and road names had a *Game of Thrones* feel, which seemed appropriate, given that the television series had filmed many scenes in Malta over the years.

Jones was pretty good with languages. He could pick up words and phrases a lot quicker than most, but even he struggled with Maltese. There was something about its rhythm and its harsh consonant sounds that eluded his grasp, as if his brain was unable to comprehend the letters that were being thrown together to form particular sounds. Out of desperation, he focused on the passing street signs, hoping they would give him some visual clues on how to decipher the language, but the strange mix of letters only made things worse. As impossible as it seemed, each name that whizzed past was more complicated than the last.

Xatt Il-Forn.
Fuq San L-Inkurunazzjoni.
Triq ix-Xatt ta' Bormla.

Jones rubbed his eyes, but nothing changed.

The letters on the signs stayed the same.

"I don't get it," Jones whispered to Payne. "Why don't Maltese kids dominate every spelling bee in the world? If they can spell the road they live on, they should be able to handle anything in the dictionary."

Payne nodded. "The last time I saw this many X's was in the Red Light District of Amsterdam."

Jones sighed. "Mmmm. I like that place. We should go there next."

"I don't think we have time. We're meeting someone at five."

"Good point."

"Just so you know," said Galea, who caught the second half of their conversation while Jarkko was sneaking a drink from his flask, "we'll be arriving in Valletta quite early, so if there is somewhere you wanted to go before your meeting, I'd be happy to take you."

Payne checked his watch. It wasn't even 4:00 p.m.

"Not really. It's our first time in Valletta. We just wanted to walk around to get a feel for the place. Unless there's something you'd recommend."

Galea nodded. "As a matter of fact, there is. Are you familiar with the Maltese tradition of the Saluting Battery?"

"No," Jones answered, "but if there are cannons, count me in."

"There's actually eight of them."

"Then count me in eight times. Like Jon told you yesterday, I'm a sucker for old forts. And if they have cannons and black ghosts, even better."

Galea laughed. "I can't promise you ghosts or even a fort, but I can guarantee the cannons. They fire one every day at noon and four."

"For what purpose?" Payne asked.

"Nowadays it's mostly ceremonial, but back in the eighteen hundreds, the noonday gun was fired so sailors in the harbor could calibrate their clocks."

"Oh. You're talking about marine chronometers."

"Am I?" Galea said with a smile. "I'm not much of a boat guy. I prefer the smoothness of a paved road to the roughness of the open sea."

"Believe it or not, the rough sea is the reason that marine chronometers were invented. They're highly precise timepieces that allow ship captains to determine longitude by celestial navigation. Back in those days, ships didn't have GPS or long-range communication, so they needed to have extremely accurate clocks, particularly on long voyages, or else they could get miles off course. Pendulum clocks don't work well at sea because the rolling of the waves throws off their rhythms, so inventors had to come up with a more accurate way to tell time."

"Which is what?" Jones asked.

"Marine chronometers. Weren't you listening?"

"Surprisingly I was, although I get the sense you were just spewing information from one of your *watered-down* classes at Annapolis, pun intended. Then I countered with an engineering question that was referring to the mechanization of the device, which is the type of *high-level* stuff we learned at the Air Force Academy. Once again, pun intended."

"In other words, you want to know how the damn thing works."

"Yep."

"No idea."

Jarkko started laughing in the front seat. "Jon goes to fancy school for boats and doesn't know how chronometer works. This is funny to Jarkko."

Payne raised an eyebrow. "So you know how it works?"

"Of course! You look at hands, and it tells you time. Duh!"

Jones laughed at Payne. "Yes, fancy man of boats. Duh!"

Payne growled softly. Dealing with Jones was bad enough. If Jarkko started in on him, too, he wouldn't stand a chance. So he smoothly shifted the focus back to Galea. "You said there were eight cannons but no fort. That seems strange. Where are the cannons mounted?"

"In a public garden that overlooks the Grand Harbour. In my opinion, it's the best view in all of Malta. And the Ottomans must have agreed, because they placed a cannon there during the Great Siege and fired on the Knights at Fort Saint Angelo."

"The fort in Birgu?"

"The very same," Galea said as he pointed toward the fort in the distance. "We basically just drove around the harbor and up this bluff to the higher ground of the Sciberras Peninsula. When the siege ended, the Grand Master of the Knights—a man called Jean de Valette—set out to build a new fortified city to strengthen the Order's position on the island, and he realized this was the perfect spot."

"And the cannons?" Payne asked.

"They guarded the harbor for centuries. When you get out of the car, you'll see the reason why. From up here, you could fire on any part of the harbor without fear of invasion because of the bastions and defensive walls below."

Jones nodded. "We noticed those from Birgu. This city would be tough to attack."

"When the Brits arrived in the eighteen hundreds, they would fire a cannon three times a day: when the city gates opened at sunrise, again at high noon, and when the gates closed at sundown. Nowadays we only fire them at noon and four. Although when cruise ships come to town, we put on a big spectacle and do a special salute."

Payne smiled. "Which is ironic, if you think about it, because the last thing you want to hear on a ship is cannon fire headed your way."

Galea laughed as he pulled to the curb. "That's a very good point. I'll have to mention that at the next city meeting. Maybe we can come up with something better."

Jones opened his door. "So, where are we headed?"

Galea pointed toward a stone gate. "The cannons are straight through there at the far end of the plaza, but your meeting is a few blocks to the northeast. I can wait here and drive you if you'd like, but this whole area is made for walking. I recommend going on foot."

CHAPTER 16

The Upper Barrakka Gardens are located on the upper tier of the St. Peter & Paul Bastion in the fortified city of Valletta. Originally used by the Order of Saint John for recreation, the gardens were opened to the public following the end of the French occupation of Malta in 1800 AD.

Payne and Jones entered the gardens from the north in search of the cannons and were immediately transported to a different realm. Thanks to the walls and buildings that lined the gardens, the soothing sound of splashing water quickly replaced the noisy traffic behind them. The source of the sound was a giant fountain that sat in the middle of a plaza that was shaded by a canopy of coniferous trees. Wooden benches faced the fountain, while an assortment of brightly colored flowers filled the gaps between stone paths and sculptures.

Jones stopped next to an oddly shaped tree and stared at its twisty limbs. It was unlike anything they had back in Pittsburgh. He glanced over his shoulder and spotted Jarkko, who was several steps behind them and lost in his own little world. He was whistling a tune and dancing a jig to a band that wasn't there. Whether it was the vodka in his system or the promise of treasure, he seemed extremely happy.

Perhaps it was the presence of his long-lost friends.

"Jarkko," Jones called out. "Come over here. I have a question."

Jarkko happily obliged. He danced his way over to Jones and greeted him with a brotherly hug. "What is it, my friend?"

"You've been here before, right?"

"Yes. Many times. Maltese women keep Jarkko warm in winter. Why?"

"Do you know what kind of tree this is?"

"No. What kind of tree is this?"

Jones shook his head. "No. I was asking you."

"How Jarkko know about tree? Jarkko fisherman, not farmer."

"Sorry, I thought maybe—"

"You point at fish, Jarkko will tell you. You point at tree, Jarkko feel dumb. Why you make Jarkko feel dumb?"

"Sorry, man, I didn't mean to—"

"Ugh! And splashing sound from fountain make Jarkko have to pee."

"Well, don't do it here."

"Of course Jarkko don't do it here! Jarkko not animal. Jarkko not going to whip out willy and pee in park in front of kids and babies. What is wrong with you?"

"Nothing is wrong with me. I just wanted to know what kind of tree this is!"

"Then why you talk about my willy?"

Jones honestly didn't know how to answer that without upsetting Jarkko further, so he was beyond thrilled when he heard his name being called from ahead.

"DJ," Payne shouted, "the ceremony is starting."

Jones breathed a sigh of relief. "I gotta go look at some cannons."

Jarkko nodded. "And I gotta go pee with mine."

"Meet you here in a little bit."

"Okay. Sounds good."

Then they hustled off in opposite directions.

Payne was waiting for Jones near a series of stone arches that lined the rear of the gardens. Built by an Italian knight named Fra Flamingo Bambini in 1661 AD, the terraced arches were originally roofed, but the damaged ceiling was removed following the Rising of the Priests, a Maltese rebellion that was squashed by the Order of Saint John in 1775 AD.

"What was that about?" Payne asked.

"I wanted to know what type of tree it was."

"How's Jarkko supposed to know that? He's not a farmer."

"Wow. That's exactly what he said."

Payne smiled. "I know. I could hear him from here."

Jones laughed as they walked under the first set of arches. Made of large, tan bricks, the massive arches soared over them by at least fifteen feet. "Wow. These are awesome."

"Wait," Payne assured him. "It gets better."

They walked across a long, narrow plaza made of decorative

bricks and headed for the second series of arches. As they got closer, Jones could finally see what Payne was referring to. The rear arches opened to a wide terrace that overlooked the breadth of the Grand Harbour. They could see everything Galea had promised and a whole lot more.

"Holy balls," Jones muttered as he made his way through the small crowd that had gathered for the ceremony. "This view is un-believable, but where are the cannons?"

The duo slid twenty feet to the left until they found an open spot along the metal railing. Only then could they clearly see the lower level of the gardens—a grassy terrace that jutted out from a hidden set of arches that supported the plaza that they were stand-ing on. A central stone walkway bisected the green grass below, leading to a wide strip of tan bricks at the edge of the bottom plaza that served as a mounting point for eight black cannons.

"My, oh my," Jones said in appreciation. "Those are smooth-bore, breech-loading thirty-two pounders. They could take down a cruise ship before the lifeboats even hit the water. Truth be told, I'd pay good money to see that happen. It would be awesome."

A foreign couple standing next to him gave him a look of concern.

Jones quickly realized his faux pas. "Not with people on it. I just meant a ship."

His explanation didn't seem to work as the couple scurried away.

Payne couldn't help but laugh. "First Jarkko, and now them. You're on quite a roll. Want to make fun of my dead parents while you're at it?"

"Shut up," Jones mumbled. "I'm watching the ceremony."

In truth, there wasn't much to the ceremony, at least compared to the ones that Payne and Jones had participated in over the years—which, at times, involved hundreds of soldiers, marching bands, and complex choreography to showcase their discipline. And yet, there was something about the simplicity of the saluting battery that was somehow captivating.

A single soldier in a tan uniform marched out to the cannons. He selected the gun for the ceremony (in this case, the fourth from the left), opened the back of the artillery, and loaded it with a three-pound charge of gunpowder. Orchestra music began to swell over the public address system as the soldier attached a cord to the trigger and stepped to his left while facing the crowd on the terrace. With the cord in his right hand, he shifted his focus to the timepiece he held in his left. His gaze never left the sweeping dial of the second hand as it ticked toward the top of the hour. A moment before it reached its apex, he shouted a word of warning to stand clear, and then he pulled the cord in front of his chest with a violent flourish.

White smoke burst from the muzzle as the cannon roared.

In that instant, Payne and Jones were transported again, this time to their former lives—where the sound of gunfire often meant death and destruction. Although they knew it was going to happen, the loud blast made them flinch like thoroughbreds at the start of a race. Their hands instinctively inched toward the weapons they had concealed under their shirts, while their gaze shifted to center mass on the man that had pulled the trigger.

Just like they had been trained to do.

The polite applause of the crowd broke their focus and brought them back to reality. No words were spoken, but each man realized what the other had done.

And it brought a smile to their lips.

It didn't matter if they were jobless, or retired, or somewhere in between: they would remain deadly until the day they died.

"You ready?" Jones asked.

"Been ready."

"Then let's go find us a treasure."

Before he had killed Sergei Bobrinsky in the tower in Tallinn, Ivan Volkov had obtained as much information as possible about his soon-to-be-extinct smuggling operation. In particular, he was interested in the deliverymen who had received their payments before he'd received his.

In Volkov's mind, that money belonged to him.

And he was willing to do just about anything to get it back.

He had become even more intrigued when he had found out that one of the smugglers had received his compensation in the form of rare Russian documents. Volkov had an appreciation for his country's history, particularly its violent past when *real* Russians handled their issues with the same brutality that he preferred. Back then, the ruling class would beat people in the street just to let them know that they could—and no one would even complain about it.

How he missed the good old days!

Of course, there were some things about the present that he enjoyed as well—like the cadre of hackers on his payroll. In little time, they had been able to track down everything he had needed to find the mysterious Finn, including his yacht's location in Birgu.

Volkov had loaded his private jet with many of his best men and had landed in Malta that morning. From there, they had headed to the Grand Harbour Marina where they had narrowly missed him and his two apparent bodyguards.

Volkov knew nothing about the black-and-white duo, except that they would be severely outnumbered when his Russian-trained soldiers moved in to question the Finn.

And when that happened, he was certain the duo would meet their doom.

CHAPTER 17

Payne, Jones, and Jarkko left the Upper Barrakka Gardens after the cannon ceremony and headed northeast, deeper into the heart of Valletta. Their meeting place was less than fifteen minutes away, so they took their time and enjoyed their stroll.

Unlike the frantic energy of Paris or Rome, the pace of Valletta was relaxed. Other than a few taxis hustling for fares, no one seemed to be in a hurry. Locals lounged at curbside tables, and tourists relished the sights. Merchants stood in open doors and welcomed customers inside. Perhaps it was the gorgeous weather or the scent of nectar in the air, but everyone seemed to be at ease, as if they felt fortunate to be in this jewel of a city in the center of the sparkling sea.

With time to kill, Payne and Jones ducked into a store and bought gym bags. They weren't sure where their adventure would take them next, but they decided to be prepared. Once they got back to Jarkko's yacht, they could retire their trash bags forever.

"Ooh la la," Jarkko mocked. "Fancy bags for fancy garbage."

"Or hopefully for fancy treasure," Jones said with a laugh.

"Wait! Jarkko is new to this. Does Jarkko need treasure bag, too?"

"Let's hope," Payne said as he checked his watch. "But we can worry about that later. We have about five minutes to get to our meeting."

"No worries," Jarkko assured him. "Library is around corner."

The National Library of Malta is located in Republic Square in the center of the city. Designed by Polish-Italian architect Stefano Attar in 1776 AD, the Bibliotheca (as it is often called) is an early example of neoclassical architecture in Malta. Although the entire city of Valletta is considered a UNESCO World Heritage Site, the library is one of its most scenic structures. Noted for its symmetrical façade and its mix of Doric and Ionic columns, the library sits in the rear of a stone plaza that once housed the treasury of the Order of Saint John.

Despite the square's history, an open-air cafe had invaded the piazza, filling its space with green tables and white patio umbrellas. Customers ate and drank and checked their phones in the same place the knights used to count their money and store their treasure.

Centuries later, it seemed like the perfect place to start their hunt.

All they had to do was follow the scent of gold.

Payne led the way through the center of the crowded plaza, walking past a restored statue of Queen Victoria from 1891 AD and heading toward the front entrance of the library. The doorway was located underneath a balustraded balcony that jutted out from the second floor and was supported by massive cylindrical columns. Jones knocked on one of the pillars as he walked past to feel the sturdiness of the stone, and it brought a smile to his face.

Growing up as a bookworm, Jones had spent a lot of time in libraries and had fallen in love with them at an early age. But they didn't build them like this where he was from. He was used to one-story shacks that smelled like mildew and urine, not neoclassical façades and arched loggias. Whenever he traveled in Europe, he always tried to visit the libraries in major cities. Not only to examine their old-world collections, but also to marvel at their architecture.

Somehow it helped him appreciate how far he had come.

Payne reached the towering front entrance before the others and tried to enter, but the door didn't budge an inch. "Damn. It's locked."

Jones pointed at a nearby sign. "And apparently closed for the day."

Payne inspected the sign and growled. It wouldn't open again until early the next morning. "Well, it was fun while it lasted. Want to get some chow?"

Jones rolled his eyes. "Quit thinking with your stomach."

"You know that's not possible."

"Trust me, I know," he said as he tried the door himself. "But it doesn't mean I want to eat every two hours."

"Hold up. Did you think I was lying about the door?"

"Possibly. I once saw you kill a man for Jell-O."

"Bullshit! It was pudding, and I only broke the guy's arm."

"You aren't helping your case."

"I don't care. It was worth it. It was the best damn pudding I ever ate."

"Move," Jarkko ordered as he pushed his way past the bickering friends. "Let Jarkko try door. Jarkko not tall like Jon or black like David, but Jarkko strong like bull."

Jones grimaced. "You racist motherfucker."

But Jarkko ignored him. He was too busy spitting on his callused hands and rubbing them together ferociously in order to improve his grip. Thankfully, his spit wasn't necessary. A split second before he grabbed the handle, the lock clanked open from the inside and the door swung wide, revealing one of the most beautiful women they had ever seen.

Dark brown hair. Dark brown eyes.

A perfect tan complexion.

And just the right amount of curves.

All of it draped in a summer dress.

Jarkko blinked several times, naturally assuming that she was a vodka-induced mirage because beauty like hers was seldom seen in the wild. Normally it was contained to the runways of Milan or the red carpets of Los Angeles, but rarely in a place with so many books. The sheer lunacy of the situation blew Jarkko's mind, so much so that he found it difficult to speak.

Thankfully, she had plenty of experience dealing with drooling men, so she took charge of the situation and introduced herself.

"Hello," she said with a thick British accent. "You must be Petr's friends. My name is Croft. Lara Croft."

For the briefest of moments, all three men held their breath as they tried to wrap their heads around her famous name. Then, one by one, they caught on, realizing it was just an icebreaker—her way to make fun of herself before her looks became an issue.

"What's your name?" she asked with her arm extended.

Jarkko reached to shake her hand, but at the last second, he remembered he had spit in his palm to improve his grip. Unwilling to defile such a beautiful creature, he yanked his arm back so violently that he elbowed Jones in the gut behind him.

"Sorry," he mumbled. "You don't want to touch Jarkko. Jarkko is dirty."

She smiled and pinched his cheek. "Maybe I like dirty."

Jarkko blushed for the first time in years and was unable to speak for a minute or so.

Despite being elbowed, Jones recovered quickly and forcefully pushed Jarkko aside in order to introduce himself. "My friends call me DJ, but you can call me David. No, wait. I got that backwards. Ah, screw it. Call me whatever you want."

She smiled and shook his hand. "Believe it or not, I actually know who you are."

"You do?" he said, surprised.

Her smile widened. "Unless I'm mistaken, you're David freakin' Jones!"

His eyes got big. "Holy shit! You're right! I *am* David freakin' Jones. How in the hell do you know me? And more importantly, how do you know my middle name?"

"Ladies talk, you know."

Jones started to say something inappropriate, but then he stopped, realizing whatever he said would undoubtedly ruin this moment of sheer bliss, so he simply smiled and said, "Yep."

In a matter of seconds, she had disarmed two-thirds of the group.

But the last member would prove more difficult.

As a handsome heir to a billion-dollar fortune, Payne had a lot of experience dealing with attractive women of all shapes, sizes, and ethnicities. Much to his chagrin, they threw themselves at him in the most awkward of ways, often before he knew anything about them. Most men in his position would undoubtedly take advantage of the situation—sleeping with countless women in order to satisfy their every sexual need—but Payne had been taught by his parents (and later his grandfather) to respect the opposite sex. Every once in a while he would let his guard down and succumb to temptation, but for the most part, he was looking for the love of his life, not a series of one-night stands.

And it was a good thing, too, because she was just his type.

"Hi," he said as they locked eyes. "My name is Jonathon Payne."

She stepped forward, grabbed his hand, and shook it in total silence. But he didn't mind in the least.

In that moment, no words were uttered, but a lot was being said. And it took both of them by surprise.

"Sorry," she said a few seconds later when she eventually let go of his hand. "You're probably going to be needing that."

"That's okay. I have another."

"Me, too," she said with a giggle. Then she lifted it up and showed it to him, as if he needed the proof. "And here it is."

Payne lifted his other hand as well. "And here's mine."

Then she laughed like a teenager in love.

"Good Lord," Jones mumbled as he watched the scene. He was quite familiar with the effect that Payne had on women, but he rarely saw his friend reciprocate it. "If you two start playing patty-cake, I swear to God I'm going to shoot you both."

"What was that?" she asked without an accent.

"Sorry," Jones said. "I didn't mean to interrupt whatever was going on with you two, but I have a question. Actually, two questions."

She blushed slightly. "Then I have two answers. Fire away."

"One, I think it's pretty obvious that Lara Croft isn't your real name, so I wanted to know what to call you. And two, what happened to your accent?"

She laughed. "Truth be told, the British accent was part of the Lara Croft gag. How did I sound, by the way?"

"You nailed it," Jones admitted.

She smiled and took a slight bow. "Thank you, sir. I'm glad to hear it. I actually spent a lot of time moving around as a child, so I have a pretty good ear for accents and languages."

"Good to know," Jones replied. "And your name?"

"Sorry," she said with a laugh. "It's Marissa. Marissa Vella."

CHAPTER 18

With introductions out of the way, Marissa led the group inside before she locked the door behind them. As she did, she explained the library was a research facility that didn't lend out books or periodicals but was still open to the public on a daily basis. Thankfully, it was well after closing time, so she felt they would have the place to themselves.

To reach the main reading room on the second floor, the group climbed a staggered neoclassical staircase. Jones whistled in appreciation as he ran his hand over the pillared railings and marveled at the intricate ceiling that seemed to glow from the natural daylight that seeped through the side windows that lined the stairs.

"I love old buildings," Jones said to Jarkko as they lagged a landing behind the others. "They don't make them like this anymore."

Jarkko nodded and pointed at Marissa's rump. "Or like *that*."

Jones grinned. "Certainly not very often."

Jarkko threw his arm over Jones's shoulder and pulled him close. "Jarkko have important question to ask David."

Jones grimaced at the thought of saliva on his shirt. "Go on."

"When we look for treasure in Greece, we get help from beautiful blonde with eyes the color of sapphires. She was student of history, yes?"

Jones nodded. "You're talking about Allison Taylor."

"Yes! Allison! Very beautiful woman."

"Yes, she is. And very bright. She's doing quite well for herself."

"And when you find catacombs in Orvieto and hidden treasure in Mexico, you get help from old girlfriend. You have shown pictures to Jarkko. She is very *bellissimo*."

Jones smiled. "Actually, Maria did most of the finding. All we did was shoot some bad guys along the way."

"Also student of history?"

"She was back then, but now she's a well-known historian.

And author. And lecturer. Truth be told, her work ethic puts me to shame."

Jarkko nodded. "Yes, it does."

"Ouch," Jones said, half-offended. "What's your point?"

"Allison is beautiful. Maria is beautiful. And Marissa is beautiful, too. But when Jarkko go to school, smart girls never beautiful. This make Jarkko sad and confused. Why is this true?"

"Ah," Jones said as he stopped on the stairs to explain things. "You're talking about the Jonathon Payne effect. That guy could hit a bus full of nuns, and all of them would be naughty ex-center-folds who were rethinking their vows. After a while, you simply don't question it. Heck, why do you think I'm friends with the guy? It sure as shit ain't his personality."

"Come on! Let's go!" Payne called from the top of the stairs. "You can hug each other in your free time, once you get back to Jarkko's yacht."

Jones rolled his eyes. "See what I mean?"

Jarkko laughed and patted him on the shoulder. "You are funny guy. Jarkko is glad to punch car in face and save your life. Sorry about spit on shirt."

Jones grimaced at the stain. "That's okay. Your drinking problem probably killed most of your germs anyway."

"Let us hope. Otherwise, David will get bad rash."

Jones froze. "Wait. What?"

But Jarkko ignored him as he trudged up the stairs, laughing.

Suddenly alone, Jones grumbled to himself about hygiene and manners and a bunch of other things as he continued his solo climb. But when he reached the top landing, his mood instantly brightened. Off to his right sat a massive room that almost defied belief: it looked like something out of the Wizarding World of Harry Potter.

The arched ceiling of the main reading room soared more than thirty feet above him and ran as far as he could see—without any poles, columns, or visible supports to hold it up. That left nothing but wide-open space and the occasional table in a spectacular chamber that was lined from floor to ceiling on all four sides by wooden shelf after wooden shelf of ancient books.

Jones walked into the room and spun in a circle to soak it all in. His gaze instantly went to the long wooden ladders that leaned against some of the stacks. The ladders had to stretch twenty feet in length, yet they didn't even reach the second level of shelves that ringed the room up near the ceiling. As far as Jones could tell, the upper level could only be accessed by trapeze or catapult because on first glance he didn't spot any doors on that level.

Marissa studied his face as he entered. "Pretty cool, right?"

He nodded. "It certainly is."

"I had the same reaction when I first saw it. Love at first sight."

"I can see why. How long have you worked here?"

"Who said I worked here?"

Jones laughed. "No, I'm serious."

"I *am* serious. I don't work here. I actually snuck in the back door about five minutes before you arrived."

"Jon," he called out. "Marissa's a burglar. Just thought you should know."

Payne turned from a long row of display cases near the main entrance to the room. They featured a wide assortment of documents about the history of Malta but also showcased an original copy of *Les Propheties* by Nostradamus that had caught his eye. "What was that?"

Marissa smiled. "David called me a burglar."

Payne rolled his eyes. "Why? Did he say you stole his heart or something ridiculous?"

"Yuck!" Jones said. "I would never use a line like that while I'm sober. I called her a burglar because she doesn't work here and snuck into the place."

"Duh," Payne said. "She told me that when you were hugging Jarkko."

She glanced at Jones. "Why were you hugging Jarkko?"

Jones raised both of his hands. "Just so you know, I wasn't hugging Jarkko. *He* was hugging *me*. But that's beside the point. For the sake of the group, why don't you fill us in on your life? I mean, it's obvious you know us from somewhere. Why don't you start there?"

"I know you from the Ulster Archives," she said with a smile. "I worked with Petr for several months, and he used to go on and on about the two Americans who protected him from gunmen and stopped his facility from burning down. Obviously I asked for all the details, and he told me stories about you, and Jon, and all of your secret adventures. Truth be told, he talked about you so much I feel like I know you already."

Payne laughed. "You aren't the first person to say that. Although I haven't seen it, I hear he has a hidden wall with pictures from our trips."

"You mean the Payne and Jones shrine? Oh, it definitely exists. I've seen it with my own two eyes. I'm pretty sure he burns candles whenever you're on a mission."

Jarkko grinned. "Maybe that is how Archives catch fire. He is so worried for Jon and David that he build massive bonfire to get you jobs and homes."

She scrunched her face. "I don't get it."

Payne shook his head. "Never mind. Inside joke."

"Speaking of jobs," Jones said, "you *really* don't work here?"

"No," she stressed. "I really don't. However, when I'm in town, I come by and volunteer—binding books, raising money, organizing collections, or whatever they need. In return, they let me come here at night and conduct my research in private. The security guard lets me in."

"What kind of research?" Payne wondered.

She looked at him and smiled. "Actually, shouldn't I be asking you that question? After all, I was the one summoned to help you, not the other way around."

Payne grinned. "Summoned? You weren't summoned. Were you?"

"That depends," she said as she pulled out her phone. "Petr sent me a text with close to fifty exclamation marks, urging me to meet an unknown group at the front door of the library at five for a research project with worldwide ramifications."

"No, he didn't."

She showed him the message. "Oh yes, he did."

Payne laughed as he read the text. "Petr is rarely subtle, which is one of the things I love about the guy. He wears his emotions on his sleeve."

"He does indeed."

"So, you know *nothing* about our current project?"

"Nope. Only what you just read."

"But you're interested in helping?"

She pointed at her clothes. "I got dressed up and everything."

"No, you didn't."

"Oh yes, I did," she assured him. "I had no idea who I was

going to meet. It could've been royalty, or an author, or someone actually important."

"Ouch," Payne said.

"Double ouch," Jones echoed.

She smiled at them. "Had I known it was going to be two guys in T-shirts with matching gym bags, I would have stayed in yoga pants. Seriously, was there a sale or something?"

Jarkko grinned. "Don't complain. Earlier today, they use trash bags for belongings."

"Really?"

"Yes!" he assured her. "Jarkko thought they were homeless!"

She broke into a wide grin. "And now I get the inside joke."

Jones tried to explain. "We didn't want to bring our luggage, so—"

Payne grabbed his arm. "Let it go. You'll only make things worse."

Jones took a deep breath and conceded the point.

"Guys," she said, laughing. "Don't worry. I'm glad you're not perfect. After listening to Petr's stories, I assumed you were immortal. It's good to know you're flawed like me."

"Like *I*," Jones teased. "But what's grammar amongst friends?"

"See! We're all messed up in our own special ways. The key is we recognize our flaws, and we're able to laugh about them. Of course, some of our flaws are funnier than others. I mean, garbage bags. Seriously? What are you, ten?"

Payne was certainly capable of defending himself in a verbal sparring match, but at this point in time, he was far more concerned with evaluating Marissa as a potential team member than he was with protecting his dignity.

As the former leader of the MANIACs, he had been forced to make split-second decisions in the field about the validity of assets and information—decisions that would potentially risk the lives of his men and their missions. Whether it came from his training or his natural instincts, Payne was known for the tuning-fork accuracy of his gut feelings.

Sometimes they defied all logic, but they always proved right.

Every single time.

And this was one of those times.

For whatever reason, he sensed that something was off.

Whether it was Marissa, or the library, or their isolation, he felt his stomach tightening, his heart racing, and the hair standing up on the back of his neck.

Something bad was about to happen.

He just didn't know what.

"Time to go," Payne announced out of the blue.

Jones glanced at him, concerned.

"What do you mean?" she blurted, confused.

"It was great meeting you. It really was, but my team has to roll."

"To where?" she asked.

"Jon," Jones said as his eyes darted around the room. "What is it?"

"Gut," Payne answered, which is all that he needed to say. A second later, his best friend was in combat mode, looking to secure all personnel.

Jones immediately grabbed Jarkko's arm and pulled him toward the door. "Time to go."

"Go where?" Jarkko demanded.

"Don't question it. Just do it."

Jarkko nodded. He didn't have to be told thrice. Instead, he reached under his puffy shirt and pulled out his gun as he rushed toward the exit.

Marissa spotted his weapon and screamed in panic.

A split second before Jarkko was shot.

CHAPTER 19

The Russian didn't have a choice.

The instant he breeched the reading room, he saw an armed man charging toward him like an angry bull, so he raised his gun and fired. His first shot missed Jarkko and hit a display case, shattering glass and sending razor-sharp fragments into the air. Jarkko lifted his gun and tried to return fire, but the Russian got off shot number two before Jarkko could pull his trigger.

The second bullet struck Jarkko in the middle of his chest, stopping his forward momentum and dropping him to his knees as he lost his ability to breathe. Liquid gushed from the hole in his shirt as he slumped to the floor, desperately gasping for air.

In that moment, he didn't care about treasure.

Or soup.

Or beautiful, bouncy women.

All he wanted was one more breath…and then possibly another.

Thankfully, Jones was there to save the day, with his weapon raised and his aim true. He pulled his trigger and shot the first Russian right in his face.

One moment, he had a nose.

The next he didn't.

Just like that, the guy was dead.

Unfortunately, many more were to come.

In the background, Payne rushed toward Marissa and tackled her to the floor as the booming gunshots echoed in the chamber. Based on her initial scream and the panic on her face, he sensed she wasn't part of the problem, but he wasn't willing to bet his life on it.

"Are you armed?" he demanded as he patted her down for weapons.

"No!"

"Do you know who they are?"

"Of course not!"

Temporarily satisfied, he grabbed a wooden table and threw it on its side. Then he grabbed her by the arm and dragged her behind the barrier. As he did, a chunk of glass sliced the back of her leg, but she felt no pain as blood oozed from her wound and stained her dress.

"Look at me!" he shouted as he grabbed her face.

She blinked a few times, trying to focus.

"Marissa! Stay *here* until I come back for you!"

"What about Jarkko?"

He ignored her question. "Do you understand?"

"Yes."

"I'm serious. Tell me you understand."

"I understand!"

Payne nodded and forced a smile to try to calm her down. "Don't worry. This shit happens all the time. Everything will be fine."

But deep inside he had his doubts.

Not because of a lack of training.

But because of the lay of the land.

Unlike most libraries that had row after row of tall shelves that would have provided him with options, this facility kept all of its books on the walls of the perimeter. What was left in the middle was a manmade canyon with wooden tables and chairs, reading lamps, card catalogs, glass display cases, and an ancient globe that might work as temporary cover but would be quickly overrun if they were facing superior numbers.

And he sensed those numbers were on their way.

Which meant they had to act quickly.

Without even looking, Payne had a mental image of the entire space. His brain had absorbed it when he had walked into the room, the same way a mechanic could identify a car by the sound of an engine or a chef could list twenty ingredients with a single taste. It was simply the way he viewed his environment, his window into the world. It allowed him to see all the angles and possible barriers long before his opposition.

It allowed him to stay one step ahead.

In the blink of an eye, Payne knew what they needed to do. With Jarkko down and ammo limited, they needed to secure higher ground.

And Jones was the man for the job.

Whereas Payne was built like a rhino, Jones was like a gazelle. He was agile, and sleek, and could run all day without even breaking a sweat. And when it came to climbing, he could scurry up walls with a heavy field pack, Yoda on his back, or a garbage bag full of stuff.

To him, it didn't matter.

He was like a ninja without a mask.

"DJ!" Payne shouted across the room. "Go high!"

Jones heard the command and actually grinned as he sprinted toward the closest ladder.

Tactically speaking it was a brilliant move because it would give them the high ground in a shooting gallery of wide-open space, but almost as importantly to Jones, it would give him a chance to climb the twenty-foot wooden ladder that he had been eyeing ever since he had stepped into the room. It had been calling to him like a jungle gym when he was a kid.

Some children liked to play on the swings.

But Little DJ always wanted to climb.

There was something about it that made him feel alive.

Or in this case, keep him alive.

The instant he reached the ladder, he tucked his gun in his shorts and climbed with the speed of an elevator. Hand over hand, legs pumping fast, like a master of parkour.

Earlier he had noticed that the last rung of the ladder stopped underneath the lip of the second level, but for someone like Jones, it was barely an obstacle to overcome. He simply sprang from the ladder with a death-defying leap and grabbed the metal railing that lined the upper ledge.

Then he flipped onto the balcony with a flourish.

Just like he had done on the playground.

All told, the entire process had taken less than ten seconds.

It was a good thing, too, because more Russians were on their way.

In the grand scheme of things, henchmen knew they were henchmen.

They *knew* what they were signing up for.

Yet they did it anyway.

Whether by birth or by girth, they had applied for a job to protect a local criminal, shady businessmen, or coked-out oligarch, all in hopes of making enough money for a better life—one in which they might possibly hire some henchmen of their own someday.

It was the circle of life in the criminal underworld.

One that kept on spinning and spinning and spinning.

Like a giant game of Russian roulette.

Only in this particular version, *several* Russians would die.

To the confusion of the men in the stairwell, the first henchman had decided to abandon their plan and had started firing the moment he had entered the door. Perhaps he thought he would look heroic or movie-star cool and be honored for a job well done. Or maybe the idiot forgot their mission and just decided to wing it. Whatever his rationale, he had paid for it with his life.

All of which put the second henchman in an interesting position.

He was standing near the doorway, ready to charge into the room to question a group of supposedly unarmed historians, when he saw his comrade get shot in the face. Back where he came from, guns and bullets were a part of his life, but it didn't mean he wanted to die in the middle of a Maltese library for a boss he didn't actually like, so he did something that the first guy had stupidly failed to do.

He appointed himself as team leader.

"Go! Go! Go!" he yelled in Russian while the rest of the henchmen stormed past him into the reading room with their weapons raised and their blood running hot.

Meanwhile, he stayed in the stairwell where it was safe.

Because the truth was he didn't want to be a henchman.

He wanted to be a plumber.

With Jones heading skyward, Payne sprinted toward Jarkko.

Despite his height, Payne stayed low as he scooted across the floor. Glass crunched underfoot as he made his way between the rows of display cases. Although their tops were transparent, their bottoms were made of paneled wood, giving him some cover as he scrambled toward his fallen friend. He put his left hand down for balance while keeping his gun hand free, all the while checking the door for incoming threats.

Jarkko was sprawled on the floor up ahead, lying on his side.

From his distance, Payne couldn't tell if he was dead or alive.

A second later, it hardly mattered.

Because the floodgates opened and the Russians came in.

CHAPTER 20

To the surprise of no one, Jarkko had seen his fair share of violence during his colorful life. In the last year alone, he had been stabbed by a saber, hit over the head with a watermelon, bitten by a horny zebra, and zapped in the balls with a cattle prod—although it should be noted that he had asked a leather-bound dominatrix to do that last one. Yet through it all, despite several close calls in barroom brawls around the globe, he had never, ever been shot.

So when he saw the gun flash and felt the impact of the bullet in his chest, he did what most people tended to do: he fell to the floor in agony. But while he was down there, struggling to breathe, he noticed something that made him think he had left reality.

The hole in his puffy shirt wasn't bleeding blood.

It was bleeding vodka.

Jarkko laid on his side and waited for the angels to take him.

And he waited. And he waited.

He waited so long he was tempted to drink the vodka that he was leaking.

Eventually it dawned on him that his chest wasn't throbbing that much anymore and he had miraculously caught his breath, so he decided to sit up and take a closer look at his wound.

And that's when he realized what had happened.

The bullet hadn't hit flesh.

It had hit the flask in his shirt pocket.

Sure, the impact had stung like hell.

But his drinking problem had saved his life.

Out of the corner of his eye, Payne saw Jarkko sit up and laugh.

Although he wouldn't know the specifics until later, Payne was thrilled to see his friend alive. But he realized his status would be short-lived if he didn't address the problem pouring through the door to the reading room. One after another they charged forward, as if they had been made on an assembly line, five nearly identical men, each as deadly as the last.

Payne rose from his crouch behind the display case and aimed his weapon. He fired two quick shots, hitting the lead henchman in center mass. The Russian stumbled forward while wildly firing a shot of his own before he crashed to the floor. His shot sailed high and wide and struck one of the shelves along the wall, just above Marissa's head.

But this time she didn't scream.

Instead, it pissed her off.

She had seen her fair share of violence in her life, most of it inflicted on her mother when Marissa was just a kid, so her first instinct had been to cower in fear. But over the years, she had learned how to turn that fear into fuel, which was what she hoped to do now. With trembling hands, she grabbed the table that she was hiding behind and carefully peeked over the top.

Up ahead she saw Payne, coolly standing in the line of fire, willing to take on the entire Russian force that was streaming through the door. As impressive as it was, she knew it wouldn't last for long if he ran out of ammo or was surrounded by superior numbers, so she did the one thing he had told her not to do: she left her hiding place.

Summoning all of her courage, she sprinted across the width of the library and dove over the circulation desk along the opposite wall. Shaped like a parenthesis, it sat on a raised wooden platform above the tiled floor and gave her more options than before, back when she had been trapped on the glass-covered floor behind the overturned table.

Unfortunately for her, her frantic dash to freedom actually had an inverse effect on her safety, because it attracted the attention of one of the goons, who charged toward her with his gun raised and violence on his mind.

A moment later, his mind was splattered on the wall—thanks to a well-placed shot from Jones, who had watched Marissa's sprint from his perch on the second level. He wasn't sure whether to praise her courage or curse her stupidity, but her brave and reckless act had actually helped Payne on the frontline, giving him a brief respite from the constant barrage of gunfire that he had endured once they had spotted his position near the display cases.

Unlike the floor below—which was wide open but dotted with obstacles—the space up high was quite narrow and virtually free of hiding spots. The only camouflage was a series of framed paintings that hung at regular intervals on the decorative railing that lined the upper floor. The gap between the railing and the bookshelves along the walls was barely a few feet wide, meaning Jones had very little space to maneuver while providing cover from above.

Ultimately he decided to crouch down behind a painting of a Maltese knight that hung diagonally above the main entrance to the reading room. From there, he had eyes on his team and could pick off anyone coming or going through the door, but most importantly of all, he could guide his personnel like a coach from the press box.

With a series of hand signals, he let Payne know where every-one was.

Six henchmen had entered, and three of them were dead.

The other three had scattered around the room.

Jarkko was back in the game after an initial scare. He was tucked safely in the front corner between a display case and a bookshelf, ready to reenter the fray.

Marissa was behind the circulation desk, without a weapon.

If she had stayed where Payne had told her to stay, she would've been directly behind him and well protected along the wall, but she had gotten bold and decided to make a move. Alt-hough it had temporarily helped his cause at the time, it now put him at a disadvantage.

To protect her, he had to cross the field of fire.

"Jarkko," Payne whispered as he dashed behind the display case where his friend was crouching. "Are you hurt?"

Jarkko shook his head. "Jarkko is wet, but Jarkko is fine."

"You pissed yourself?"

"No!" Jarkko insisted before he looked at his damp shirt and pants. "Well, maybe. Jarkko's piss and vodka smell the same."

"Can you shoot?"

"Yes! Who should Jarkko kill?"

"The bad guys."

"Where are they?"

Payne pointed. "Out there. But so is Marissa."

"That's not good."

"No, it's not. Do you know what covering fire is?"

"Yes. Jarkko former soldier."

"Really? You never told me that."

Jarkko shrugged. "You never ask."

Payne was about to respond, but he noticed movement above. He glanced up and saw Jones signaling down to him. One of the henchmen was making his move toward Marissa.

Payne cursed under his breath. They had to act now.

"On three, I want you to shoot across the way."

"At what?"

"Anything but Marissa."

"Okay."

"Three."

Jarkko stood and did what he was told, firing a few quick shots toward the shelves in the back of the room. His covering fire had the desired effect, forcing the Russians to temporarily scramble for cover while Payne left the safety behind the display case and dashed across the floor. Instead of diving headfirst over the desk and risking a concussion, he slid across its wooden surface on his hip and used his feet to stop his momentum as he crashed into the alcove.

"Ouch," he mumbled as he scrambled to his knees and looked for someone to shoot. Fortunately, the only person he saw was Marissa, who had armed herself with a stapler but was staring at him like *he* was crazy.

"What are you doing here?" she demanded.

"Saving you."

"I don't need to be saved."

"Fine," he said. "Then I can leave."

She grabbed his arm. "Don't be hasty."

Payne smiled at her before he glanced at Jones, who was signaling from his perch. Two Russians were toward the back of the room, hiding behind a card catalog. The other one was lurking behind an overturned table in the middle of the chamber. Payne nodded in understanding, then signaled back to Jones, letting him know that Jarkko had another chance to help their cause.

Only this time he would get to aim at the Russians.

CHAPTER 21

Jarkko was in the corner, still laughing at his good fortune, when he heard a voice from above.

A few minutes earlier, he would have assumed it was an angel calling his name, but now he knew it was his jobless friend David, who had apparently jumped thirty feet to the upper level and was hiding behind a painting of an old guy in a red blouse.

Jarkko glanced up at him and waved.

Jones smiled and signaled for Jarkko to move along the wall behind the display case to a spot near the center of the room. From there, he would have a direct shot at one of the goons.

Jarkko's grin got even wider.

If there was one thing he liked more than vodka, it was killing Russian scum.

As a native of Finland, he and his homeland lived under the constant threat of a Russian invasion. They all knew it was coming; it was just a matter of time. And when it happened, there wasn't a damn thing that they could do about it, because their military lacked the resources and manpower of the empire to their east.

It was one of the reasons he did so much illegal business in Russia.

He liked screwing them any chance he got.

With his gun raised and his shirt wet, Jarkko did what he was told. He creeped behind the display case until he reached its end. From there, he spotted the exposed leg of a Russian, who was crouching behind a table directly across from the circulation desk. He posed a direct threat to both Payne and Marissa, who were temporarily out of harm's way but would be in the line of fire if the Russian pressed forward.

So Jarkko made sure that didn't happen.

He pulled his trigger and fired a single shot into the Russian's knee. The goon screamed out in pain while falling backwards on his ass, which conveniently exposed him to a headshot.

A second later, Jarkko silenced him forever.

Payne didn't need to look. He knew the Russian was dead. He had been in enough firefights to recognize the sudden silence that came with a kill shot.

That meant two gunmen were left.

Both hiding in the rear of the library.

If Payne had wanted to escape, this would have been the time to do it. He could tell Marissa to run toward the door while the rest of his team slowly retreated toward the exit while firing just enough shots to keep the Russians pinned in place in the back of the chamber.

But the truth was Payne didn't want to leave.

He wanted answers.

That meant he needed to capture one of the goons alive.

Payne signaled to Jones, who signaled to Jarkko, who signaled to Payne, until all of them knew what they were doing. The only one who wouldn't participate was Marissa, who had traded in her stapler for a pair of scissors. She was using it to tend to the gash on the back of her leg. She cut off a strip of duct tape that she had found in one of the drawers and used it to seal her wound until she got stitches or a proper bandage.

While she worked, she didn't wince or complain.

Which brought a smile to Payne's face.

A lot could be learned during pressure situations.

And this revealed that she was tough.

Payne glanced at her leg. "Want me to kiss it and make it better?"

Considering their circumstances, the comment was so unexpected she had to cover her mouth to keep from laughing. "If you get me out of this alive, I might just let you."

"Then it's a date."

"Whoa, cowboy. I said *might*. Besides, you still have work to do."

"No worries. I'm working on the problem as we speak."

Truth be told, Jones was the one doing most of the work—because he was crawling on all fours from his perch above the door to the ledge that lined the wall across from the circulation desk. Payne had noticed that it went directly above the two card catalogs where the Russians were hiding, which would give Jones the decisive high ground in a shootout.

Meanwhile, Jarkko was told to stay put near the display cases.

If the Russians ducked underneath the ledge to avoid Jones's wrath, Jarkko would be there to pick them off. And if the Russians ran toward the center of the room, Payne would pop up from behind the desk and gun them down.

As far as Payne could tell, they had every angle covered.

Regrettably, Payne was wrong.

Jones could crawl almost as skillfully as he could climb, so he had no problem making his way through the narrow gaps to his new perch above the card catalogs. Once he got into position, he snuck a quick peek over the edge to inspect the Russians below.

They were down there, whispering to one another.

Each held a gun in his hand.

Jones leaned back against the wall and waved his arms above his head to get Payne's attention. From across the room, Payne nodded and then signaled instructions to his men.

First to Jones, then to Jarkko.

For this to work, they needed to be in sync.

Both men nodded back, ready for action.

Jones took a deep breath as he stood on the narrow ledge. With his back against the bookshelves, he couldn't be seen by the goons below, but the instant he stepped toward the decorative railing, he would be exposed. As far as he was concerned, it was worth the risk because he would have a clear downward shot at the Russians. If he fired quickly, he would be able to take them out before they even knew what hit them.

Unfortunately for Jones, that's not what happened.

And the thing to blame was the library he loved.

The moment he stepped forward to line up his shot, the floorboard underneath his left foot creaked, a sound that screamed in the quiet room.

The Russians looked up and saw the face of their foe staring down at them, so they raised their guns and fired. Both shots missed wide as Jones got off a shot of his own that clipped the shoulder of one of the men. He screamed out in pain and darted underneath the ledge that was holding Jones. The other Russian joined him, temporarily out of Jones's range.

"Shit," Jones mumbled.

Payne cursed even louder across the way.

From his position near the display cases, Jarkko had a shot at the Russians, who were partially protected by one of the ladders that leaned against the stacks. Forced to hurry, Jarkko's first shot clipped one of the thick side rails of the ladder.

Wood splintered near the injured Russian's head, but he didn't flinch due to the adrenaline coursing through his veins. Instead, he turned and fired two shots that hit the side paneling of the case next to Jarkko, who fired right back and hit the ladder once again. This time a chunk cracked off and punctured the Russian's flesh. He yelped in pain and slumped to the floor as blood gushed from his cheek, matching the liquid that leaked from his shoulder.

"Fuck you, you commie bastard!" Jarkko yelled in Russian.

Staring at the splinter in his comrade's face, the healthy hench- man got an idea. He glanced upward at the boards underneath the ledge and realized that they were ancient. So he turned his gun sky- ward and waited for another creak, at which time he pulled his trigger.

Jones was staring at the floorboards beneath his feet when they erupted in a barrage of gunfire. Shot after shot after echoing shot, delivered so precisely that they burst through the old floor and em- bedded themselves in the ceiling above, narrowly missing Jones, who managed to jump back on the bottom bookshelf while some- how keeping his balance.

A moment before the floor had been solid, but now he could see straight through.

And grinning at him from below was the healthy Russian.

CHAPTER 22

Payne knew their plan had gone to shit the instant the floorboard had creaked, which is why he had cursed so loudly behind the circulation desk.

Now he was forced to enter the fray and leave Marissa behind.

Despite his size, Payne was incredibly light on his feet. He had the ability to sneak through jungles, deserts, forests, or snow, without making a sound—so the tiled floor of a public library was hardly a challenge.

Directly across from the circulation desk was a long chain of tables that had been pushed together, each draped by a green tablecloth that hung below chair level. Payne knew it would give him adequate cover as he moved closer to the Russians. After signaling Jarkko, he covered the distance between the desk and the tables in less than a second, then he scooted along the floor until he reached the far end of the row.

Now Jarkko was to his left and the goons were on his right.

In a matter of seconds, blood would be spilled.

The henchman who wanted to be a plumber had remained in the stairwell while his comrades were gunned down, one after another. Although he was racked with guilt, there wasn't much he could do since one of their foes had positioned himself above the main door. The plumber realized if he charged forward to help, he would quickly be another corpse on the floor.

So he waited. And he waited. And he waited some more.

Until his patience paid off.

The gunman above the door finally left his perch and made his way toward the back of the room, followed by the smuggler in the puffy shirt. And last but not least, the muscle-bound warrior left the circulation desk, leaving the woman behind.

If the plumber was going to make a move, this was the time to do it.

So he took a deep breath and crept forward.

Jones knew he was in deep shit when he saw the bastard's grin. Soldiers from Russia rarely showed positive emotions when engaged in battle. They preferred to stay cold and clinical, just like their training, so a smile that wide meant something horrible.

Then he saw what it was through the hole in the floor.

The henchman from hell had a grenade in his hand.

And then he didn't.

Because he had leaned forward and tossed it onto the ledge.

At that moment, Jones had a decision to make—and less than a second to make it. Should he grab the grenade and throw it back toward the goons? Or would the damn thing go off before it left his hands? And even if he managed to redirect it, would the ancient ledge with the bullet holes be able to sustain the blast?

Of course, he could always catch the grenade and try to throw it far away, but during the past several seconds, he had lost sight of his friends—thanks to the barrage of bullets that had been pumped through the floorboards. He didn't want to endanger their lives, so he ruled that out the instant it crossed his mind.

Unfortunately, that left him with no good options.

And one really dangerous one.

So he opted for that and made the most of it.

Using the iron railing like the monkey bars he had mastered as a kid, Jones jumped over the top bar while twisting his body. This allowed him to catch the bottom rail and swing back underneath the ledge where the two goons were hiding.

The grin left the henchman's face when Jones crashed on top of him, slamming his head against shelf after shelf as Jones rode him all the way to the floor. At some point the impact shattered the goon's skull, because the bumpy ride ended with Jones on top of a dead Russian leaking brains while staring at a live one with a gun in his hand.

The injured henchman couldn't believe his luck. One of their targets had literally fallen from the sky and landed at his feet. Despite his pain, he raised his arm and put the gun in Jones's face. But before he could squeeze the trigger, the grenade exploded above, producing a thunderous blast and a bright burst of light that filled the entire room.

And it happened directly over Jones.

Payne had watched the events play out from his position behind the table.

He saw the grenade go up and Jones come down.

Right on top of the healthy gunman.

Payne stepped forward to make sure his friend was okay when he saw the injured Russian point his gun at Jones, so Payne did the only thing he could.

He raised his weapon and fired.

With everyone's focus toward the back of the room, the plumber crept in silence. He had no interest in tangling with one of the enemy gunmen, so he went after another prize.

Based on everything he had seen, the plumber knew that he would be the only henchman to survive this battle. He also realized if he left the library uninjured and empty-handed, that his boss would interpret that as failure, something to be punished with torture…or worse.

Which put him in a difficult position.

He had to return with something, but what?

And then he saw it.

The perfect trophy to take back to Volkov.

He snuck quietly toward the circulation desk where the injured woman sat alone, armed with a pair of scissors and a roll of tape. With a gun in his hand, he crept closer and closer until he was so damn close that he could practically hear her breath.

And that's when he made his move.

There on the floor sat two matching gym bags.

Purchased by the enemy an hour before.

He grabbed the first one and quickly filled it with books and papers and anything he could find. Then he grabbed the second bag and immediately did the same.

Now the bags were filled with stuff.

Library stuff.

He could work with that.

He was about to turn and run for the door when he sensed some eyes upon him. He glanced up and noticed Marissa. She was hiding behind the desk with her scissors raised. At some point she had spotted him and had retreated to safety.

As far as he was concerned, she had the right idea.

So he followed her lead.

He grabbed the two gym bags and ran for the door.

The bullet left Payne's gun a split-second before the grenade went off. It whizzed through the air and struck the injured Russian in his head at the same time the device exploded.

The goon's gun hand went limp as thunder roared above.

Thankfully for Jones, the grenade was merely a flash-bang—a nonlethal explosive that was meant to temporarily disorient an enemy's senses—otherwise the entire side of the library would have come crashing down on him and the dead goons.

As it was, it was still enough to knock Jones silly and scare the shit out of everyone else in the room. Books vibrated on shelves and tables rattled as Payne and Jarkko turned from the blast and did their best to protect their ears and eyes.

Each of them had seen the grenade in the air, so they were semi-prepared.

Across the way, Marissa had no idea what had happened.

After watching the plumber sneak away, she remained in the alcove behind the desk until the coast was clear, but even then, the thunderous sound echoed in her mind.

As did the multiple deaths she had witnessed.

Volkov's plan had been simple.

His henchmen were supposed to enter with stealth, disarm the Finn and his unsuspecting bodyguards, and then summon Volkov by phone for the inquisition. His cadre of hackers had turned off the surveillance cameras from afar, so he didn't have to worry about being seen.

Once inside the library, he had planned to find out everything he could about the Russian documents that the smuggler had received as payment from Bobrinsky and anything else that he could profit from before he disposed of the Finn and his men.

Some would think that Bobrinsky's brutal death in Estonia had more than offset the perceived slap in the face, but Volkov had felt differently.

He would not be satisfied until everyone had suffered.

And yet, as he sipped his iced tea at the café outside the library, he was the one doing the suffering. His team had entered the building several minutes earlier, and he hadn't heard a word from them since. That was very unlike this particular crew. They were elite soldiers, who had trained in the Russian military before taking positions in his organization. He had seen them in the field on many occasions and was confident in their abilities.

Obviously something had gone wrong.

But what?

He stared at the burner phone in his hand to make sure that it had a signal. Then he casually glanced around the plaza to see if anything seemed amiss. Everywhere he looked, people were enjoying their day, completely clueless of what was happening inside the library.

Just like he was.

Volkov was too seasoned of a criminal to do something rash—like sneaking inside to see for himself—but the longer he sat there, the more exposed that he felt.

Perhaps it was a mistake to send the entire team inside.

Maybe I should have kept someone by my side.

And then it happened.

One of his men opened the front door of the library. He stuck out his head, checked for possible resistance, and then stepped outside. In his hands were the two gym bags that the Finn's bodyguards had purchased in Valletta and had carried with them to the library.

Volkov watched with fascination as his henchman took a deep breath, collected himself, and then headed toward the street ahead. He was halfway across the plaza when he spotted Volkov at a café table. They locked eyes for the briefest of moments— barely enough to register the glance—but in that instant, Volkov learned everything he needed to know.

His plan had failed miserably.

And the rest of his men were dead.

CHAPTER 23

Interpol Headquarters
Lyon, France

Nick Dial leaned back in his chair and smiled.

Somehow he had gotten through the day without a crisis.

His meetings had gone smoothly. His employees had behaved. He even had time to eat lunch without any interruptions, an event that happened roughly once a decade.

All things considered, it had been a good day for Dial.

Which was a rarity during the past few years.

As the director of the homicide division at Interpol—the largest international crime-fighting organization in the world—Dial was tasked with coordinating the flow of information between police departments whenever a murder investigation crossed national boundaries. All told he was in charge of 192 member countries, filled with billions of people and hundreds of languages.

All of which kept him extremely busy.

Just not in the way he would prefer.

He would much rather be on the streets than in an office.

For the first few years, he had been thrilled with his position. He wrote the rules. He set the budget. He handpicked the personnel. On a few occasions, he even went into the field to work on high-profile cases, including one that involved multiple crucifixions and another that involved several dead scientists in Stockholm.

Dial didn't get involved because he had to.

He did it because he wanted to.

Being an investigator was in his blood.

Unfortunately, the election of a new secretary general at Interpol had changed Dial's ability to get his hands dirty. Dial's new supervisor wasn't a former cop; he was a politician. And he had introduced Dial to a concept that he had quickly come to despise: *optics*.

It didn't matter if Dial was effective when assisting police departments in the field. His new boss was only concerned about the possibility of an international incident, which could potentially lead to bad press. An angry Dial had protested fiercely. He didn't give a shit about perception; he only cared about justice. But he had been told in no uncertain terms that his participation in an active case would lead to his suspension and/or termination.

And just like that, he hated going to work.

Somehow his dream job had become a nightmare overnight.

As luck should have it, a few of his friends were going through similar problems with their high-profile careers. One in particular had finally pulled the plug after ten difficult years. Dial had been tempted to call him during lunch to get an update, but had decided against it due to the time difference in the States. He knew his buddy had been a night owl when he had a job. There was no telling how late he would sleep in retirement.

With nothing better to do, Dial decided to write him an email to see how things were going. He pulled out his cell phone, scrolled through his contacts, and found the name he was looking for. His finger was just getting ready to click the envelope icon when—

Ding-a-ling-a-ling!

The sound was so loud and piercing that he could feel it in his—

Ding-a-ling-a-ling!

Dial cursed loudly as he tried to turn down the volume, but for some strange reason, the master volume didn't have any effect on this—

Ding-a-ling-a-ling!

"What the fuck!" Dial yelled at his phone. Not only had this never happened before, but he didn't even recognize the sound effect. His normal ringtone wasn't a—

Ding-a-ling-a-ling!

"Answer your phone!" screamed Henri Toulon from outside Dial's office. He was one of Dial's best investigators but a royal pain in his—

Ding-a-ling-a-ling!

Now Dial was pissed. He stared at his locked screen, but no name or number appeared. In fact, the only thing on his display was a large, green—

Ding-a-ling-a-ling!

Toulon screamed even louder. "I swear to Buddha, if you don't answer your phone, I'm going to shoot you in your—"

Ding-a-ling-a-ling!

Dial finally relented and hit the green button. "Who the fuck is this?"

There was a slight delay before he heard a response.

"The Pentagon calling for Director Nick Dial."

That took the starch right out of his shorts.

"The Pentagon?" he said in a much calmer tone. "For me?"

"That depends. Are you Director Nick Dial?"

"Yes," Dial said as he stood from his desk and closed his office door. As he did, he flipped off Toulon, who was already doing the same to him. "What's this about?"

"Please hold."

So he held.

Seriously, what else was he going to do?

It was the goddamn Pentagon.

A few seconds passed before there was a click on the line, followed by a few more clicks, a couple of pops, and then finally a voice.

"Nick? Are you there?"

Dial recognized the caller at once. "Jon? Is that you?"

"Hey buddy, how ya doin'?" Payne asked casually.

"How am I doing? Holy shit, how do you think I'm doing?"

Payne noticed his irritation from hundreds of miles away. "Is this a bad time?"

"No, Jon, it's not. It's not a bad time at all. At least, it wasn't until the air-raid siren—or whatever that fuck that was—went off on my phone!"

"Air-raid siren? What in the hell are you talking about?"

"Believe it or not, I was just getting ready to write you an email when my phone started making the most god-awful sound. It was this hideous ding-a-ling that just wouldn't quit until I answered your call."

"Nick, I hate to break it to you, but that's how phones work. They keep ringing until you hit the button and pick up."

"Aha! You knew about the button!"

"All phones have buttons! Seriously, man. Have you been drinking? I know work's been kind of rough for you lately, but you shouldn't be hitting the bottle at the office."

"The Pentagon! Your call came through the Pentagon!"

"Wait," Payne said defensively. "How did you know that?"

"Because the goddamn operator said this is the goddamn Pentagon! I thought there had been a missile launch or something!"

"Randy!" Payne shouted into his phone in case Randy Raskin—the computer genius who worked as a researcher in the Pentagon's subbasement but was Payne and Jones's high-tech secret weapon—was still listening. "I just needed a clean line, not an introduction!"

"Did you just call me 'Randy'?" asked Dial, who was getting more and more confused by the second. "And why do you need a clean line to speak to me?"

"Let's start there. Are you somewhere you can talk in private?"

Dial nodded. "I'm in my office, and I sweep it daily for bugs. I haven't found one yet, but I know my asshole boss is looking for an excuse to push me out."

"Wait. I thought you wanted to leave?"

"I do, but I want to leave on my own terms. I don't want to get fired."

"In that case, maybe we should end this call right here."

"Not a chance. First things first: who is Randy? And how did he hack my secure phone? This thing is supposed to be unhackable."

Payne took a deep breath. "That's a long story."

"Well, you have my attention. In fact, you have my whole building's attention. Seriously, you have no idea how loud that sound was."

"Trust me, it could've been worse. Randy once took the audio track of a gay porn movie and uploaded it to DJ's phone as his ringtone. Anytime he received a call, he'd start hearing grunts and splashes and all kinds of nasty stuff, all at full volume. DJ tried his best to ignore it, but after two days, he was so embarrassed and angry that he literally shot his phone."

Dial laughed. "You're right. That would've been worse. So who is this guy?"

Payne knew that Dial still had a high clearance from his time at the FBI, so he felt comfortable giving him some basics. He didn't reveal Raskin's full name for security purposes, but he was able to explain some of the ways that Raskin had assisted them during their military days and how a friendship had grown from there.

Dial sat down and took it all in before he asked the question that still hadn't been answered. "And why did he hack my phone?"

"I'm guessing boredom. To someone like Randy, a secure phone at Interpol probably sounded like a challenge. Obviously it wasn't since my phone rang for less than thirty seconds before I heard your voice, so yeah, you should probably look into that— especially if you think your boss is trying to bug your office."

Dial shook his head. "No, you misunderstood my question. Why did you feel the need to call your hacker friend at the Pentagon to place a call to me in the first place?"

"Oh, that. Well, it seems that DJ and I may have gotten ourselves into a little situation, and we were hoping our good buddy at Interpol may be able to lend us a hand."

Dial groaned. "Define *little*."

Payne glanced at the carnage in the library. From where he was standing, he could see multiple bodies, plenty of blood, and several bullet holes. Plus, for some strange reason, Jarkko was working the arms of one of the dead goons like a creepy puppeteer, just flipping and flopping his lifeless arms around, much to the amusement of Jones.

"Actually," Payne admitted, "*little* may be an understatement."

CHAPTER 24

There were very few people in the world that Payne and Jones respected more than Nick Dial, and the feeling was quite mutual. Together they had faced a lot over the years, and during that time, they had grown from casual acquaintances to trusted friends.

The trio had met several years earlier at a pub in London that catered to Americans called Stars & Stripes. It was the type of joint where *football* meant helmets and shoulder pads, not yellow cards and hooligans. At the time, Payne and Jones were still in the military, and Dial was just starting his career at Interpol. The three of them had hit it off right away, and they had kept in touch ever since—occasionally bumping into each other in foreign lands.

Once at an airport in Italy.

Another time in the mountains of Greece.

It was during that particular adventure that their friendship was truly forged, watching each other's backs while battling a vicious foe and solving an ancient riddle on Mount Athos. By the end of the trip, Dial had met a hard-drinking fisherman named Jarkko and a famous historian named Ulster, both of whom would play major roles in the story that he was about to hear.

Dial took a deep breath. "How bad is it?"

Payne surveyed the scene. "On a scale of one to a hundred, I'd rate it a six."

"Whew!" Dial said, relieved. "I can handle a six. After that air-raid alert from your hacker friend, I was expecting a whole lot worse."

"Unfortunately, the six stands for the number of dead bodies that—"

"Seven!" Jones shouted from across the way.

"Hold on, Nick. We're still counting corpses here." Payne lowered his phone and shouted back to Jones. "Who the hell is number seven?"

"They killed the security guard on their way in. *And* they stole our gym bags."

"Seriously? Why the hell would they steal our gym bags?"

"Because our gym bags were awesome."

"Any surveillance?"

"On the gym bags?"

"In the library!"

"Nope. They killed that, too. The whole system is kaput."

"Call Randy and see if he can help with anything—including traffic cameras on the surrounding streets. And please tell Jarkko to quit touching the bodies."

Payne got back on the phone. "Sorry about that. Kind of hectic here. We're trying to get as much done before the police arrive. They'll only slow us down."

"Whoa! Whoa! Whoa!" Dial growled as blood rushed to his face. He could literally feel his body temperature rise while he listened to the update. "You need to start from the beginning, because right now I'm about to blow a fucking fuse."

"Was it something I said?"

Dial didn't find it funny. "Stop that shit right now, or I swear to God I'll hang up this phone and hang you out to dry. This isn't the time for jokes. This is when you fill me in on everything, and I decide if I need to put out an alert for your arrest."

Because of the complex nature of their friendship, Payne often forgot that Dial had been trained to handle death in a much different way than he had. In the world of the special forces, Payne and Jones had been taught to kill and move on without looking back, mostly because the military feared they might not be able to handle it if they paused long enough to see how much destruction they had brought into the world in the name of peace. After a while, they had built up such a tolerance to violence that they were able to joke about things that others wouldn't.

Not out of disrespect, but in order to keep their sanity.

Meanwhile, Dial viewed things quite differently.

As an investigator, he had been forced to study the moment of death, to closely examine all of the grisly details that soldiers tried to forget. He knew it was in the minutiae where murderers made mistakes, and that's what was needed to catch a killer. Once a case was over and Dial was throwing back beers with his colleagues, the dark humor would come out—in hopes of washing away the stains that still remained—but until then, his job was to uphold the law.

Or, at the very least, keep it in view.

And that's where things got tricky.

Dial was no longer an investigator. He was an administrator. It wasn't his job to go to a crime scene and look for clues. His duty was to pass on as much information as possible to the police forces involved in any crimes that crossed international borders. However, as the director of the homicide division of Interpol, he realized his opinion carried a lot of weight.

With a single phone call, he could start or stop an investigation.

Which was why Payne was calling him now.

Without Dial's help, they would be in deep shit.

And Payne knew it.

"Sorry, Nick. I truly am. I'm still amped up on adrenaline, trying to make sense of what just happened. Because I'm telling you, it doesn't make sense."

Dial noticed the change in Payne's demeanor and appreciated it. Like Payne, he had been shot at multiple times in the line of duty and realized it brought a rush of emotions that were tough to contain. With that in mind, he took a deep breath and tried to calm down as well.

"First things first: are you and DJ okay?"

"Yeah, man, we're fine. Banged up, but fine. Sorry, I should have led with that. Truth be told, my head's still ringing from the grenade."

So much for calming down.

"Grenade? You used a fucking grenade?"

"Not us, Nick. *Them.* Just a flash-bang, though. Otherwise, DJ wouldn't be standing."

"Who the hell is *them*?"

"Listen, I'll gladly fill you in on everything, but I need you to do something for me A-SAP. Reach out to the police in Valletta and let them know there was an assault on their national library that's been stopped. Tell them who we are, and make it clear we're the good guys. Otherwise, they're liable to come in here with a SWAT team, running hot."

Dial knew Payne well enough to trust his assessment of the situation. If he said the threat had been thwarted, then Dial believed him. He immediately opened his office door and called out to Toulon, who was no longer flipping him off. "There's been a shootout at the national library in Valletta. Seven down, but the situation is contained. Let them know we have a team inside. If the locals have any questions, they can call me direct."

"What team?" Toulon asked as he searched his computer screen for the contact information of the National Central Bureau in Malta. It was the duty of local NCB offices to monitor their territories and report pertinent facts to Interpol's headquarters in France.

"Payne and Jones."

Toulon had met them when they had stopped by Lyon to check out Dial's office and to get a better sense of Interpol's system of operations. Despite his reputation for hating everyone, Toulon had actually hit it off with the duo, much to the surprise of Dial. "Are they okay?"

"So far, but they won't be if tactical units storm the building with them inside."

"On it. Give them my best. I love those guys."

"Sorry about that," Dial said to Payne as he closed his office door once again. "Henri says hi, by the way. Not to me, ever. Only to you."

Payne smiled. "Thanks for doing this. I truly appreciate it."

"No problem. I want you guys safe. That way I know you're healthy when I kick your ass for putting me in this situation. I thought I told you the last time I couldn't keep bailing you out, but it's like déjà vu all over again."

"I'm telling you, this one is different—so different that my first call was to the Pentagon. The team that attacked us was Russian."

"Russian? What the fuck are Russians doing in Malta? Actually, what the fuck are you doing in Malta? And why the fuck am I swearing so much?" He took a deep breath before he collapsed onto his chair. "Seriously, Jon, I'm getting too old for this shit."

"You and me both. But we had no choice. They came in firing."

Payne did his best to summarize the events of the past forty-eight hours—when they had arrived in Malta, how they had bumped into Jarkko, why they had spoken to Ulster, and where they had met up with Marissa. The only question he couldn't answer was, *who*?

Who were the Russians?

That was the element that had him baffled.

The one thing that didn't make sense.

Thanks to their former line of work, Payne and Jones were still considered valuable assets to the U.S. Government. Not only did they work for the Pentagon as consultants on a regular basis, but their knowledge of classified missions from the past two decades made them possible marks for foreign operatives.

But the Russians didn't treat them as assets to be potentially flipped.

They viewed them as targets.

Literal targets.

Opening fire without saying a word.

Why in the world would they do that?

Payne and Jones realized that the Cold War was heating up again, and the two superpowers were constantly probing each other for weaknesses. But this attack reeked of desperation, as if they needed to stop the duo from doing something before they got away. Otherwise, why stage an assault in a national building on foreign soil?

And yet, if their goal had been to kill them, why did the Russians show up with sidearms and flash-bangs? Why not go full tilt and bring in actual grenades and automatic weapons? Against that type of firepower, the duo wouldn't have stood a chance.

All of which led Payne to believe that this was related to their search.

Possibly a shakedown for information that simply went wrong.

Payne didn't have proof, but that's what his gut was telling him.

And Dial happened to agree.

"Okay," Dial said. "I believe you. I'm willing to put my ass on the line for you yet again in order to keep this quiet. I'm not quite sure how we're going to do that—maybe give credit to the local cops for stopping such a horrible threat. I'm sure the media will eat that up. But dammit, Jon, you need to stop hunting for treasures. Don't you have enough cash as it is?"

Payne laughed. "I'm not in it for the money. I'm in it for the history."

"Bullshit!" Dial exclaimed. "You're in it for the hunt. It's the same thing that I'm currently missing from my life, the one thing I can't get while I'm tied to a fucking desk."

"You're welcome to join us, Nick. Last time turned out all right."

"I appreciate the offer—I really do—but I get the sense you need me here. At least until you figure out who is after you."

Payne glanced across the room at Jones, who had just finished taking pictures of all the dead Russians and using a special program on his phone to scan their fingerprints. Thanks to the Payne Industries tech in his device, he was able to upload that information securely to Raskin, who would then go through his numerous databases until he got a hit. "Due to the slow response time of the local police—who I'm told were quite heroic in their efforts to take out the Russian horde that stormed the library—we'll probably have some names before dinner."

Dial smiled. "They still aren't there yet?"

"Nope. Unless they're setting up a perimeter. Don't blame them, though. This entire room is lined with books. My guess is no one outside heard a thing."

"Meaning you could have walked away from the scene. Thanks for not doing that."

"Come on, Nick. We respect you and the law way too much for that. Plus, in this case, we were completely innocent."

Dial grinned. "Not exactly."

"What's that supposed to mean?"

"Are you familiar with the gun laws in Malta? I'm guessing, no. I'm also guessing that the weapons you used to innocently kill six foreign nationals were either smuggled into Malta by your private jet or Jarkko's sex yacht. I'm also guessing that those weapons have no serial numbers and were probably wiped clean at the scene, both of which are illegal acts. Unless, of course, you guys got really sloppy and decided to buy your weapons in country from a Russian arms dealer, who then followed you to your meeting at the library in order to steal back his merchandise, thus forcing you to kill him and his men in self-defense."

Payne laughed. "But other than that, *completely* innocent."

Dial noticed the laughter and decided to make him sweat. "Seriously, Jon. You need to be more careful. Personally, I don't care where you got the guns, but you better have a good answer for the local cops because someone is going to ask."

"Any suggestions?"

"Only one, but you aren't going to like it."

"Why not?"

"Because I think your best option is to tell them that DJ is your bodyguard."

"Excuse me?"

"Listen. You don't have a badge, and DJ has a private-eye license. Simply say that you hired him to provide personal protection on your business trip."

Payne shook his head vehemently. "Listen to me, and listen to me good: I would rather go to jail for six consecutive life sentences than tell anyone that DJ was my bodyguard. He would never—and I do mean *never*—let me live that down. He would literally get business cards that said he was my bodyguard and hand them out to everyone at the Pentagon. Sorry, Nick, I'm willing to eat some shit, but I'm not going to eat that turd burger."

"Hey, you asked for my opinion, and I personally think that's your best option. But if your stupid pride won't let you go that route, you can always fight dirty."

"Meaning what?"

"Just blame it on the black guy."

Payne finally caught on. "Oh my God, you're fucking with me. I was just attacked by six angry Russians, yet you're busting my balls for reaching out. Good for you!"

Dial couldn't help but laugh. "Serves you right, you prick. I was having a good day until you called, now I'll be here all night doing paperwork. Thanks a lot."

"At least you'll have Henri and his ponytail to keep you company."

"Screw you."

Payne grinned. "Tell that furry Frenchman I said hello."

"Will do. Same to DJ and Jarkko. And Jon?"

"Yeah?"

"Lose my number."

CHAPTER 25

Volkov wasn't used to failure.

Occasionally he was forced to deal with incompetence and outright betrayals, but rarely failure. It happened so infrequently that he didn't know how to react.

Somehow he had managed to keep his cool outside the library. When the henchman with the gym bags had started to walk toward his table, Volkov had shaken his head and held up his phone to let the goon know that he would call him instead. Then Volkov had paid his bill and left the plaza before the police had even arrived.

After that, he had walked the streets of Valletta until he was far enough away from the chaos at the library to summon his driver. Once he was safely inside the tinted town car, Volkov called the henchman and told him where they would meet.

The plumber knew he couldn't tell Volkov the truth about the library.

Not if he wanted to live.

So while he waited to be picked up, he hid in an alley behind a dumpster and concocted his version of the shootout, all in hopes of surviving the day.

When the town car arrived, he hustled from his hiding spot and climbed into the back seat where Volkov eagerly awaited details about the library. To make sure the driver couldn't listen, Volkov raised the soundproof partition before he started his questioning.

"What the hell happened?" he demanded as the car pulled away from the curb. "I want to know everything!"

"They were waiting for us," the plumber explained. "The moment we stepped into the room, they started shooting. I don't know if someone tipped them off or they had access to the camera feeds outside the building, but they knew we were coming."

"Impossible!" Volkov blurted. "The cameras were down."

"Sir," the plumber said as he mixed fact with fiction, "I've never seen anything like it. These guys weren't normal bodyguards. They were elite soldiers with unorthodox tactics. The only reason I'm still alive is because of the woman."

Volkov had seen Marissa when she had unlocked the library door but knew nothing about her except her beauty. "How so?"

"When the shooting began, she dove over the main counter and started loading documents into these gym bags," he blatantly lied. "We figured they must have some importance, so I dealt with her while the rest of my team took on the bodyguards. My initial plan was to kill her without mercy, but since we knew nothing about her or how she relates to the Finn, I opted to spare her life in case you wanted to question her at a later date."

The plumber took a deep breath in order to sell his lie. "But I'm telling you, sir, it was the *toughest* decision of my life. It took all of my discipline and military training to stop myself from pulling that trigger and splattering her brains against the wall. Instead, I had to settle for kicking her in the ribs and taking her bags while she writhed on the floor in agony."

He shook his head with fake angst. "I hope I did the right thing."

Volkov considered the henchman's statement as he stared out the window at the harbor. There were so many unanswered questions in his mind that he didn't know what to ask. "Yes, comrade. You did the right thing. I am glad that you showed restraint. The woman may prove useful in the future. Too bad the rest of your team didn't possess your valor."

"They fought hard, sir. You would have been proud."

Volkov barely heard his reply. His thoughts were focused on the bags instead. "While you were waiting, did you look inside?"

The henchman shook his head. "Of course not, sir. I got them for you."

Volkov reached out and grabbed the first gym bag from the floor. It was much heavier than he thought it would be. Whatever the woman was trying to take had some bulk.

Much to his surprise, Volkov could feel his heart race.

The mystery of it all made him feel alive.

Like a child waking up on Christmas morning.

Unfortunately, it was followed by a stocking full of coal.

Because the bags were filled with crap.

Nothing but crap.

"What is this?" Volkov shouted as he rifled through multiple pamphlets about Valletta, several takeout menus, a Maltese phonebook, and various other pieces of junk.

The henchman stood his ground. "I don't understand! Why would the woman risk her life to save this meaningless shit? Unless…"

Volkov stared at him. "Unless what?"

"Unless it was a ploy of some kind. Maybe she wanted to distract us while the Finn stole something of real value from the library."

"Like what?" Volkov demanded.

The henchman shrugged. "Sorry, sir, I can't imagine. The library was quite large, and I was focused on the woman and retrieving the bags. I know nothing about the Finn or his motivations. He could have been after anything."

Volkov nodded with sudden clarity. He had planned to go back to Russia to regroup, but he suddenly realized that he needed to learn more about the smuggler—or else this entire trip had been a waste. With a touch of a button, he lowered the car's partition so he could speak to the driver. "Change of plans. Instead of the airport, take us to the Grand Harbour Marina."

The henchman grimaced in frustration. His plan had worked perfectly until then. He was so close to going home he could almost taste it. "Sir, are you sure that's wise? His men cut through our squad with little difficulty. I'm not sure how much protection I can offer you."

Volkov cocked his head slightly. Until that moment, he had believed everything the henchman had told him, but now he wasn't so sure. How did a soldier go from bragging about his "discipline and military training" and his deep desire to "splatter brains against the wall" to cowering in fear?

He probably didn't—unless he had been a coward all along.

Volkov closed his eyes and thought back to the moment when the henchman had opened the library door. In his mind, he saw it quite clearly: the look on the henchman's face.

It wasn't relief from surviving the fight.

It was embarrassment from sneaking away.

"Maybe you're right," Volkov said as he opened his eyes and

focused on the henchman. "If his bodyguards are as good as you say, perhaps retreat would be prudent."

"You're the boss, sir. I'll do whatever you say. But I think that is probably wise."

In that instant, Volkov knew that he was correct.

The henchman had been playing him all along.

And for that, he must pay the ultimate price.

Volkov reached into his pocket with his one hand, while raising the partition with the other. He didn't mind killing in front of witnesses; in fact, he normally enjoyed the rush. But in this case, he didn't want to get arterial spray on the windshield.

The last thing he needed was to be pulled over.

Corpses were so hard to explain.

Volkov calmly waited until the partition clicked shut before he flicked open his blade. A split-second later, he unleashed his frustration in a torrent of displaced rage.

Throat. Hands. Arms. Face.

Whatever got in his way.

He just kept on slashing and slashing until there was no goon left.

Just blood and bone and meat.

Volkov wiped his hands on the dead man's pants before he placed the call to his hackers. He told them where he was headed and ordered them to shut down surveillance in that area.

A minute later, the cameras at Grand Harbour Marina went offline.

Not only the security feed, but every camera on every boat in Birgu.

As if the entire marina had been sucked into a technological black hole.

Volkov had no idea how they did it, but they were worth every ruble.

Now he would be free to search the Finn's yacht in private.

CHAPTER 26

Malta was a peaceful country with an average of five murders per year, so the police were less than thrilled when they arrived at the scene and found seven dead bodies and significant damage to their national library. But as expected, a phone call from the director of the homicide division of Interpol to the commissioner of the Malta Police Force was enough to convince the local authorities not to arrest Payne and his friends.

At least for the time being.

The main sticking point—as Dial had feared—was the arsenal they had used in their supposed act of self-defense. Back in the States, Payne and Jones would have come clean about their weapons, knowing full well that they would never get arrested because of their connections to the Pentagon, but they couldn't do that here.

Gun laws were a tricky thing in foreign countries, so they ultimately decided to lie to the police in order to cover their asses and to protect Jarkko from potential smuggling charges. Although they knew Dial would stand by them through thick and thin, they highly doubted he would do the same for a hard-drinking Finn that he barely knew.

With little time to think of a cover story, they decided to tell the police that Payne had disarmed one of the Russians in their initial breach and had used his weapon to take down another. As luck should have it, the second goon had a backup pistol as well. That allowed Payne to arm Jones and Jarkko, who evened the odds and joined the fray.

The police were skeptical at first, until they learned about Payne's background in the military. Once they found out he had been an elite soldier in the special forces, they started to come around. Before long, he was teaching them some of his best moves and offering to pay for any damage to the library that wasn't covered by insurance.

And yet hours passed before they were finally allowed to leave the library. The sky was dark by then, and Payne was soooo hungry he was tempted to kill again just to get some protein. Thankfully, Jones persuaded him to buy some takeout instead on their way to Jarkko's yacht, which they had decided to use as mission headquarters. Not only would it provide them with more privacy and mobility than their hotel suites, but it also had the rest of Jarkko's armory.

Something they would need if the Russians returned.

One of the biggest drawbacks about lying to the police was the simple fact that they were forced to leave their weapons behind. With a fully armed enemy possibly lurking around every corner, the short drive from Valletta to Birgu felt incredibly long. As Galea's sedan made its way through the ancient neighborhoods, the streets took on an ominous feel, as if they had been transported back to a time when sword-wielding marauders invaded with regularity.

Payne and Jones had been initially reluctant to call Galea. Not because they didn't trust him, but because they didn't want to put him in danger. Ultimately they decided to be upfront with their driver and let him make his own decision; otherwise, they would have been forced to use a cab or hitch a ride with the police. Once they told Galea what they had been through at the library, he had insisted on picking them up and driving them to wherever they wanted to go. As a proud Maltese, he felt it was his duty to help visitors in their time of need.

Needless to say, his gratuity was going to be huge.

Despite the excitement of the day, their energy was low by the time they reached the marina, but all of that changed as they walked along the dock toward the yacht. Jarkko led the way past several boats of varying shapes and sizes. They bobbed gently in the calm waters of the harbor. Payne was directly behind him, followed by Marissa and Jones, both of whom were carrying the food since Payne had picked up the tab.

Jones was just getting ready to comment on how peaceful things seemed after the chaos at the library when Jarkko suddenly stopped.

"Not good," he whispered.

"What's wrong?" Payne demanded.

Jarkko pointed at his yacht. "Jarkko no leave lights on."

Payne glanced ahead. One of the cabin lights was lit. He turned back and looked at Jones. "Did you touch any lights?"

Jones crouched and lowered their food. "Definitely not."

Payne looked around and realized how exposed they were on the dock. If the Russians had set up an ambush, there was nowhere to run. "Marissa, can you swim?"

"Yes," she said, nervously. "Why?"

"If bullets start to fly, hit the water. Don't stop swimming until you're out of harm's way. Just hide in the darkness along the quay until the police arrive."

She put her bag of food on the dock. "Please don't take this the wrong way, but I'm starting to regret meeting you guys."

Payne smiled. "Don't worry. DJ hears that all the time."

Jones winced. "Ouch. Friendly fire."

"Let's hope that's all we're facing."

Jones glanced back toward the street. There were several cars on the road where Jarkko had punched a Fiat earlier in the day and plenty of people strolling on the sidewalk, but no one looked suspicious. "How do you want to play this?"

Instead of answering, Payne hopped onto a nearby fishing boat that was tied to the dock. He spotted a long metal pole that was equipped with a three-pronged spearhead. He pulled it from its rack and handed it to Jones.

Jones swooshed the trident through the air a couple of times before he stabbed an imaginary foe in the darkness. "Hell, yeah! I'm gonna go Aquaman on their ass!"

Jarkko stared at him with envy. "Why is David the Aquaman?"

Payne tossed him a flare gun. "Because you're the Human Torch."

Jarkko nodded. "Okay. Jarkko be Mister Torch."

Now it was Marissa's turn to pout. "Wait just a second. Why do they get weapons and I have to swim? Somehow that doesn't seem right."

"Show of hands," Payne said as he pulled a fishing knife from its sheath and admired its blade in the dim light. "Who among us hasn't been in the military?"

Marissa self-consciously raised her hand.

Payne nodded and stepped off the boat. "And there's your answer."

"Just because you guys served, doesn't mean—"

Payne cut her off. "Listen. I admire your bravery and appreciate your spirit, but we're heading to a potential gunfight with weapons from Gilligan's Island, so as much as I'd love to stand here in the open and have a lengthy discussion with you about my sexist ways, I need to pull rank and ask you to pipe down before you get us all killed."

"Fine," she whispered. "But for the record, I never called you a sexist."

"And just so you know, I'm definitely not."

"Good. Glad to hear it."

"But while we're gone, do us a favor and keep our dinner warm."

She couldn't help but smile. "Oh my God. You're such an ass!"

Payne laughed as he crept away in the darkness. Jones and Jarkko followed closely behind, each of them scanning the surrounding boats for any signs of an ambush while Marissa grabbed their food and hid in the shadows.

Jarkko's yacht was up ahead on the right in the second berth from the end. As the trio moved forward, their footsteps were masked by the incessant sounds of the sea.

The rippling waves.

A distant motor.

A clanging bell.

Payne stopped just short of the yacht and stared at the water around its hull. If someone was moving around on board, he might be able to see the slightest tremor.

But he saw nothing.

And more importantly, he *felt* nothing.

Back at the library, a gut feeling had notified him of an imminent attack. But as he crouched in the darkness near the stern of the boat, he sensed no threat at all.

Payne waited until Jones and Jarkko were by his side before he announced his next move. "I'm going in. If you see anything suspicious, scream and let me know."

"How's your gut?" Jones asked.

"Hungry. But unconcerned."

"Even so, be careful. Look for tripwires in case they rigged this thing to blow."

He appreciated the concern. "Don't worry. I'll be fine."

"I'm not worried about you. If the boat explodes, I might get hurt."

Payne rolled his eyes as he stepped onto the yacht. He moved with speed but never hurried, always making sure his stride was clear before he took another. When he peeked into the first cabin window, he saw what he expected to see: the interior of the boat had been tossed.

After that, Payne moved from window to window, just to make sure the yacht was empty, but he felt confident the Russians were long gone. His instincts told him that they had probably searched the place while he and his friends were being questioned by the police. All of which supported his theory that the gunfight in Valletta was a robbery gone wrong.

But what were the Russians looking for?

The letter?

Or something else?

As things stood, Payne barely had knowledge of the treasure itself, let alone anything about the historical period when it surfaced or an understanding of the people involved. For him to fully comprehend what they were up against meant he had to learn more about the past, and the best person to teach him was the woman he had gone out of his way to protect.

Ultimately, he knew she would be the key to everything.

CHAPTER 27

Jarkko cursed several times in multiple languages when he saw the interior of his yacht. Liquor bottles and glassware had been smashed, mattresses and furniture had been slashed, and some of the navigational equipment on the bridge had been destroyed.

The Russians had done more than search the boat.

They had expressed their displeasure.

Payne immediately checked to see if they had found Jarkko's hidden armory. Thankfully, the secret closet hadn't been spotted, and his arsenal remained intact. Payne quickly armed himself and handed weapons to the others in case the Russians returned.

Much to his surprise, Marissa took a Beretta and checked its clip with a practiced hand. She may have never served in the military, but it was pretty apparent she had been around guns at some point in her life. He made a mental note to ask her about it later, but for the time being, they had more important things to worry about.

After a quick search, it was obvious the Russians had found the documents that had started Jarkko's journey. Ironically, he had been uncomfortable with bringing the collection to their initial meeting with Marissa, so he had left the boxes in his stateroom for safekeeping.

And that decision had cost him everything.

Payne knew his friend was hurting, so he approached with trepidation. Jarkko was standing on the flybridge, just staring out at the harbor. His swearing had stopped a few minutes earlier and had been replaced by total silence. "I'm sorry about your yacht. I know how much it means to you. Is there anything I can do?"

Jarkko shrugged. "Yacht is just a thing. She can be fixed."

Payne nodded. "Do you think she can run?"

Jarkko forced a smile. "Why? Are you looking to buy?"

Payne shook his head. "Right now, we're sitting ducks. We

could be attacked by land or sea. I'd feel a lot safer if we were in the open water. Easier to see people coming."

Jarkko gritted his teeth. "Jarkko *wants* them to come."

"I do, too—but on *our* terms. Why give them an edge?"

Jarkko nodded in understanding. "You get ropes. Jarkko start yacht."

Although Payne had been around boats for most of his life, he had little experience with yachts. Growing up in the Steel City, he used to watch the massive barges as they crawled at a snail's pace before unloading their freight on the local wharfs. Then at Annapolis, he was introduced to the best ships in the naval fleet before he tested their full capabilities in combat. And once he had retired from the military, he had bought a pleasure craft for lazy summer days on Pittsburgh's three rivers, but it was half the size of Jarkko's boat.

Measuring seventy feet in length, the sleek yacht had twin V12 engines and a maximum speed of forty knots but was built for entertaining. With spacious foredeck seating and a separate area for sunbathing, several people could stay outside, while several others remained in the air-conditioned comfort of the glass-lined saloon. Private stairs led to the master stateroom on the lower level, while a separate stairwell led to three other cabins, each with a private bathroom.

Despite its current state, it was one impressive vessel.

Payne hustled to the stern, where he went to work on the ropes. The first line came off the bollard with ease, but a second line went into the water underneath the pier. Payne tugged on the line with one hand, and it hardly budged.

"What's the holdup?" Jones asked from above.

Payne glanced up at him. "You know anything about yachts?"

"Not really, but I do know this: Jarkko's yacht is nicer than your plane."

"Believe it or not, I agree with you. I might ask him to trade."

Jones laughed as he walked down the rear stairs toward Payne. "If you do, never turn on a black light. I can't even imagine the stains that Jarkko's made on this thing."

Payne grimaced. "Good point."

Jones kept laughing. "Truth be told, if the Russians touched anything in his bedroom, we may not have to hunt them down. They're probably already dying of syphilis."

"Well, you're the expert."

"Says the guy who gave it to me."

"Wow!" Payne blurted. "I have no idea who you were trying to insult with that one, but it just kind of blew right up in your face, didn't it?"

"You know what I meant."

"Honest to God, I have no clue what you meant!"

"Me, neither," Jones admitted as he signaled to move on. "So, why did you ask me about yachts when I asked you about the holdup?"

Payne pointed at the rope. "Because I have no idea what this line is for. For some damn reason, it goes underneath the pier. I pulled on it, but it's caught on something."

Jones tucked his weapon under his shirt. "Here. Let me help."

Payne grabbed the line with both hands while Jones did the same. By pulling together, the rope slowly emerged from the murky depths of the marina.

One foot, then two.

Five feet, then ten.

And then much to their surprise, two *actual* feet appeared.

Both of them tied to the end of the line.

"What the fuck!" Jones shouted as he let go of the rope and hopped backward in disgust. "Is that a body?"

Payne struggled to keep the line in place. "Dammit, DJ. Keep pulling!"

"Why? I don't need a body. I already have one."

"Come on," Payne growled. "We need to see who it is."

Jones swore under his breath, but he grabbed the rope.

A minute later, they were hauling the faceless henchman onto the pier. Jarkko heard the commotion and came running, just in time to see Volkov's handiwork. The corpse had so many slashes that they were tough to count—a process made difficult by teeth marks.

The goon had wanted to be a plumber, but he had ended up a seafood buffet.

Nothing more than dinner for the creatures of the deep.

As much as he hated to do it, Jones took out his phone and scanned the dead man's fingerprints. Most of them were still intact. Then he opened the man's mouth and took a single photograph of his teeth. There was no way they were going to identify him with facial recognition, but maybe his dental work would give them a lead.

"Guys," Payne whispered as Jones continued to work. "Nothing about this makes sense. Not this. Not the assault at the library. None of it. Bodies are piling up, and I have no idea why. Who the hell are we facing, and why are they so damn pissed?"

Jones winced in disgust as he wiped his phone on his shirt. "Obviously it has something to do with the treasure, or else they wouldn't have stolen Jarkko's collection."

Payne agreed, so he glanced at Jarkko. "Who else knew about the collection? Did you tell anyone? Someone you slept with? Someone at a bar? Someone you slept with at a bar?"

Jarkko shook his head. "Jarkko tell no one! Jarkko is sure!"

"Fine," Payne said. "What about the guy you got it from? Could he have told someone? You said he was Russian, right? Maybe he's the source of the leak."

Jarkko shrugged. "Jarkko don't know. Jarkko no talk to him since Jarkko get collection. Should Jarkko call and ask?"

Payne nodded. "At this point, I don't see how it could hurt. Whoever we're facing already has the damn collection, so what do we have to hide?"

Jones glanced at his phone. It was still slimy. "I'll send these prints to Randy and see if he found out anything about the other goons. Maybe that will give us a lead."

Payne took a deep breath. "And I'll call Nick. He'll want to know about the body."

Jones laughed. "Good luck with that."

"Trust me, I'd rather be calling Randy."

"I'm gonna tell Randy you said that. It'll probably make his day."

"Why bother? If I know him, he probably tapped our phones and has been listening to us the entire time. Haven't you, Randy?"

There was a slight delay before all of their phones beeped once.

CHAPTER 28

Marissa had seen the dead body on the pier and wanted no part of it. She had been around enough corpses in the past few hours to last her a lifetime.

With nothing better to do, she decided to clean. Not because she viewed it as her job, but because it was the right thing to do. Although she had just met Jarkko, she had noticed the distraught look on his face when he had first entered his yacht and wanted to do anything she could to help ease his pain. As an added bonus, she found that cleaning actually helped relieve her stress in times of turmoil. There was something about putting things in their proper place that was reassuring to her, as if she had some control in the chaos that surrounded her.

The behavior had started when she was just a kid. Anytime her parents would fight—which was quite often and frequently violent—she would look for things to organize in her bedroom.

Books on the shelf. Toys in their chest. Clothes in her closet.

Anything to take her mind off her real problems.

And she did the same thing on the yacht.

By the time the police had finished questioning the guys and had given them permission to leave the marina, the interior of the boat didn't look so bad. There was little she could do about the slashed couches, other than sealing them with duct tape, but everything else had improved dramatically. So much so, Jarkko picked her up and gave her a massive bear hug.

It lifted her in more ways than one.

Thankfully, Nick Dial had worked his magic with the police commissioner; otherwise, they wouldn't have been allowed to leave at all. But since there was no blood evidence on board the yacht and Jarkko had no intention of pressing charges against the vandals, Dial had argued that they should be allowed to leave for their personal safety—and for the safety of the marina.

The commissioner had quickly agreed.

After discussing it over with Jones and Jarkko, Payne decided the safest place for them wasn't the harbor, since it was bordered by land on three sides and filled with hundreds of boats. So Jarkko headed to the waters of St. George's Bay. It was a short boat ride from Birgu and next to Payne and Jones's hotel, so the duo was quite familiar with the surrounding terrain.

For them, it was hard to believe that less than twelve hours had passed since their morning breakfast at the Corinthia Hotel. During that meal, their biggest concerns had been what boat to rent, what attractions to see, and how to carry their things. Now they were worried about a Maltese treasure, crazed Russians, and catching syphilis on Jarkko's yacht.

Through it all, the one thing that hadn't changed was Payne's appetite.

It was as predictable as the setting sun.

While being questioned by Dial and the police, Payne had nibbled on an assortment of goods from Jarkko's pantry: nuts, crackers, dried fruits, and a Finnish meat product that turned out to be reindeer jerky. Although the snacks had temporarily satiated the beast inside, they had failed to slay the demon. It had kept growing and growing until it demanded to be fed. The instant they passed Fort Tigné and turned north into the Mediterranean toward St. Julian's, Payne left his post on the stern and headed inside the yacht.

A sliding glass door opened into the rear of the glass-lined interior. A galley equipped with a refrigerator, stove, sink, oven, microwave, dishwasher, and marble counters sat on his left, while a dining area with a long wooden table and cushioned benches sat on his right. Further up the center aisle was the main social area. It had a large couch, love seat, and coffee table. Beyond that was the helm and the private stairs that led to the stateroom at the front of the yacht.

But Payne didn't care about any of that.

His sole focus was finding food.

For the third time in the past few hours, Marissa had surprised him. Earlier it had been her impressive dexterity with the Beretta that had opened his eyes. Then she had taken it upon herself to tidy up the yacht while he was dealing with the police. And now she was in the kitchen, heating up the takeout that he had bought for the group upon leaving the library. He knew some women wouldn't have pitched in after his earlier crack about keeping their dinner warm, but she had taken it the way he had intended it—as nothing more than a silly joke.

"Wow," Payne said, "dinner smells great."

Marissa was standing in front of the electric stove, stirring a pot of spaghetti and meatballs. "Thanks. I dumped it out of the containers all by myself."

"Ouch," he said as he entered the galley and grabbed a piece of garlic bread from a hot baking sheet. "I was being serious. It smells really good. And the yacht looks unbelievable. I can't believe you whipped it into shape so quickly."

She glanced back at him and realized that he was being sincere. "Sorry. I didn't mean to snap. It's been a long and confusing day. Some of it still hasn't sunk in."

"That's probably a good thing."

"You're probably right."

"How's your leg?"

"Sore, but I'll survive."

Payne sidled up next to her and tried to dip his bread in the simmering tomato sauce, but she smacked his hand with hers.

"Ouch!" he said with a laugh.

She held up her wooden spoon in a threatening manner. "That's the second time you used that word. Don't make me cause a third. Now get out of my kitchen."

Payne grinned. "It's technically a *galley*, so—"

"Out!" she ordered with a smile. "Make yourself useful and get the others. And tell them to wash their hands. I can't believe how many corpses you've touched today."

Payne was about to bite into his garlic bread when he realized she was right. He discreetly tossed the piece in the trash on his way to disinfect whatever he could.

Once the yacht had reached the bay and Jones had searched the interior for listening devices, the four of them gathered in the dining area for their late-night meal. In addition to the spaghetti and meatballs, they also had an order of lasagna, some chicken parmigiana, a container of cheese ravioli, a large house salad, and several cans of soda from Jarkko's refrigerator.

Despite their need for sustenance, Payne felt they should remain vigilant during dinner, so they turned off the interior lighting and ate in candlelight. This allowed them to see out of the glass-lined interior in a full 360 degrees. He highly doubted the Russians would attack again after suffering so many losses in Valletta, but nothing about their behavior had made sense to Payne, so he wasn't going to take any chances.

With no unbroken plates to eat on, they made do with the take-out containers and baking sheets. Not that anyone was complaining. All of them were so famished after such a grueling day that they ate in near silence for the first few minutes. It wasn't until Jones cracked a joke that they snapped out of their food-induced trances and had an actual conversation.

Jones spoke in a high-pitched, motherly tone. "So, kids, how was your day? Did anything exciting happen at school?"

Payne looked at Jarkko, who looked at Marissa, who looked at Payne. Then all of them burst out in laughter over the absurdity of their situation.

Jarkko spoke first. "Jarkko punched car and made puppet out of dead Russian."

Payne pointed at him. "I saw that! What the hell were you doing?"

"Trying to make David laugh."

Jones nodded. "And it worked."

Marissa went next. "I dove over a freaking counter to avoid gunfire. I did not expect that when I woke up this morning."

"You looked like your namesake," Payne teased.

"My namesake?" she asked, confused.

"Lara Croft."

She laughed. "Oh my God! I totally forgot about that. I guess you're right!"

Jones leaned back on the cushioned bench. "As for me, I got to climb. And jump. And kill. Pretty much my perfect day."

Payne laughed at the absurdity of his statement. "Truth be told, I was pretty impressed by your moves. That flip you did was like something out of an action flick. Unfortunately, your landing was straight from a disaster movie. You crashed and burned big time."

"What do you mean? I took out two Russian gunmen while evading a grenade. I hardly call that a disaster."

"Actually," Payne corrected as he twirled pasta on his fork, "you took out *one* Russian gunman. I shot the other guy in the face before he could shoot you in yours."

Jones played the scene back in his mind. "Is *that* why his head exploded? I thought it was from the grenade. Oh well, perfect day ruined because of Jon."

Jarkko looked at Payne. "And what about you?"

"What do you mean?" Payne asked.

"What was your highlight?" Jarkko wondered.

Payne put down his fork and wiped a pretend tear from his eye. "I'd say sitting here and eating dinner with all of you."

Jones threw a piece of bread at him. "Boooo!"

Jarkko and Marissa quickly joined in. "Boooo!"

"Fine!" Payne said as he tried to defend himself from flying carbohydrates. "If I had to choose one thing from today, I'd probably say that soup at lunch. It was soooo good."

Jarkko nodded. "Best soup ever."

Marissa pretended to pout. "I spend the entire day whipping up a fancy Italian feast, and the highlight of your day was the soup at lunch? What about meeting me?"

Payne gave it some thought as he chewed. "That was third."

"Third?" she blurted. "What was second?"

"Weren't you listening? I shot a guy in his face to save DJ's life." Payne reached over and grabbed Jones by his cheeks. "Look at this mug. How could I let anyone hurt this mug?"

Jones pushed him away. "Bad touch. Bad touch."

"Besides," Payne said, "your highlight wasn't meeting me; it was diving over a counter. I did the same damn thing like two minutes later."

She smiled. "Maybe so, but I stuck my landing."

"I stuck mine, too," Payne claimed. "Stuck it right against the wall. I hit so damn hard I think I cracked my ass." He started to stand up. "Here, do me a favor and take a look."

She grabbed the wooden spoon from one of the takeout containers. "Sit your ass back down. Remember what I told you before— don't make me use this!"

Jones looked at her funny. "What in the hell are you going to do with the spoon? And if you did it before, *please* tell me you washed it before you served the spaghetti."

Jarkko kept eating. "Jarkko don't mind. Sauce taste good."

Jones grimaced. "Dude! That's disgusting."

"What?" Jarkko said. "Marissa is good cook. David should thank her."

Payne nodded and raised his can of soda. "Actually, everyone should be thanking her. Somehow she brought a sense of normalcy to this otherwise abnormal day. Thank you for making us feel at home."

Jones and Jarkko followed his lead and lifted their sodas in salute.

Marissa sheepishly smiled and clinked their cans before she set hers down on the table. Through it all—from the urgent text message from Petr Ulster, to the shootout at the library, to the madness of the marina—one thing had been nagging her, one thing that she desperately needed to find out, and she felt this was the time to do it.

"Guys," she said, "I appreciate the toast and the kind words. I really, truly do. Today has been unlike any other day in my entire life. And yet, as I look across the table at each of you, there is one tiny thing that keeps echoing over and over in my brain. No matter how hard I try, I just can't get this question out of my head."

"Go on," Payne encouraged. "What's troubling you?"

She took a deep breath before she spoke. "Why the hell am I here?"

CHAPTER 29

Because of the chaos of the day, one crucial thing had slipped the minds of the three men staring back at Marissa: she still hadn't been briefed about the treasure.

Over the past few hours, she had picked up bits and pieces on her own. She knew the Russians had stolen a collection of documents from Jarkko's stateroom. She also assumed that the collection tied in with her expertise, or else she wouldn't have been contacted in the first place. But no one—including Petr Ulster—had told her any specifics.

And that needed to change for the sake of her sanity.

"Holy crap," Jones said as the realization washed over him. "You've been under fire since the library, facing the same shit that we have, yet you have no idea why." He shook his head in amazement. "Great job, Jon. Way to keep your troops in the loop."

Payne looked at Jones. "Wait. Why is it my fault?"

"Because I don't want it to be mine. Duh."

"Fine! I'll take the blame, but I think it's only fair to point out that I've been kind of busy trying to keep us alive and out of jail, so excuse me if I didn't find time to schedule a briefing."

"Guys," she assured them, "no one's to blame. We were attacked before you had a chance to tell me. Then there were too many cops around to discuss it or too many calls to make to pull me aside. I swear I'm not mad at anyone. I'm just confused. So I'd appreciate if someone could fill me in from the very beginning. Otherwise, I think I may just lose my shit right here, and I don't want to do that in front of people that I actually like."

So the men explained everything, each of them filling in sections of the backstory while the others continued to eat. Through it all, Marissa said very little. She asked a few questions for clarity's sake, but other than that, she just let them talk until they had nothing more to say.

Once they were done, the men tried to gauge her reaction—to see if they had risked their lives for nothing. But she gave them little as she processed the information. Not to torture them, but because she needed some time to think. Jones started to crack a joke to end the painful silence, but she raised her hand and signaled for him to stop while she finalized one last thought.

"Okay," she said. "Now I'm ready."

Payne furrowed his brow. "For what?"

"I'm assuming this is when you guys ask me a million questions, so fire away."

Jarkko went first. "Do you have boyfriend?"

She couldn't help but laugh. "Oh my God! We were just attacked by Russian gangsters because of a box of documents that I might know something about, and your first question isn't about your stolen collection or the likelihood of Maltese treasure. It's about my social status?"

Jarkko nodded. "Not asking for Jarkko. Asking for friend."

She kept on laughing. "Next question!"

Jones shook his head at Jarkko. "Dude. Bad start."

Jarkko shrugged. "Sorry. Jarkko is sober and not thinking clearly. Give Jarkko second chance. Jarkko will ask better question. Jarkko promise."

Jones nodded. "Go on. But it better be good."

Jarkko stroked his chin in thought. "Do you have girlfriend?"

Jones and Marissa burst out laughing. There was just something infectious about Jarkko's delivery and sly grin that made his humor tough to resist. And considering how furious he had been when he had first seen the damage to his yacht, they were just glad to see him joking around. But for some reason, the comment rubbed Payne the wrong way. Maybe it was Payne's continued confusion about the Russians' aggression or his innate knack to take control of a group that had lost its focus, but he sensed that this was a time for information, not humor.

"Knock it off!" Payne growled in the authoritative tone that he had perfected in the military. "Marissa risked her life to help us today. She's not some floozy at a bar. She's a highly respected historian, so show her the respect that she deserves."

Just like that, the yacht was silent.

And all eyes were on Payne.

He dialed it back a notch before he continued. He wasn't mad at his friends. He simply needed them to know that it was time for business. And in order to establish Marissa's voice as one of authority, he felt she needed a proper introduction. "When I spoke to Petr, he told me that you had trained at the Archives for several months and felt that you could be a massive help to us, but he never told us about your area of expertise. Perhaps you could start there."

She sensed what he was doing and gave him an appreciative nod. "I have a DPhil in history from Oxford with a specialization in Maltese history. My most recent project has been focused on the Hypogeum of Ħal-Saflieni—a Neolithic subterranean structure dating back to the Saflieni phase in Maltese prehistory. But I am quite familiar with other eras as well, everything from the Megalithic Temples of Malta to the modern-day iterations of the Knights Hospitaller."

Jarkko whistled, impressed. "Jarkko must apologize for earlier joke. Jarkko now realizes you have no boyfriend or girlfriend. You are far too smart to date."

Marissa smiled. "Thanks, I think."

Jones jumped right in. "A couple questions. What the hell is a DPhil in history?"

"Doctor of Philosophy in history. It's Oxford's fancy way of saying PhD."

"So you're British?"

"Only when I pretend to be Lara Croft."

Jones laughed. "The reason I ask is because your lexicon is very American. If I had to guess, I'd say you went to undergrad in the States, but not somewhere pretentious like Harvard or Yale. I say that because I haven't noticed any northeastern vowels in your speech patterns."

"Very good," she said. "I went to undergrad at Stanford."

"But you aren't American."

She shook her head. "My mother was from Malta, hence my interest in Maltese history. And my father is from—well, my father is a long story. Suffice it to say, I grew up all over, which is why I have such a good ear for accents. Then again, I guess you do, too."

Jones nodded. "It was part of our training in the special forces. We had to make split-second decisions in the field based on whatever information we could get, and sometimes our ability to distinguish between friend and foe came down to word choice and accents."

"Interesting," she said, and she meant it.

"Tell us more about your research. You said the Hypogeum was a megalithic subterranean structure dating back to Maltese prehistory. How old is that?"

"The Hypogeum is *Neolithic*, not megalithic. And it dates back to 3,300 BC. To put that in perspective, that's roughly eight-hundred years older than the Great Pyramid of Giza."

"And it's here in Malta?"

She nodded. "It's located underneath the town of Paola in the South Eastern Region of Malta. It was discovered in 1902 AD in the middle of a crowded neighborhood when workers cutting a cistern for a new housing development broke through its roof."

"Damn. I'd love to see that. Maybe you can show us."

She shook her head. "No way. Not until this is over with. I don't want the Russians anywhere near that place. It's far too important to Malta."

"Fair enough," Jones said. "It will give me something to look forward to."

She smiled. "Me, too."

Payne chimed in. "And what can you tell us about the Knights Hospitaller?"

"Quite a bit. What do you know already?"

"Not much," he admitted. "Prior to bumping into Jarkko, I'd never heard of them—at least not by that name."

"For good reason," she explained. "They have been called many names over the years. In the beginning, they were known as the Order of Knights of the Hospital of Saint John of Jerusalem, and it was founded during the First Crusade after the conquest of Jerusalem in 1099 AD. The organization was a religious and military order with its own Papal charter, tasked with the defense and care of the Holy Land. Back in those days, the two most formidable military orders in the Holy Land were the Hospitallers—as they were known then—and the Knights Templar. Most people have heard of the latter, but the Hospitallers have a much longer history."

"Maybe so," Jones cracked, "but the Knights Templar have a *much* cooler name. What the hell is a Hospitaller anyway?"

She smiled. "To understand that, you have to understand the group's origins. Some scholars disagree on the specifics, but most believe that a group of caregivers founded a hospital in Jerusalem in the eleventh century on the site of the monastery of Saint John the Baptist. Their goal was to provide care for poor, sick, or injured pilgrims coming to the Holy Land, regardless of their faith or race. The devotion of the hospital workers was eventually recognized by Pope Paschal the Second in 1113 AD with an official edict known as a papal bull. Entitled *Pie postulatio voluntatis*, it officially decreed the establishment of the Hospitallers as a lay-religious order under the sole protection of the Church. The bull also gave the Order the right to elect its grand masters without interference from the Church or external authorities. As I mentioned, the group initially cared for pilgrims in Jerusalem, but the Order soon started to provide pilgrims with armed escorts—and those escorts eventually grew into a substantial force. Thus, the Knights Hospitaller became a military presence without losing its charitable roots."

Jones nodded in understanding. "Okay. Now their name makes sense. It was an order of knights that originated from the Hospital of Saint John in Jerusalem."

"Exactly!" she blurted, glad that someone was paying attention. "And do you know where that papal bull from 1113 AD is located?"

Jones guessed. "The Vatican Archives?"

She shook her head. "The National Library of Malta."

Jones groaned. "Seriously? I hope we didn't shoot it."

She laughed. "If you did, you would have been arrested for sure, because it's the library's most treasured possession."

Payne rejoined the conversation. "Please don't take this the wrong way, but why is it in Valletta and not the Vatican—or even Jerusalem? Or am I skipping ahead?"

She smiled. "You are *definitely* skipping ahead. But that's okay, because the Knights skipped around a lot, too. Keep in mind, their organization has been around for over nine hundred years, and unlike the Knights Templar, it still exists today."

CHAPTER 30

Marissa paused for a moment to take a sip of water. It had been a while since she had spoken so much about history. Normally her research was done in private, far from the prying eyes of other academics, who may be tempted to steal her ideas. Although she wasn't used to violence or bloodshed, she was accustomed to defending her turf in the cutthroat world of academia.

"As I'm sure you're aware," she said as she glanced around the table, "the *city* of Jerusalem was overrun by Saladin and his Muslim forces in 1187 AD, but the *Latin Kingdom* of Jerusalem held on until 1291 AD, at which time the Order sought refuge in the Kingdom of Cyprus."

Jones grinned. "I was aware, but I doubt Jon was. He majored in football."

Payne rolled his eyes. "Just because you can remember stuff from your childhood doesn't mean you should blurt it out."

Jones gave him a quick salute with his middle finger.

Marissa laughed. "Unfortunately, the Knights quickly found themselves immersed in the politics of Cyprus and realized that they would be better off somewhere else. They eventually gained control of Rhodes—the largest of the Greek Dodecanese islands—and a number of neighboring islands after a four-year military campaign that ended in 1310 AD."

Jarkko sighed. "Jarkko has been to Rhodes. Good island. Great women."

She smiled at him. "When you weren't cavorting with the locals, do you remember seeing a large medieval castle in the city of Rhodes?"

Jarkko nodded. "Very big. Hard to miss."

"That Gothic fortress is called the Palace of the Grand Master. It served as the administrative center of the Order during its time on Rhodes—a highly prosperous era when the organization temporarily became known as the Knights of Rhodes."

"Little-known fact," Jones said to show off his knowledge. "The state of Rhode Island is actually named after the Greek island of Rhodes."

"Really?" Marissa said. "I mean, it makes sense given the spelling, but I guess I never really thought about it until now. Good to know."

Jones tipped an imaginary cap. "You're welcome, my lady."

Payne remained focused. "Why was the Order so prosperous in Rhodes?"

"Believe it or not, it was because of their biggest rival: the Knights Templar. By the beginning of the fourteenth century, the Knights Hospitaller and the Knights Templar had grown so powerful that they were hard to control by European nobility, so the newly elected pope sent a letter to the grand masters of the two organizations asking them to merge. Neither leader was amenable to the idea, but the pope persisted and invited the two grand masters to France to discuss the matter. Unfortunately for Templar Grand Master Jacques de Molay, King Philip the Fourth of France owed a tremendous amount of money to the Templars from his war with the English, so he seized the opportunity to free himself from his debt. On Friday the Thirteenth of October in 1307 AD, King Philip ordered the grand master and hundreds of French Templars to be arrested at dawn. The arrest warrant claimed many things, including fraud, financial corruption, worshiping idols, and spitting on the cross."

"Damn," Jones said. "That's a baller move. Have the pope invite your biggest creditor to town for a chitchat, and then arrest his ass before he can leave."

Marissa smiled. "Since you like trivia, here's some for you. Many historians believe that Friday the Thirteenth is considered unlucky because the Templars were arrested on that day."

Jones nodded. "Good to know."

She tipped her imaginary cap. "You're welcome, my lord."

Jones glanced at Payne. "I like her. She's fun. Can we keep her?"

Payne rolled his eyes. "And how did that help the Knights Hospitaller?"

Marissa explained. "To use DJ's term, King Philip continued his baller moves by pressuring the pope to take his side. In November of 1307, Pope Clement issued the papal bull *Pastoralist praeeminentiae*, which instructed all Christian monarchs in Europe to arrest all Templars and seize their assets. The pope called for papal hearings to determine the Templars' innocence or guilt, but those were the days of the Inquisition, so you know how those trials turned out."

Jones nodded. "Like a black man with an all-white jury in Mississippi."

"Exactly," she said. "And King Philip used that to his advantage. Citing the public scandal that had been generated by the Templars' forced confessions, the king threatened military action against the Church unless the pope complied with his wishes to disband the Order. It took nearly five years, but Pope Clement eventually agreed. In 1312 AD at the Council of Vienne, Clement issued a series of papal bulls, including *Vox in excelso*, which officially dissolved the Knights Templar, and *Ad providam*, which turned over most of the Templar's assets to the Hospitallers."

"Hold up," Payne said in order to clarify things in his mind. "I've seen lots of references to the Templars' massive treasure in pop culture—"

Jones cut him off. "*National Treasure, The Da Vinci Code, The Last Templar*—"

"And so on," Payne added to silence Jones. "But you're telling me the Knights Templar were disbanded seven hundred years ago and all of their holdings were given to their rivals? Which means the Knights Hospitaller—and *not* the Templars—was the Order with all the loot?"

She nodded. "That's exactly what I'm saying."

Jarkko grinned at the news. "Jarkko has boner as big as treasure."

Jones grimaced in disgust, then slid away from Jarkko on the cushioned bench.

Payne ignored them both. "If that's the case, why are the Templars so much more famous than the Knights Hospitallers? As I mentioned, I wasn't aware of them before today."

Marissa replied. "Truth be told, I think the aura around the Templars first started when they were unfairly persecuted by King Philip and Pope Clement. When you combine the sudden arrests of the Templar, the conflicting stories about their forced confessions, and the fact that many of the Templars' leaders—including Grand Master de Molay—were burned at the stake in very dramatic proceedings, you can understand why legends were born about the group. In many ways, their abrupt downfall was very Shakespearean. Which, in this case, is actually an anachronism since it preceded Shakespeare by over two-hundred and fifty years."

Payne pressed forward. "So what happened to the money? Did the surviving Templars actually give it the Hospitallers, or did they hide it away for Nick Cage to find?"

Jones grinned at the movie reference. "Nice!"

Marissa smiled. "I'm sure the Templars hid some of their wealth, but the majority of their assets were given to the Hospitallers. By this time, the Order was so wealthy that it took on the features of a state—minting their own money and maintaining diplomatic relations with other nations. New knights came to Rhodes from all over Europe, and it was natural for them to associate with those who spoke their language and shared their traditions. So the Order decided to group the Hospitallers according to eight ethno-linguistic divisions known as *langues* or tongues. It's been a while since I learned these, but let me see if I can remember them all."

She counted on her fingers to try to keep track. "There was Crown of Aragon, Auvergne, Crown of Castile, the Kingdom of England, France, the Holy Roman Empire, Italy, and...shit! I can't remember the last one. Not that it matters. I mean, seven out of eight isn't—*Provence*! The last one was *Provence*! Sorry. I always forget that one because it eventually became a part of France. That was eight, right?"

Jones nodded. "*Oui.*"

She laughed before she took another sip of water. "Anyway, each of these langues was led by an administrator known as a *pilier*, and each langue had an *auberge* as its headquarters. That's also where the knights were housed by region."

Jarkko frowned. "Jarkko no speak French. What is this *auberge*?"

She answered. "It's the French word for 'inn', but in this case, it isn't a completely accurate translation because some of the buildings were quite massive. For instance, the Auberge de Castille in Valletta was completed in 1574 AD, but it currently serves as the Office of the Prime Minister of Malta. It's the Maltese equivalent of the White House."

"Speaking of Malta," Payne said, "I'm still trying to figure out how it fits into things. Right now the Hospitallers are living in

Rhodes, and my energy level is starting to drain. Perhaps you can fast-forward a bit to Valletta."

"Sure thing," she said with a smile. "While on Rhodes, the Knights were forced to become a more militarized organization in order to defend themselves against invading forces, including hordes of Barbary pirates. Then in 1522, an entirely new challenge arrived. Sultan Suleiman the Magnificent of the Ottoman Empire sent more than four hundred ships and over a hundred thousand men to the island to force them out once and for all. Under the leadership of Grand Master Philippe Villiers de L'Isle-Adam, the Order had roughly seven thousand men yet were able to last for nearly six months before the defeated Hospitallers were allowed to withdraw to Sicily. For roughly eight years, the Hospitallers sought a new place to call home until Charles the First of Aragon—as King of Sicily—gave them Malta, Gozo, and the North African port of Tripoli in perpetual fiefdom in exchange for an annual fee. Any idea what that fee was?"

Jarkko grinned. "Jarkko know this one. Answer is F-word."

Marissa laughed. "Not *the* F-word, but Jarkko is actually correct. The annual fee was a single Maltese falcon, which was to be sent to the King's representative, the Viceroy of Sicily, on All Saints' Day. This was known as the Tribute of the Maltese Falcon, and it was honored by the Knights until they were expelled from Malta in 1798."

"Obviously I'm familiar with the film," Payne said. "I remember watching *The Maltese Falcon* with my grandfather when I was just a kid, but I didn't know about the history behind the tribute."

Marissa explained further. "In the novel by Dashiell Hammett and the movie with Humphrey Bogart, the Maltese Falcon was actually a statue of gold and jewels made by the Knights of Malta as a gift for Charles the First, but it was captured by pirates and passed from owner to owner around Europe for centuries. So even though many people don't recognize the name of the Hospitallers, they're still vaguely familiar with their organization."

Payne nodded. "As I mentioned, I didn't recognize the Order by their original name, but as soon as Petr said the Knights of Malta, I immediately knew who he was talking about."

"And for good reason," she said, "because they truly made their reputation while they were here. And as I'm sure DJ will attest, the

Knights of Malta is a much cooler name."

Jones agreed. "You're right. It's pretty badass. Not as cool as the MANIACs, but definitely better than the Order of Knights of the Hospital of Saint John of Jerusalem."

She looked at Jones. "Who are the MANIACs?"

Payne shook his head. "That's a story for another day. Right now let's focus on the Knights. How did they make their reputation in Malta?"

She smiled. "By accomplishing the impossible."

CHAPTER 31

Marissa glanced around the table to make sure she had everyone's attention before she continued her lecture about the Order of Saint John.

"When the Knights first arrived in Malta in 1530 AD, they continued their actions against the Barbary pirates, who were Ottoman corsairs operating off the Barbary Coast in Northwest Africa. Since Tripoli was part of the Knights' fiefdom, the Order did whatever they could to protect their assets and control the sea. Unfortunately, this drew the ire of Sultan Suleiman the Magnificent, who had allowed the Knights safe passage to Sicily upon their defeat in Rhodes. Wanting to wipe out the Order once and for all, the sultan sent an invasion force of over forty thousand men to besiege the five hundred knights that were stationed in Birgu in 1565 AD. The ensuing battle was known as the Great Siege of Malta."

Jones smiled. "Our driver was telling us about the siege earlier today. He insinuated that it was one of the biggest military upsets of all time."

She nodded in agreement. "At the time of the siege, the Ottomans were considered an unstoppable force that would slowly but surely seize control of the Mediterranean before taking over Europe. In order to conquer Malta, the Ottomans assembled one of the largest armadas since antiquity. The fleet consisted of nearly two hundred vessels, most of which were galleys filled with weapons and professional soldiers. Meanwhile, the home team had approximately six thousand men, more than half of which were slaves, servants, and Maltese citizens. So yeah, I'd say it was a remarkable upset—one that got pretty nasty at times."

"In what way?" Payne wondered.

"After capturing Fort Saint Elmo at the entrance of the harbor and positioning cannons on Mount Sciberras—which is the modern-day location of Valletta—the Turks decided to taunt the

Order by nailing the bodies of the fallen knights on mock crucifixes and floating them across the bay. In response, Grand Master Jean Parisot de Valette beheaded all of his Turkish prisoners, loaded their heads into his cannons, and fired them back at the Turks."

Jarkko grinned. "First time in history when getting head is bad thing."

The group laughed at the absurdity—and accuracy—of the comment.

"Anyway," Marissa said with a grin, "once the Ottomans established the higher ground on Mount Sciberras, they started their bombardment of Birgu across the harbor."

"We were up there," Payne said. "Before we visited the library, we stopped by to see the saluting battery in the Upper Barrakka Gardens."

She smiled, glad that they had witnessed a Maltese tradition prior to the chaos at the library. "Then you know it's a direct shot to Fort Saint Angelo, which is where the seventy-year-old de Valette and his forces were headquartered. Despite facing far superior numbers, the Knights held on for another three months in the hot Maltese summer until a relief force led by the Viceroy of Sicily finally arrived. All told, the Ottomans had fired an estimated one hundred and thirty thousand cannonballs at the Order, and yet the Knights of Malta still managed to win the war."

Payne whistled. "I don't know what's more impressive: the one hundred and thirty thousand cannonballs or the fact that the Knights were led by a seventy-year-old man during the sixteenth century. Based on life expectancy, that has to be the equivalent of a ninety-year-old man today."

"You're probably right," she said. "And he didn't just rule from a throne at Fort Saint Angelo. He actually led the charge into battle on multiple occasions, even fighting against the Turks in hand-to-hand combat. For his remarkable valor, the Church offered him a position as a cardinal, but he declined in order to maintain his independence from the papacy and to start the rebuilding process on Malta. That included the commissioning of a fortified city on Mount Sciberras that would eventually take his name."

"Valletta," Payne said to the group.

"Duh," cracked Jones from across the table. "The dude's name was Valette."

Payne started to defend himself but thought better of it. "Go on."

She smiled and nodded. "Thanks to the Order's miraculous victory, money flowed in from royal families across Europe, all of them looking to win the Knights' favor. Even the Vatican contributed to their cause. Pope Pius the Fifth sent his military architect—an assistant of Michelangelo's named Francesco Laparelli—to design the city. It officially became the capital of Malta in 1571 AD when the leader of the Order moved his seat at Fort St. Angelo to the Grandmaster's Palace in Valletta. Sadly, the grand master who made the move was Pierre de Monte, and not Jean Parisot de Valette, who had passed away before his city was complete. In the years that followed, seven auberges were built for the Order's seven langues, and the Knights settled in for the long haul until Napoleon came knocking in 1798 AD."

Jones groaned. "As a student of history, I know that was rarely a good thing."

"And it certainly wasn't for the Knights of Malta. Napoleon was leading a force of thirty thousand men on his way to Egypt, and the Order was a shell of its former self, filled with undisciplined knights with split loyalties. On top of that, many of the local citizens were tired of the Order's presence in Malta, so their support couldn't be counted on in a time of crisis."

"That's a bad combination," Payne said.

"But it gets worse," she assured them. "Although Grand Master Ferdinand von Hompesch was warned of the approaching armada, he did nothing to fortify the island's defenses. Then when the French fleet arrived, Hompesch openly provoked Napoleon by denying his request to get water provisions for his men, allowing only two French ships in the harbor at one time. Until that moment, Napoleon hadn't declared war on the Maltese islands, but he viewed Hompesch's denial as a provocation and ordered the invasion."

"How long did it last?" Payne wondered.

She held up her index finger. "One day."

"Damn!" Jones said. "Napoleon didn't mess around."

"He certainly didn't," she said with a shake of her head. "And yet, Maltese scholars still wonder why Hompesch didn't take the French threat more seriously. I mean, when Grand Master de Valette learned about the approaching Turks, he took a number of steps to prepare for the upcoming siege. He poisoned wells with bitter herbs and dead animals to ruin the enemy's water supply.

He also harvested all crops, including unripened grain, to deprive the enemy of local food supplies. But Hompesch did no such things. Instead, he sat on his ass in Valletta and did nothing until it was time to negotiate the Order's surrender, which handed over sovereignty of the islands of Malta to the government of France."

As a student of war, Payne could think of a number of reasons behind the grand master's lack of action, but none of them were good. "Out of curiosity, what nationality was Hompesch?"

Marissa looked at him, confused. "Hompesch was German. In fact, he was the first German ever to hold office as grand master. Why do you ask?"

Payne smiled. "Because if he was French, I'd say he threw the fight."

She laughed. "It's funny you should say that, because nearly two-thirds of his Knights were of French descent, so Hompesch really couldn't be sure where their loyalties were until he saw them in battle. Furthermore, the rules of the Order explicitly stated that the Knights couldn't fight against fellow Christians, which complicated things further. Then, when you factor in what I told you about the locals, it's pretty darn obvious that he wasn't going to win that war."

"Did he even try?" Jones wondered.

"There was some fighting in western Malta before it eventually fell to the French, but it was token resistance at best. During the entire battle, the French only lost three men. After that, it was all over except for the paperwork. Hompesch surrendered on June the eleventh, signed the treaty on June the twelfth, and a week later, he was on a ship to Trieste, Italy, where he established a temporary new headquarters for the Order."

Jones grunted. "Was Hompesch involved in the fighting like de Valette?"

She shook her head. "Heck no. He remained in Valletta the entire time."

Jones rubbed his chin in thought. "Interesting. Very interesting."

Payne knew that look quite well. Anytime his friend was close to a breakthrough, he would temporarily leave the real world and disappear into that computer brain of his, the one that produced the highest score in the history of the Air Force Academy's MSAE (Military Strategy Acumen Examination) and had organized hundreds of operations with the MANIACs. He had a way of seeing things several steps ahead, like a chess master.

"What are you thinking?" Payne wondered.

Jones grinned at his best friend. "I'm thinking you should have figured this one out before I did, given your proclivity for magic."

Payne did, in fact, enjoy the art of prestidigitation and had been collecting magic tricks ever since he was a boy. His grandfather had started the collection for him, buying him a deck of magic playing cards when Payne was only five, and the gift had turned out to be habit-forming. For many years, it had been a way to spend time with his grandfather as they learned and practiced tricks together. Then, when Payne's parents were killed by a drunk driver, he had used magic as a diversion, his way to escape the real world and focus on the miraculous instead.

But unlike most skilled magicians, who seemed to love sequins and crave the spotlight, Payne was more of a closet magician, half-embarrassed of his abilities and unwilling to showcase his talents to anyone but his closest friends. Occasionally, he would use sleight of hand to baffle total strangers in public in order to amuse Jones, but other than that, he preferred to keep his magical skills and knowledge to himself.

Of course, that wasn't possible now that Jones had blown his cover.

Thinking as a magician, Payne replayed what he had just learned about Hompesch and his curious, if not baffling, strategy in 1798 AD and realized that Jones might be onto something. "Holy shit. He didn't throw the battle. The battle was a misdirect."

Jones nodded. "I mean, it makes sen—"

Payne interrupted him. "You're right. But man, it would take some serious balls. How do you send men to risk their lives while—"

Jones cut him off. "But *were* they risking their lives? Given what we know about—"

Payne grinned. "You're right! How much danger were they actually—"

Jones laughed. "Man, if this is true—"

Payne nodded. "Then it's one of the ballsiest escapes of all time!"

Jarkko glanced across the table at Marissa, who glanced back at Jarkko, and both of them were dumbfounded. For the past few seconds, they had witnessed Payne and Jones having a conversation without needing to fully voice their thoughts, almost as if the two of them were sharing a brain. Sometimes couples had the ability to finish each other's sentences, but this was beyond that since Payne and Jones didn't even need to utter their thoughts out loud.

They simply knew what the other was going to say.

Jarkko spoke first. "Tell Jarkko truth. Were you involved in comic-book science experiment? That would explain fighting skills and ability to speak without words."

Marissa agreed. "I'm with Jarkko. That was pretty freaky."

Payne looked at her. "Was it?"

"Doesn't matter," Jarkko said. "Important thing is Marissa's desire to be with Jarkko. So question has finally been answered. Marissa now has boyfriend."

"Wait!" she said, not wanting to be misunderstood.

Jarkko dropped his head. "And now she is single."

Payne ignored Jarkko and focused on Marissa. "What was freaky?"

Before she answered, Marissa glanced at Jarkko to make sure he was okay. He gave her a quick wink to let her know that he was just messing around. She breathed a sigh of relief before she focused on Payne's question. "Your conversation with DJ. Or should I say your non-conversation with DJ?"

Payne laughed. "Yeah, sorry about that. When we were in the military, we were in so many tough spots together where words needed to be kept to a minimum that we developed this weird vocal shorthand that allowed us to communicate without saying much."

Jones grinned. "We used to drive the guys in our unit crazy."

Payne nodded. "Even though it saved their lives—"

"—on multiple occasions," they said in unison.

Jarkko frowned. "Jarkko can't tell which is ventriloquist and which is dummy."

"No dummies here," Jones bragged, "since we figured out what happened."

"Actually," Payne said to soften his boast, "it's just a theory."

"A *really* good theory. It fits everything we know."

"Maybe so, but—"

"Guys," Marissa said, "stop talking to each other and talk to us. What's the theory you're bragging about? I'm assuming it deals with Hompesch. At least that's what I gathered from your freaky half-statements and insane ramblings."

Jones glanced at his best friend. "Go on. The floor's all yours."

Now it was Payne's turn to tip his imaginary hat.
Jones grinned and tipped his in return.
Then Payne explained one of the greatest tricks of all time.

CHAPTER 32

Payne glanced at his friends as he tried to figure out where to begin.

"Okay," he said, "here's what we know about Grand Master Hompesch. In 1798 AD, he finds out that an unstoppable force is headed his way. Even though Napoleon is bringing ten thousand fewer men than the Magnificent Sultan did for the Great Siege, Hompesch realizes that his own men are fat off the land, their loyalties are divided, and the locals are unlikely to offer support. He also knows that his allegiance is to the Order itself and *not* to Malta. This is a key piece of the puzzle, one that I didn't think about when you first depicted the impending battle. You had described the Order as the home team during the Great Siege, and that was accurate in 1565 AD—but that doesn't apply here, because the Order was no longer welcome in Malta."

Jones nodded. "That explains why Hompesch didn't poison the local wells or fortify the defenses around the harbor. As far as he was concerned, that would have been a wasted effort on his part because he had no intention of risking his life to save the locals who wanted him gone. Plus, he didn't want this battle to last any longer than it needed to because that would only result in additional deaths of his men. You see, his goal all along wasn't to fight. It was to *escape.*"

Payne smiled at the thought. "In order to pull this off, you would need to have a team of willing associates that you could trust explicitly. You obviously couldn't trust any French knights because of possible divided loyalties, but you probably could trust men from your homeland. Tell me, was there a langue for Germans at the time of the French invasion?"

Marissa nodded excitedly. "Over the centuries, the original eight langues were forced to change with the times. The Crown of Aragon and the Crown of Castile no longer existed as medieval states, and the other langues had morphed as well. If I remember correctly, the German knights would have been housed in Auberge d'Allemagne in Valletta. Strangely, very little is known about the structure other than it was the only auberge to be intentionally demolished. That happened way back in the early nineteenth century."

Jones laughed. "Of course it was demolished! It probably had evidence about Hompesch's escape. You can't afford to leave that standing."

Payne rolled his eyes. "Don't start with your conspiracy theories, or we're gonna lose all credibility with our audience."

Marissa smiled at Jones. "I promise, you won't lose me. I *love* conspiracy theories. The crazier, the better."

Jones grinned. "Then wait until I tell you where spiders come from! You won't believe it!"

Payne shook his head. "Come on, DJ. Stay focused! We're on a roll here."

Jones nodded. "Sorry, man. You're right. Treasure first, spiders later."

Payne realized that he had about five seconds to get the conversation headed in the right direction or else Jones was going to launch into a monologue about alien arachnids. "As I was saying, Hompesch would need a team of willing associates that he could trust to pull this off, and my guess is that he found them at Auberge d'Allemagne. Did I say that right?"

Marissa nodded her head. "*Oui.*"

Jarkko was confused. "Pull off what?"

Payne smiled. "If DJ and I are correct, Hompesch used a classic misdirect to conceal what he was actually doing. Think about what we know: When Napoleon first arrived in Malta, Hompesch wouldn't let his fleet into the harbor to get water. In fact, his men made a big production out of it, saying that only two French boats could come into the harbor at a time. Why in the world would he do that? Why risk pissing off an ill-tempered general with far superior numbers over something as mundane as water provisions?"

Jarkko guessed. "To buy time."

Payne nodded. "That's what we were thinking. Marissa already told us that Hompesch wasn't fortifying their defenses, or poisoning wells, or even moving his troops into position. He was sitting on his ass in Valletta—her words, not mine—until it was time to negotiate the Order's surrender. So the question is, what was he buying time for?"

Jarkko grinned. "For treasure!"

Payne smiled. "The thought had crossed my mind."

Jones picked it up from there. "I'm not sure what you know about Napoleon's military career, but Malta wasn't his main objective on this trip. It was merely a pit stop for the French on their way to Africa. At the time, Napoleon was getting ready to launch a major expedition to seize Egypt. His goal was to establish a French presence in the Middle East, where he could link up with Muslim enemies of the British in order to secure a trade route to India. So the last thing he wanted to do was lose a bunch of men and supplies in a meaningless battle with the Knights."

Payne nodded. "And Hompesch would have known that."

Marissa cut them off. "If that's the case, why piss off an ill-tempered general—your words, not mine—at all? Why not just negotiate a treaty and be done with it?"

Payne couldn't help but smile. Not only was Marissa highly intelligent, but she was more than eager to engage in the verbal jousting that he enjoyed with his quick-witted best friend. Over the years, he had come across very few people—let alone beautiful women—who could keep up with their verbal repartee, but she was matching them jab for jab.

"Here's the thing," Jones explained. "Fighting a war on foreign soil is very expensive—particularly when you're battling extreme elements as well. And that's what Napoleon would be facing as he marched across Egypt. In order to pay for everything, you either need to start your journey with a massive war chest, or you need to accumulate resources along the way. And since the Knights of Malta were one of the richest organizations in the world but no longer able to defend themselves, Napoleon was probably salivating at the thought of their riches."

Marissa chimed in. "Just to be clear, the Knights of Malta had lost a lot of their assets over the centuries and were no longer as wealthy as they once were. When I was fast-forwarding for Jon's sake, I skipped over the Protestant Reformation, which decimated the Order's holdings in Europe and weakened the stability of the Catholic Church. Don't get me wrong: the Knights were far from broke, but they weren't nearly as rich as they were at the height of their power."

Jarkko groaned. "Jarkko's flag now at half-mast. Jarkko will keep you posted."

Jones grimaced and moved even further away on the bench.

But Payne ignored them both. He was too focused on Marissa.

"Believe it or not," Payne said to her, "your comment only strengthens our theory."

"How so?" she wondered.

Payne did his best to explain. "If the Order had tons of riches throughout Europe—and I'm talking about literal tons of gold and jewels—then they probably didn't need to tangle with Napoleon at all. But now that I know their assets were centralized in Valletta, then the entire future of the Order rested on the shoulders of Grand Master Hompesch. But here's the rub: because of divided loyalty amongst the knights and the fact that two-thirds of his men were French, Hompesch couldn't move the Order's wealth in advance of Napoleon's approach. Hompesch needed to wait until there was something massive going on to distract his men."

Marissa smiled. "So Hompesch wasn't sitting on his ass while waiting to sign the treaty. You think he was actually killing time while waiting to move the treasure?"

Payne nodded. "It's a classic misdirect. He sends a bunch of knights—I'm guessing French, just to fuck with them—down to the waterfront to tell freaking Napoleon that he can only send two ships into the harbor at one time. Then he sends another group of knights—I'm guessing French, just to fuck with them some more—to defend the western flank of Malta from advancing French troops, knowing full well that they're unlikely to put up much of a fight. But that's okay as far as Hompesch is concerned, because the only thing that matters to him is moving the Order's wealth without being seen by disloyal French knights."

Jones jumped back in. "Meanwhile, Napoleon is sitting in his high chair, getting ready to throw a hissy fit, because he's being disrespected by a stupid German, who is making the French fleet wait their turn at the water fountain. But Napoleon's mood quickly brightens when he finds out the Maltese people are aiding his cause and that the knights in the west are providing minimal resistance at best. So Napoleon heads to the negotiating table in great spirits, thinking he has just defeated the legendary Knights of Malta while losing only three men. Meanwhile, what he doesn't know is that the so-called stupid German had emptied the Order's massive vaults under Napoleon's massive nose while he was waiting for a drink of water."

Payne laughed at the thought. "Like I said before—if our theory is correct and Hompesch actually pulled this off—it was one of the ballsiest escapes of all time."

CHAPTER 33

Although Marissa had been filled with doubt when Payne and Jones had started to explain their theory about Hompesch's escape, she had found herself getting caught up in their momentum as they somehow managed to present a creative hypothesis that utilized all of the facts that they had been told about the Order's last days on Malta. But as a highly trained academic, she knew there was a major difference between imaginative conjecture and substantiated fact, so she felt it was her job as the historian on this adventure to explain the difference to them.

"Guys," she said. "It's a great theory, and I *really* want to believe it, but as far I can tell, it's just speculation. Don't get me wrong: I found it highly entertaining, and maybe even plausible, but what do you have that actually supports what you're thinking?"

Payne took a moment to absorb her comments before he replied. "As the newest member of our team and someone who was kept in the dark on the true nature of our mission until a few minutes ago, it took a lot of guts to express your doubts about our theory. And yet, in the interest of group morale after a highly stressful day, I feel there is only one appropriate response."

She stared at him, unsure. "What's that?"

He picked up a scrap of bread and threw it at her. "Boooo!"

Jones and Jarkko quickly joined in. "Boooo!"

She laughed as she swatted the projectiles away like Godzilla. "That's okay. I'm used to butting my head against popular opinion. I've been doing it my entire academic life. It's the only way you can truly make a difference in scholarly pursuits."

Jarkko shook his head. "First you break Jarkko's heart. Then you shatter Jarkko's dreams. Maybe it's time for Marissa to swim to shore."

She playfully stood from the table. "No problem. I'll leave if you want me to go. But your odds of finding the treasure will go down significantly if you make me walk the plank."

"Perhaps," Payne said with a laugh, "but if you want to fit in with this crew of pirates, you'll learn that we've had a lot of success with wild speculation. Why spend your days buried in books when you can just make up an awesome theory as you go along?"

"Because," she countered, growing annoyed, "the key to proving any hypothesis is through methodical research based on established facts, not wild conjecture. Otherwise, you can't effectively determine anything. You'll just waste your time, stumbling in the dark, while the real work is being done by people who happen to enjoy spending time in libraries."

"And yet," he argued, as his passion started to rise, "our goal on this particular mission isn't to write a thesis paper that will be approved by a board of faculty members or published in an academic journal to be admired by their peers. Our goal, in case you forgot, is to find a damn treasure—something we've managed to do multiple times without you."

Marissa winced, completely unprepared for a personal attack. But her shock didn't last long. She quickly lashed back with a retort of her own. "I'm glad you're so confident in your abilities. I'm sure your success in Greece and Mexico will come in quite handy when you're staring at a document written in Maltese or trying to figure out why Grand Master Hompesch was writing letters to the emperor of Russia in the first place. Or did you forget about that part? Even if your speculation about Napoleon is correct, you know absolutely nothing about the next piece of the puzzle, and you sure as shit won't be getting it from me."

Marissa punctuated her comment by turning angrily from the table, storming up the center aisle toward the helm, then opening a side door that spilled onto the foredeck seating area at the bow of the yacht. She was tempted to slam the door behind her to voice her fury, but it was thin and made of glass, so she simply left it open in a final act of defiance.

Jones watched the whole thing play out before he offered comment. He turned toward Payne and shook his head. "And that, my friend, is why you're still single."

"Screw you," Payne growled as he picked up another scrap of bread and fired it against the wood-paneled refrigerator in the galley. In a yacht lined with windows, it was the only solid surface in his throwing range that he knew he wouldn't shatter.

Jones stared at him. "Keep it up, asshole, and you'll be friend-less, too."

"Uh, oh," Jarkko said as he stood from the table. "Time to talk feelings. Jarkko doesn't do that when Jarkko is sober. Besides, Jarkko has to pee. Boner is gone, but bladder is full."

Payne and Jones nodded, both of them realizing it was for the best. Neither would open up with Jarkko listening.

Ivan Volkov was filled with rage as he stared at the laptop com-puter on his private plane. His flight to Malta had been completely full of henchmen, but his journey home was mostly empty—all thanks to the Americans on his screen.

During the past few hours, Volkov's cadre of hackers had dug through surveillance video from Birgu and Valletta and had de-termined the identities of the smuggler's bodyguards. Much to Volkov's surprise, they weren't bodyguards at all but famous treas-ure hunters, who had unearthed so many precious artifacts in the past decade that their discoveries were going to be featured at the Smithsonian Institute in Washington, D.C.

Volkov took some solace from his defeat at the library when he discovered that Payne and Jones were also two of the finest sol-diers that the U.S. military had ever produced. Both of them were rated as special forces-plus, a term that Volkov had never heard of until his hackers had unearthed a heavily redacted file from a joint mission with the CIA that had been leaked by a whistleblower to a dark web message board. Volkov had asked his men to get per-sonnel files on the duo, but they claimed the firewall at the Penta-gon was so far above their capabilities that it wasn't even worth their time to try.

Even Russian hackers refused to mess with Randy Raskin.

Still, the Finn's involvement with Payne and Jones was intriguing.

Volkov doubted that two famous treasure hunters would be wasting their time with a Finnish fisherman in the National Li-brary of Malta, unless the Finn was contributing something signif-icant to their cause. And Volkov rightly assumed that their meet-ing in the library had something to do with the documents that he had stolen from the smuggler's yacht—the documents that the Finn had received as payment from Sergei Bobrinsky.

Despite the failure that Volkov had endured in Malta, he realized that he had actually come out ahead on the ledger sheet. Not only did he recover Bobrinsky's payment from the Finn, thereby righting the original wrong, but Volkov was now on the trail of a potential fortune—one that seemed to be tied to his homeland, based on the documents that he had read.

If so, Volkov didn't care how talented the Americans were.

In Russia, he would undoubtedly have the advantage.

CHAPTER 34

Payne knew he had been an asshole to Marissa. He didn't need Jones to tell him that. And yet, whenever Payne got worked up about something, Jones managed to slice and dice through all of the bullshit and the bravado to help him figure out what was wrong. Roughly half of the time, it was because Payne was hungry, but after watching Payne devour a multi-course Italian feast, Jones assumed it was something else—and he had a pretty good idea of what it was.

But before he could lay out the specifics, he knew what always came first. It was almost as predictable as Payne's appetite, yet it came from an organ slightly above Payne's stomach.

A heartfelt apology in three...two...one...go.

"DJ," Payne mumbled as the shame of his outburst washed over him. "I'm sorry for lashing out. I shouldn't have yelled at Marissa, and I certainly shouldn't have yelled at you. Neither of you deserved it. I just got...I don't know. I just got riled up."

"No worries," Jones said as he bumped Payne's fist as a peace offering. "You've yelled at me before, and you'll yell at me again. And that's okay because I yell at you, too. Not *nearly* as often as you do—you're like the fucking Hulk—but you know, every once in a while."

Payne cracked a smile. "Mostly during your period."

Jones shook his head. "Wow. Just wow. Your apology was going so well until right then. Sometimes you make it really tough to stick around. Good thing I love your plane."

Payne groaned in regret. "Sorry, man. You're right. You're absolutely right. Bad time for a personal insult. What the hell is wrong with me?"

Jones started to stand. "Hold on. I'll go get my list. It's pretty substantial."

Payne smiled. "I bet it is."

"Actually," Jones said as he sat back down, "I'm far too tired to go over the whole thing. If it's okay with you, why don't I jump right in and focus on the good stuff?"

Payne nodded. "Proceed."

"As far as I can tell, you aren't hungry."

"Not at the moment."

"And despite the late hour, you don't seem overly tired."

"I'm okay."

"Are you thirsty?"

"No."

"Are you cold?"

"No."

"Can you breathe?"

"Yes."

"Is it raining?"

"What?"

Jones repeated the question. "Is it raining?"

Payne glanced outside. "No."

"Okay," Jones said, seemingly satisfied. "Then my original theory is correct."

Payne stared at him. "I hate to be the bearer of bad news, but you're acting weirder than usual. Maybe I should go and talk to Jarkko instead."

Jones shook his head. "Jon, you know better than that. *Never* insult your therapist."

"You're not my ther—"

"You know damn well I'm your therapist. Now shut your mouth and pay attention, or you'll be alone for the rest of your miserable life."

"Truth be told, I'm really not that miserable."

"You will be if I put my foot up your ass. Now shut the hell up and listen to me, or I swear to God you'll be shitting laces for a week."

Payne didn't like it, but he shut the hell up. He knew better than to mess with Jones whenever he got feisty. Although Payne would bludgeon Jones in a clean fight because of their sheer difference in size, Payne realized that Jones was a crafty fighter—some would even say *dirty*—who was willing to do anything it took to take down his opponent.

"Good," Jones said. "Obeying me is the first step to happiness."

Payne tried his best not to roll his eyes.

Jones continued. "Just to be clear, I wasn't being weird when I asked you those questions. I was merely ruling out your basic biological needs in order to determine the root of your outburst. Both of us know that food and sleep are big triggers for you, but since you aren't hungry or tired, we can rule those out for now. You aren't cold or thirsty, which means you have warmth and water, and you're breathing okay, which means you have air. Then I asked if it was raining to see if you had adequate shelter, which I'm guessing you do since you're on a multi-million-dollar yacht. So as far as I'm concerned, you're only lacking one basic biological need."

"Which is?"

"Sex."

Payne shook his head. "I told you, man, I don't swing that way."

Jones snapped. "I wasn't offering."

"How am I supposed to know that? You said obeying you is the key to happiness, then you tell me I need sex. If you were in my shoes, wouldn't you think—"

"Speaking of shoes, remember what I told you earlier?"

"Yeah, yeah, yeah. I'll be shitting laces for a week."

"Exactly!"

"Fine! I'll shut up. But I'm only doing it to shut *you* up."

"Are you done?"

Payne nodded but said nothing.

"Good," Jones said as he took a deep breath to calm down. "Now where was I?"

"You wanted to bang me."

"Come on, man! Be serious. Or this session is over. Which also means this mission is over, because if you don't apologize to Marissa in the correct fashion, she certainly isn't going to help us. Not after your ridiculous outburst. Or did you forget that?"

Payne grunted, but he knew Jones was correct.

"Fine," Payne muttered. "Proceed."

"When was the last time you had a girlfriend?" Jones asked.

"Excuse me?"

"Not a one-night stand or a one-week fling, but an actual girl-friend?"

Payne growled. "You know the answer."

"Say it anyway."

Payne growled louder. "It's been a while."

"Why do you think that is?"

"Because I'm a picky bastard."

"And why do you think *that* is?"

Payne stared daggers. This was unlike their typical sessions. This one was cutting deep. "You better get to your point real quick before I actually hulk out. Because if *that* happens, the mission won't be the only thing that comes to an abrupt end."

Jones stood his ground. He was one of the few people in the world with the courage to do so, and he was doing it for a good reason. He sensed his friend was close to a major breakthrough, something that had been holding him back for years. "No worries, Jon. I can tell I'm upsetting you with this particular approach, so I'll change course just a bit. Why did you join the Navy?"

"Excuse me?" he said defensively.

"Don't get me wrong. You made a great choice. I swear, I'm not insulting the Navy. I'm just curious. I mean, you came from a wealthy family, so you certainly didn't need a scholarship. Your grades were exceptional, so you could've gone to Pitt or Carnegie Mellon while living in your family mansion. Or you could've gone away to school and partied your ass off. But you didn't. You chose the hardest option of all. You went to Annapolis. Why'd you do that?"

Payne shrugged. "You know the answer. My grandfather thought I needed discipline."

Jones shook his head. "That's bullshit, and you know it. You weren't a troubled kid in high school. You were the golden boy— a star in football and basketball with a great GPA. You never got into trouble. You did volunteer work. You were every teacher's wet dream. And don't even try to deny it. We've spent way too much time together to lie about our pasts. You know my shit, and I know yours. So why the hell did your grandfather send you to the Naval Academy?"

Payne shrugged again. He truly didn't know.

So Jones voiced it for him. "He sent you there because you needed a way to funnel the rage from the death of your parents before it chewed you up and destroyed you for good. He knew you didn't need beer pong and sorority girls. You needed to be a part of something that would help save lives and protect people, since you were unable to save theirs. That, my friend, is why your grandfather sent you to a military academy instead of college. Not because you needed discipline, but because you needed to fill the hole that your parents left behind."

Payne instantly knew that Jones was correct.

Somewhere deep inside, Payne had known the truth all along.

However, hearing the words out loud had made an impact.

So much so, that Payne found it hard to breathe.

Jones grabbed a bottle of water from the far end of the table and slid it to Payne, who nodded his thanks before he opened it and took a long sip. Despite Payne's revelation, Jones knew they were only halfway done. He still had to get his friend to understand his earlier outburst, which was connected to the same psychological trauma that had occurred when he was a child.

Jones also knew he had his friend's attention. And even though he was reluctant to dump so much on Payne at one time, Jones realized that they had to work through this issue, or else the entire mission was going to blow up in flames.

"Believe it or not," Jones said in a calming voice, "that hole in your life did more than drive you to greatness in the military. It's also the reason you push people away. You do everything you can to discard potential loved ones from your life before they can leave you, and it all goes back to the loss of your parents. It's merely a mechanism to protect yourself."

Payne nodded in agreement. He knew that to be true.

Jones continued. "For as long as I've known you, the only woman you've ever let into your life—and I mean *really* let in, where she got to see the good, the bad, and the ugly—was Ariane Walker, and when that didn't work out, you quit trying to find love."

Ariane had been the first and only love of Payne's life. She was smart, beautiful, funny, and self-sufficient—everything he looked for in a woman. And even though he hadn't proposed, he was getting ready to when she was abducted by a group of sadists who were hell-bent on revenge. They had taken her and several others to an isolated plantation in Louisiana where the prisoners were brutally tortured until the secret motivation behind their selection was revealed.

Payne and Jones had ultimately managed to save the abductees and punish the criminals involved, but the near-death experience had changed Ariane's priorities. She had immediately quit her job in Pittsburgh and moved to Colorado to be next to her sister and recently born nephew. Payne knew how traumatic the situation had been for Ariane and had done his best to make the long-distance relationship work, but in the end, she had chosen her family over him.

And it had haunted him ever since.

Payne stared at Jones. "What does Ariane have to do with this?"

Jones started to laugh but managed to bite his tongue. "Come on, Jon. I could practically see sparklers in your eyes when you met Marissa, and that paled in comparison to the fireworks in hers. I swear to God, I thought the two of you were going to spontaneously combust."

Payne grinned. He hadn't felt an instant attraction like that since—

"Shit," he said aloud, suddenly understanding the connection.

Jones nodded. "In the therapy business, that's known as an *aha moment.*"

Payne rolled his eyes. "You aren't my therapist."

Jones laughed at that. "Aren't I?"

"Fine!" Payne admitted. "You're my fucking therapist. But I refuse to pay for this session since you only calmed me down to keep the mission alive."

Jones theatrically put his hand over his heart. "Dude, that hurts. And if you truly believe that, you don't know anything about me at all. I would *never* go against my oath as a therapist for something as mundane as a mission. However, I would definitely do it for your plane."

Payne laughed. "Yeah, that makes more sense."

Jones stared at him. "Why are you still sitting here?"

"Where else would I—"

"Seriously?" Jones said, cutting him off. "Do I have to spell it out for you?"

"Marissa! Right! Almost forgot." Payne started to stand before he sat back down. "And what am I supposed to say to her?"

"Oh my God! I *do* have to spell it out for you." Jones shook his head in disbelief. "Start with an apology—a sincere apology *without* insults of any kind. Then take it from there."

Payne stood. "Right. I'll be back in a flash."

"No!" Jones blurted. "Don't come back in a flash—unless she tries to stab you or something. You're on a yacht. The moon is out. Use it to your advantage."

Payne nodded. "Good idea."

"Oh, and Jon?"

"Yeah?"

Jones glanced at his watch and noted the time. "On your way out, send in my next patient. I want to talk to Jarkko about his drinking problem."

CHAPTER 35

Marissa felt like a total idiot. She couldn't believe that she had stormed off like a petulant teenager over a comment that was technically accurate. The truth was that Payne and Jones had done more for history over the past decade than all of her former professors combined. And even though the duo's methods were far from traditional, it was hard to argue with their results.

They weren't risking their lives to write a research paper.

They were searching for a long-lost treasure.

And thanks to her dramatic exit, she had blown her chance to help.

She cursed under her breath as she stared at the surrounding harbor. From the cushioned seat in front of the helm, she could see the rising grandeur of the Corinthia Hotel on her left and the neon lights of Dragonara Casino to her right. But as her gaze swept along the waters of St. George's Bay, she wasn't truly seeing anything.

Her mind was too focused on the events of the day.

Over the past twelve hours so much had happened that it was tough for her to believe. It had started with an urgent text message from Petr Ulster, followed by an amazing opportunity to work with two men that she admired, topped off with a gunfight in one of the few places that she used to feel safe. To say her day had been an emotional rollercoaster would be the understatement of the year.

No wonder she had lost control inside.

She was still surging with adrenaline.

And yet, she couldn't stop beating herself up over the way she had stormed out. She was a fighter, not a quitter, but in this case, she had practically run from the confrontation as she scorched the earth beyond her with a series of fiery barbs.

She had no idea why she had done that.

To figure things out, she tried to block out the rest of her day to focus solely on her interactions with Payne. Until things had fallen apart at the very end, she had found him to be everything she had imagined and more.

During her time at the Ulster Archives, she had heard so many stories about his exploits from Ulster that it had been impossible not to be impressed. For her, it was more than just his recent adventures with Jones, but also his career as a highly decorated soldier and his position as CEO of Payne Industries, where he seemed to spend most of his time doing charity work. She didn't care about his money. She cared about his deeds and the man himself. Like a schoolgirl with a crush, she had followed his exploits from afar, never expecting to have the opportunity to meet him in person, let alone work with him on one of his missions.

Her heart had leapt with joy when she saw him standing outside of the library. Somehow she had managed to play it cool when she had introduced herself to Jarkko, partly because she was in character as Lara Croft at the time. But her façade had started to crumble during her conversation with Jones. She was nearly as familiar with him as she was with Payne, but she had kept it together until she shook his hand and called him "David freakin' Jones".

That's when she had started to lose it.

That's when the fangirl had surfaced.

By the time she had reached Payne in the greeting line, she knew she was in serious trouble. Her heart was pounding, her cheeks were flushed, and her eyes were as wide as saucers. For someone like Marissa, who went through life with headphones on in order to keep people away, these emotions were as foreign to her as the Maltese language was to Payne.

She didn't have the first clue how to proceed.

Growing up in boarding schools around the world, she didn't have much experience with the opposite sex, and the encounters that she'd had were mostly unpleasant. Because of her extreme beauty, she had been targeted by every creep who saw her from the moment that she hit puberty. At the age of thirteen, she was being propositioned by men of all ages, who had offered her everything imaginable for unspeakable deeds in return.

Most people assume that beautiful women have it easy.

But beauty has its drawbacks, too.

To keep the predators at bay, she had built up walls, and she had been hiding behind them for years. Unlike many social-minded women who traveled in packs and used velvet ropes to separate themselves from undesirables, Marissa avoided cliques and clubs altogether, preferring the company of books to those who were only drawn to her looks. Although she'd had a boyfriend or two at Stanford—a school where the best and brightest intermingled, allowing her to temporarily experience human interaction without being placed on a pedestal by her classmates—she had very little familiarity with the feelings that had surfaced today with Payne.

When their eyes had locked and their hands had touched, she had experienced a rush of emotions that was so electric that she was afraid she was going to fry. And as their gaze had lingered, she had sensed that Payne had felt it, too. That he had somehow looked past her beauty and the towering walls that she had built to protect herself, and had seen the real person inside, the one who longed for the type of connection that her parents never had. Although she wasn't a romantic at heart, she still wanted to find someone who made her feel alive.

And she had felt that way and more when they had met.

But less than twelve hours later, she was pushing him away.

Marissa cursed again, this time in Maltese, a trait she had picked up from her mother before her untimely passing. It didn't take a degree in psychology to figure out why Marissa had lashed out at Payne the way that she did. She had interpreted his comments about finding treasures without her as a sign that he was going to discard her, much like Marissa's father had done with her and her mother. So instead of waiting for the axe to fall, Marissa had done the chopping herself, cutting Payne out of her life even though it was the last thing that she wanted.

And to make matters worse, she had done it in front of his friends.

She knew very little about men, but she knew that was a no-no.

The male ego was such a fragile thing.

Marissa was tempted to dust herself off and return to the scene of the crime to make her amends before his wounds had a chance to fester, but before she found the courage to do that, she heard the gentle creak of the side door, the same one she had stormed out of only minutes before. When she glanced over and saw Payne squeezing through the narrow portal, she felt her cheeks flush once again. But this time, she was better prepared to handle it. She took a deep, cleansing breath to calm her nerves, coolly brushed the hair away from her face, and tried to figure out what she was going to say to apologize for her outburst.

"Marissa?" Payne said as he peeked around the corner. "May I come out?"

She bit her lip and nodded. "Yes, of course. Believe it or not, I was actually getting ready to come inside."

"Oh," he said, disappointed. "Don't let me keep you. If you want to go inside—"

"No!" she blurted, much louder than she intended. So she softened her voice and tried again. "No, that's not what I meant. I was coming inside to speak to you."

"Really? That's great!" He pointed at the cushioned bench that she was sitting on. It was one of the few pieces of furniture that hadn't been slashed by Volkov. "Do you mind if I join you?"

She patted the seat next to her. "Please, take a load off. It's been a taxing day. And this bench is perhaps the most comfortable thing I've ever sat on. I'm not sure what it's made of, but I'm guessing it's the substance they would use to wrap a box of bubble wrap."

Payne laughed as he sat down. "That's a pretty sophisticated metaphor. Try not to use those in front of Jarkko. His head might explode."

She smiled. "I don't know about that. He pretends to be dumb for comic effect, but I get the sense that he may be smarter than the rest of us."

Payne nodded as he squeezed the seat cushion with both of his hands. "You're right about both things. This seat *is* unbelievably comfortable—so much so I want my coffin to be lined with this stuff. And Jarkko is highly intelligent. He speaks five or six languages and knows the seas better than any instructor I ever had at the Academy. I'm lucky to call him my friend."

"Good. I'm glad to hear you say that."

He glanced at her. "Why's that?"

She smiled. "I like it when we agree on things."

"Me, too," he said as he turned his body to face her. "Listen, about my outburst inside. I honestly didn't mean to—"

"No!" she blurted. "Stop right there! It's *totally* my fault. I shouldn't have reacted the way that I did. This is your mission—"

"No," he said as he vigorously shook his head. "There's no need to fall on your sword. I raised my voice in an inappropriate manner and said something I didn't mean to say in the heat of the moment. Seriously, I have no idea where that came from. That's not like me at all."

She shook her head, too. "It *wasn't* inappropriate! You were exactly right. You have accomplished more in your lifetime than I could possibly accomplish in mine, yet I was lecturing you about your methodology. Obviously your tactics work just fine, and it was foolish of me to insinuate otherwise."

"Stop. Just stop. You know damn well that we don't stand a chance in hell of finding the treasure without you. Sure, we've had some success in the past, but our team will be much stronger if you're on it. So please accept my apology and come back to the squad."

"Only if you accept my apology for storming out like a drama queen."

He nodded and stuck out his hand. "Deal?"

She grabbed his hand and smiled. "Deal."

For the briefest of moments, their hands lingered, skin on skin, as they stared at each other in the moonlight. But unlike the giddy awkwardness of their initial introduction, this somehow felt right, as if they were meant to be entwined—and that sensation freaked them out more than the gunfight at the library. They both let go at the exact same time, running from the feelings that both of them shared, while turning their attention to the undulating sea.

"You know," Payne said just to fill the silence. "For a moment there…"

She glanced at him, hopeful. "What?"

His mind churned, looking for the right thing to say. "For a moment there, I thought we were going to get into a fight while we were trying to apologize."

"Me, too!" she said with a disappointed smile. "We kept talking over each other, trying to take the blame, when both of us knew that you were clearly at fault."

Payne laughed. "Hold up! Is that how you remember it? As a highly trained historian, you sure take a lot of liberties with the past. I think if you take a closer look at your terms of surrender, you'll see that we agreed on joint custody of the blame."

"*My* terms of surrender? I distinctly remember you offering your apology before I followed your lead, which means it was *your* surrender, not mine."

"Holy crap," Payne said. "We're doing it again. What is wrong with us?"

She shook her head in frustration. "I have no idea."

Then they sat in silence for several uncomfortable seconds.

"Anyway," Payne said as he stood from the bench, "it's great to have you back on the team. There are four cabins on board, so each of us will have our own space. Choose whichever one you want, and make yourself at home. I know Jarkko will try to offer you his stateroom, but for health reasons, I highly recommend one of the guest cabins."

She stood as well. "Are you coming inside?"

Payne shook his head. "I'm a troubled sleeper, so I always take first watch. I'm ninety-nine percent confident that the Russians won't be coming back tonight, but I need to make sure."

"If you'd like, I could keep you company for a bit."

Payne smiled. "As much as I appreciate the offer, I think it's best if you got your rest. It's been a long, emotionally draining day, and we'll need you at the top of your game in the morning when we figure out our next move."

She nodded. "You're probably right. Some rest will do me good."

"Jarkko has some clean clothes and supplies down below. After you take a shower, have DJ take a look at your wound. I know from personal experience that he's a master at first aid."

"Okay," she said as she squeezed past him to get to the side door. As she did, they briefly touched, chest against chest. "Don't stay up too late. You need your rest, too."

Payne nodded. "Don't worry. I'll be fine. I've done this before."

She sighed as she turned and walked away. "Yeah. Me, too."

CHAPTER 36

Thursday, June 14
St. Julian's, Malta

Payne opened his eyes in the starboard guest cabin and slowly focused on the two oval windows in the right-hand wall. Bright sunlight poured into the wood-paneled room, revealing two side-by-side bunks separated by a narrow gap and a stretch of beige carpet.

When Payne had crawled into his berth just before dawn, he had chosen the less-damaged mattress on the left and had fallen right to sleep. Prior to that, he had spent half the night on watch regretting what he had said to Marissa, and the other half regretting what he didn't say. Although his therapy session with Jones had helped him to better understand his intimacy issues, he wasn't ready to get involved with a woman he didn't know.

Particularly one he kept arguing with.

Besides, he had more important things to focus on. There was a treasure to be found, Russians to be dealt with, and a hearty breakfast to be eaten.

But definitely not in that order.

Much to Payne's surprise, he spotted a suitcase sitting inside his cabin door. It was the same suitcase he had bought (and filled) at the Point Shopping Mall and had left in his hotel room the day before. On a trip filled with luggage misadventures, this was the most curious of them all. He had no idea how his bag had surfaced on a yacht in the middle of the Mediterranean.

Lacking the sustenance to think clearly, he half-assumed that he was still sleeping and the suitcase was just a figment of his imagination, but when he opened it up, it didn't contain a mass grave of rotting corpses, a disease-ridden village filled with dying children, or any of the horrific images from his military career that

183

had haunted his dreams at various times over the years.

Instead, it was stuffed with clean clothes and toiletries.

Needless to say, it was a pleasant development.

Payne grabbed a quick shower in the tiny bathroom before he went about his morning routine. Ten minutes later, he was wearing brand-new threads—a black T-shirt, khaki cargo shorts, low-cut socks, and black tennis shoes—and ready for chow.

Fortunately for the safety of everyone on board, Payne detected the aroma of food and followed it to the galley, where he found Jones standing next to several cartons of takeout on a fancy silver platter. Payne glanced out of the glass-lined saloon and realized they had pulled up close enough to the rocky shoal behind the Corinthia Hotel to get ashore.

"Good afternoon, princess," Jones said as he fist-bumped his friend. "I was just getting ready to wake you. I didn't know if you'd want breakfast or lunch, so I ordered both. Call me crazy, but I had this weird feeling that you'd be hungry when you got up. Am I psychic or what?"

Payne nodded his appreciation. "Thanks for the food and my bag."

Jones shook his head. "Don't thank me. Thank the hotel. I didn't want to leave my post while you were sleeping, so I called the front desk and said we had spent the night on the yacht and asked them to fetch some things from our room. They didn't even blink an eye. Then they asked if they could do anything else to make our stay more pleasant. And I go, 'as a matter of fact, there is'. I said we're hungry and need some grub, and they say, 'shall we bring it to the yacht?' And I go, 'hell yeah! Bring that shit out to the yacht.'"

Jones laughed at the memory. "At this point, I'm feeling like a total rock star, and they say, 'is there anything else we can do for you, Mister Payne?' Because, you know, I'm using your credit card, so I'm obviously pretending to be you."

Payne rolled his eyes. "Obviously."

"So I go, 'my girl Marissa needs some new clothes'—because, she does. I mean, her dress was torn and covered in blood, and we don't have time to drive over to her place. So she reluctantly gets on the speakerphone, tells them her size, and they say, 'no problem.' At this point, Jarkko is starting to get jealous, so he grabs the phone from Marissa and tells the hotel that his liquor supply is empty, which doesn't faze them at all because we're fucking rock stars on a boat. So he orders some really nice spirits—I'm talking top-shelf stuff that I've never even heard of and will definitely cost you a fortune—and once again, they go, 'no problem.'"

Jones rubbed his chin theatrically. "Which got me thinking. I mean, they said 'no problem' for everything we requested, so now I'm wondering, where do they draw the line? I'm literally wondering, what could I ask for that *would* be a problem? I mean, these people aren't wizards. There has to be something I can ask for that would actually cause them to say, 'sorry, Mister Payne, we just can't do that—that's beyond our capabilities as hotel genies to grant you this wish.' So I glance at Jarkko, who's still holding the phone, and I can tell he's thinking the same thing as I am. Somewhere in that depraved mind of his, he's running through a list of items that are so outrageously forbidden that even he couldn't obtain them on short notice."

"And?" Payne asked, growing more curious.

"Obviously Jarkko is feeling the same rock-star vibe as I am, because that crazy bastard goes, 'we require an albino tiger for a Viking blood ceremony.'"

Payne laughed. "He did not."

"I swear to Odin, he did."

"What did they say?"

"Jon, I'm not shitting you. There was a slight pause, then the hotel genie whispers, 'does it have to be alive?' Which freaks out Marissa but gets Jarkko so excited that he starts to chant in a Viking dialect that has been dead for centuries. So I grab my phone from Jarkko, who is now dancing with a kitchen knife, to keep this conversation going, and I say, 'that depends. Give me an ETA for each scenario.' And he goes, '2:00 p.m. for alive and 2:01 p.m. for dead'—which, I'm guessing, means the genie is going to kill the tiger himself."

Payne kept laughing. "The guy called your bluff."

"Here's the thing, Jon. I don't think the genie was bluffing. There's actually a billionaire on Malta that *has* an albino tiger, and I truly believe in my heart that he was willing to drive over there and put a bullet in its tiger brain in order to meet our needs as a guest of his hotel."

Payne laughed louder. "How'd it end?"

"Believe it or not, this genie starts pressuring me for an answer. He goes, 'which would you prefer, dead or alive?' Seriously, what kind of question is that? Who would actually say that to a guest? Well, you know me. I'm pretty quick on my feet, so I say, 'we need time to consult the oracle.'"

"Oracle? What oracle?"

"Come on, Jon! I made that shit up to buy us some time. I don't want this tiger-killing genie to think we were just messing with him or else he might spit in our food, so I told him we'd call him later with the oracle's decision. And do you know what he says? He goes, 'no problem.'"

Payne grinned. "Of course, he did."

Jones nodded. "So, now you have a tough decision to make."

"Decision? What decision?"

"For one reason or another, Jarkko is under the impression that *you're* the oracle, so you have to decide if we want the tiger to be dead or alive."

"Easy choice. No tiger at all."

"Well, good luck telling Jarkko that. He's pretty excited about the ceremony."

As Jones finished his story, Marissa emerged from the forward cabin and crept up the stairs. She was wearing a red-and-white sundress that wasn't really her style but fit better than the other clothes that had been delivered by the hotel. Although she had dressed up for the library meeting the day before, she had viewed it as a professional obligation. She typically preferred clothes that hid her curves and flawless skin, all in hopes of blending in with the crowd.

Payne saw her appear from the steps down below and literally gasped at the sight. He instantly forgot about Jones and the albino tiger. His sole focus was on her.

"Wow," Payne said as he walked over to greet her. "You look amazing."

She blushed. "Really? You don't think it's too girly?"

"No," he said. "It's perfect. You look perfect."

She smiled and greeted him with a kiss on each cheek. "That's how we say hello in Malta."

Payne practically drooled over the scent of her hair. She had been injured in a gunfight just yesterday, but somehow managed to smell like strawberries. "Great tradition."

"Did you eat?" she said as she made her way toward the galley.

"Of course not. We were waiting for you."

"Then I'm flattered. David led me to believe that your stomach doesn't wait for anyone."

"It doesn't," Jones assured her. "And if he tells you otherwise, he's full of shit. I've seen him cut in line in front of an admiral in order to feed the beast."

Payne laughed. "That was one time on an aircraft carrier, and he was taking too long to decide. I mean, he could keep track of the entire Northern Fleet in his head, but he couldn't choose between beans or potatoes. Give me a break."

"See," Jones said as he pointed at Payne. "These are things you need to know. Truth be told, I'm not really his friend. I'm more like his keeper. An unpaid keeper."

"Says the guy who uses my credit card more often than I do."

"I'm not doing it for me; I'm doing it for you. If you don't use your card, you may lose valuable reward points and money-saving perks. How many times do I have to tell you that?"

Payne patted him on the back. "Well, thank you for your service."

"Speaking of thanks," Marissa said, "thank you for the clothes. I didn't want to do it, but David insisted. He said time is a priority, now that the Russians have Jarkko's documents."

"He's right," Payne said. "I wish I hadn't slept so late, but I guess we can figure out our next step over brunch. That is, if Jarkko's around."

Jarkko heard his name and trudged up the stairs. "Don't worry. Jarkko is coming. But Jarkko has bad news."

They could tell from the look on his face that he was upset.

Marissa walked toward him, concerned. "Are you okay?"

He shook his head. "Jarkko did what Jon suggested last night. Jarkko make phone call to colleague who gave collection to Jarkko to see if he told Jarkko's name to Russians. Unfortunately, colleague couldn't come to phone because colleague is dead."

Marissa gave him a quick hug. "Oh my God. I'm so sorry to hear that. Were you two close?"

He shook his head again. When he couldn't get Bobrinsky on the phone, he had called a mutual acquaintance for insight. "Not friends like Jon and David, but business associates. Jarkko did business with Sergei for long time. He a good man. A family man. And that is what makes Jarkko angry. Jarkko look online for details, and Jarkko sees his family is killed, too."

Payne cursed as he absorbed the news. "When did it happen?"

Jarkko pulled out his phone and looked at the article on his browser. Although he had read the story twice, the details were still sinking in. "On Saturday in Estonia. Apparently, Russians go to Tallinn and kill him and family in famous tower."

Jones pondered the news. "Why was he in Estonia?"

Jarkko shrugged. "If Jarkko has to guess, Sergei takes family to Estonia to run from problems and start new life. Jarkko tell you yesterday during soup that Sergei is good man with large debt. His wife gets very sick, and Sergei borrows money from wrong people to help with cure. When Sergei can't pay, he gets desperate. That is why he gives collection to Jarkko. Sergei likes Jarkko and makes sure Jarkko gets payment first. Perhaps this upsets man with larger loss. Jarkko does not know this for sure. This is just Jarkko's guess."

Payne gave it some thought. "Your theory makes sense. I knew there had to be a reason why the Russians came after us with so much anger. They attacked us at the library. They shredded your yacht. They even tied a corpse to your stern. Obviously that goes beyond a simple treasure. They were attacking you on a personal level."

Jarkko took a deep breath. As he did, he trembled with emotion. "Jarkko is *so* sorry. Jarkko did not know this would happen. If Jarkko knows, Jarkko would not risk lives of friends for stupid treasure. No treasure is worth friendship, so Jarkko thinks it's time to say goodbye."

"Fuck that!" Payne said as he marched over to Jarkko and looked him straight in the eye. "This is *not* your fault, and we are *not* going to abandon you in your time of need. You've dealt with Russians even more than I have, so you know damn well that they aren't going to stop—not after we killed so many of their comrades. They're going to scurry home to Mother Russia, multiply like cockroaches, then come after us with everything they've got."

Jarkko nodded in agreement. "You are right. They will not stop. They will keep coming and coming until we are dead or we cut head off snake."

Jones stared at him. "Does the snake have a name?"

Jarkko nodded. "It's Volkov. Ivan Volkov."

CHAPTER 37

From his office at Interpol headquarters, Nick Dial growled into his cell phone. "Ivan Volkov? You're fucking around with Ivan Volkov? Do you have a death wish?"

"Not really," Payne said from the outdoor table on the stern of the moving yacht. Spread out in front of him were several takeout containers, filled with an assortment of food: a cheeseburger with fries, pasta salad, fruit salad, and a stack of pancakes. As Jarkko piloted the craft into deeper water and away from other boats, Payne grabbed some fries and dipped them in ketchup. "But you know damn well I'm not going to back down from a challenge."

"A *challenge*?" Dial blurted as he stood from behind his desk. "You call going up against one of the most powerful criminals in Russia a *challenge*?"

"Yep," he said as he chewed quietly. "Why? What would you call it?"

"A death wish!"

Dial took a deep breath as he stomped across his floor to his office door and shut it for privacy. He had spent half the night trying to come up with information about the Russian attack in Malta, only to have news about its mastermind handed to him by Payne.

Not that he was upset about the call itself.

The truth was he was thrilled that Payne had kept his word and had phoned the minute he had come up with news about the gunmen. Dial's frustration stemmed from the slow trickle of data that had come from I-24/7, which was the global police communications system that Interpol used to connect law enforcement officers in all of its member countries. Unfortunately, the system was completely reliant on the National Central Bureaus and police departments around the globe. Until information was added to the appropriate databases, Dial couldn't access it on the network. And since the secretary general had banned Dial from investigative work, all he could do was sit on his ass in France while his friends' lives were in danger in Malta.

For a man like Dial, that was hard to handle.

"Listen, Jon, and listen good. Even though Russia is one of Interpol's member countries, I cannot help you or DJ if you go to Moscow to take on Volkov. My fancy title doesn't mean shit to the *Politsiya*. Their entire police force operates under the Ministry of Internal Affairs of the Russian Federation, and they barely tolerate our presence. I can't even imagine how the Minister would react to a phone call from me—a fuckin' American—but you better believe it wouldn't help your cause in a Russian prison or my chance of continued employment at Interpol."

"On the bright side, you've been looking for a change."

"Don't fuck with me, Jon. I'm not in the mood."

"Would your mood improve if I helped you clear a murder case?"

"Good Lord," Dial said as he started to pace his office. "Who'd you kill now?"

Payne laughed as the yacht slowed to a stop. "Not me. *Volkov*."

Dial stopped. "It might."

"Does the name Sergei Bobrinsky mean anything to you?"

"Bobrinsky?" he said as he tried to think. Thousands of murders happened every day in his member countries, so the odds of him knowing a single name were pretty slim. But for some reason, that particular name had made his radar. "Where did he die?"

"Estonia," Payne said as he continued to eat.

"Tallinn!" Dial blurted. "He died in the tower in Tallinn!"

Payne wiped his mouth with a napkin. "That's the guy."

Dial sat in his office chair and reached for his computer mouse. "I'm gonna put you on speakerphone, if that's okay with you."

"Only if I can do the same with you."

"Honestly, I'd rather you didn't."

"Don't worry," Payne said, realizing Dial's job was on the line. "No one is around. I'm merely trying to eat."

Dial smiled as he clicked through files. "When *aren't* you trying to eat?"

Payne laughed. "Good point."

"In that case, go ahead. But if I hear mooing sounds and gunshots in the background, I'm gonna bust you for animal cruelty."

Payne picked up his cheeseburger, completely unaffected by

the comment. "Speaking of which, how long would you put someone away for killing an albino tiger?"

"Excuse me?"

"Asking for a friend."

"A long, long time."

"Good. I'll let him know."

Dial stared at his computer screen. While Payne was rambling, Dial had pulled up the case files from the Bobrinsky murder on the I-24/7 network. "If it's okay with you, can we get back to Estonia? As far as I can tell, it's an open investigation. How do you know it was Volkov?"

"Is this off the record?"

Dial laughed. "Of course this is off the record! I'm the head of the entire division, and I'm hiding in my office like a teenager—a teenager with chest pains and ulcers."

"Just making sure," Payne said as he reached for the pancakes. "Wait. Are you serious about the health shit, or were you just busting my balls?"

"A little of both. Anytime you call, I feel my blood pressure going up."

"That's better than your dick going up."

Dial laughed. "Touché."

"Anyway," Payne said, "I got the intel from Jarkko, who got it from one of his business associates in Russia. It turns out that Bobrinsky was the one who jumpstarted our treasure hunt when he gave Jarkko a collection of Russian documents as payment for services rendered. Unfortunately, Bobrinsky owed Volkov a substantial debt, which is likely the reason that he came after Jarkko at the library. We think it was to make a point about priorities. If you owe money to Volkov, you better pay him first or everyone—including family—gets punished."

Dial listened as he scanned one of the reports on his screen. "Makes sense to me, and it fits the evidence found at the scene. Bobrinsky was carrying three fake Estonian passports. Very high quality. The type a desperate man would buy to smuggle his family out of Russia. Truth be told, I'm not quite sure why he would stay so close to home. If I owed money to Volkov, I would move to a different hemisphere to protect my family, but that's just me. Maybe Bobrinsky had contacts in Tallinn who were going to help him from there."

Payne shrugged. He had no clue. He wasn't the type to run. "I've been to Tallinn more than once for business conferences. It's a thriving, high-tech city with tons of cameras. There has to be surveillance footage of Volkov and his goons."

Dial shook his head. "The murders took place in Old Town, which is the medieval part of Tallinn. There are cameras there, but not nearly as many as the bustling downtown. According to this report, there was a Wi-Fi blackout in the area at the time, so there's no footage of the murder. However, the cameras conveniently came back on *after* the bodies were found."

Thanks to his work at Payne Industries, Payne knew that Tallinn had a free, citywide Wi-Fi network that would ping the moment he landed at the airport. The city also had some of the best high-tech wizards on the planet. If someone had managed to hack their network—much like the network in Valletta had been hacked at the time of the gunfight—then they were extremely talented, the type of hackers who could potentially mess with a presidential election.

"If it's okay with you," Payne said, "I'd love to share this information with Randy Raskin. Maybe there's something he can do to recover some footage."

Dial nodded. "That's fine with me. Anything to keep him from messing with my phone. I can't get his *ding-a-ling* out of my mind."

Payne laughed. "You may want to rephrase that."

"Shit. You know what I meant."

"Wait until I tell DJ."

"Please don't."

"No worries. This call never happened."

"What call?" Dial said with a smile. "Seriously, though, thanks for the intel. I'll let you know if I learn anything else about Volkov."

Payne nodded. "I appreciate it. And I'll obviously do the same."

CHAPTER 38

Because of the time difference between Malta and America, Payne was reluctant to call Raskin so early in his morning. Although the computer whiz worked ridiculous hours and had a cot in his sub-basement office at the Pentagon for the occasional sleepover, Payne knew from experience that Raskin was a lot more receptive to favors later in the day, once he was fueled by several cans of Mountain Dew and bored with his actual work.

While continuing to eat his brunch, Payne slowly but surely typed out a summary of his conversation with Dial in a lengthy email and added a list of other things that he hoped Raskin could accomplish once the hacker's caffeine meter had reached a peak level. Payne was great at a lot of things, but typing wasn't one of them. His hands were too big for most keyboards and mobile devices, so he was forced to peck at keys with his index fingers.

Not that he was complaining.

If he had been given the choice at birth between the small, nimble hands of a surgeon or the strong, meaty hands of a black-smith, he would always pick the latter. In his line of work, he pre-ferred to pack as much punch as possible.

Payne finished his meal and his email at roughly the same time. He clicked the send button on his phone, then gathered the takeout cartons from his feast before opening the sliding glass door at the back of the saloon. The others were cleaning up their car-tons as well, having eaten approximately the same amount of food combined as Payne had eaten by himself.

"How's Nick?" Jones asked, already knowing the answer.

"Stressed," Payne said as he closed the door behind him.

"One of these years, I'm going to ask that question, and you're going to blow my mind and say something different."

"Don't exaggerate. You know damn well sometimes I say 'angry'."

Jones laughed. "Good point."

"Seriously, though, I think he's long overdue for a therapy session. I was kind of hoping you could fit him into your busy schedule."

"Sure thing. I'll pencil him in between 'kill Russians' and 'find treasure'."

Payne dumped his cartons into a trash bag that looked identical to their luggage from the day before. "Speaking of which, we still need to finish our history lesson."

Marissa glanced at him as she washed silverware in the sink. "I thought that was the plan for brunch. Then you ran outside to make your call."

"Sorry," he said as he walked into the galley to explain. "I promised Nick I would call him the instant I found out about the gunmen, and I always do my best to keep my word."

She smiled at him. "I wasn't complaining, and I admire the trait. I was merely pointing out to the group that the delay was completely your fault."

Jones chimed in. "Just so you know, it always is. With Jon, it isn't 'three o'clock'. It's 'me o'clock'. For some reason, he thinks the world revolves around him."

Marissa and Jarkko laughed at the comment, much to Payne's chagrin.

"Wow," Payne said as reached over his shoulder and pretended to remove a dagger. "You're gonna stab your best friend in the back to make a mediocre joke."

Jones grinned. "Truth be told, I thought it was pretty funny."

Marissa smiled. "And accurate."

Jarkko nodded. "Jarkko laughed because it's true."

"Ouch," Payne said as he tried not to smile. "So, that's how you're gonna play it. I step outside for one minute, and you guys start a mutiny."

"Not mutiny," Jarkko said with a shake of his head. "This is Jarkko's ship, so Jarkko is captain. You are merely cabin boy. That is why you sleep in smallest bedroom."

"Wait." Payne glanced at the others. "Did I really?"

Jones laughed. "That's what you get for taking first watch."

"Fine!" Payne snarled with mock outrage. "If that's how little you respect me, I'll let someone else run today's briefing."

Marissa grabbed a towel to dry her hands. "Let's be honest, Jon. I'm the one with all the expertise on the subject matter, so I can take over from here."

Jarkko grinned. "That works for Jarkko. Jon is good cabin boy, but not Jarkko's type. Jarkko would much rather stare at Marissa."

"Me, too," Jones said as he grabbed a seat at the table. "Besides, do we really want a has-been like Jon running the meeting? The guy doesn't even have a job."

"Neither do you!" Payne snapped as he sat down next to Jones. "Which is why I'm not running the meeting. Duh."

Jarkko nodded. "Also because you are homeless."

"Knock it off!" Marissa growled, trying to imitate Payne's voice from the night before. "Enough with the jokes. It's time to get serious!"

The three men stopped talking and stared at her.

"How was that?" she asked with a smile.

Jones burst out laughing. "That was awesome. *Much* better than Jon. You sounded like a studio wrestler."

Jarkko shook his head. "More like dominatrix. Dungeon name could be Mean Marissa."

Jones stared at Jarkko. "Dude! Enough with the jokes."

Jarkko stared back. "Who's joking?"

Payne glanced at Marissa. "See what I have to deal with?"

"Boys," she said as she took her seat at the table. "And I do mean *boys*, because *men* wouldn't be acting like that in front of a lady."

Jarkko lowered his head in shame. "Sorry."

Jones put his hand on Jarkko's shoulder. "He's done. I promise."

"Glad to hear it," she said as she tried to remember where she had left off the previous night. "Unless I'm mistaken, the last thing I mentioned before I stormed out of here like a spoiled brat was Napoleon's invasion of Malta and Grand Master Hompesch's surrender."

Payne stared at her, impressed. Not only had she managed to settle down Jones and Jarkko, but she had also taken responsibility for her less-than-ideal behavior. That was the sign of a great leader, someone who realized that he or she wasn't above culpability. "That sounds right. You said a week after Hompesch surrendered that he was on a ship to Italy, where he established a temporary new headquarters for the Order."

She nodded. "Hompesch went to Trieste, which is an affluent city in northeastern Italy, roughly twenty miles from modern-day Croatia. At the time of his arrival in 1798 AD, Trieste was part of the Habsburg Monarchy and a very prosperous seaport. But Hompesch never viewed it as a permanent home for the Order. Instead, he used it as a base to negotiate."

"Negotiate what?" Jones wondered.

"That's a very good question—one I'm afraid I can't answer with much certainty. Until our discussion last night, I would have said that he was trying to find a new home for the Order, just like other grand masters had done over the centuries. Keep in mind, this organization had moved from Jerusalem to Cyprus and then to Rhodes before they had even arrived in Malta, so this type of thing wasn't new to the Order. However, unlike all of those other moves, the organization was lacking the one thing that they had always possessed in the past: money."

Payne nodded in understanding. "*Unless* they had a treasure."

"Exactly!" she said with excitement. "If Hompesch possessed the treasure that we're looking for, then he would have had some serious bargaining power. He could have bought an island, or bribed a monarch, or done something to keep the Order flourishing, but none of those things happened. Instead, most of the remaining Knights viewed him with shame because of his actions in Malta, and he was forced to resign his position a year later."

Jarkko grimaced with confusion. "Why shame?"

Payne explained his theory. "If Hompesch accomplished what we hope he did—meaning he smuggled the Order's fortune off the island with the help of a few trusted men—then the majority of the knights wouldn't have known what had really happened in Valletta. Instead, they would have viewed him as an incompetent coward, someone who didn't prepare for Napoleon's attack and, even worse, surrendered to him after a single day of minor fighting. As a former soldier, I can speak from experience that word spreads awfully quick amongst the troops if a leader is viewed as a coward. To soldiers, the only thing worse is a traitor."

Jones picked it up from there. "But if Hompesch was forced to resign a year later, then that means one of three things most likely happened. One, there was never any treasure, and all of this is a wild-goose chase. Two, the French spotted Hompesch's escape attempt and grabbed the treasure for themselves. Or three, Hompesch was a weaselly crook who kept the treasure all to himself. The question is, what does history say?"

All three men glanced at Marissa, looking for answers.

She greeted them with a confident smile.

"If it's okay with you," she said, "I'd like to address your points in reverse order. Let's start with number three. Hompesch resigned under pressure in 1799 AD. Soon after his dismissal, he settled in the city of Ljubljana, which is the modern-day capital city of Slovenia. But back then, it was known as Laybach and was under Hapsburg rule. He stayed there until 1804 AD, when he moved to Montpellier in France, where he lived in poverty. Less than a year later, he died of asthma and was buried in the Church of Saint Eulalie in a simple tomb."

"In other words," Jones said, "he didn't keep the treasure for himself."

She nodded. "That seems highly unlikely."

"Okay. Moving on. What about scenario number two? Could the French have spotted his men and kept the treasure for themselves?"

She shook her head. "Also highly unlikely, and here's why: Napoleon *loved* to brag. At that point of his military career, he was trying to accomplish as much as humanly possible in order to win over his countrymen in order to fulfill his ultimate goal of becoming emperor of France. If he or his men—who he ruled with an iron fist—had seized a major treasure from the famous Knights of Malta, he would have trumpeted its capture for maximum effect. Additionally, if he had come up with such a significant source of wealth before his march through Egypt, he would have undoubtedly used the treasure for food and supplies."

She looked at Jones. "Sorry. I'm not sure why I'm telling you that. Last night you were the one filling us in on Napoleon's objectives in Egypt. Do you remember anything about a huge surplus of gold or jewels coming from Malta?"

Jones shook his head. "Nope. Nothing like that, so I guess we can rule that out, too."

Marissa nodded. "Which leaves us with number one—the dreaded scenario that none of us want to talk about. What if there was no treasure and all of this was a wild-goose chase?"

She took a moment to look them in the eye. "I hate to be the bearer of bad news, but this is, by far, the most likely scenario. During all of my years studying Maltese history, I have never heard a thing about a secret treasure hoarded by the Knights until you showed up in Valletta. And as far as I can tell, the only evidence we have—make that *had*—about a treasure was a letter from Emperor Paul the First of Russia to Grand Master Hompesch. Unfortunately, it was stolen by Ivan Volkov before I had a chance to verify the authenticity of the letter."

Payne chimed in. "Just so you know, I sent a picture of the letter to Petr before he even texted you about meeting us, and he verified the authenticity of the handwriting. He said it matched other surviving documents that were written by Paul the First."

"Good to know," she said as she considered the new information. "That increases the possibility of a treasure by roughly one percent in my mind. However, as a historian—and that's my role on this team—I still have to express my doubt. Serious, soul-crushing doubt. I know that's hard to hear, but if you want to know my opinion as an expert on Maltese history, I have to tell you the truth. I honestly don't think there was a treasure."

CHAPTER 39

Marissa's skepticism about the treasure dampened the hope on the yacht. And she could sense it, too.

As she glanced around the table, she could see the disappointment on the faces of all the men, and it instantly filled her with regret.

At that moment, she realized that she had learned nothing from the night before. Despite the harsh criticism from Payne, she was allowing her book smarts to get in the way of creativity and innovation. She was so focused on what she had learned in classrooms and libraries that she wasn't allowing herself to believe that textbooks could be wrong.

So she opted to do something about it.

"Despite my doubt about the treasure," she said in a much cheerier tone, "I am familiar with one particular crew of pirates that's had a lot of success with conjecture and wild speculation. Following nothing but their gut instincts and minimal knowledge of history, they managed to sneak onto Mount Athos and make one of the biggest archaeological discoveries of all time."

Jarkko whispered to Jones. "She's talking about us."

Jones whispered to Payne. "Minimal knowledge of history?"

She ignored them and continued. "And since we've reached the part of our journey where textbooks end and imagination begins, I think it is in everyone's best interest if I relinquish control of this briefing to the best cabin boy in the world, Mister Jonathon Payne."

Jones and Jarkko pounded on the table to express their approval.

Payne grinned while nodding at Marissa.

She smiled and nodded back.

"My first order of business," Payne announced, "is to thank Doctor Marissa Vella for her time as mission commander. Although this crew works best when playing it fast and loose, we will still need her vast expertise as we rewrite the history books that she loves so much."

Jones and Jarkko pounded on the table once again.

Marissa smiled and dabbed a fake tear from her eye.

"Okay," Payne said, slowly turning serious. "Now that the transition is over, I was hoping we could get some additional information from our esteemed historian. Unless I'm mistaken, you haven't mentioned any relationship between Russia and Malta—other than Jarkko's letter. But when I spoke to Petr on the phone yesterday afternoon, he said there were a number of significant connections, particularly when it came to the Order of Saint John."

She sensed his change in tone and shifted back to her former role. "As usual, Petr is correct. Coincidentally, the relationship between Russia and the Order of Saint John started exactly one hundred years before Napoleon's arrival in Valletta. In 1698 AD, Peter the Great sent a delegation to Malta to observe the training and abilities of the Order and its fleet. The Russian contingent was led by Field Marshal Boris Sheremetev, who arrived with a letter of introduction from the czar and a second one from Holy Roman Emperor Leopold. At first, there was mutual distrust between the two sides, but after a week of flowery speeches, given in Latin, where Sheremetev spoke of Russia's unrelenting war against the hated Turks, the Knights started to view Russia differently. They sensed that this great power to the east might be their best hope against the encroaching powers of the west, which viewed Malta as the key to the Mediterranean. With preservation of the Order in mind, the Knights discussed several future ventures with Sheremetev, including the possibility of a Russian naval base in Malta."

Payne grunted, completely repelled by the notion. "I can't even fathom the worldwide ramifications of a Russian naval base in the Mediterranean. It would've been incredible for them, but catastrophic for the rest of the world, particularly during the Soviet era."

Marissa nodded in agreement. She knew modern-day Malta would be a much different place if Russia had established a permanent stronghold on her island. "Prior to leaving Malta, Sheremetev established diplomatic relations with the Knights and was given a diamond-studded Cross of Devotion by the Order in return. This marked the beginning of a special relationship between the Knights and the Russian crown."

She took a sip of water before she continued her lecture.

"Throughout the eighteenth century, Russia sent military officers for special training with the Knights of Malta, and in return, the Order sent ambassadors to Russia to lay the groundwork for a continued partnership. By the time Manuel Pinto da Fonseca was elected as grand master of the Order in 1741 AD, there was a growing trust between the two allies. Unfortunately, Pinto's reign was marred by his lavish lifestyle. During his thirty-two years as grand master, he did a number of impressive things—including the creation of the University of Malta in 1769 AD. However, he is best remembered for the massive debt that he accumulated during his tenure, which forced the Knights into bankruptcy shortly after his death in 1773 AD."

Jarkko groaned. "Sorry. Jarkko not happy."

Payne nodded. "I can understand why. If the Knights went bankrupt twenty-five years before Napoleon even arrived, maybe Marissa is right. Maybe there wasn't a treasure."

Marissa flashed an ironic smile. Suddenly their roles were reversed, and she was the one providing optimism to the group. "Don't give up hope just yet. The Order's fortune is about to change. After a short and unsuccessful reign by Pinto's successor—a Spaniard named Francisco Ximenes de Texada—the Order got things right by electing Emmanuel de Rohan-Polduc as its grand master. As a member of the wealthy and influential Rohan family of France, he sought to win the respect of his knights by fortifying their defenses in Malta and strengthening their finances. During his first few years, he acquired the properties of the Order of St. Anthony in France, several assets from the Knights of the Holy Sepulchre in Poland, and most importantly of all, expanded the Order of Saint John into Russia."

"Interesting," Jones said as his mind swirled with theories. "Very interesting."

"How so?" Payne asked.

"What? A brother can't find something interesting?"

"Sorry, I thought you had more to offer than an adjective."

"Maybe I do," Jones said, defensively. "But I would prefer to hear the lady out before I dazzle you with my insight. Besides, I also threw in an adverb."

Payne rolled his eyes. "Sorry about that. Please continue."

"No problem," she said as she picked up from there. "Believing that Russia was the key to the Order's future, Grand Master de Rohan sent a young adventurer by the name of Bailiff Count Giulio Renato de Litta to Saint Petersburg in 1789 AD to assist with the reorganization of Russia's Baltic Fleet. Blessed with a diplomatic and military mind, the twenty-six-year-old knight soon distinguished himself in battle, serving as a commander with the Russian Imperial Navy in its ongoing war against Sweden. For his heroic service, he was honored with the Order of Saint George—which was bestowed upon him by Catherine the Great—and promoted to the rank of Rear Admiral in the Imperial Navy."

"Really?" Payne said, impressed. "For a foreigner to be given the Order of Saint George—which is still the highest military honor in Russia—and a promotion to Rear Admiral while he was in his twenties is remarkable to me. He must have been revered by the crown."

She nodded. "Despite his age, de Litta had made his way into Empress Catherine's inner circle. When Grand Master de Rohan found out about this, he viewed it as an opportunity to strengthen the relationship with the crown, so he appointed de Litta as Minister of the Order in Russia to curry favor with the empress. But before they could take advantage of the situation, Catherine died quite unexpectedly in November of 1796 AD, and her son, Paul, ascended to the throne. Initially, this seemed like bad news since de Litta was so well liked by the empress, but as fate should have it, the accession of Paul the First actually strengthened the connection between Valletta and Saint Petersburg."

"In what way?" Jones wondered.

Marissa took another sip of water to soothe her throat. She simply wasn't used to talking this much. Not that she minded one bit. The truth was she found it exhilarating to be holding court with people that she actually admired. Her social circle was extremely small, consisting mostly of former classmates and professors who were scattered around the globe. Normally the only people that she talked to in person were the librarians that she encountered while doing her research and the employees at her favorite restaurants.

Other than that, she went through life alone.

"Fourteen years before Catherine's death—way back in 1782 AD—she sent her son Paul, then a Grand Duke, to Malta to visit Grand Master de Rohan in Valletta. Although it was her intent to solidify her relationship with the Order with this gesture of admiration and respect, it was actually Paul who came away impressed. The man who would eventually become Paul the First was fascinated by the lore of the heroic Knights, so much so that within a year of becoming emperor, he signed the Treaty of 1797 with the Order of Malta. This agreement did two important things. It established a Roman Catholic Grand Priory of ten commanderies in Russia, and more importantly, Paul was officially named as the temporal Protector of the Order."

Jones rubbed his hands together. "Now we're getting somewhere. So a year before Napoleon shows up in Valletta, Paul the First agrees to be the Order's secular protector. I'm assuming that means its *military* protector, as opposed to its *spiritual* protector, which would still be the Catholic Church."

She nodded. "That's correct."

"And who ratified the treaty on behalf of the Order: de Rohan or Hompesch?"

She smiled, impressed by the question. "Although de Rohan had negotiated the agreement with Paul the First, de Rohan passed away before the treaty was signed, so it was Hompesch, his successor as grand master, who actually ratified the deal."

Jones had figured as much. "So starting in 1797 AD, Malta and Russia are officially tied together with this deal, and more significantly, Hompesch and Paul the First are tied together as well. I think that's something we need to keep in mind when we discuss Jarkko's letter."

"Why's that?" Jarkko asked.

"Because Hompesch's surrender to the French meant that Paul had failed to do his job. He had failed to protect Malta in its time of need. Unless, of course, he knew about Hompesch's plan all along. In which case, all is forgiven."

Jones shifted his gaze to Marissa. "After the fall of Malta in 1798, how was Paul treated by the Order? Did they shun him like Hompesch?"

"No," she said with a laugh. "Quite the opposite. Not only didn't they shun Paul the First, they actually elected him as the new grand master of the Knights."

CHAPTER 40

Before Jones could ask the hundreds of questions that were surging through his brain, Payne's cell phone started to vibrate. He glanced at its screen to silence it but decided to take the call instead when he saw who was on the line.

"Hold that thought," he said to Jones. "It's Petr."

Payne excused himself and walked away from the group to avoid being rude. He hated it when someone answered a call at a crowded table, forcing everyone around them to either talk over the phone conversation or sit there quietly while waiting for the call to end. In a world full of social-conscious millennials that would stage protests over the slightest insults, he couldn't believe the lack of manners that existed in society today.

"Hang on," Payne said as he answered Ulster's call. He opened the sliding glass door at the back of the boat and took a seat at the table where he had devoured his brunch. From there, he saw nothing but the turquoise water of the Mediterranean. "Sorry about that."

"Jonathon?" Ulster mumbled, confused. "Can you see me? Because I can't see you."

Payne pulled the phone from his ear and glanced at his screen. It was filled with Ulster's full name and several digital buttons, but that was all. He laughed to himself before he returned the phone to his ear. "Petr, I hate to be the bearer of bad news, but the reason we can't see each other is because you didn't make a *video* call."

"I didn't?" Ulster blurted before laughing at his own mistake. "Jonathon, my boy, promise me that you won't tell David about this blunder. No need to prolong my embarrassment."

"No worries, Petr. Your secret is safe with me."

"Great! See you soon!"

Then without warning, Ulster hung up his phone.

"Petr?" Payne said when he heard the click. "Are you there?"

Payne glanced at his screen and laughed when he realized what Ulster had done. In a weird way, it made him love the man even more. Despite having a mastery of human history, Ulster often struggled with the modern world and his place in it. Although he was smart enough to realize that he would be left behind if he didn't adapt his life and business to the technological age, he frequently encountered bumps along the way.

Payne realized as much and assisted whenever he could, literally building customized technology at Payne Industries and donating it the Archives. The equipment helped Ulster's staff of academics and interns scan the millions of pages of history that were being protected in the vaults at Küsendorf and upload them to a digital cloud that was set to go public in the near future. Payne had also hired a bunch of elite coders, handpicked by Randy Raskin, to develop software that would translate ancient languages and dialects into modern ones.

Software that Payne and Jones had used on prior adventures.

And yet, there was only so much he could do with Ulster himself. The phone that Ulster had called on was another piece of Payne Industries tech. Built with secured communications in mind, it was the same model that Payne and Jones carried. Payne had personally taught Ulster how to use the device when he had given it to his friend as a birthday gift, but Ulster's tendency to lose himself in thought and bumble in the real world was one glitch that software wouldn't fix.

Not that Payne would ever want to.

Bumbling was part of Ulster's unique charm.

Payne grinned when his phone vibrated again. This time it was an actual *video* call. So either Ulster had figured out which button to push or his butler Winston had done it for him. Either way, Payne touched his screen and accepted Ulster's call.

"Much better!" Ulster pronounced as he stared from Payne's phone.

"Indeed it is," Payne replied. "How are things at the Archives?"

Ulster smiled. "I wouldn't know, because I'm not there."

"Really?" Payne said, half-surprised. "It normally takes a special occasion to drag you out of the comfort of your reading rooms. Where are you headed?"

Ulster shook his head. "Instead of supplying you with that

morsel of information, I thought perhaps we could have round two of yesterday's guessing game. I'm sure you can remember that I deduced *Birgu* as your location, and I'd like to see you do the same."

"Petr," Payne said, "I appreciate the opportunity to even the score, but I'm rather busy at the moment. Besides, I don't possess your keen observational skills or your encyclopedic knowledge of geography. Truth be told, I'm sure my guesses would only disappoint you in the end."

"Nonsense!" Ulster said dismissively. "You could *never* disappoint me. I certainly hope you realize that by now. Furthermore, my current location is somewhere that you've been rather recently. I'm confident that you'll figure it out if you follow my breadcrumbs."

"Fine!" Payne said with a laugh. No matter how hard he tried, he always fell for Ulster's boyish charm. It was like being friends with a *really* smart toddler. "I'm glad that you've decided to take it easy on me. Otherwise, I'm sure I wouldn't stand a chance."

"Okay, Jonathon. I'm starting the clock," Ulster announced. "Where am I?"

Payne stared at his phone, but the video image didn't change. All he could see was Ulster's grinning face. "You're on my screen."

"I know I'm on your screen, but *where am I* on your screen?"

Payne shook his head. "No, Petr, I mean I can *only* see you. For this to work, you need to take the phone away from your face and show me your surroundings."

"But if I do that, how will I know what you're guessing?"

"By my voice. You'll still be able to hear me like a speakerphone."

"Ah, yes! Of course! How silly of me!" Ulster lowered his voice to a whisper. "Once again, I must insist that you don't tell David, or else——"

"Hold up. Why are you so scared of DJ? Has he been bullying you?"

"No, certainly not," he said with a shake of his head. "The truth is I get the feeling that I'm something of an intellectual mentor of his, and if he hears about my occasional lapse of common sense, it might shatter the delicate pedestal that he has placed me on. And the last thing I would want to do is ruin the heroic image of me that is engrained in his psyche."

"Hang on," Payne managed to say before he hit the *mute*

button and turned his phone toward the Mediterranean. Then he exploded with laughter. He laughed so loud and so long that Jones threw his shoe at the window behind Payne's head in order to get him to shut up.

Payne wiped the tears from his eyes before he hit the *unmute* button and turned the camera phone back toward himself. "Sorry about that."

"No worries," Ulster said with a grin. "I actually enjoyed the intermission. Out of curiosity, does my phone have the same screensaver as yours? I'm hoping it does, because it was rather lovely. It was so realistic that I felt like I was actually there."

"Sorry, Petr, that wasn't a screensaver. That was actually a live video feed. Right now I'm on Jarkko's yacht in the middle of the Mediterranean."

"Oh dear," Ulster muttered as his face flushed with embarrassment. "I certainly hope that you're still near Malta. Otherwise, this will be something else to keep from David. And Winston. And the rest of my household staff."

Payne furrowed his brow as he tried to figure out why Ulster was getting so worked up, and then it hit him like a lightning bulb. All along, Ulster had been giving him clues about his location in order to make it easier on Payne:

> *I deduced Birgu, and **I'd like to see you do the same**.*
> *My current location is **somewhere that you've been recently**.*
> *I'm confident you'll figure it out if you **follow my breadcrumbs**.*

Suddenly, Payne felt like the detective character in *The Usual Suspects* who worked out the identity of the villain by using all the clues in plain sight.

Payne groaned. "Please tell me you aren't in Birgu."

Ulster nodded and forced a grin. "Surprise!"

Payne took a deep breath. "Petr, please don't take this the wrong way, but what are you doing here? You should've called first."

"Well, truth be told, when *you* didn't call or text to let me know how your meeting went with Marissa, I naturally assumed that it went poorly and you were too disappointed to tell me. After an evening of little rest where I spent half of my night worrying about letting you down and the other half imagining what type of treasure that Grand Master Hompesch was hiding—*and* if I'm being totally honest, the *third* half devouring an entire fruit torte that my chef had made with exotic delicacies like mango, papaya, and kiwi. He topped it off with hand-whipped cream that contained the slightest hint of almond extract that somehow brought out the natural flavor of the fruit. I'm not quite sure what possessed him to be so bold on a weeknight. Normally his mid-week desserts are—"

"Petr!" Payne blurted, but it hardly slowed him down.

"Actually," Ulster said with a laugh, "now that I've said it aloud, his dessert choice makes *perfect* sense. He must have heard that I was working with my Chinese collection in the Forbidden Room—a name that still makes me chuckle—and he decided to test my puzzle-solving brain, as I encourage my staff to do. Of course you know in some cultures 'kiwi fruit' is actually called 'Chinese gooseberries'—which, if I'm still being honest, is another word that makes me giggle. Say it with me, Jonathon: *gooseberries*. Too funny!"

"Petr!" Payne repeated, this time a little louder.

"Anyway, as I was saying before my stomach got in the way, my restless night inspired me to leave the cocoon of safety that I have woven around myself in the confines of the Archives for the open water and fresh air of a new adventure. As you certainly know, I rarely head out into the field unless I am surrounded by people I like and trust, and I can't think of two people I would rather spend time with than you and David. I don't mean to embarrass you when I say this, but while I was preparing our exhibition for the Smithsonian, I found myself missing the adrenaline-fueled escapades that we have shared in the past. So much, in fact, that I caught the first and only flight from Switzerland to Malta in order provide my expertise on your latest mission. Of course, I realize that just showing up was a trifle bold on my part, but I can assure you that my massive belly is dwarfed by my historical expertise, even after last evening's dessert. Speaking of desserts, have you ever had a *trifle*? It's a delightful mix of sponge cake and—"

"Petr!" Payne shouted, loud enough to stop Ulster's momentum.

"Sorry, my boy, was I rambling again?"

Payne nodded without words, if only to figure out what he wanted to say. As much as he would love to have Ulster's expertise at his disposal, he realized that Ulster was more of a liability than Marissa when it came to future attacks. At least she had the ability to run and jump and load a weapon—something he still needed to ask her about—whereas Ulster's main exercise came from opening his refrigerator door.

"Petr," Payne explained, "the reason I didn't call you yesterday about our meeting with Marissa is because we were attacked at the library by a group of Russian gunmen. We're all fine, but we're still trying to sort through the mess."

"Oh my heavens!" Ulster said as absorbed the news. "Don't ask me how, but I *knew*—simply *knew*—that you were wading into trouble. I warned you, Jonathon. Didn't I warn you?"

"You did, Petr, but—"

"And everyone's okay?"

"Yes, Petr. A little banged up, but—"

"Including Marissa?"

"Yes, Petr, including Marissa."

Ulster breathed a sigh of relief. "Well, thank heavens for that. Since I was the one who had arranged the meeting, I don't know what I would have done if harm had befallen her. If I may be so bold, where are you right now?"

"About a mile offshore. We decided it would be best if we stayed away from people while we figured out our next move. Out here, we can see potential threats on the horizon."

"But you feel you're currently safe?"

Payne nodded. "I do. I definitely do."

"Good! Then swing into the harbor and pick me up, and we can return to your current locale. If you're merely a mile offshore, we can be back to safety within an hour."

"Petr, as much as I'd love to have you, I don't think you understand—"

"No, Jonathon, it's *you* who doesn't understand." Unlike his playful tone from earlier, Ulster's voice now possessed an edge that Payne was unaccustomed to hearing. "As far as I'm concerned, you have a decision to make. Either your yacht is safe or it isn't. Right now, that's all that matters to me. If it *is* secure, then swing by Birgu or wherever you'd like me to go, and pick me up so I can assist you with your grand adventure. Although Marissa is an expert on Maltese history, I can assure you that her knowledge pales in comparison to mine on all things Russian, and that expertise will most definitely come in handy with Catherine the Great, Paul the First, and all of the other pieces in your historical puzzle. On

the other hand, if you feel your yacht *isn't* safe from Russian gunmen, then I must insist that you drop off Marissa at once. I will
happily take her back to the Archives where we can help you via
mobile device while under the protection of armed guards."

"Petr, it isn't that simple."

"Actually, Jonathon, it is. As far as I'm concerned, those are
your choices. Pick one, or risk losing me as an asset."

CHAPTER 41

Although Payne didn't like Ulster's ultimatum on multiple levels, he realized that Ulster was correct. If the sea was safe enough for Marissa, then it was safe enough for Ulster.

After all, how much running could they do on a yacht?

And yet, Payne didn't want to risk going into the busy harbor in the middle of the afternoon to get him. In his mind, there were far too many boats to adequately defend themselves against possible threats, so he told Ulster to take a cab to the Corinthia Hotel where they would pick him up in the relative seclusion of St. George's Bay.

Upon his arrival, Ulster was directed to the rear wharf by a member of the hotel staff, who also assisted with Ulster's luggage. Unlike Payne and Jones, who hopped onto a plane with nothing but the clothes on their backs, Ulster brought more than enough bags for everyone, including two that were filled with nothing but snacks.

Despite the tension during their video call, Payne was happy to see Ulster when they pulled near shore. In fact, all of them were. There was just something about the way he carried himself that put people at ease, which was highly ironic since he was the biggest introvert of the group. Until Payne and Jones's first trip to Küsendorf, Ulster had rarely ventured from the Archives. Every year he would force himself to attend a fancy gala or two in order to raise money for a new museum or library, but other that, he simply preferred to stay at home and work.

But their adventure across Europe—during which they had found out the truth about the crucifixion of Christ—had opened his eyes to the world around him. Although he could speak multiple languages and identify spots on the globe with nothing more than a glance, he realized he had never been to most of the places that he had lectured about. Ever since then, he had vowed to travel more often. Ulster still wasn't racking up tons of mileage, but trips like this were becoming more and more frequent.

"Petr!" Jones shouted as he hustled off the yacht to greet his friend with a hug. "It's great to see you in the flesh. It's been far too long."

Ulster grinned with delight. "I couldn't agree more, which is why I packed my bag and hopped on the first flight to Malta."

Jones peeked over Ulster's shoulder and stared at his assortment of luggage. "Did you say 'bag'—*singular*? How long are you planning to stay? A decade or two?"

Ulster laughed. "If that's how long it takes, then so be it. I wanted to be prepared for all contingencies, including pedestrian meal service. That is why I asked my personal chef to pack a few of our favorite things, including those chocolate Swiss rolls that you love so much."

"The ones that look and taste like fancy Ho Hos?"

"Those are the ones," Ulster said with grin.

"I love those! Which bag are they in?"

"Truth be told, I don't know. My staff did all the packing."

"Doesn't matter," Jones said as he patted his friend on the arm. "I was going to carry your bags anyway. Not in one trip, though. I'm not a freakin' pachyderm."

"Excellent Scrabble word, David. Remember it for later!"

Marissa stood back until their conversation was finished before she stepped forward. Although she had communicated with Ulster via text the day before, she hadn't seen him in quite some time. "Petr, it's so good to see you!"

Ulster did a double take. "Marissa, is that *you*? Oh my heavens, how you've changed! The last time I saw you, you were hiding yourself in an oversized sweater and baggy jeans. Now you're tan, and leggy, and breathtakingly beautiful. You have blossomed like a flower, my dear, and I couldn't be happier for you."

Marissa put her hands to her heart and nearly started to cry. She had always wanted her father to say something like that to her, but since she knew that was never going to happen, it was nearly as good coming from a mentor like Ulster. She quickly gathered her composure and greeted him with a kiss on each cheek. "It appears I'm not the only one who has shaken up their wardrobe. You look like an explorer searching for El Dorado."

Dressed in a white, vented shirt, beige capri pants, and a matching African safari hat, Ulster went through a series of action poses to show off his outfit. "I have to admit, I've been waiting to wear this ensemble for quite some time now, but somehow it didn't feel right in the Alps."

"Well, it certainly looks right in the Mediterranean."

"Truth be told, I never knew men could wear capri pants until I saw them in a catalog. They looked so comfortable on the model that I decided to give them a try. And do you know what? I love them! The breeze on my calves travels straight to my toes!"

"I'm glad to hear it!"

"And look at your dress! I love that shade of red on you. Unfortunately, I can no longer wear red because it makes me look like Father Christmas, but on you, it looks enchanting."

"Stop it!" she said as she touched his cheek. "You look *great*, and your beard makes you look *distinguished*. Just like the world's best historian should."

"Well, thank you for saying so, my dear. It's been quite a while since a beautiful woman complimented a part of me besides my brain, so feel free to keep the flattery coming!"

She laughed and took his arm in hers. "Are you ready to come aboard?"

"I certainly am," Ulster said as he glanced around. "But where's Jonathon?"

Jones heard the question as he walked past Ulster on his way back to grab more of Ulster's luggage. "Jon's on watch and Jarkko's at the helm until we're back at sea. We don't want to take any chances with such precious cargo."

Ulster laughed. "My luggage isn't *that* expensive. Granted, the collection did set me back several Swiss francs on my last trip to Zurich. Or should I say *Winston's* last trip to Zurich, because as both of you know, I'm not the type to go on shopping sprees. Instead, I look in catalogs or go online from the comfort of my office, and then I send Winston in the helicopter to fetch whatever I desire. In my opinion, everyone should be doing that. It saves so much time."

"Great tip," Jones said with a grin. "Now that I'm rich, I may have to hire a white guy to do all of my chores. Just like you do."

Ulster nodded. "I highly recommend it."

"But just so you know, when I mentioned 'precious cargo', I wasn't referring to your luggage. I was talking about you and Marissa. On our way back to shore, Jon lectured my ass on the importance of keeping you two safe. I'm not quite sure what you said to him, Petr, but it sure riled him up. The last time I saw him like this was…well, it was last night with Marissa."

"Oh dear," Ulster groaned. "I was afraid of that. I think I was a tad too aggressive during my plea to join the team. It had started off as a humble request to help you on your journey, but when I heard about the incident at the library, I'm afraid my parental instincts kicked in and I became so worried about you—" He glanced at Marissa and held her arm tighter. "That I might have issued an ultimatum. I told him if he didn't let me keep an eye on you—whether on the yacht or on the shore—then I would no longer accept his calls."

"Wow," Jones said, completely shocked by Ulster's atypical behavior. "Now I know why Jon was so cranky. He doesn't do well with demands or threats. Obviously you mean the world to us, and you've built up a lot of goodwill with Jon over the years, so I think you're in the clear. But if you had been a stranger, that gambit of yours would have blown up in your face—followed, quite possibly, by a fist."

"Petr," Marissa said as she stared at her mentor. "I appreciate your instinct to take care of me, but I'm a grown woman now who can make her own decisions. For you to risk your friendship with Jonathon over my wellbeing was incredibly shortsighted and foolhardy. However, and I mean this from the bottom of my heart, I do appreciate the gesture."

Ulster smiled. "You're welcome, my dear."

Jones stared at the luggage that remained on the pier. "And since you're a grown woman, I think it's only fair to treat you as my equal. So stop yapping with Petr and help me with his bags, or else we're going to be here until sundown."

"Sorry, DJ, I can't," she said with a laugh. "You heard Jon. I'm 'precious cargo'. The last thing he would want is for me to break a nail."

"The same with *moi*," Ulster said with a chuckle. "Besides, I need to speak to Jonathon to make amends before he sends a fist in my direction. Although my beard and chins would certainly soften the blow, I get the sense I would fall quicker than the Knights to Napoleon."

"Ha!" Jones said. "Some expert you are. They threw that fight on purpose."

Ulster frowned. "Whatever do you mean?"

"Long story," Marissa said as they turned to board the yacht. "I'll fill you in on everything. Needless to say, it's been an interesting twenty-four hours."

"Don't worry about me," Jones shouted. "I'm used to doing shit like this. Just another brother carrying bags for the man. The least you could do is give me a tip."

Ulster stopped and turned back toward Jones. "Oh my goodness! How foolish of me! I can't believe myself sometimes!"

Jones quickly changed his tune. "Petr, I was joking. I'm happy to grab your stuff. And the only tip I need are those chocolate Swiss rolls of yours."

Ulster shook his head as he walked closer. "Relax, David. I know how you like to tease. That's not why I came back. The gentleman who brought my bags to the dock asked me to give you a message before we departed, and I nearly forgot to pass it along."

"What kind of message?" Jones asked.

"I'm assuming it's some kind of code, so I wrote it down just to be safe." He reached into his shirt pocket and fished out his reading glasses. "Nice fellow, but rather intense. Maybe even a bit star struck. I've been called numerous things during my life—historian, archivist, professor, humanitarian, even philanthropist—but this was the first time someone called me an *oracle*."

"Oh crap," Jones muttered. "That's bad."

"Not at all!" Ulster assured him. "In fact, it's quite the opposite. Although most people think of oracles as priests or priestesses who acted as mediums for the gods in classical antiquity, the modern definition of the word is someone who is regarded as an infallible authority of a particular subject. Obviously this gentleman is a fan of my work as a historian and was merely bestowing upon me the respect that he felt I deserved. As hard as this is to believe, did you know that the word 'oracle' actually derives from the Latin word—"

Jones cut him off. "What's the message?"

"Ah, yes! The message! I almost did it again, chatting on and on about ancient things when my attention should be focused on the world in front of—"

"Petr!" Jones said, growing concerned. "The message!"

"My apologies!" he said as he pulled out the slip of paper and read it to Jones. "Here's what he wanted me to say: *We have the tiger. Dead or alive?*"

"On the boat!" Jones shouted. "Everyone on the boat now!"

CHAPTER 42

Ulster's arrival (and luggage) changed the housing situation on the yacht. Jones gave up his cabin and moved in with Payne even though it was the smallest room on board. Since one of them would always be on watch, they figured it would still be like rooming alone.

Not that it really mattered to the former MANIACs.

Over the years, they had bunked together in some of the worst conditions imaginable—the heat of the desert, the cold of the Arctic, the humidity of the jungle, and everything in between. Compared to those extremes, a few nights on a luxury yacht was hardly something to complain about. That is, if they even stayed on board for that long.

As Payne stared at the turquoise waters of the Mediterranean from his position near the bow, he couldn't help but feel like he was lost at sea. His initial enthusiasm about Hompesch's escape had been temporarily muted by a lack of evidence to support his theory. In fact, with each new detail that he learned about Hompesch's past and the Order's connection to Russia, he found himself drifting further and further away from his original hypothesis.

His gut told him that they would be okay.

But for the time being, he couldn't see the shore.

While scanning the horizon for trouble, Payne heard a noise behind him and turned to see who it was. Because of his girth, Ulster was struggling to squeeze through the narrow glass door from the enclosed helm. Once he made it through, Ulster could barely keep his balance as a mischievous Jarkko lurched the wheel back and forth while revving the engines, all in hopes of toppling the round historian.

"Stay there," Payne shouted from his perch. "I'll come to you."

Designed for sunbathing, the entire front of the boat was lined with the same soft padding that covered the bench that he and Marissa had sat on the night before. Using his muscular arms and legs, Payne resembled a silverback gorilla as he crawled across the pad with incredible speed and dexterity, so much so that Ulster thought he was going to attack.

Ulster shrieked as he fell backwards onto the bench. "Please don't hit me!"

Payne rushed forward to check on his friend. "Are you okay?"

"What's that?" Ulster asked, temporarily confused.

"Are you okay?" Payne repeated.

Ulster touched his own body just to be sure. "Yes, I do believe I am—thanks to this miracle substance underneath my rump. The last time I felt something so soft was the chocolate mousse I devoured on Tuesday night. I'm telling you, Jonathon. My tongue danced with delight!"

Payne breathed a sigh of relief. "You need to be careful when you move about the sundeck. One false move, and you'll—wait! Did you ask me not to hit you?"

Ulster nodded, more than a little embarrassed. "I'm afraid I did, but please allow me to explain before I upset you further. Given the tension of our last conversation and David's graphic account of your dealings with past ultimatums, I came up here to apologize for my reprehensible behavior, but when I saw you charge forward like a majestic bull, my fight-or-flight response kicked in, and—I think it's safe to say—I chose flight."

"More like *fright*," Payne said. "You shrieked like a little—"

"And I'm not proud of it, not in the least. So please do me a favor and—"

"Yeah, yeah, yeah. Don't tell David. Trust me, I know the refrain by heart. But if you want my advice, I think it's time to stop worrying about DJ and all of his crazy nonsense. I mean, he actually thinks the hotel is going to slaughter an albino tiger for a Viking blood ceremony."

"Believe it or not," Ulster said as he fished the message out of his pocket and handed it to Payne, "he might be onto something. The bellhop asked me to give you this."

Payne read the note and grunted. He had no idea what an albino tiger cost, but if the charge appeared on his hotel bill, he was going to make Jones pay for it. "Still, for you to believe that I was actually going to hit you is more than a little disappointing to me."

Ulster nodded. "I know it is, but—"

Payne cut him off. He had more that he needed to say. "But that pales in comparison to the disappointment I felt when you used our friendship as a bargaining chip to join us on this mission. After all we've been through, I would have hoped that you viewed DJ and me as more than just pawns that you were willing to discard if you didn't get your way. As far as I'm concerned, your ploy was beneath you as a gentleman and a scholar."

Ulster's cheeks and ears turned bright red as he lowered his head in shame. He knew he had gone too far when he had made his threat on the phone, but it wasn't until he had heard Payne's words and seen the disappointment in his face that it had really hit home.

The two of them sat in silence, side by side on the bench but with a chasm in between, as Jarkko slowed the yacht to a stop in the open water. Without the rumble of the engines or the rush of the wind to speak over, Ulster lowered his voice to a whisper before he spoke again.

"Jonathon," he said as his words cracked with emotion, "what I did was inexcusable and will never, ever happen again. Your friendship means more to me than I could ever put into words, and if you're willing to forgive my deplorable crime, I will spend the rest of my life making it up to you. Furthermore, if you feel that my presence is an intrusion in any way, just say the word and I will strap my luggage together into a makeshift raft and paddle back to shore."

Payne forced a smile. "That won't be necessary."

"Thank heavens. Because I doubt I have the stamina to make it."

Payne shook his head, still focused on the issue at hand. "Here's the thing that's bothering me. I simply don't understand why you did it. Why would you risk our friendship over something as trivial as a mission? I've known you for many years, Petr, and I have never seen you act callous or ruthless to anyone. So please help me understand your actions, because right now I feel like you're hiding something—and that's making it very tough to forgive you."

Ulster took a deep breath before he found the words to explain. "Just so you know, what I'm about to tell you is *not* an excuse, because what I did was inexcusable. But you asked for some context to explain my actions, and out of respect of our friendship, I'm more than willing to provide it. But please, I beg of you, keep this to yourself."

"Dammit, Petr. I told you to stop worrying about DJ."

He shook his head. "I'm not worried about David. I'm worried about Marissa."

Payne furrowed his brow. "Go on."

Ulster turned and faced his friend. "When Marissa first came to the Archives for her internship, she wasn't the woman that you see today. Back then, she was a sullen, fractured child in her early twenties, who possessed a brilliant mind but zero confidence. Truth be told, I didn't think she would last a day, let alone the summer, so I made it my mission to keep an eye on her and help her with the transition. During that first week, she worked hard but always kept her distance, never wanting to bother me with questions, as if she wasn't worthy of my time. But as the days went on and my persistence lingered, I somehow managed to crack through her defenses, and much to my surprise, hidden under-neath her gruff exterior was a remarkable creature full of humor, passion, and ambition. In all of my years as a mentor, I never saw someone change so much, and I truly believe it was because of the attention I showed her, as if she was a flower dying of thirst that finally sprang to life because of a sprinkle of kindness."

Ulster shook his head. "Trust me, I know how that makes me sound, and the purpose of my story was not to flatter myself but to illustrate my connection to her. So when I heard about the inci-dent at the library, I felt incredibly guilty for putting her in that situation in the first place, particularly since the night before I had expressed my concerns about this particular treasure and had failed to warn her about it. The next thing I know, my parental instincts kicked in—instincts that I didn't even know I had—and before I could stop myself, I was issuing an ultimatum."

Ulster glanced at Payne. "But like I said, my explanation is not an excuse. I am merely providing context for my actions. I take full responsibility for what I did, and I'm willing to live with the consequences—though I hope it doesn't involve my rowing ashore."

Payne smiled and patted Ulster on his knee. He knew that his friend was embarrassed and full of regret, and now that he under-stood the impetus behind Ulster's actions—and the connection that he shared with Marissa—there was no sense in prolonging the inevitable.

"We're cool," Payne said as he reached his hand toward Ulster. "I'm glad we cleared the air, and I'm thrilled to have you as a part of the team."

"Thank heavens!" Ulster said as he grabbed Payne's hand in both of his and shook it enthusiastically. "You've made me so happy I think I'm going to burst."

Payne pulled his hand away. "If you're gonna be sick—"

"No worries, my boy. That's not what I meant. I actually took some dimenhydrinate before my flight, so I should be sedated for a few more hours. Unfortunately, in spite of my prodigious appetite, I have trouble swallowing pills, which forced me to buy a suppository instead. Truth be told, when I landed on my rump, I'm fairly certain that I felt it move deeper into my bowel. At least I hope that's what it was, or else I landed on a pencil."

Payne laughed and grimaced at the same time.

"Goodness me," Ulster said, "I can't believe I voiced that aloud. Either the drug is lowering my inhibitions, or I broke the seal on my candor and everything is spilling out."

"Are you sick or not?" Payne demanded.

"*Not*," Ulster stressed. "I was speaking metaphorically, not physically."

"So you're good?"

"Yes, I'm good. And I promise, no more talk of my derrière."

"Glad to hear it."

"And Jon?"

"Yeah."

Ulster smiled. "Please don't tell David."

CHAPTER 43

Before the team gathered for another lesson, Marissa got Ulster up to speed, detailing the history she had covered with the group and the theories that they had formulated about the treasure.

Ulster was particularly intrigued by the possibility of Hompesch's gambit with Napoleon. Like Marissa, he realized that there was little evidence to support such conjecture, but unlike his former student, he seemed to be much more optimistic about the likelihood of a treasure and escape attempt. When she asked him why, he merely gave her a smile and said he would share his theory at the appropriate time.

"Are you ready for us?" Jones asked as he entered the glass-lined saloon through the rear sliding door. He walked up the center aisle past the galley on his left and the dining table on his right until he reached the main social area in the center of the yacht.

"We certainly are," Ulster said from his position on the love seat. It sat off to the right in front of a massive window that stretched from the ceiling to the floor. Marissa sat next to him, the two historians, side-by-side, ready to give a joint lecture.

Although Volkov had slashed most of the furniture, Marissa had done her best the night before to stuff the padding back into the pillows. She had also found several clean sheets in a linen closet below deck and had used them as slipcovers to line the furniture. All things considered, she had done a remarkable job to make the room look undamaged.

Jones stepped around the wooden coffee table to his left and plopped down on the enormous couch. It sat across the aisle from the love seat and was designed to seat eight people. The sectional was lined with three different colored sheets, making it look more like a trio of separate couches than a singular combined one. With the local islands on his mind, Jones announced that the purple sheet on the left was Gozo and claimed it for himself.

Jarkko heard the pronouncement and hustled into the room before Payne. He dove headfirst over the coffee table onto the main portion of the couch and landed with a cushioned thud. The entire section was covered with a striped sheet made up of an assortment of colors. "Jarkko is captain, so Jarkko claims Malta. That means cabin boy is stuck with Comino."

"That's fine," Payne said as he sat on the small sectional to the right. It was draped with a patterned sheet that resembled green bamboo leaves. "I ate Comino for breakfast yesterday morning and found it delicious."

Jarkko turned and plopped his dirty bare feet on the coffee table. "Jarkko has seen Jon eat. Jarkko believes he could consume entire island."

Ulster and Marissa looked to Payne for an explanation.

"Long story. I'll tell you later," Payne said.

"If it involves food, I shall certainly listen," Ulster said with a grin. "Speaking of which, I restocked the pantry with an assortment of delicacies from the Archives. Feel free to eat anything you'd like *except* the can of Beluga caviar. I brought that as a peace offering for Jarkko."

Jarkko sat up. "For Jarkko?"

Ulster nodded. "I know how disappointed you were in your settlement from Mount Athos. Unfortunately, due to the monks' deep religious ties, there was simply no way I could send you caviar and strippers as part of your payment. However, thanks to a Russian friend of mine, I was able to get my hands on a can of Beluga Gold, which is not even sold in stores. Please accept it as a token of my appreciation for your contribution to the team's discovery."

Jarkko grinned. "Thank you, Petr. You are forgiven. You may keep strippers for self."

Ulster laughed. "Wonderful! I'll teach them to read and put them to work."

Payne smiled at the thought. "As much as I'd like to discuss that, what do you say we get back to Valletta? If I remember correctly, we left off with the Treaty of 1797."

"That's right," Marissa said as she joined the conversation. "Hompesch ratified a deal with Paul the First in 1797 AD that made Russia the secular protector of Malta. Unfortunately, there was little that Paul could do from his throne in Russia to protect Malta from the invading French fleet. He simply didn't have the time to react to their arrival or the resources necessary to stop Napoleon on his journey across the Mediterranean."

Payne furrowed his brow. "Then why did the Order hold him in such high regard?"

"Because Paul gave them shelter after the storm."

Ulster explained further. "Keep something in mind: Napoleon didn't kill the knights or take them prisoner. He had more important thing to worry about on his way to Egypt. Instead, the terms of Hompesch's surrender detailed a multitude of things, including an annual pension for himself and the exile of the Order from Malta."

Marissa chimed in. "As I mentioned yesterday, the Order was made up of knights from all over Europe. Some of those men returned home to fight for their homelands in this particularly turbulent time. But a large percentage of the knights who remained loyal to the Order opted to go to Saint Petersburg instead, where Paul the First welcomed them with open arms. This infusion of refugee knights gave rise to the Russian tradition of the Knights Hospitaller and eventually led to Paul's election as grand master of the Order."

Payne shook his head. "Hold up. I'm confused. I thought you said that Hompesch went to Trieste, Italy, where he established a temporary headquarters while looking for a new home."

Marissa smiled, glad that her lesson had sunk in. "You're not confused at all. Both of these things occurred at the exact same time. Hompesch went to Italy, and most of his men went to Russia. And this separation led to a brief period where the Order had two grand masters."

"Sweet!" Jones said from Gozo. "Please tell me they dueled to the death."

Ulster laughed. "I'm afraid not, David, although that certainly would have been exciting. Instead, they resorted to something almost as scintillating as a clash of swords: politics!"

Jones and Jarkko both booed from the couch.

Payne smiled. "I'm with them. Boooo!"

Ulster grimaced, confused. "Since when do we boo knowledge?"

Marissa whispered. "Since last night."

"I'm not sure I like it."

She shrugged. "It's much better when *we* do the booing."

"We get to boo, too? That *does* sound like fun. Please tell me when!"

She smiled and took his arm in hers. Although she had remained in touch with Ulster via phone over the past few years, they had been apart for far too long in her opinion. She didn't realize how much she had missed her mentor until she had seen him on shore.

"If it's okay with you," Payne said to keep the briefing on course, "please summarize the politics and give us the shortened version. Or else there may be a revolt."

Ulster's eyes lit up. "As a matter of fact, there *was* a revolt! After Napoleon's arrival, the French rapidly dismantled the institutions of the Order, including the Roman Catholic Church. Property was looted and seized to pay for his expedition to Egypt, which generated considerable anger among the deeply religious population of Malta. Their rage erupted on the second day of September, long after Napoleon's departure, during an auction of Church property. Within a week, thousands of Maltese citizens had driven the French garrison into Valletta. A year and a half later, the French were vanquished for good as the British took control of Malta."

Ulster finished his statement with a satisfied grin. "I must admit, I think that's the shortest lecture I've ever given. I should try summarization more often."

Payne cleared his throat. "I hate to burst your bubble, but the lecture you just gave—as concise and compelling as it was—was actually on the wrong topic."

Ulster frowned. "Really? What was I supposed to be talking about?"

"Politics."

"Yes, of course! Why didn't you stop me earlier? Please, if I ever start to ramble about something that I shouldn't be rambling about, I won't be the least bit offended if you cut me off with a word or two before I—"

"Petr!"

Ulster blinked. "Yes! Just like that. Well done, Jonathon!"

Marissa smiled. "Why don't you let me take it from here?"

"Please, my dear, I'm all ears. Well, *some* belly, but mostly ears. Actually, who am I kidding? I'm a giant belly who can barely hear, but I'll still do my best to listen."

"Politics," Payne repeated from Comino.

"On it," she said with a nod of her head. "To understand the politics involved, we must assume that either Hompesch didn't have a treasure *or* he accomplished the task of hiding the treasure with only a few trusted men. That would mean that ninety-nine point nine percent of the knights who were exiled from Malta thought that he was an incompetent coward, one who actually had the gall to negotiate a pension for himself from the French as part of his surrender."

"*No bueno*," Jones said.

"You're right. Not good at all. So when the majority of the knights arrived in Saint Petersburg—where they were given a hero's welcome by Paul the First, despite their loss to the French—who do you think the knights favored: Hompesch or the emperor?"

Jarkko grinned. "Jarkko guess emperor!"

She smiled. "Jarkko is right!"

"Jarkko *always* right. What Jarkko win?"

"Possibly a golden treasure filled with incredible riches," Jones announced in the voice of a game-show host. "But only if you shut up long enough for us to find it."

Jarkko laughed. "Steve Harvey make good point. Jarkko shut up now."

"*Steve Harvey*? You racist motherf—"

"Knock it off!" Payne shouted before Jones could finish. "Please continue."

"Thank you, Jon," Jones said with a smile. "You racist motherf—"

"Not *you*! I was talking to *Marissa*."

"Fine!" Jones mumbled. "Let the white girl talk."

Payne rolled his eyes. "Please, Marissa. Go on."

Marissa nodded. "With the majority of the knights in Russia, they felt it was within their right to elect a new grand master, and Paul willingly accepted the title. Meanwhile, Hompesch kept his title as well until 1799 AD, when he was forced to abdicate under pressure from the Austrian Court. Ironically, that left Paul as the *de facto* grand master of the Catholic order even though he was the leader of the Russian Orthodox Church at the time."

"How did the Vatican feel about that?" Payne wondered.

"Actually," she noted, "the reason I said 'de facto' and not 'de jure' is because Paul's election was never ratified under Roman Catholic canon law. Of course, they had their own troubles to worry about. When Malta was captured, Pope Pius the Sixth was a prisoner of the French, who had defeated papal forces in Rome in 1796 AD. The pope eventually passed away in August of 1799, and it wasn't until March of 1800 that Pope Pius the Seventh was crowned—although it wasn't much of a crown. Since the French had seized the tiaras normally used by the Holy See, Pius the Seventh was anointed as pope while wearing a papier-mâché papal tiara."

"That's awesome!" Jones said with a grin.

Jarkko laughed as he pulled out his phone to search for an image. "Pope wearing paper hat! That make Jarkko laugh! Jarkko want to see picture!"

"Jarkko," Jones explained. "They didn't have cameras back then."

"Jarkko now sad, but Jarkko still laughing."

Marissa couldn't help but smile. "After his election, Pius the Seventh was a tad indecisive on the subject. At first he supported Paul as grand master, perhaps as a way to curry his favor while in exile himself, but he eventually ended up abstaining over the complex issue. Of course, none of this mattered after 1801 AD, when Paul was killed by a band of dismissed Russian officers, who strangled and trampled him to death in his own bedroom."

"Good Lord!" Jones exclaimed. "What in the name of David Carradine was going on at that orgy? How in the hell do you get trampled to death in your own bedroom?"

Jarkko nodded. "Jarkko knows. But Jarkko not telling."

Ulster made a disgusted face. "It wasn't a sex party. It was an assassination, most likely caused by his affiliation with the Knights. Paul was so enthralled by their code of chivalry that he tried to force it upon Russian nobility. His attempt to improve the lives of the lower classes actually alienated many of his trusted advisors, who helped orchestrate the regime change. His son, Alexander the First, took over the country but *not* the Order, and that led to a period of chaos that eventually contributed to the end of the Knights Hospitallers."

"The end?" Payne blurted. "I thought you said the Order still existed today."

Marissa nodded. "It does, just not in its original form. As I mentioned yesterday, the Order always seemed to adapt with the times, and their old model stopped working in the nineteenth century. As countries came and went quicker than you could draw a

map, the Knights Hospitallers morphed into several smaller orders, including the Sovereign Military Order of Malta. The organization settled in Rome in 1834 AD and is widely considered the
modern-day continuation of the Hospitallers. All told, the Order of
Malta—as they are often called—has over thirteen thousand
knights, dames, and auxiliary members, plus more than forty thousand
employees, and over eighty thousand volunteers around the globe."

"That's a lot of people," Payne said.

"And they do a lot of good," she stressed. "They help the elderly, the homeless, children, victims of natural disasters, and so
many more in their times of need."

"So," Jones said, "they're like a charity."

Ulster shook his head. "They're actually much more than that.
As a sovereign order, they maintain diplomatic relations with over
one hundred states. They enter into treaties. They have permanent observer status at the United Nations. They even issue their
own passports, coins, and stamps. Their main headquarters in
Rome has extraterritorial status, meaning it is treated like an em-
bassy and exempt from local laws. And even though I'm not privy
to the latest numbers, their annual budget is reportedly close to
two billion dollars."

Payne whistled. "That's a lot of money. Given the amount of
charity work that I do, I'm surprised I've never heard of them."

"I'm not," Marissa said. "Despite their size, they don't have
diplomatic relations with the United States. Most of the work they
do is in South America, Africa, and, of course, Europe—where the
legend of the Knights of Malta still has meaning."

"Okay," Payne said in summation. "Unless I'm mistaken,
we're caught up on the history of Knights Hospitallers, Paul the
First, and Grand Master Hompesch. Now comes the tough part.
We have to figure out if the Order had a treasure, and if they did,
how did Hompesch get it out of Malta? Unfortunately, I'm kind
of at a loss on where to begin."

"Then it's a good thing I'm here," Ulster said with a twinkle
in his eye. "Because I have a pretty good idea how Hompesch got
the treasure out of Valletta."

CHAPTER 44

Saint Petersburg, Russia

Ivan Volkov knew next to nothing about world history. Not because he wasn't intelligent, but because the ancient past bored him to tears.

Even as a child in school, he had despised academics. He had done just enough to pass his classes in order to stay out of trouble, while spending most of his time after school causing it. Despite his small and wiry frame, he had been the most feared kid on the playground, using his ferocity and rage to scare boys who were twice his age and size.

Where he grew up, everyone called him *the wolf.*

Partially because of his surname.

But mostly because he was an animal.

He had used that reputation to work his way through the ranks of the Russian underworld until he had enough cash and contacts to launch his own empire, and he had announced his arrival in a sea of blood and carnage, killing multiple crime lords in a single night.

Ever since then, he had been feared by everyone.

His men, his rivals, even the Russian police.

No one was willing to tangle with Ivan Volkov.

That is, until the incident in Malta.

Although word of the shootout hadn't reached Russia and probably never would since all of those henchmen were dead—including his driver, who Volkov had killed upon their arrival in Moscow—he wasn't willing to take any chances. He needed to take care of the Finn and his American friends before the news of their victory could possibly spread, while also claiming the treasure that he assumed they were searching for.

Unfortunately, Volkov had no idea where to start.

On his flight home, he had browsed through most of the documents that he had stolen from the Finn's yacht, but he couldn't make sense of them. He wasn't familiar with the Knights of Malta or the history of Valletta. And even though he had heard of Catherine the Great, he knew nothing about her son Paul I or his dealings with the Order.

Eventually Volkov had realized that he needed an expert, someone who could take the historical collection in his possession and turn it into actual gold, but since neither King Midas nor Rumpelstiltskin was available, he decided to journey north to Saint Petersburg in order to visit the State Hermitage Museum.

According to his phone, it was the second-largest museum in the world (behind only the Louvre in Paris) and was founded by Catherine the Great after she had acquired an impressive cache of paintings from a Prussian merchant named Johann Ernst Gotzkowsky. Volkov didn't care about the Prussian or his stupid paintings, but he figured a museum that was built by the empress was bound to have an expert or two on the lives of her family.

Unwilling to risk boredom by going inside an actual museum, Volkov sent in a few new henchmen to find someone who had knowledge of the subject matter. Thirty minutes later, they brought out a curator named Boris Artamonov, who looked almost as old as the museum itself.

Dressed in a rumpled sport coat with patches on the elbows and brown tweed pants, he showed no fear as he slowly shuffled along between the goons toward the idling limousine, as if this type of thing happened every day. Of course, growing up in the Soviet Union, he had lived through many things far worse than a stroll along the Neva River. When a tour boat near the quay passed him by, he waved to the people in the late-afternoon sun.

Volkov didn't know whether to be offended or impressed.

The old bastard wasn't the least bit scared.

He was just happy to still be alive.

The bigger of the two goons opened the limousine door while the other helped Artamonov inside. Instead of showing any fear, he actually smiled at Volkov.

"Hello," he said in Russian. "My name is Boris. What's your name?"

Volkov nodded to the henchman, who shut the door from the outside, leaving the two alone. "My name is Volkov. Ivan Volkov.

Does that name mean anything to you?"

Artamonov shook his head. "Not at all. Are you famous?"

"More like *infamous*."

"Sorry, Ivan. I don't follow the news. I prefer to spend my time in the past."

"I'm curious. What did my men tell you about my situation?"

"They said you needed my help. So I'm here to help."

"Just like that?"

Artamonov shrugged. "I used to work as a full-time curator, but now I'm just a part-time volunteer. Honestly, I've got nothing better to do."

Volkov smiled an actual smile. For him, this was a refreshing change of pace—particularly after the debacle in Valletta. "If I may be so bold, what is your specialty at the museum?"

"Over the years, I have worked in just about every building and every department imaginable. I started at the Small Hermitage, which housed the original collection, but then I moved to the Old Hermitage, then the New Hermitage, and the Hermitage Theatre, followed by the Winter Palace. That's my personal favorite. It's where Catherine the Great used to live."

"So I read," Volkov said as he leaned forward with excitement. "And what if I told you that I recently discovered a number of ancient documents about Empress Catherine and her family? Would you be willing to explain their significance to me?"

Artamonov glanced at his watch. "That depends. Will you buy me dinner?"

Volkov grinned. "I think that could be arranged."

"Dessert, too?"

"If you'd like."

Artamonov shrugged. "In that case, why not?"

Payne and Jones had seen a similar twinkle in Ulster's eyes on previous occasions, and it usually meant one of two things: either a meal was about to be served, or he was about to blow their minds with a historical fact that would undoubtedly help their cause. Jones obviously hoped for the latter, but Payne would have been fine with either result.

No matter the time of day, he was always willing to eat.

Ulster started with a question. "When Marissa told you about the Great Siege of Malta, did she talk about the cannon placement of the Ottomans?"

Payne answered. "Yeah, she said they positioned them on top of Mount, um…" He glanced at Marissa for help. "How do you pronounce it again?"

"Mount Sciberras," she replied.

Payne nodded. "They put them on Mount Sciberras and then bombarded Birgu with over a hundred thousand cannonballs. And just so you know, we actually visited the Upper Barrakka Gardens and watched the saluting battery before the library. Very cool stuff."

"Indeed!" Ulster said with a grin. Since everyone in the group had already been there, it would make what he was about to reveal even easier to explain. "After the Order's miraculous victory, Grand Master Jean de Valette realized that Birgu was far too vulnerable along the harbor to be able to protect it. He also realized that money would come pouring in from Europe once word spread about his victory over the dreaded Turks. Looking to put his own personal stamp on the region, he selected the Sciberras Peninsula as the site of his new city, laying the foundation stone himself in March of 1566 AD."

Payne pointed at Marissa. "We actually know all of this. Your former intern did a wonderful job filling us in on the basics. You should offer her a permanent job."

Ulster smiled at her. "If she wants one, she can have it. I've been trying to lure her back to the Archives for years, but she's been too busy shooting up libraries."

Marissa laughed. "Once I'm out of bullets, I'll give you a call."

"Excellent!" Ulster said. "In the meantime, would you mind terribly if I highlighted a few pertinent items from your lecture about Valletta? I think perhaps I can shine a light on a shadow or two that you might have overlooked."

"It would be my honor. You know how much I love listening to you talk."

"Which," he joked, "is one of my favorite things about you!"

She laughed and squeezed his arm tight.

"David!" Ulster said out of nowhere.

Jones was listening but snapped to attention. "What'd I do?"

"Don't worry. You're not in trouble. I was just hoping you could help our discussion. Being a former soldier and a history buff, I'd like your thoughts on the following: What would have been your first priority if you were building Valletta in 1566 AD?"

"Whores. You can never have enough whores."

Jarkko laughed. "David's right. They keep the knights happy."

"Boooo!" Marissa said as she elbowed Ulster.

"Boo is right," Ulster said with a grin. "Boooo!"

Payne glared at Jones. "Come on, man. Be serious."

Jones frowned. "Sorry. My bad. Just trying to keep things loose."

"Just like the whores," Jarkko whispered to him.

Jones fought hard not to smile. "Considering their recent battle with the Ottomans and their ongoing fight with the Barbary pirates, I would think the fortification of the city would be high on my list. You just said the main reason that they moved from Birgu was because they were looking for somewhere more secure, so I'm assuming that's what Valette did."

Ulster nodded. "You are correct. He built bastions as high as forty-seven meters, which is approximately one-hundred-fifty feet tall to you and Jonathon."

Payne chimed in. "We saw the bastions when we sailed in and out of the harbor. We also saw them from the overlook in Sliema on our first night here. They're impressive."

"Maybe so," Ulster said, "but they're also a problem. If you build a medieval city on top of a bluff and your enemy surrounds you down below, how do you get supplies? Back then, there were no planes or drones to drop things from the sky, so what were the knights to do? And if you don't know, think back to our first adventure together. What did they do in Orvieto?"

"A well!" Jones said, remembering Pozzo di San Patrizio, a historic well that was commissioned by Pope Clement VII, who had taken refuge in Orvieto during the sack of Rome in 1527. "They dug nearly fifty feet into the plateau until they hit water."

"And the Knights did something similar, digging deep into the soft limestone of the Sciberras Peninsula in order to build a system of cisterns and sewers. But while they were down there, they also did something else. They built hundreds of chambers, some of them small but many as tall as three stories high, from one end of the city to the other. They did this to store their most precious supplies in case of a siege, whether that be food, weapons, or——"

"Treasure!" Jarkko shouted.

Ulster grinned. "To reach these chambers, they also built an intricate network of tunnels, some of which were so top secret that only the grand master himself knew where they went. Which got me thinking. If the Knights of Malta did, in fact, have a secret treasure, there's only one place they would have kept it—and that's underneath the city of Valletta!"

CHAPTER 45

Marissa smiled at her mentor. Although she knew that tunnels existed underneath the city of Valletta, she had never thought to mention them during her history lesson. Not because they weren't pertinent, but because they weren't the type of thing to be described in textbooks or taught in classrooms. They were merely interesting footnotes.

Suddenly Ulster's comment about shining 'a light on a shadow or two that she might have overlooked' made perfect sense to her in two completely different ways. On one hand, he was talking about the dark underworld of the tunnels themselves, which was obviously going to play a big role in Hompesch's supposed escape attempt, but he was also talking about her tendency to be so focused on the black and white that she missed the gray stuff in between.

That's where the real history could be found.

Hiding in the shadows of the spotlight.

"Petr's right," she said as she squeezed his arm. "If the grand master had a secret treasure, he wouldn't have kept it at the Order's treasury, which was located in Piazza Tesoreria—the square outside of the national library. He would have kept it elsewhere underground."

"Have you been in the tunnels?" Payne asked.

She nodded. "I've been in some, but certainly not all. Recently the government opened up a few tunnels to the public as tourist attractions. Some of the chambers are as tall as modern buildings and reinforced with elaborate brickwork. The problem is there are so many tunnels, I wouldn't even know where to begin. The Order certainly built a number of them when they constructed Valletta, but in the four centuries since, countless more have been added by locals who dug into the ground for a variety of reasons."

She smiled as a story came to mind. "The Knights weren't the only group who tried to conceal things in the limestone of the

Sciberras Peninsula. During World War Two, the British—who still controlled Malta at that time—decided to build a submarine base *underneath* Valletta. They brought in the equipment and started to build a secret lair that would be large enough to store one of their subs. Halfway through the construction, they realized that the expense of the lair was going to cost twice as much as the sub they were trying to hide, so they stopped the project and used the leftover money to build an additional submarine."

"Was it yellow?" Jones asked with a grin.

She laughed at the Beatles reference. "I can't answer that, but the half-built lair still exists to this day. The Brits don't like talking about it, but I know where it is."

Payne smiled. He had been around the military long enough to know how often they wasted money on ridiculous projects. He also knew that they rarely liked to talk about them. "What about the other tunnels? Would you know how to access those?"

"Some," she said as she used her hands to illustrate the problem. "Unfortunately, they crisscross the peninsula like a game of Dig Dug. Some start high and go deep. Others stay straight for blocks. And dozens were built as fallout shelters during World War Two. Most of those zigzag back and forth to diffuse shockwaves from enemy bombs."

Payne shook his head. "Unless I'm overlooking something, we're not interested in those. We're looking for the ancient tunnels that were built by the Knights themselves."

She nodded in understanding. "One of the major tunnel systems has an entry point in the basement of the national library. I'm assuming the tunnel originally led to the Conservatoria—the place where the Order's treasury stored its gold and silver bullion until the last quarter of the eighteenth century. But it was moved to make way for the library. Of course, all of this would have been done under Grand Master Emmanuel de Rohan-Polduc, the immediate predecessor to Hompesch. Call me crazy, but if I'm Hompesch, there's no way I would have used a tunnel that was built by Rohan's men. Not at a time when French knights couldn't be trusted."

Ulster grinned with pride, glad that Marissa was connecting the dots on her own. Although he was in Malta to help the team find the Order's treasure, he viewed every situation as a teaching moment. If he had wanted to, he could have jumped in and dominated the conversation, but he preferred it when those around him came to realizations on their own.

In his mind, how else were they going to learn?

But at some point, Ulster knew that he needed to reenter the discussion in order to get them to where they needed to go. "I agree with Marissa. I think we're probably looking for a tunnel system that was known to a select few. Possibly one that has been forgotten by time."

Jones grimaced. "And how are we supposed to find that?"

Marissa answered. "If you'd like, I could make some calls to local historians to see if they have any suggestions. Maybe one of them could—"

"Are you nuts?" Jones said with a laugh. "You want to endanger the lives of others by getting them mixed up in this shit?"

"You're right," she said as she shook her head in embarrassment. "I can't believe I forgot about the Russians and all the guns. You guys must be rubbing off on me."

Jarkko grinned. "Jarkko would like to rub—"

"If you finish that sentence," Payne threatened, "I swear to Poseidon that I will drag you from the couch by your hairy feet and throw you off your yacht."

Jarkko frowned. "But Jarkko captain."

"Then act like one."

Jarkko glanced at Marissa. "Jarkko sorry."

She nodded her forgiveness to Jarkko and her thanks to Payne. Both of them smiled in return.

"Anyway," Ulster said, "I think I have an answer to David's question."

"What question is that?" Jones asked.

"The one about finding the correct tunnel."

"Oh yeah," Jones said. "That *was* a great question. What's the answer?"

Ulster grinned. He had been holding back an important piece of information since his arrival. "Late last night, while I was awaiting the call from Jonathon that never came, I started to think about Grand Master Hompesch and his treasure. Obviously the tunnel system underneath the city immediately sprang to mind, and it dawned on me that I had seen some ancient blueprints of Valletta at one point in my career. Unable to sleep after devouring the delightful fruit torte that I told you about—you know, the one with the mango, papaya, and Chinese gooseberries. Did I happen to mention the hand-whipped cream?"

"Focus," Payne ordered.

"Yes, of course, how foolish of me! Anyway, with no sleep in my future, I decided to putter downstairs to my collections to see if I could dig up—pun intended—anything on the construction of the city. As Marissa will surely attest, I have a fair amount of information on Malta in the Archives. An island system such as theirs, which sits at the crossroads of the Mediterranean, has been touched by more civilizations over time than just about any place on earth. It truly is a remarkable place that has seen empires come and go. And yet, as I flipped through my records, I was unable to locate the document that I had certainly seen before."

Marissa chimed in. "Unless you acquired it during the last few years—which is certainly a possibility given your facility—I can say with near certainty that the document was not in your Maltese collection. And the reason I can say that with such confidence is because *I* was the intern who helped you reorganize that entire section."

She turned to the group. "You see, the problem with Maltese history is that it has been mixed with so many other cultures over the centuries—whether that be the Phoenicians, the Greeks, the Byzantines, the Normans, and so on—that it is next to impossible to sort through the overlaps. For instance, if you find an ancient scroll from the Roman Empire on Gozo, do you put it in your Roman collection or your Maltese collection? In the Archives' original system, before the dawn of computers, it was up to Petr to connect all of the threads in that genius brain of his and remember that he had placed that scroll in his Roman room."

"Unfortunately," Ulster admitted, "my genius brain has seen better days, so sometimes I'm not as fast or reliable to make those connections, which is why we are scanning everything into the computer system that Jonathon was kind enough to donate…. Wait. Where was I?"

Payne smiled. "You were flipping through Maltese records."

"Right!" Ulster blurted. "As I was flipping through my Maltese collection, I came across a document that described the Vatican's contribution to the rebuild of Malta after the Great Siege, and just like that, it came to me. I was looking in the wrong place. I shouldn't be looking in my Maltese collection at all. I should be in my Vatican vault!"

Jones's eyes lit up. "The pope's dude!"

Payne glanced at him. "Excuse me?"

Jones stood up in his excitement. "I know where Petr is going with this!"

"Oh!" Marissa said, catching on. But she was so swept up in the moment, she completely blanked on his name. "Michelangelo's assistant!"

"That's him! The Italian guy!"

Jarkko jumped up, too. "Jarkko remembers name. It was Francesco Lasagna!"

"Boom!" Jones said as he started to dance. "It was Frankie Lasagna!"

Ulster burst out laughing. "Although I could go for a nice slice of lasagna covered in Bolognese right about now—which I do believe I saw in a takeout container in the yacht's refrigerator— the man you're referring to was actually named Francesco Laparelli."

Jarkko grinned. "That's what Jarkko said: Francesco Lasagna."

Payne cursed to himself. He hated being the last one to figure out things. "Now I remember. He was the Vatican's military architect, the one sent to Malta to design Valletta."

"Exactly!" Ulster said with a smile. "So I hustled over to my Vatican vault and scrolled through my files on Pope Pius the Fifth, and there it was: the original blueprints of the city of Valletta by Francesco Laparelli."

"That's fantastic!" Marissa said before she gave it some thought. "I'd love to see the original plans, I truly would. But how will they help us? The tunnel system that we're looking for would have been dug *after* Laparelli's death in 1570 AD. In case you forgot, the Valletta project was actually completed by his assistant, a Maltese architect named Girolamo Cassar. He went on to build many things in Malta including the auberges."

"Trust me, my dear, I'm well aware of Mister Cassar and quite happy that he was the builder who finished the project."

"Why's that?" she wondered.

"Two reasons," Ulster said with confidence. "Unlike Francesco Laparelli, who answered to the Vatican and the pope himself,

Girolamo Cassar was a Maltese citizen, who learned his craft under Evangelista Menga, the resident engineer of the Order of Saint John. Therefore, Cassar's loyalty would have been to the Knights—particularly after 1569 AD when he was admitted to the Order. Like the Knights themselves, Cassar made his name during the Great Siege when he risked his life on multiple occasions to repair the fortifications that were damaged by the constant barrage of Ottoman cannons. By the time that he rose to replace Menga as the resident engineer of the Order, Cassar was highly respected and trusted by his fellow Knights."

She nodded in understanding. "Meaning that Cassar probably designed many of the tunnels under the city of Valletta, including the secret ones."

"Exactly," he said with a nod.

"Okay. All of that makes perfect sense. What's the second reason?"

Ulster grinned. "Guess who has Cassar's portfolio in his suitcase."

CHAPTER 46

Considering their luggage misadventures, Jones laughed when he heard Ulster's comment. "I hope to hell Cassar's portfolio wasn't in *my* bag, because it was stolen at the library."

Payne nodded. "Mine, too."

"Really?" Ulster asked. "Why did they steal your bags?"

"Because our bags were awesome," Jones replied.

"Guys!" Marissa said. "Petr just revealed a major piece of information, and you're talking about your gym bags. How about a little focus?"

Jarkko nodded. "Jarkko agrees with Mean Marissa. Time to talk treasure."

Jones saluted him. "Sorry, captain."

Jarkko grinned and saluted back.

She faced Ulster. "I can't believe you didn't tell me about this sooner. Who discovered Girolamo Cassar's portfolio? And when did you acquire it?"

Ulster answered her question with a brainteaser. "Technically, my dear, I haven't acquired anything. And yet, technically, I have!"

Jones glanced at Payne. "I think we broke Petr."

Payne shook his head and smiled. "No, DJ, we didn't break Petr. He's never been better. He told us everything we needed to know with his riddle."

Now it was Jones's turn to be confused. As much as Payne hated to be the last one to solve anything, Jones's frustration was even worse since he prided himself on his mental acumen and detective skills. As far as he was concerned, Payne was the muscle of the group while he was the brain. It was an insight that Jones had shared with his best friend many times over the years, which made moments like these almost unbearable.

"Ugh," Jones said, "give me a clue."

Payne smiled at him. "Dumb Jon need no clue. Why Einstein

need help?"

Jarkko looked at Payne. "Why you make fun of Jarkko?"

Payne shook his head. "I wasn't making fun of you. I was making fun of DJ."

"By talking like Jarkko?" he said, confused.

"Guys!" Marissa said. "You're doing it again. Quit joking around!"

Payne nodded as he stood up. "Sorry. Couldn't resist. Petr, which bag is your computer in? I'll go get it for you."

Ulster smiled, glad that someone had figured out his puzzle. "It's in my shoulder bag. Unfortunately, the screen is fairly small for a group so large. Would you, by chance, know how to hook it up to a television? You know tasks such as those aren't my forte."

Payne pointed at Jones. "DJ's the man when it comes to—hint, hint—*technology*."

Jones groaned in understanding. "Oh, now I get it. You didn't *technically* acquire the portfolio, because you don't *actually* have it in your possession. But someone sent it to you on your computer, which means you acquired it *technically*."

Ulster applauded. "Well done, David. I'm glad to see you haven't lost a step."

"That's right," Payne cracked. "He's *always* been a step behind me."

Jones ignored the comment and shifted his focus to the task at hand. "Hey Jarkko, did Volkov break that big-ass TV in your bedroom?"

Jarkko shook his head. "Volkov knock on floor but did not smash. Why?"

"Would you mind if I brought it up here for some show and tell?"

Jarkko furrowed his brow. "What is this 'show and tell'?"

Jones explained. "Petr's going to *show* us where Hompesch hid the treasure, then we're going to *tell* him how we're going to retrieve it."

Jarkko hopped to his feet. "Jarkko likes show and tell. Jarkko help you carry."

Five minutes later, the group was sitting on the massive couch and staring at the 60-inch television, which rested on the wooden coffee table in the middle of the glass-lined saloon. Thanks to the television's network connection, the contents of Ulster's laptop were being wirelessly mirrored onto the larger screen, much to Ulster's delight.

"David," Ulster said as he typed in his passcode to unlock his computer. "It is quite obvious that you are far more tech-savvy than I. Would you mind taking control of the mother ship while I proceed with my lecture?"

"Sweet," Jones said as he grabbed the laptop. If Ulster hadn't suggested it, Jones would have. He knew from experience that Ulster was barely one step above the Amish when it came to technology. "Just tell me what you want me to do."

Ulster pointed at a blue folder on his computer desktop that was labeled CASSAR. "Please open this folder and display its contents on the television screen."

Jones clicked a few buttons on the laptop, and a series of blue file icons spread across the computer and television screens at the exact same time. "Now what?"

Ulster struggled to lean forward on the couch. Between his size and the damage to the pillow underneath his plump derrière, he felt like he was sitting in quicksand. He rocked back and forth, trying to generate enough momentum to reach his feet so he could point at a file on the television screen, but he quickly realized that he was fighting a losing battle. "Jonathon, my boy, do you happen to have a pointer of some kind that I can use during my lesson? I'm afraid if I keep rocking like this, I may cause a tsunami that wipes out Malta before we retrieve the treasure."

Payne looked at Jarkko. "Do you have anything like that?"

Jarkko rubbed his chin. "Jarkko has rifle. Will that work?"

Ulster laughed. "Well, that would certainly be unique! However, if you don't mind, I would prefer something a little less lethal."

Jarkko grimaced. "Switchblade?"

"Hang on," Marissa said as she hustled into the galley. She opened the pantry door and grabbed the mop that she had used to clean up the broken glass from the night before. She quickly unscrewed the mop head and brought the handle back to Ulster. "Will this work?"

"It's perfect," he said as he swung the neon-green plastic handle in front of him like a light saber. "Although I must admit, this is the first time I've held a mop in years!"

"Use the Force, Petr," Jones cracked. "Clean the room, you must."

Everyone laughed except Ulster, who didn't get the *Star Wars* reference.

"Anyway," Ulster said to change the topic, "if you would be so kind as to click on the file labeled VALLETTA 2 – 1575 AD. That will get this ship back on course."

Marissa glanced at her mentor. "Hold up! You still haven't told us about the portfolio. Where was it discovered? And how did you obtain it?"

Ulster smiled. "Believe it or not, Jonathon helped me obtain it."

"I did?" Payne asked. "How'd I do that?"

Ulster was happy to explain. "Word is starting to spread amongst the academic community about the digitization of my files at the Archives, which is being done with the device that you built at Payne Industries. As you've probably heard me preach, the majority of the world's historical artifacts are not currently available for public consumption. Most are being stored in museum vaults for preservation or being hoarded by private collectors. My goal at the Archives has always been to promote the sharing of historical knowledge for the betterment of mankind."

Marissa knew all of this. "And that helped you obtain it, how?"

"Sorry!" Ulster said with a grin. "I knew I was leaving something out. Thanks to the digitization of the files, I have recently heard from a number of like-minded historians, who were interested in acquiring the Payne Industries technology in hopes of following my lead. Over the past few years, Jonathon's tech division has developed multiple versions of these scanning devices, some of which have greatly increased in speed and precision. Instead of putting the older models in a dusty closet at the Archives, I obtained Jonathon's permission to send them to some trusted colleagues. We figured they could use them as training tools while also scanning their documents for the digital cloud that we are planning to launch in the future."

He leaned back as he spoke to the group. "With so many people interested in this project, I got to pick and choose whom I sent these devices to. One particular enthusiast contacted me and asked for a sneak peek at some files that we had already scanned at the Archives, and I asked him what he could offer in return. This gentleman, who shall remain nameless, let it be known that he had acquired Cassar's portfolio from a black marketeer for his private collection. When offered the opportunity to view the portfolio—something that I never even knew existed—I agreed to send him one of Jonathon's units in order to add the collection to my digital library."

Ulster turned his focus to Marissa. "Although the Archives acquired these files a few weeks ago, I didn't have an urgent need to study them prior to Jonathon's call. As you know, I'm not really a fan of the digital medium. I would much rather touch paper than push buttons. Truth be told, I only remembered the portfolio *after* I found Francesco Laparelli's blueprints in my Vatican vault. I literally had to wake up one of my archivists in the middle of the night and have him search through our digital submissions in order to find the proper files. He was kind enough to load them onto my laptop, so I could share them with you today."

She leaned forward in anticipation. "I'll be honest, I can't wait to see what you've found. I'm so excited my hands are shaking."

Jones followed his earlier instructions and clicked on the file labeled VALLETTA 2 – 1575 AD. The computer sprang to life, sending a sixteenth-century blueprint of the city to both screens. There were so many tiny details in the ancient drawings that everyone focused solely on the television. Unfortunately for Payne and Jones, they quickly realized that they would be reliant on the others, because the language used in the document was definitely not English.

Payne furrowed his brow. "Is that Latin?"

Marissa gasped in amazement. For a historian like her, the significance of this document went far beyond a treasure hunt. In her eyes, the document itself was a treasure. "Most of the words are written in an ancient form of Latin, but not all of them. For some reason, Cassar also mixed in some Maltese, but I have no idea why. You would think he would have used a standard language for an official document."

Ulster grinned. "Who said this was an official document?"

She looked at him, then back at the screen. "Wait. So you think this blueprint was for his eyes only?"

"The thought had crossed my mind, particularly when I compared it to the original." Ulster turned toward Jones. "David, if you would be so kind, please open the file that's named: VALLETTA 1 – 1575 AD. Then, if you could, please place it to the left of the other blueprint."

Jones looked at him. "One on the left, two on the right?"

Ulster nodded. "Exactly."

Jones clicked a few buttons and made it happen. "There you go."

The two documents appeared side by side on the television screen. At first glance, the blueprints seemed to be identical, but as the group studied the two images, they slowly realized that there were a number of subtle differences.

"No Maltese," Marissa said as she snatched the handle from Ulster's hand and pointed it at the screen. "The first document has no Maltese. The entire thing is written in Latin."

Ulster nodded. "I noticed that as well."

She pointed at the second document. "And these lines *here* and *here*, they don't appear in the first document. Same with these lines over *here*. And over *here*."

Ulster smiled. "And what do all of those lines have in common?"

She glanced at her mentor. "All of them were labeled in Maltese."

Ulster grinned. "Correct."

"Hold on," Payne said while trying to understand the significance of the files. "Unless I'm mistaken, you're suggesting that the document on the right—the one with all the extra lines—is a coded blueprint that Cassar kept to himself. And you believe that all of those extra lines represent tunnels? Tunnels that were intentionally omitted from the official blueprint on the left?"

Ulster continued to grin. "I do indeed."

Payne stared at the plump historian. "And if I forced you to put a percentage on your certainty, what would that number be?"

Ulster kept on grinning. "Ninety-nine percent."

"Really?" Payne blurted. "That's pretty damn high. Why so confident?"

"Let me show you," Ulster said as he grabbed the handle from Marissa and pointed it at the screen. "David, please open this folder here. The one labeled TUNNELS."

Jones did as he was told, and its contents soon filled the screen. Inside that folder were dozens of files, all of them labeled with its own number in sequential order. The list of files was so long that it extended beyond the scope of the screen. "Now what?"

Ulster pointed his handle. "Open files one through five."

A moment later, five new blueprints filled the screen. But unlike the extensive plans of Valletta that referenced the tunnels with little more than vague lines, these plans were very precise, each one showing specific dimensions of individual tunnels that were to be built between the sewers and cisterns of the new capital city.

Ulster kept on grinning. "The reason I'm so confident that those lines were tunnels is because Girolamo Cassar took the time to draw them in great detail for us."

"Holy shit!" Marissa said as she stared in disbelief. "Where do they lead?"

"Now *that*, my dear, is an interesting question. Where do you think they went?"

She racked her brain, trying to think of the most logical locations, then it dawned on her that she didn't need to guess. She could simply look. "DJ, clear those files off the screen and go back to Cassar's coded blueprint."

"Yes, ma'am," he said while clicking away. "Here you go."

She leapt to her feet to take a closer look at the screen. "Can you zoom in on the middle of the city? I want to read the Maltese, but I can't with the—better! Much better! Thanks!"

Jones nodded from his seat on the couch. With his view of the television temporarily obstructed by Marissa, he stared at the image on the laptop's screen. Even though he couldn't read Maltese, he noticed the same word over and over. "What does *Berga* mean?"

She immediately stopped and looked at him. "That's it! That's where the tunnels went!"

Then, without a word of explanation, Marissa turned back toward the television screen and started calling out places in Maltese. She did it in such a rhythmic cadence that she almost sounded like she was chanting. "Berġa ta' Alvernja. Berġa ta' Provenza. Berġa ta' Aragona. Berġa ta' Kastilja. Berġa ta' Italja. Berġa ta' Franza. And Berġa ta' Alemanja."

Jones listened to the words as she said them, and he quickly picked up on the theme. The word *Berga* was obviously a noun, and the words that followed described it. He didn't know what *Alvernja* meant, but *Provenza* sounded like 'Province'. And *Aragona* sounded like 'Aragon'. And *Kastilja* sounded like 'Castile'. And Italja sounded like 'Italy'.

On the other side of the couch, Payne was going through the same process. Halfway through her list, he was racking his brain trying to remember where he had heard all of those places before. At some point during her lecture, she had mentioned all of those words together.

Then it hit them both at the exact same time.

Berga stood for 'auberge'.

The inns where the individual langues had housed their knights.

"Auberges!" they shouted in unison. "I said it first! No, *I* said it first!"

Meanwhile, Ulster looked on with delight.

He had started the ball rolling; now they were learning on their own. And they were having fun while doing it.

He glanced at Marissa. "It seems you are a better teacher than I, for you managed to teach the boys Maltese in a single night!"

Jarkko raised his hand. "Jarkko have question."

"Yes," Ulster said as the excitement settled down. "What is it?"

Jarkko looked at him, confused. "Did Petr find treasure?"

"No," Ulster said with a comforting smile, "I'm afraid not. Although I certainly wish that was the case, all we've managed to do is locate a system of tunnels that I believe may have enabled Grand Master Hompesch to move the treasure underneath the city. After discovering these tunnels in the middle of the night, I woke up a second staff member and asked him to go through anything he could find in Valletta's modern-day infrastructure to see if any of these tunnels had been discovered or damaged in any way. As far as I can tell, much of the system appears to be situated in areas of the city untouched by public works. Of course, this doesn't mean that we will be able to locate them or even find them viable, but at this point in time, I do believe the quickest way to test our theory is to take a field trip underneath Valletta. And while we're down there, perhaps we will find further evidence about the treasure itself."

"I'm in," Jones blurted.

"Me, too," Payne said.

Jarkko nodded his head. "Jarkko likes to dig."

Ulster glanced at Marissa. "What about you, my dear?"

She smiled. "You had me at Cassar."

CHAPTER 47

After giving it some thought, Payne and Jones realized that they didn't have the necessary equipment to journey through the subterranean world underneath Valletta. They had no idea what they were going to find down there, and since they felt responsible for the safety of the rest of the group, they didn't think it was wise to go without the proper tools.

Thankfully, Payne had a private plane at his disposal and a manufacturing facility in Italy less than an hour flight away. With a quick call to Samuel McCormick, the new CEO of Payne Industries, Payne was put in touch with the right people in Rome, and they were willing to assemble everything that Payne needed for a successful mission.

Unwilling to leave his friends in case of an enemy attack, Payne sent an empty plane to Italy, where the necessary equipment was loaded on board before the jet returned to Malta. It was met at the airport by Mark Galea, who traded in his chauffeur's hat and Mercedes sedan for work gloves and a panel van. He loaded all of the crates into the back of the truck while fantasizing about the size of his gratuity.

He had a feeling that it was going to be a personal best.

While that was going on, Jones, Ulster, and Marissa went through the rest of Cassar's portfolio in order to figure out the best way to access the tunnel system. Marissa pointed out that Cassar had designed and built the majority of the original auberges in Valletta, which gave further credence to the hidden tunnel system underneath the inns.

Unfortunately, Cassar's tunnel system would have been in place for more than two hundred years prior to the French invasion in 1798 AD, so the three of them felt that it was unlikely that Hompesch would have solely used the original tunnels. Not only would the tunnels have been known by too many men over the centuries—including disloyal French knights—but they realized a secret treasure would need to be stored completely out of view.

The question was, where?

Marissa's initial thought was underneath the Grandmaster's Palace, which was built by Cassar in 1574 AD. And upon closer inspection of the file labeled VALLETTA 2 – 1575 AD, they realized that it was part of the same tunnel system as the auberges.

Which, of course, made perfect sense.

If the grand master had wanted to hold a secret meeting with some of his knights, they could have used the underground network of tunnels to reach the palace without being seen. Stories had spread over the years that the Knights used to ride underneath the city on horses while hauling supplies on carriages, yet a massive system like that had never been found.

Perhaps, this was where the rumors had started.

But Marissa also realized that the Grandmaster's Palace had gone through many renovations over the centuries, including a major one in the mid-1700s. Later on, after the French arrived, they renamed it the Palais National, which was then changed to the Governor's Palace when the British seized control of Malta in 1800 AD. Nowadays, the building is officially known as The Palace, and it currently houses the Office of the President of Malta.

Jones laughed at the thought of the call that Payne would have to make to Nick Dial if they were caught by Maltese police in a tunnel underneath the Office of the President, but Marissa didn't find it quite so funny since she actually lived in Malta. Since they all agreed that Hompesch would have been foolish to keep the treasure in the same location as his French predecessor, they highly doubted they would find anything other than an abandoned tunnel under the former Grandmaster's Palace.

With that in mind, they kept searching elsewhere.

Always on the lookout for a good conspiracy, Jones remembered something he had pointed out to Marissa the night before. He had found it strange that Auberge d'Allemagne (the inn for the German knights) was the only auberge to be intentionally demolished. He reasoned, if Hompesch—the only German grand master in the history of the Knights of Malta—needed men he could trust, he would have found them at Auberge d'Allemagne.

Expecting an argument, Jones was pleasantly surprised when

Ulster and Marissa agreed with his reasoning. Although none of them (including Jones) believed there was a conspiracy to demolish the inn—since it was the British, not the Order, that had razed the auberge in 1839 AD to make way for St. Paul's Pro-Cathedral— they felt it made perfect sense that Hompesch would have used the German auberge as his base of operation. They were even more enthused when they looked through modern municipal plans and realized that the substructure of the Anglican church did not appear to encroach upon the original tunnel system built by Cassar.

It came close, but it did not connect.

Of course, they had no way of knowing if the construction of the cathedral or other buildings in the area had accidentally collapsed the German leg of the tunnel system. The only way they would know for sure was by going under Valletta to see for themselves.

While Payne handled the arrangements for their subterranean mission and Jones helped Ulster and Marissa determine the precise location of their upcoming search, Jarkko was tasked with keeping an eye out for trouble. He highly doubted that they would be attacked on the open sea, but just to be safe, Jarkko moved the position of the yacht every fifteen minutes or so.

In his line of work, he had done business with all types of criminals, but Jarkko and his smuggling associates around the globe particularly despised Russian thugs. There was just something about the way that they carried themselves that pissed Jarkko off, as if they were ethnically better than criminals from other parts of the world.

Worse still, he found they often let their egos get in their way.

Which was the main problem with Volkov.

For one reason or another, he had interpreted Jarkko's dealing with Bobrinsky—one of the few Russian criminals that Jarkko actually liked—as a slap in his face. In response, Volkov had thrown a temper tantrum on Jarkko's yacht to let him know that he was gunning for him.

Initially, Jarkko hadn't been scared by the damage to his yacht. He had dealt with Russian scum for years and knew how to take care of himself, but everything changed when he had found out the name of the man throwing the tantrum. Though he had never met Volkov, he had known a few people who had, and none of them had lived to talk about it.

Jarkko had put on a happy face for the others and was thrilled to temporarily have the distraction of the treasure, but he knew enough about Volkov to realize that a war was coming—one that Jarkko doubted he could win. Not only did Volkov have hundreds of goons at his disposal, but he apparently had a team of hackers on his payroll, who were capable of disabling traffic cameras and erasing surveillance footage with a few keystrokes.

With that type of support, the Russian had little to fear.

To survive, Jarkko knew he needed to strike first.

As he stared at the turquoise sea, a plan started to form, one that would require the help of his friends. Even before Malta, he had admired Payne and Jones for the way they had treated him on their Greek adventure. He knew in his heart that he didn't truly deserve a piece of their finder's fee. After all, he was merely a boat for hire, and they had paid him well above his normal rate. But they went out of their way to make sure that he was given a slice of their pie.

In his world, people like that were hard to find.

And he wanted to do whatever he could to protect them.

Unfortunately, Jarkko realized that his friends were involved whether he asked for their help or not. He knew Volkov wasn't the type of man who would forgive Payne and Jones for killing his henchmen. If anything, he would go after them twice as hard just to prove a point. Then he would go after Marissa, and Ulster, and anyone else who had helped Jarkko.

That was simply the way Volkov did business.

He would keep coming and coming until he was stopped.

With that in mind, Jarkko decided to pull Payne aside to have a man-to-man talk, one to be held out of earshot from the people that he hoped to protect. He waited until Payne was off the phone with his contacts in Rome, then called him to the padded bench in front of the helm. It was the same bench that Payne had sat on with Marissa the night before and with Ulster earlier that day. And every time, Payne was stunned by its softness.

"Did I do something wrong?" Payne asked as he leaned back and smiled. "I can't remember the last time I was pulled aside by a ship's captain. Probably back at the Academy."

Jarkko shook his head. "Not time for laughs. Jarkko in trouble."

Payne could tell he was serious. "What kind of trouble?"

Jarkko took a deep breath before he let his emotions out in one rambling burst. "Jarkko pretends everything is okay, but everything is *not* okay. Ivan Volkov is bad man. He knows Jarkko's name, and he knows about you. No way Russian hackers wipe files without looking. You are famous man. David is famous man. Volkov will search internet until he finds names, then he will come after you. Then Marissa. Then Petr. Then everyone you know. Then everyone they know. Jarkko has lost many friends to men like him, but Volkov is worst of bunch. In Russia, they call him 'wolf', because he enjoys hunt. That is why he went to Tallinn to kill Sergei Bobrinsky. That is why he came to Malta to kill Jarkko. You saw what he did to his own man. He is animal. He will not stop until he tastes blood—or we taste his."

Payne said nothing as he absorbed the impact of Jarkko's warning. Instead, he just sat on the bench staring at the sea, while running scenarios through his mind.

From the moment Jarkko had told him about the slaughter of Bobrinsky and his family, Payne had realized that Volkov would need to be dealt with. He knew Nick Dial would prefer something legal, but from Payne's personal experience dealing with some of the worst terrorists in the world, he knew that megalomaniacs like Volkov wouldn't play by society's rules.

His sole goal was to get revenge in the loudest way possible.

And for someone like Payne, that was a scary thought.

Not because he and Jones couldn't take care of themselves—because they certainly could. But because they couldn't protect their entire circle of friends and associates from someone who didn't follow the rules. What if Volkov's next move was an attack on Payne Industries? Or their upcoming exhibit at the Smithsonian? Or the Ulster Archives? Or about a hundred other places he could think of?

How could they protect everyone at once?

It simply wasn't possible, even for men like Payne and Jones.

Unless they dealt with the problem head on.

"Believe it or not," Payne said to break the silence, "I knew we would eventually have this conversation. I wasn't sure when, but I knew it was coming. And I happen to agree with you. I think we need to be the aggressor in this situation, or else we'll be looking over our shoulders for the rest of our very short lives."

Jarkko nodded. "What about David?"

Payne smiled. "If DJ had his way, we'd already be in Moscow."

"Bad idea. Must not hunt wolf in Russia. Must make wolf come to you."

"I agree," Payne said. "But we can't bring him here. He's already caused enough problems in Malta. We need to lure him somewhere else."

"Jarkko agrees. And Jarkko knows where. But Jarkko needs help."

Payne looked at him. "Help with what?"

Jarkko grinned. "Setting trap."

CHAPTER 48

The Pentagon
Arlington, VA

Despite its name and shape, the Pentagon is jokingly referred to as the "squarest" building in the world by Washington insiders, since it was filled with letter-of-the-law soldiers in perfectly pressed uniforms doing so many monotonous tasks that the entire place was incredibly boring and mechanical. Of course, that type of regimented precision was needed to run something as massively complex as the United States Department of Defense.

And yet, not everyone who worked at the Pentagon was expected to show up in starched white shirts and recently polished shoes. Deep in the subbasement of the Pentagon lurked a computer researcher named Randy Raskin, who was able to track down just about anything in cyberspace. Thanks to next-generation computer technology and his high security clearance, Raskin was privy to many of the government's biggest secrets, a mountain of classified data that was there for the taking if someone knew how to access it. His job was to make sure the latest information got into the right hands, whether that be CENTCOM, Capitol Hill, the White House, or two former MANIACs with a penchant for mischief.

Over the years, Payne and Jones had used his services on several occasions, and that had eventually led to a friendship. Raskin often pretended he didn't have time for them, or their frequent favors, but the truth was he admired them greatly and would do just about anything to help. In fact, one of his biggest joys in life was living vicariously through them—whether that be their missions in the special forces or their recent travels around the globe.

Someday he hoped to join them on one of their grand adventures, but for the time being, he was perfectly content monitoring their escapades from the warmth of his fuzzy blue bathrobe, which he often wore over his wrinkled clothes inside his chilly office. In order to prevent his computers from overheating, the room temperature was set to a nippy fifty-eight degrees.

"Research," said Raskin as he answered the phone on his headset while continuing to type. If he had taken the time to see who it was, he would have been a tad less formal.

Payne smiled at the sound of his voice. "Mister Raskin."

Raskin stopped typing. "Asshole!"

"Wow," Payne said with a laugh. "What did I do to deserve that?"

"How soon one forgets."

Payne grimaced. "Seriously, I'm at a total loss here. Did I forget your birthday or something? Because if I did, you're shit out of luck. I can barely remember *my* birthday, let alone yours."

Raskin shook his head. "Which is *why* I send you hourly reminders whenever we're getting close. I mean, what good is having a billionaire as a friend if he doesn't buy you fancy gifts?"

"Beats me. I'm not friends with any billionaires."

"Touché."

"So, why am I an asshole?"

"I am soooo tempted to place a conference call to DJ right now, just so he can answer that question for me. I'm sure he has a substantial list."

"It gets longer every day."

"That's what *she* said."

Payne rolled his eyes. "Seriously, what's the deal?"

"Hold on," Raskin said as he clicked away on his omnipresent keyboard while staring at one of the six computer screens that filled almost his entire field of vision. "So you don't remember sending me a long-ass message from a yacht in Malta with a bunch of next-to-impossible tasks for me to complete once, and I quote, 'you've had enough caffeine that you're pissing pure Mountain Dew'?"

Payne grinned. "Oh, you're talking about my email. Of course, I remember that! Truth be told, I thought that part was rather poetic."

"And accurate," Raskin said with a laugh. "You know me well enough by now to know the magical moment when urine turns to Dew occurs shortly after lunch."

"Which is why I sent you an email instead of calling you at dawn."

"Well, thank you for being so courteous with your list of demands."

Payne shrugged. "I do what I can."

"Where do you want to start?"

"Dealer's choice."

"Fine," Raskin said. "Let's go in order. Number one, you wanted to see if I could recover any surveillance footage from the murder that took place in Tallinn. I'm guessing to get evidence against the Russian prick who attacked you at the library. Correct?"

"That's affirmative."

"Unfortunately, Jon, the answer is 'no.' I can't recover any footage because the security cameras were remotely turned off *before* the murder occurred. Despite my considerable talents, I'm not a time-traveling wizard who can turn back the clocks to turn on surveillance cameras in order to get you secret footage. Trust me, if I could do that, I wouldn't be sitting in a windowless office in my bathrobe. I'd be running the porn empire that I've always dreamt about in a penthouse office in my bathrobe."

"Let's talk about your wet dreams later. Or hopefully, not at all."

"Works for me. Moving to number two. Can I get any surveillance footage of Volkov in Malta? The answer is once again 'no.' And the reason is the same reason as number one, but with a caveat. Do you know what that is, or do I need to explain it?"

"*Caveat* is fancy fish eggs, right?"

Raskin laughed. "I'm going to assume you're joking. Otherwise, a Naval Academy education is not nearly as good as my admiral pals claim it to be."

"Look at you—friends with billionaires and admirals. You're such a fame whore, I don't even know you anymore."

"Yep," Raskin said as he adjusted his bathrobe, "I'm living the good life. No doubt about that. Want to poke me again with a stick, or can I get back to your list of demands?"

"Proceed."

"Here's the caveat I was referring to," Raskin explained. "I've never seen a surgical, rolling blackout like this before. It was as if Volkov had a device in his pocket that wiped out cameras as he approached them. It started when his plane landed in Malta, and it followed him around the city like a black cloud. Airport surveillance, traffic cameras, library cameras, and so on—one camera after another went out until he got back on the plane and left for Moscow. But he didn't fry them with some kind of electromagnetic pulse. They turned back on after he passed."

"But you don't think it was a device."

"No," Raskin said with a laugh. "If that technology existed in pocket form, I would have asked you to build one for me. Instead, I think Volkov was carrying a very precise GPS unit that sent his whereabouts back to Russia, where a team of hackers worked their magic from afar. Truth be told, it's pretty impressive stuff."

"In other words, these guys are good."

"Better than good. These guys are *great*."

"Better than you?"

"Whoa! Whoa! Whoa! Don't talk crazy now. I was merely giving these guys a compliment, not handing them my championship belt as the world's best hacker."

"Please tell me you don't actually have a title belt."

"Not yet, but now I know what I want for my next birthday."

Payne smiled. "So far, it doesn't sound like you've done anything to earn a gift. If my count is correct, you're oh-for-two on my list."

"And he's back to the stick."

"Just speaking the truth."

"Like I did when I called you 'an asshole'?"

"Ouch."

"That's right! This hacker has claws."

Payne laughed. "Fine. I'll play nice, if only to get this moving along."

"Yeah," Raskin said as he continued to multitask, "like *you're* the busy one. It must be tough lounging on a smuggler's yacht in the middle of the Mediterranean. Meanwhile, I'm literally sending schematics to an assault team that is getting ready to breach a terrorist cell in a country that I'm not allowed to mention because my security clearance is higher than yours."

"Seriously? Do you need to go?"

Raskin stared at his screens. "Fuck it. They have guns. They'll be fine."

Payne laughed. "Then let's move on."

Raskin glanced at Payne's to-do list. "Numero three. You need some background information on Sergei Bobrinsky's business. No sweat. I can help you out with that. I just need a few more details on what you're looking for."

"No problem," Payne said. "According to Jarkko, Bobrinsky used to conduct most of his business on the dark web. That's where he would buy and sell his goods, whether it be artwork, antiquities, or ancient documents. Unfortunately, Jarkko wasn't a customer. He worked in, um, logistics, so he doesn't know the specifics of Bobrinsky's listings."

"Since when did 'smuggling' become 'logistics'?"

Payne grinned. "Since I bumped into Jarkko in Malta."

Raskin laughed. "That's what I figured."

"Anyway, as you probably know from following my every move like a stalker, Volkov stole a collection of ancient documents that Jarkko had received from Bobrinsky a few days before he fled with his family from Russia to Estonia. We're kind of hoping that Bobrinsky didn't have time to remove his listing about the collection from the dark web. If we're lucky, maybe there are pictures of the documents, or at the very least, descriptions of what the collection contained. Anything to help us catch up to Volkov."

"Sure thing," Raskin said. "That shouldn't be tough for someone like me. In fact, even if Bobrinsky deleted the listing, I still might be able to help."

"How so?" Payne asked.

"Remember before when I said I *wasn't* a time-traveling wizard? Well, the truth is I lied. When it comes to the World Wide Web, I actually do have the ability to go back in time. I realize you don't have a firm grasp on the technology involved with computer networks—despite your former title as CEO of Payne Industries—but suffice it to say, my friends over at the NSA spend a whole lot time of taking snapshots of the web and web traffic. They literally have city blocks of storage space that is strictly dedicated to saving and indexing those pictures."

"For what?" Payne wondered.

"Evidence," Raskin said before he launched into an explanation. "Let's pretend our boys at the FBI figure out that there's going to be a major terrorist attack, and it's being led by a virtually unknown activist named—I don't know—John Smith. The FBI does a quick search of the current Internet and finds nothing on this guy, because he isn't a total idiot and deleted his social media accounts two years ago. So what does the FBI do? They call in a favor from the NSA—because that's how this game is played, with fucking favors—and the NSA sends over a report on John Smith's online activities since he was given his first password in kindergarten."

Payne whistled. "That's awesome and fucked up at the same time."

"Tell me about it."

"Please do me a favor and *never* tell DJ. For some reason, he's really gotten into conspiracy theories over the past year or two. If he hears about this, he's liable to shit himself."

"Actually," Raskin said, "do *me* a favor and never repeat that to anyone. I'm not quite sure what the security level is on that particular topic. I may have just committed treason."

"No worries. Just call Nick. I'm pretty sure you have his number."

Raskin laughed. "Trust me, I have a lot more than that."

"Speaking of hacking, I was kind of hoping you'd be willing to help me out with a certain Russian problem that I've been having."

"Are you referring to Volkov or his hackers?"

"Both."

"Hell yeah! Let's kill those bastards!"

Payne smiled. "Wow. I thought it was gonna take a lot more begging than that."

"Sorry," Raskin apologized, "that comment wasn't to you. That was directed to the assault team. They just breached the terrorist's warehouse and—dammit! I almost did it again. I almost blabbed to you about an ongoing mission. Now you know why I rarely use the phone. Well, *that*, and I don't really like people all that much. Anyway, what were you saying about the Russians?"

"I was hoping you could help me take them out."

"No thanks. I'm kind of busy."

Payne nodded. "Now that's more like it. What's it gonna take?"

Raskin paused. "A piece of the treasure."

"Excuse me?" Payne said, surprised. "What treasure?"

"Don't play dumb. You know damn well I know about the treasure. More importantly, I know that you gave Jarkko a cut of your finder's fee for your discovery in Greece. I also know you didn't give me diddlysquat for all the intel I provided during that treasure hunt or any of the others. And if you don't recall what intel, I'll be happy to pull out my notes."

"I'm just glad you said 'notes'."

"I'm serious, Jon."

"I'm serious, too."

"No," Raskin stressed, "like *really* serious. I could lose my job for helping you like I do. The least you can do is compensate me for my risk."

"Fine," said Payne, who didn't have an issue with paying Raskin for his services. The truth was that he had been quietly setting money aside in a private offshore account that was to be given to Raskin upon his retirement, knowing full well that Raskin would be flagged and investigated if he suddenly had an extra million or two in his personal checking account. "We'll give you a cut of the treasure, but only if you help us with our Russian problem. Because the truth is if we don't take care of Volkov, we won't be around long enough to find anything."

"Do you have something in mind, or do you need me to come up with that, too?"

Payne shook his head. "We have a plan. We just need you to set the trap."

Raskin grinned. "Then consider it set, because the championship belt is staying with me."

CHAPTER 49

Mark Galea climbed out of the black panel van when he saw the yacht pull up to the private dock. It was located in a deepwater marina that was a ten-minute drive to Valletta. In Payne's opinion, it was far enough from the city to avoid prying eyes but close enough to the tunnel system to give them an escape route if something happened to go wrong.

Payne was the first and only one off the yacht. He held a gun in his hand but concealed it behind his back as he made his way toward their driver. Although he trusted Galea, he had no idea if the Russians had followed him there or had compromised him in any way. Payne seriously doubted either possibility, but he wasn't willing to risk everyone's life on it until he had a chance to get the lay of the land and examine the expression on his driver's face.

"So let me see if I got this straight," Galea said as he made his way across the gravel parking lot toward Payne. "When I picked you up at the airport, you had no luggage. Then when I picked you up at the mall, you suddenly had luggage. Then when I picked you up at the hotel, you had trash bags filled with fancy rubbish. And now, when I pick you up at a private marina, you have absolutely nothing, but *I* have an entire van filled with mysterious wooden crates."

Galea shook his head at the ridiculousness of it all. "You, my friend, are the most interesting man in the world."

Payne laughed as he tucked his gun into his belt under the back of his shirt before he stuck out his hand to shake Galea's. "I don't know about that, but you are certainly the world's most accommodating driver. Thanks for doing all of this for us. I know it required a lot of trust on your part, and I'm truly appreciative of your time and effort."

"My pleasure," Galea said with a smile. "Just promise me that this isn't the beginning of the American invasion of Malta that David teased me about."

"Nope," Payne assured him. "Pretty much the opposite. We hired a local historian, and we're going to explore some of the tunnels underneath Valletta. We want to see what Malta's former occupants built underneath the city before they departed your beautiful country."

"Thank goodness," Galea said. "I'm so used to driving on the left-hand side of the road, I truly don't know what I'd do if America took control of Malta. I'd rather retire and move to London than drive on the right-hand side like you crazy Yanks."

"Wow. I can't remember the last time someone called me a 'Yank', but I'll let it slide since it's approaching midnight and you have a van full of guns and explosives."

"Pardon?" Galea blurted.

Payne laughed. "Just kidding. DJ told me to say that. He said it would freak you out."

"And it did."

"Good. Consider us even for the Yank comment."

Galea nodded. "Will do."

"If you'd like, I'm more than happy to show you the contents of the crates. Although I get the sense if you were truly worried, you would have taken a peek before I arrived."

Galea smiled. "You're right. I would have. But I researched you online after the shootout at the library, so I know who you are and trust you completely."

Payne assumed as much. "We trust you as well."

"Glad to hear it."

"Great. Then why don't you start opening crates while I get my team?"

"Works for me."

Payne turned and walked back toward the dock. He was halfway there when he spotted a fully armed Jones and Jarkko near the stern of the yacht. "We're clear. Get the others."

A few minutes later, Payne was introducing his historians to Galea, who set down one of the crates to shake their hands. Inside the boxes was everything they needed for their upcoming adventure: lights, ropes, archaeological gear, clothing, and footwear, plus a number of electronic devices that would aid them in mapping the tunnels and getting them through impediments.

Although Payne and Jones were comfortable in their T-shirts and shorts, Marissa convinced them to put on full-length, water-resistant clothing and boots by showing them a few videos that she had taken on her phone while exploring some of the public tunnels during the past few years. Due to broken drainage systems, many of the tunnels had at least a foot of water in them. She didn't think conditions would be quite that bad, since it wasn't the rainy season, but she felt the best way to protect their electronic equipment—and themselves from scrapes and insect bites—was with the proper clothing.

Marissa climbed into the van and closed the door behind her. When she emerged a short while later, she was wearing black boots, black cargo pants, and a snug black sweater that stretched when she moved. "I feel like a ninja."

Payne smiled. "You look like one, too. A really sexy ninja."

"You mean a *kunoichi*," Jones said.

"Excuse me?"

"A *kunoichi*. That's the proper name for a female practitioner of *ninjutsu*. I mean, if you're gonna give a girl a compliment, you might as well get the terminology right."

Ulster nodded. "David is quite correct. Marissa is technically a sexy *kunoichi*."

Marissa blushed and kissed Ulster on the cheek. "Thank you, Petr."

Ulster smiled. "You're welcome, my dear."

"Hold on!" Payne complained. "I'm the one who gave you the compliment in the first place, but Petr ends up getting the kiss. What's up with that?"

Ulster chuckled. "Obviously she likes me more."

Marissa nodded. "It's true. I do."

"Fine," Payne said as he grabbed his change of clothes. "If you need me, I'll be getting undressed inside the van."

Jones grinned. "Worst pickup line ever!"

Payne held in his laughter until he closed the door behind him.

A few minutes to midnight, Galea parked the van down the street from St. Paul's Pro-Cathedral. Founded in Valletta in 1839 AD, it was one of three cathedrals of the Anglican Diocese of Gibraltar in Europe, but since the church wasn't the main cathedral of the diocese, it was stuck with the designation "pro-cathedral" in spite of its size and grandeur.

Considered a local landmark, its spire stood nearly two hundred feet tall and was constructed with Maltese limestone in a neo-classical style, and yet none of that mattered to the team leader inside the van. The sole reason they were there was because of what *used* to occupy the space before the church: the Auberge d'Allemagne, the inn for the German knights.

Although Ulster and Marissa didn't expect to find a treasure underneath the streets of Valletta, they hoped that the tunnel system built by Cassar might provide them with more clues about the Order's secret treasure. According to the letter from Paul the First, Hompesch had contacted him previously to ask for Russia's assistance to move the Grand Master's treasure out of Malta and past all of the threats lurking in the Mediterranean. Paul responded that he would happily assist with the endeavor, but his letter was dated in April of 1798, less than two months before Napoleon's arrival. So the historians had no way of knowing what happened next.

If anything had happened at all.

Marissa still wasn't confident that there ever was a treasure. She felt that Hompesch could have created a fictional hoard in order to assure Paul's assistance in the Order's upcoming battle against Napoleon. But when Russian ships didn't arrive in time to protect the Knights from the French armada, Hompesch had no choice but to surrender in shame.

In her mind, that was the scenario that best fit the history books.

Hompesch wasn't a hero. He was a coward.

Like she had always been led to believe.

Ulster, on the other hand, was far more open-minded. Unlike his former student, he had a lot of experience rewriting the history books that she clung to. He was doing his best to open her eyes to a wide range of possibilities, and he felt a trip through a secret tunnel system underneath the city that she knew so well was just the elixir to do it.

Sitting in the passenger seat of the van, Payne stared out of the windshield. He wanted to make sure they were completely alone before he opened the cargo door to let out his team in the alley. "What kind of patrols should we expect at night?"

Galea shrugged from the driver's seat. "Normally very few, but you might have heard there was a shootout at the library and a dead Russian found in the Grand Harbour Marina. I'm not quite sure how that's going to affect the local watch."

Payne smiled. "Fair enough."

Galea glanced at him. "Why are you so worried about the police? Tell me the truth: are you getting ready to rob the church?"

"I knew he'd wuss out," Jones teased from the back.

"Not at all," Galea said with a laugh. "Take whatever you want from Saint Paul's. That wouldn't bother me one bit. I'm *Catholic*, not Anglican. I'm on your side in this holy war."

Jones laughed. "That's more like it!"

Marissa rolled her eyes. "I can assure you there will be no thieving on my watch. We're merely going to inspect the tunnels, not plunder a cathedral."

Jarkko groaned. "Marissa make bad pirate. Sexy ninja, but bad pirate."

"*Kunoichi*," Ulster stressed. "A sexy *kunoichi*."

"Gesundheit," Jarkko said.

Payne glanced at Galea, who was more than a little bit amused by their antics. "I know what you're thinking, but I can assure you that I wasn't drunk when I assembled this team. Jarkko might have been, but I wasn't. These are some of the top people in their fields."

Galea laughed. "I'll be sure to tell that to the rescue squad when you get lost underground. Maybe they'll try a little harder to find you."

Payne smiled and handed him a Payne Industries phone. "Before you call for outside assistance, please try us first. There's special technology in our devices that should allow us to communicate through the limestone foundation of the city. If we get into any trouble, we'll reach out for help, and the same goes for you."

Galea shook his head. "I'm not worried about me. I'm worried about you. If you don't survive, I don't get paid."

CHAPTER 50

Friday, June 15
Underneath Valletta

As the clock struck midnight, Payne lifted the manhole cover with a crowbar and dropped a fluorescent glow stick down the entry shaft. It landed on a dry walkway fifteen feet below the alley. Although they weren't actually going to rob the nearby church, they were all dressed in black in case the Russians happened to make an appearance in the dark tunnels below.

Payne doubted they would, but he preferred to take precautions.

With gloves on his hands and a pack of equipment strapped to his back, Payne climbed through the opening and began his descent into the world underneath Valletta. Metal steps attached to the inner wall led him to the walkway below, where he picked up the glow stick and used it to examine his immediate surroundings.

As expected, he was in the middle of a long utility tunnel with a slightly arched ceiling that ran north and south for as far as his eyes could see. Roughly ten feet in height and six feet in width, the corridor had several utility lines mounted to the ceiling above, along with motion-activated lights every thirty feet or so. Once their eyes adjusted to the gloom, there would be no need for flashlights for this part of their journey.

"We're clear," Payne whispered up to his team.

Jarkko went next, followed by Ulster, Marissa, and then Jones. All of them carried equipment on their backs except the rotund historian, who could barely squeeze through the tight entry shaft and struggled to climb down to Payne. Once they were all safely at the bottom, Galea put the manhole cover back into place, sealing them into the tunnel system before he drove away.

No sense drawing extra attention to their point of entry.

Payne glanced at his team. "Everyone good?"

Ulster smiled. "Winded, but enthused!"

Marissa placed her hand on his back. "If you need a break, please let us know."

Jones pointed at Payne. "That goes doubly for you. If you start to get hungry, *please* get something to eat. The last thing we need is for you to hulk out in a tunnel. You could bring down an entire city like Sokovia. The Avengers are *still* taking heat over that."

Jarkko laughed. "Jarkko has been to Sokovia. Beautiful women!"

Marissa whispered to Ulster. "Where in the world is Sokovia?"

Ulster whispered back. "What's an Avenger?"

Payne ignored their banter as he pulled out his phone.

Prior to leaving the yacht, Jones had uploaded very precise GPS data to their devices that would reveal where they were in relation to the secret tunnel system designed by Cassar. The corridor they were standing in ran extremely close to the ancient system, nearly breaching it in more than one location. Payne's plan was to walk in the comfort of the maintenance shaft until they reached one of those points, specifically the one underneath St. Paul's Pro-Cathedral.

That is where he hoped to cross over to the older tunnels.

"Quiet," Payne whispered as he wrote EXIT on the wall with a piece of white chalk to mark the shaft in case anyone got lost or separated. "I know everyone's excited, but we're currently trespassing down here. The less we talk, the better."

The team quieted down as they fell in line behind Payne, who turned north and walked toward the substructure of the church. He shifted his gaze between the corridor and his phone as digital blips kept him in tune with the ancient tunnel that ran near the modern one. They walked over fifty feet before Payne started to slow down. According to their calculations, they were getting close to the spot where they had planned to punch through the concrete.

He walked a few more feet before he stopped.

"Okay," he said as he turned to his right and made a mark on the wall. "If our calculations are correct, 'X' marks the spot. Cassar's tunnel system is right through there. Unfortunately, to find out if we're actually correct, we need to break a few more laws."

"Several," Jones stressed. "And the local cops are already pissed at us."

Payne nodded. "So now is your last chance to back out. Because once I start busting through this wall, our culpability goes to a whole different level."

Jarkko grinned. "Jarkko is staying."

Ulster smiled. "So is Petr."

Marissa nodded. "And Marissa."

Jones shrugged. "I'm screwed either way. If the cops see me out at this time of night, they're gonna shoot me on sight. So I might as well stick around for the fun."

Payne laughed as he pulled the pack off of his back. Although it was stuffed with an assortment of small digging tools (designed for archaeological fieldwork), it did not contain any sledgehammers or explosives. Instead, he planned to bust through the wall using a tiny device that was built by Payne Industries for the U.S. military.

Nicknamed the *magic wand* in honor of Payne's love of magic, the sonic baton came in a wide variety of sizes. Some were as small as a penlight. Others were as large as a car. But the physics involved was still the same. The device produced a high-frequency sonic pulse that turned solid rock into rubble without the scorching or blast radius of an explosive.

The prototype in Payne's bag—which was the only one at the Payne Industries facility in Rome—looked remarkably similar to a cordless drill, so much so that Jarkko started to laugh when Payne took it out of its case.

"Jarkko is confused. How we break through wall with drill? We should have brought hammer instead. Jarkko is strong like *rhinoceristus*. No, like *rhinopocaurus*. Like *rynoseripitis*. Shit! Jarkko can't pronounce word, so Jarkko strong like bear."

Jones patted him on the shoulder. "You almost had it."

Jarkko shrugged. "How you say word?"

"Rhinoceros."

"*Rhynesitus*? Shit! Jarkko stick with bear."

Payne laughed as he held up the device. "I know this doesn't look like much, but it's actually much better than a sledgehammer. Have you ever seen the spring-loaded batons that firemen use? The ones that puncture safety glass to rescue accident victims? Well, this works in a similar way, only it uses a sonic pulse instead of a steel tip."

Jones was fully aware of the device's capabilities. "Back when Jon and I were in the military, we were constantly under threat of mortar fire. I can't tell you how many times we came upon a village and found people trapped underneath fallen roofs. Unfortunately, it was impractical to haul around a forty-pound hammer when you're doing recon, plus the last thing you want to do in that scenario is to start pounding debris on top of the wounded."

"So when I left the military," Payne explained, "I tasked the engineers at Payne Industries to come up with a lightweight device that soldiers could carry in the field that could cleanly cut through stone. It took several years of research, but they finally got it right about a year ago. This thing is truly amazing."

Marissa glanced at the wall. "What kind of damage will it do to the other side?"

"Unlike explosives, this will be a precise cut. That's one of the reasons that I brought the chalk. I'll let you historians draw on the wall, then I'll follow your lines. Depending on the depth of the wall, this process may take a few hours, but when we're done, we'll be able to push the concrete slab to the other side. It might literally weigh a ton or two, but thankfully one of us is strong like a *rhinoceristus*. I mean, bear."

After a brief discussion, Marissa and Ulster decided to draw a full-sized door on the wall. They figured if they had, in fact, managed to locate Cassar's tunnel system that their passageway would be used by thousands of people in the coming years. But before they did any major cutting, they wanted Payne to puncture through to the other side to view and record the ancient tunnel with a video borescope, a flexible fiber-optic cable with an embedded chip that relayed images to a monitor/recording device. Not only would this allow the team to see if they had found what they were looking for, but more importantly, it would prevent them from cutting a massive door through something of historical importance.

In order to puncture through the thick wall of concrete, Payne first had to cut a notch that was wide enough for the tool and his extended arm. They settled on an eighteen-inch square at shoulder height along the left side of the chalked door. Ulster marked it with precision as Payne put on a pair of safety glasses and an industrial dust mask. Marissa recorded everything on a 4K video camera while Jones turned on a few LED lanterns for the proper lighting. Although they realized the recording could be used against them in a court of law, they were willing to take the risk. Ulster promised if they found anything of value, he would be sure to upload it to the Archives' video cloud once it was fully operational.

Or, more accurately, have his butler do it for him.

Unsure of what to expect, the group took a few steps back when Payne turned on the device, but the magic wand barely made a sound. He brought the tip of the device to the top-left corner of the small, chalked square then watched as concrete seemed to melt away.

No messy fragmentation.

No shards flying around the tunnel.

Merely dust, falling to the ground like leaves from a dying tree.

"Good heavens," Ulster said as he took a step closer to investigate. He wore glasses in his everyday life, so he wasn't concerned about debris. "That device is truly amazing."

Payne stopped for a moment. "I believe I stated that earlier."

Ulster nodded. "Well, I officially concur."

Payne glanced back at him. "I can build you one if you'd like. I may not be the boss anymore, but I still think I have a few connections at Payne Industries."

Marissa cleared her throat. "If you're giving them away, I'd like one, too."

Payne smiled at her. "How about this? The two of you can share a single device. I think it would do both of you good to see each other more often, and this will be a great excuse. Consider it joint custody."

Marissa put her arm around Ulster's shoulders. "Works for me."

Ulster nodded. "Me, too."

Jones rolled his eyes. "Call me crazy, but maybe we should save the Hallmark moments until *after* we make a discovery. While you two are hugging it up, I'm back here sweating bullets. You know damn well if we go to trial, I'm the only one who's going to see jail time."

Payne laughed. "Inmate zero-three-two-five-four-zero is correct. I need to get back to work, but the truth is I actually stopped for a reason. I need Marissa's help with something."

She stepped forward. "With what?"

Payne pointed at the notch. "I need your help with all this dust. Inside your pack is a portable vacuum. There should also be safety goggles and another mask. It will save a lot of time if you can keep sucking up this mess as I create it, like a dental hygienist in a dentist's office."

"Yuck," she said as she reached into her bag for the portable vacuum. "Can you imagine flossing other people's teeth all day?"

"Shut up!" Jones blurted from behind. "Seriously, just stop it!"

Marissa froze, unsure what had set him off.

Payne touched her arm and whispered. "DJ *hates* the dentist. Totally freaks him out. He would rather walk through a field of landmines than get his teeth cleaned. I used to mess with him on purpose, but it simply isn't worth it. I'm talking PTSD-level anxiety."

Jones shook his head. "Come on, man! Quit your damn whispering and get back to work, or else Jarkko and I are going to shoot through the concrete with our guns."

"Sorry," Payne said. "Just showing Marissa what to do."

"David," she said as she turned around. "While I'm doing this, would you mind filming our work? I don't want to miss a thing."

Jones nodded. "My hands are shaking, but I'll do my best."

Jarkko frowned. "Does this mean no guns?"

Payne's speed increased significantly with Marissa's help. Instead of stopping every thirty seconds to clear away dust and debris, Payne maintained a constant pace until he made it through the concrete tunnel and hit the limestone behind it. According to their calculations, he had roughly six more inches to go until he would hit the ancient tunnel system designed by Cassar.

Then five inches. Then four.

Then three. Then two. Then one.

Then limestone. And even more limestone.

Which is when the group started to get worried.

Because of the extra depth of the shaft, Payne found it more and more difficult to reach into the eighteen-inch notch that he had originally created. Marissa was no longer able to work beside him because he had to twist sideways and shove his entire shoulder into the hole in order to drill deeper, so she took the camera back from Jones and filmed Payne as he struggled to work.

Behind him, Ulster, Jones, and Jarkko started to discuss secondary plans. Either they could increase the size of Payne's workspace—which would allow him to drill deeper into their current spot—or they could locate the other parts of the utility corridor that nearly intersected with the ancient tunnels and opt to drill there. The three of them were in the middle of deciding what to do when they heard a muffled pop. They quickly turned to see what had happened and saw Payne pull his arm out of the notch before he removed his goggles and mask.

"Ladies and gentlemen," he said directly into the camera, "we have just breached the secret tunnel of the Knights of Malta."

CHAPTER 51

Despite Payne's proclamation, they wouldn't be sure of what they had found until they used the video borescope to view what was on the other side of the wall.

Covered in a fine layer of concrete, Payne dusted himself off, then quenched his thirst with a bottle of water while Jones readied the equipment. He had used similar devices in the military when the MANIACs were entering guarded compounds, rescuing hostages, and/or searching for IEDs, but technology had advanced at such an incredible rate that this modern iteration put the old ones to shame. Not only would they get high-definition images, but with a proper computer network, he could have literally streamed the incoming video to everyone's phone.

But in the depths of the tunnel, the team would have to crowd around the wired 10-inch touchscreen while Jones fed the flexible optic tube through the tiny hole that Payne had punctured in the inner wall. The moment Payne had heard the pop, he had stopped drilling at once and had pulled his arm out of the workspace. Then with a flashlight, he had visually inspected the hole on the far side of the notch and realized that he had definitely pierced a chasm of some kind. They assumed it was the tunnel system that they were looking for, but this would be the moment of truth.

Jones stared into the notch. "What did you do with the glow stick?"

Payne glanced at him. "It's in my pack. Why?"

Jones held up the camera end of the borescope. "There's a small lamp on the end of this tube. It's more than adequate to light a few feet, but it's not bright enough to fill a tunnel. I think the hole you drilled is wide enough for you to slip the glow stick through."

"Good idea," Payne said as he bent down to retrieve the fluorescent tube. "Any objections from the historians?"

Marissa answered as she continued to film the proceedings. "None from me. As far as I'm concerned, the more light in there, the better."

Ulster agreed. "As long as we dispose of it once we're through, I have no objections at all. I don't want to step on it and soil the tunnel floor with luminescent green."

"Dispose of it?" Jones said with a laugh. "I'm gonna sell that thing to the highest bidder. After all, it will be the first object inside the tunnel in two hundred years."

"Here it is," Payne said as he tried to hand it to Jones.

Jones just stared back at him. "What am I supposed to do with that?"

"You just said you wanted the glow stick for the tunnel!"

"Dude," he said. "Look at your monkey arms, then look at my normal arms. Do you really think I can reach the hole on the far side of that notch?"

Jarkko spoke up. "Jarkko has body part that can reach any hole."

Marissa groaned. "Come on, Jarkko! I'm filming this!"

Jarkko shrugged. "Wouldn't be first time Jarkko is filmed."

Payne rolled his eyes. Now he knew why Galea had given him such a hard time about the makeup of his team. "She's right, Jarkko. We're filming this for posterity, so please watch what you say. And DJ, there's no need for insults. You should've just asked me to do it."

Jones pointed at the camera. "Rewind the damn tape. I *did* ask you to do it! I said the hole is wide enough for *you* to slip the glow stick through."

"Move," Payne said as he bumped Jones out of the way. "And for the record, there's no 'tape' inside Marissa's camera. It is strictly a digital device."

"I know that, Jon. It was merely a figure of speech."

Marissa whispered to Ulster. "Do they always bicker like this?"

Ulster grinned. "They do, and I love it!"

With the glow stick tucked in his fingertips, Payne stuck his hand into the notch and stretched his arm as far as he could. In order to reach the hole on the far side, Payne had to twist his body and put his right cheek against the rough texture of the concrete tunnel as he maneuvered blindly in the void. It took a few tries before he was able to line up the tip of the glow stick with the unseen hole and finally push it through. But it was definitely worth the effort. Once he pulled his arm out of the notch, the hole glowed neon green.

Getting even for the earlier bump, Jones shoved his best friend out of the way in order to work the borescope. First he fed the black optical tube through the notch with his hands until the camera tip was near the hole. Then he used the touchscreen to control the unit.

Inside the tube was a series of high-tech mechanical fibers that allowed him to control the articulation of the device. By sliding his fingers across the screen, he could rotate the camera in any direction. He could also sharpen the camera's focus or change the brightness of the light. With his left hand, he snaked the tube forward, and with his right, he used the touchscreen to raise the tip of the camera until it practically crawled through the hole.

"I'm in," Jones said as the team crowded behind him to look at the screen.

Expecting to find nothing but an ancient tunnel, they jumped back in fright when they saw a green specter dancing in the chasm. Jarkko screamed and leapt back so far that he practically knocked over Ulster and the work lights behind them. All of them breathed a huge sigh of relief when they realized the apparition was merely a product of the limestone dust floating in the stale air and the light from the fluorescent green glow stick.

After they collected themselves, Jones pushed the tube forward a few more inches before he used the touchscreen to curl the camera tip back to get a better view of the wall itself. Just as they had hoped, they saw nothing but the rough texture of cut limestone.

Ulster pointed at the screen. "As far as I can tell, we haven't damaged anything of historical significance. No masonry, carvings, or artwork. It simply appears to be a stretch of tunnel. At least I think it's a tunnel. What type of range does the borescope have?"

Jones shrugged as he continued to maneuver the camera. "In this atmosphere, it's hard to say. Between the dust and the darkness, maybe ten feet. Truth be told, I was expecting a lot more range than that, but I'm getting some kind of interference."

Payne grimaced at the thought. "Interference? You shouldn't be getting any interference. That camera costs more than most cars."

"Then maybe you shouldn't have bumped me so hard."

"Unlike you, it can handle abuse. Where's the interference?"

Jones pointed to a portion of the screen that looked similar to the specter they had seen earlier, but unlike the green apparition, this one was whitish in color. "If it's not interference, it's some kind of video ghosting."

Jarkko heard the word "ghost" and took another step back.

Payne stared at the screen and reluctantly agreed with Jones. "Shit. I think you're right. That certainly isn't dust. It must be a technical glitch."

"Actually," Marissa said as she paused her camera, "I don't think it is. I've seen something similar in other tunnels around Valletta. I think what you're looking at are tree roots."

"Roots?" Jones said as he pushed the borescope forward and articulated it up and down to get the best view possible of the enigma. "I'll be damned. I think she's right. The damn things grew straight through the ceiling."

Ulster leaned closer and grinned. "Believe it or not, this is excellent news! Tree roots have less trouble growing through porous limestone than solid concrete. And from the looks of this image, this entire stretch of tunnel appears to be infested with them."

Jarkko heard the word "infested" and stepped back further.

Payne glanced at Ulster. "So, what do you think? Should I keep on drilling?"

Ulster looked at Marissa and urged her to speak up.

"Hell yeah," she blurted. "It looks like we found the tunnel!"

Buoyed by the team's excitement and no longer worried about cutting through a historical artifact, Payne was able to increase his speed significantly.

As they had done earlier, he did the sonic drilling while Marissa did the vacuuming. Every ten minutes or so, they would pause to take a break while Jones and Jarkko emptied the sweeper unit into one of the industrial-strength trash bags they had brought along. Their goal was to keep the utility tunnel as clean as possible, so as not to draw extra attention to their handiwork.

Realizing that they wouldn't be able to spend enough time inside the tunnel to thoroughly examine it in a single night, they had come up with a temporary solution to keep workers away. They had brought opaque plastic sheets to cover their improvised doorway and had printed official-looking work permits to hang next to the breach.

But that would be for later.

For now, they stayed focused on the doorway.

After working for a while, Payne realized it made more sense to cut the tunnel in moveable chunks. He'd slice a few feet of concrete, then let Jarkko lift the wedge out of the hole and stack it in the utility tunnel. Originally they had planned to push a huge slab through to the other side, but the extra depth of Payne's drilling wouldn't allow it.

Unfortunately, the process was taking longer than they had expected. They quickly realized they wouldn't be able to complete the entire doorway in the time they had available, so Payne concentrated on the middle section of the chalked entryway. He would cut just enough to allow them to crawl through and get a good look at the tunnel on the other side. After that, they would decide if it was even worth the time and effort to cut an entire doorway.

All told, it took nearly two hours to accomplish the job.

And by then, they were practically bouncing with anticipation.

After putting down the drill, Payne brushed himself off. "So, who goes first?"

Ulster pointed at Payne. "You're the team leader, and you did the bulk of the manual labor. I believe it should be you."

Payne shook his head. As he did, dust fell out of his hair "Truth be told, I had someone else in mind. I think it should be Jarkko."

Jarkko pointed at himself. "Jarkko? Why Jarkko?"

Payne explained. "Because you're the one who started us on this journey. Without your letter from Paul the First, we wouldn't have even known a treasure existed."

Jarkko pounded his chest. "This is true! Jarkko is chosen one!"

"Besides," Payne teased, "if there actually is a green ghost in there, there's no way in hell I want to be the first one through."

Jarkko took a step back. "On second thought, ladies first!"

Payne laughed. "You heard him, DJ. Go ahead."

Jones smiled. "Normally, I would take great offense to that childish insult, but in this particular case, I'm more than willing to let it slide if it means I'm the first one in. Back in the service, Jon always had to be the first one through the door. Every. Single. Time."

"That's because I was team leader, and it was the most dangerous position! I was doing that to protect you and the rest of our team!"

"Hush!" Jones ordered. "This is my moment. Not yours."

"The key word is *moment*. Not hour. Seriously, it's gonna be light soon. If we were at the Oscars, the band would already be playing."

"If we were at the Oscars, my black ass wouldn't even be allowed in!"

Payne nodded. "Good point."

Jones looked at Jarkko. "Where was I?"

Jarkko stared at him. "You were happy to be called 'lady'."

Payne groaned and handed Jones a flashlight. "Come on, DJ! Just go already. Marissa is running out of tape in her camera."

Jones laughed. "Fine. I'll go. But I'm only doing this to be honored during Black History Month. It's one small step for man, but a giant leap for me!"

And with that, he dove headfirst through the opening.

CHAPTER 52

Stunned by Jones's sudden disappearance, the group rushed forward to see if he was all right. They crowded around the gap in the tunnel wall and waited for a sign from the other side.

Five seconds passed, and then five seconds more.

But no word came from Jones.

"DJ!" Marissa shouted into the void. "Are you okay?"

Payne was used to his friend's antics, but even he started to grow concerned. He was a few seconds away from climbing through the wall to check on him, when Jones suddenly popped up and screamed while holding the fluorescent glow stick underneath his chin. Combined with his black clothing, the neon light made it appear that Jones's face was a green, floating head. Its unexpected appearance caused everyone in the group to recoil in fright.

Jarkko was so freaked out by the ghostly manifestation that he actually ran down the utility tunnel toward the exit, shouting expletives in his native tongue about the devil. In his mind, no treasure was worth eternal damnation.

Meanwhile, Jones roared with laughter.

"DJ!" Payne yelled through the gap as he clutched his chest. "I can't believe you did that! You almost gave me a heart attack!"

Jones kept on laughing. "You always give me shit about black ghosts, but now I know you believe in them—or else you wouldn't have just pissed your pants! Hell, I think Jarkko's still running. You better go catch him before he reaches his yacht."

"You're lucky I didn't shoot you. I actually reached for my gun."

"It would've been worth it!" Jones said as he wiped tears from his eyes before turning his attention to Marissa. "*Please* tell me you got that on film."

"Sorry," she apologized. "Everything happened so fast, I didn't even capture your leap through the wall. Next time give me some notice."

"Man," he whined. "Every time I do something cool, no one catches it on film. First my gymnastics in the library, and now this. I need to hire a publicist."

"David," Ulster said tentatively. "I don't mean to step on your joke or stop a potential rant, but I was hoping I could pose a query of some importance."

Jones looked at him. "Sure. What's up?"

Ulster leaned forward. "Have we located the Knights' tunnel?"

Jones smiled at the historian. In his moment of levity, he had completely forgotten about the significance of this find. "Why don't you come on over and judge for yourself?"

Ulster grinned. "I was hoping you would say that!"

Once Payne had convinced Jarkko that there wasn't a poltergeist in the ancient tunnel, the two of them helped Ulster through the narrow opening. Marissa went next, followed by Jarkko, and then Payne, who passed LED lanterns and flashlights through the gap before he made the journey himself. By the time he reached the far side, the space was being lit by multiple lights, which gave him a good view of his surroundings.

Stretching more than eight feet in height and width, the tunnels had been carved through the limestone to the dimensions in Cassar's original drawings. A tangled web of tree roots hung from the punctured ceiling, giving the space an otherworldly vibe, but as Payne ran his hand along the porous walls, he could practically feel the history of the Knights in the stone.

"What an extraordinary discovery!" Ulster announced for all to hear. "Despite the complex root structures that have grown over time and a bit of seepage from the earth above, this tunnel is in remarkable shape! I truly wasn't sure what we were going to find, but this surely exceeds the grandest of my expectations."

Marissa gawked in amazement. "I know I'm supposed to be filming this, but I'm so blown away that I need to soak it all in. I'm sure this will be the highlight of my career."

Payne smiled and put his hand on her shoulder. "Let's hope not. Remember, the reason we're down here is to look for clues about the treasure. We can film and map the tunnel structure later, but for now, why don't we focus on our ultimate objective?"

She reached up and squeezed his hand. "That sounds good, but still, thank you for this."

"My pleasure," he said as he looked at her in the glow of their surroundings. "Hopefully, this is the beginning of something bigger."

She smiled at him. "I couldn't agree more."

"Jonathon," Ulster called from afar. "In all of my excitement, I have managed to turn myself around. Tell me, my boy, which way is south?"

Marissa squeezed his hand a second time. "Go help Petr. I want to take a look around before Jarkko breaks something important."

"Good idea," Payne said with a grin. "He strong like bear but jumpy like cat."

She walked away, laughing, as Payne pulled out his phone. Despite their depth underground, it was still accurately tracking his movement and elevation. According to his screen, he was facing Marsamxett Harbour to the north in a tunnel system that supposedly had multiple corridors to the south, as it branched out underneath the heart of Valletta. Ulster was calling to him from behind, which meant Ulster had been walking south.

Payne turned and headed in that direction. "You're south of me."

Ulster called out. "Well, it seems I've hit a roadblock."

From his current position in the tunnel, he couldn't actually see Ulster in the distance. The dangling roots were quite thick at times, and they prevented the beam of his flashlight from reaching too far into the distant gloom. He used his left hand to brush them away as he weaved his way past the thickest tangles of vegetation until he could see Ulster in the tunnel up ahead.

Much to Payne's surprise, Ulster was standing in front of a roadblock.

A *literal* roadblock.

Made of cut stone, the giant wall was expertly patched together by mortar and stretched across the entire width of the tunnel, thereby cutting off this stretch of corridor from the rest of Cassar's ancient system.

Payne glanced at Ulster. "Is that a support wall?"

Ulster shook his head. "I don't believe so. I have a theory as to its purpose, but I'd love to discuss it with Marissa first. Why don't you gather the group as I continue to examine the wall?"

It took a few minutes to wrangle the others, but once they heard that Ulster wanted to share some news, they excitedly followed Payne back to the stone barricade. When Marissa saw it, she literally gasped and ran up to Ulster to compare their thoughts. As fate should have it, both of them agreed on the purpose and significance of the wall.

Ulster urged her to speak. "Go ahead, my dear. Tell them."

"Okay," Marissa said, bubbling with enthusiasm. "Although we never mentioned it to each other, both of us were privately hoping to find a wall like this."

Ulster laughed. "Excellent wordplay. Simply excellent!"

Marissa giggled when she realized what she had said. Her use of "privately" had been completely unintentional, but she was happy to have amused her mentor.

Payne walked forward and put his hand on the wall. "I think you better explain, because right now I have no idea how this is a good thing. I mean, it completely prevents us from accessing the other parts of the tunnel system without finding—oh, hang on! Now I get it!"

"Get what?" Jones demanded as he approached the barricade.

"I get Marissa's pun, *and* I get the need for this wall."

Jarkko shined his light on Ulster. "Jarkko confused. Petr explain."

Ulster grinned. "Despite my private nature and introverted ways, I have always enjoyed a good spotlight, whether that be a gallery opening in Vienna or a karaoke bar in Japan. In fact, I remember this one time I had gathered with some colleagues of mine at a geisha house in Kyoto, where they served the most delightful tea made out of—"

Jarkko made a loud buzzer sound and shifted his light to Marissa. "Sorry, Petr. Time is up. Marissa's turn to explain."

Ulster nodded in understanding as Marissa took center stage.

"History tells us that Hompesch became grand master of the Knights in July of 1797, nearly a full year before Napoleon's arrival. If our theory is correct, that's when he learned about a massive treasure that had been hidden by the Order for centuries and realized it was his best piece of leverage to protect his organization. With this in mind, he started correspondence with Paul the First of Russia in order to save the Knights from a looming war with France."

She looked at Jarkko. "With me so far?"

Jarkko nodded as she started to pace in front of the wall.

"Unfortunately," she continued, "the grand master of the Knights prior to Hompesch was a Frenchman named Rohan, who may have told some of his countrymen about the treasure before his death in 1797. Worried about the loyalty of the French knights, Hompesch realized that he had better move the treasure as soon as possible. But how does he do that without being seen?"

Jarkko answered. "Secret tunnels."

"Exactly," she said as she pointed at him. "Except the tunnels weren't that secret to the knights themselves. After all, they had been around for over two hundred years, and they led to all of the major buildings in the Order's world, including all of the inns for the knights. But as luck should have it, Hompesch was a German, and Auberge d'Allemagne—the inn for the German knights—was the northernmost structure with access to the tunnel system. Suspicious of the other langues, Hompesch confided in some of his most loyal companions and convinced them to move the treasure to the German section of the tunnel in preparation of their departure from Malta. In order to work *privately*—notice the wordplay—they built a wall in the tunnel behind them to make sure that none of the other factions could discover their secret plans."

Jones nodded in understanding. "That makes perfect sense. It also explains why the other langues believed Hompesch was a coward. They had no way of knowing what he was doing on this side of the wall. From their perspective, he was cowering with his German knights as Napoleon approached, but he was actually planning their escape."

Ulster chimed in as he walked toward the right corner of the wall and crouched near the floor. "When Jonathon left my side to collect the rest of the team, I happened to notice a date etched into this cornerstone. In German, it simply reads: JANUARY 1798."

Marissa hustled over to inspect it. "Finally! Some proof to go along with all of this speculation! I was hoping we'd find some eventually! Truth be told, speculation like this isn't my forte. But I'm guessing you already knew that."

Ulster smiled at her. "I'm quite proud of you, my dear. Putting your name on a theory with only a shred of proof to support it. That's what true visionaries do. They stretch the realm of the understood world with the power of their imagination."

Jarkko walked over to wall. "Jarkko still confused. Where is treasure?"

Marissa glanced at him. "That, my friend, is a very good question.

Do you feel like taking a walk through time?"

Jarkko stepped back. "Like ghost?"

"No," she laughed as she grabbed his arm. "More like a field trip."

She turned Jarkko away from the wall and urged him to follow her north in the tunnel. Everyone fell in behind her as she explained her theory aloud.

"Now that we have a starting date, we know that Hompesch had roughly five months to prepare for Napoleon's arrival in June after building that wall. During that time, Hompesch started correspondence with Paul the First and began to look for allies in the coming war with France, which had seized control of Italy on its way to Egypt."

As they walked, they were forced to duck and weave around the dangling roots, some of which were so thick and colorful that they looked like tropical snakes in the darkness. But Marissa was so caught up in the lecture that she was giving that she didn't even seem to notice the obstacles in her way.

"Based on his blueprints, we also know that Cassar's tunnel system was built underneath the entire Sciberras Peninsula. Starting at the Grand Harbour to the south, it passed under the Upper Barrakka Gardens and ran directly through the heart of Valletta to the north, where it went underneath the Auberge d'Allemagne on its way to Marsamxett Harbour. It also extended east and west, like an ancient subway system that ran to every auberge in Malta."

As they passed the shaft that they had carved into the tunnel system, Payne paused in its opening for just a moment to listen for noises in the utility corridor. When he heard nothing of consequence, he continued on his journey with the rest of the group.

"At some point during his correspondence with Paul the First," Marissa said as the tunnel curved sharply to its right and started to head down a 45-degree ramp that eventually curled back underneath the upper shaft, "Hompesch realized that he was on his own to deal with Napoleon. That is when Jon and DJ's escape theory comes into play. Realizing that Napoleon would plunder everything of value in Malta, Hompesch presumably ordered his most trusted men to bring the treasure down this ramp, which corkscrews through the depths of the limestone, where it would eventually be met by an awaiting ship in Marsamxett Harbour."

As they walked down the spiraling ramp, the group marveled

at the precision of the construction. In many ways, it reminded Payne and Jones of *Pozzo di San Patrizio*—the historic well in Orvieto that Ulster had used as an example in one of his lessons. That had been built in 1527 AD, approximately fifty years before the creation of this tunnel system, and had also left them in awe. By comparison, modern roads were filled with potholes within a few years of being built, yet somehow this corridor was still mostly intact more than four centuries later.

"Unfortunately," Marissa said after a long stretch of silence, "the moment the Order's treasure was loaded onto a ship, history managed to lose track of it. Perhaps there are additional clues in the documents that accompanied the letter from Paul the First in Jarkko's collection. Or maybe we'll be able to track down some external leads now that we know what we are looking for, similar to what Petr did with Cassar's portfolio. After all, until I stepped foot inside of this tunnel system, I did not fully believe that any of this was possible."

Having memorized Cassar's designs, she had timed the pace of her lecture to her immediate surroundings. "For the time being, I'm afraid this field trip must come to an end, because we have run out of research and hit the literal and metaphorical end of the road."

As if on cue, they made one final turn and found themselves facing another stone wall. Built just shy of Marsamxett Harbour to the north, it looked remarkably similar to the wall up above, with one major exception.

The cornerstone on this one read: JUNE 1798.

The date when Hompesch and his men left Malta forever.

CHAPTER 53

Moscow, Russia

When Ivan Volkov was a child, history lessons had fallen on deaf ears, but that had certainly changed yesterday. Volkov had paid close attention to Boris Artamonov, the former curator at the Hermitage, when he had described the significance of the historical documents in the collection that Volkov had stolen from Jarkko's yacht.

Suddenly, the presence of the two Americans made perfect sense.

They were seeking an unfound Maltese treasure.

Although Volkov looked forward to getting revenge on the Finn and his gun-toting friends, he was even more excited about the possibility of unearthing a staggering sum of wealth. As a criminal with connections throughout Eastern Europe, he had heard rumors about a treasure train filled with gold and artifacts that had been located in a remote part of Romania.

He knew it was somehow tied to the death of Grigori Sidorov, the leader of a Russian extremist group known as the Black Robes that had caused Volkov's organization a lot of problems over the years. But unlike the religious Sidorov, Volkov didn't make his decisions based on dogma or blind faith.

Instead, he acted on reliable information.

Cold, indisputable truths.

That's why he only hired the best hackers in the world.

They gave him an edge that no one else had.

The previous night, Volkov had tasked his cadre of computer specialists to track down any information that they could find on the Maltese treasure. He had given them several historical keywords (Hompesch, Paul I, Knights of Malta, etc.) to search for, and a number of modern ones (Payne, Jones, etc.) as well, hoping that they might stumble upon a digital breadcrumb that would give him a tactical advantage in his search for his rivals and/or the treasure.

At a ripe age of twenty-seven, Mikhail Blokhin was the most experienced member of Volkov's hackers. He was paid an incredible amount of money to do what he did and rarely had to deal with Volkov in person—which was fine by Blokhin because he knew how unhinged Volkov could actually be. Most of their communication was done via phone or computer, while Blokhin and his crew worked in a non-descript warehouse in central Moscow.

Volkov had spared no expense when arming the collective. They had the best equipment and the fastest network in the entire city, outside of the government itself. Because of this edge, he expected results, and often got violent when his employees let him down.

Of course, that hadn't been mentioned during the hiring process. Blokhin had only discovered it when his superior had been fired. Not just relieved of his duties, but tied to a pole and burned alive.

Now the pressure was on him to deliver results.

Thankfully, he had found something of value.

Volkov smiled when he glanced at his phone. He knew Blokhin wouldn't be calling with bad news. That was usually delivered by email or text, if at all. Sometimes if the news was awful enough, the man responsible would simply pack a suitcase and run.

Little did they know, Volkov always relished the hunt that followed. It usually made the bad news worth it.

Volkov answered in Russian. "Did you find something?"

Blokhin swallowed hard in his office. Whenever he spoke with Volkov, he assumed his life was on the line, and this was no exception. Even though he was calling to deliver good news, he realized that Volkov could have changed his mind about the project overnight, making this call moot and a waste of Volkov's valuable time. "Yes, sir, I did."

"Well, spit it out!"

Blokhin did the opposite. He swallowed harder. "Sorry, sir. My apologies. As you requested, I took the keywords that you provided and ran a comprehensive search on multiple networks in order to locate any threads that connected those terms in an unusual way. This was done to eliminate the type of results that one would expect in a search of this kind. Obviously historical figures like Paul the First and the Knights of Malta were going to be cross-referenced in thousands of results, but by tweaking my algorithms,

I was able to weed out high-traffic sites like Wikipedia and focus on threads that were found in non-traditional forums."

"Such as?"

"Sites about antiquities, treasure hunting, ancient maps, and so on. That's where you find purveyors of artifacts—people who are buying and selling ancient items. Most of these sites are located on the dark web or similar networks in order to protect the identity of those involved, but as you know, those sites aren't as secure as people think."

Volkov thought of Sergei Bobrinsky and smiled.

His actions had made all of this possible.

"And what did you uncover?" Volkov asked.

Blokhin stared at his computer screen. "I found a post from five days ago on an obscure Maltese forum seeking information on any communication between Grand Master Ferdinand von Hompesch and Emperor Paul the First of Russia. A reply came the following day that directed the original poster to a highly encrypted network where they could have a private conversation."

Volkov did the math in his head.

Four days ago was prior to his appearance in Malta.

But it coincided with Payne and Jones's flight from America.

Perhaps this was what had triggered their journey.

"Please continue," Volkov said.

Blokhin nearly fell out of his chair when he heard the word "please". Until that moment, he didn't think his boss was capable of pleasantries. "Using the processing power of our clustered network, I was able to crack the encryption within a few hours and view the contents of their conversation. Once we're done with the call, I can send you the entire transcript if you'd like."

Volkov groaned. "Fine! But get to the point!"

"Sorry, sir," Blokhin said as his nerves reappeared. "Their chat was more than a simple exchange of information. It was a negotiation for a collection of letters written by Hompesch in the months after he departed Malta, and they settled on a price of one million American dollars."

"You're sure of this?"

"As sure as I can be, sir. Obviously I can't confirm the veracity of the letters or their content, but I can verify the conversation itself. The transcript is quite clear."

Volkov smiled at the news. "What do we know about the posters?"

"That took a little more doing. The two parties involved obviously knew their way around computers. Both of them routed their access through multiple proxies and VPN lines in order to throw off their scent, but I was able to trace the original poster by his device itself. Few people know this, but whenever data is accessed on the Internet, the requesting device leaves a digital footprint. Normally this wouldn't be that big a deal if the user was working on a brand-name phone or computer, because there are literally millions of those devices floating around and they all have a similar footprint. But in this case, the device signature was extremely useful since the buyer in question was using a prototype manufactured by Payne Industries."

Volkov laughed at his opponent's error. Only a skilled hacker would have spotted it. "Excellent work! Truly excellent! And what about the seller?"

Blokhin was energized by his boss's praise. "It gets better, sir. As you know, we constantly keep tabs on your rivals in order to exploit their weaknesses whenever we can, and when I was trying to track down the seller through the digital mist, I started to notice some similarities in tactics between him and one of your competitors. The same proxies. The same VPN lines. The same everything. Sure, their IP information is obscured—meaning we couldn't track them to a specific location—but their pattern is still recognizable. And since I was already familiar with this particular pattern, I'm fairly confident I have identified the seller."

"Who is it?" Volkov growled.

"Your old friend Kaiser."

Volkov practically cackled with delight. Not because the two of them were comrades, but because they were bitter enemies. Two titans who clashed in the night, fighting for the same realm, each desperate to rid the world of the other.

Much like Volkov himself, Kaiser had emerged from nothing to launch a criminal empire. Starting as a supply sergeant in the U.S. military, he had realized he could make great money by delivering illegal goods to soldiers overseas. Long before Amazon, Kaiser had figured out a way to get people what they wanted faster than anyone else and had made millions in the process. But due to the proliferation of the Internet, Kaiser had been forced to change his business model and extend his network into new regions, and that included a profitable foray into Russia.

For the past decade, the two criminals had exchanged multiple body blows, yet neither had managed to knock out his opponent, despite several violent attempts.

But this seemed like a golden opportunity to finally finish the job.

That, and so much more.

In one fell swoop, Volkov could take out the Finn, the Americans, and Kaiser.

And as a billion-dollar bonus, maybe find a treasure as well.

Volkov was practically salivating. "When are they meeting?"

"Tomorrow night at nine."

"In Malta?"

"In Finland. On the southernmost island of Suomenlinna."

CHAPTER 54

Saturday, June 16
Helsinki, Finland

Unlike his flight to Malta, Payne was fully awake for his trip to Finland, if only to sort through everything that had occurred during the past thirty-six hours.

Shortly after documenting the ancient tunnel system on video, they had sealed up the historic site with sheets of opaque plastic before meeting Galea in the waiting van. Thrilled to get away unnoticed, he had dropped them back at Jarkko's yacht just before sunrise. Then they had sailed the boat back to sea for some much needed rest.

As always, Payne had taken first watch while the others got some sleep. He had been on duty for roughly an hour when Raskin had startled him with a new ringtone: the classic Johnny Rivers song, *Secret Agent Man*. Played at full volume on his phone, the tune had practically sent Payne diving to the floor for safety, but all was forgiven once Raskin had revealed the reason for his call: the Russians had found his digital breadcrumbs.

The beauty of Raskin's trap had been its simplicity. By faking a chat transcript from the beginning of the week and inserting it into a real message board, it had created the illusion that a negotiation had been conducted *prior* to Volkov's appearance in Malta, thereby lowering his suspicions and convincing him that it was a legitimate transaction. Based on everything they knew about Volkov, he would leap at the opportunity to get revenge in person, but just to make sure, they had added the name of one of his fiercest rivals to the mix to guarantee his presence.

Unbeknownst to Volkov, Payne and Jones had known Kaiser for years and had been given his blessing for the ruse. Truth be told, he was almost as eager to take out Volkov as they were, and they were more than happy to get his help with weapons and logistics.

A former supply sergeant in the U.S. military, Kaiser had started his operation in Kaiserslautern, Germany—hence the nickname—servicing the nearly fifty thousand NATO personnel living in the Kaiserslautern Military Community. Since the majority of the residents were Americans, he had realized that he could make great money by providing them with illegal exports from the States.

His business had blossomed from there, eventually turning into a criminal empire that extended all the way across Europe and into Russia. His most trusted smuggler on the Baltic Sea was a Finnish fisherman by the name of Jarkko, who had been with him for over a decade and had made a fortune in the process. Kaiser trusted him so much that he had given his name to two of his colleagues who were looking to smuggle an American historian named Allison Taylor out of Saint Petersburg before heading to Greece to look for treasure.

That was when Payne and Jones had first met Jarkko.

And it had happened in Helsinki.

Memories of Allison slowly became thoughts of Marissa as Payne stared out the window at the city below. He had purposely kept her and Ulster from this part of their plan. Not only for their safety—he didn't want them anywhere near Finland when this confrontation happened—but because he wasn't sure how she would react to his role in the upcoming battle.

To guarantee their security, he had flown them to Switzerland, where they would be protected by armed guards at the Ulster Archives while they searched for potential leads on the location of the Maltese treasure. Armed with new evidence from the Order's secret tunnel system, he hoped they would be able to find something of value in the Archives' files, much like Ulster had done with Cassar's portfolio.

Of course, Payne realized if his confrontation with Volkov didn't go as planned, the treasure hunt would be over, as would his life.

"There it is!" Jarkko said from the seat behind him. "Suomenlinna!"

"Wow," Jones muttered. "It's bigger than I thought it would be."

Jarkko snickered. "Jarkko hear this before."

Payne shifted his focus from the city to the north to the water beneath his plane. Scattered across the mouth of the harbor were dozens of brown islands, most of them small and uninhabited like rocky icebergs that never moved, but his gaze was drawn to the southeast where he spotted a stone bastion emerging from the Baltic Sea.

Spread across six islands, Suomenlinna was a massive sea fortress built by the Swedish crown in 1748 AD, back when Finland was still a part of the Swedish kingdom. Its original goal was to protect Helsinki from Russian expansionism, but it fell to them in 1808 AD, paving the way for Russia's occupation of Finland the following year. Isolated from Helsinki proper, Payne hoped that the island stronghold would protect innocents and help Jarkko defeat Volkov and his men, finally claiming a Finnish victory against Russian forces, as was its original intent.

Thankfully, they wouldn't be alone in their battle with Volkov. Kaiser was so excited about the possibility of eliminating his rival that he had flown to Helsinki on Friday morning before he had even received confirmation that Volkov's hackers had found the digital breadcrumb.

In his business, it was tough to know whom he could trust, so Kaiser had assembled a crew of his most loyal men. He had posted some on the ferryboats that serviced the complex to keep track of passengers and potential threats. He had kept a few on the island docks to monitor smaller boats, while several more patrolled the outer paths of the island with their eyes on the sea. He had dealt with Volkov long enough to know that he would come fully prepared.

As expected, Jarkko was able to help as well. Not only with men from his own network of smugglers—which was based in Helsinki and was far more vast than he had ever let on to Payne and Jones—but also with personnel on Suomenlinna. That was the main reason he had selected this island fortress as their battleground. He had sailed past it thousands of times on his way in and out of the harbor and was quite friendly with the Suomenlinna staff. He knew visitors would be long gone by 9:00 p.m. And thanks to the short northern nights, the sun wouldn't go down until long after Volkov had fallen.

That is, if things went the way they hoped.

Even with a sneak attack, Volkov realized he was at a slight disadvantage. He had roughly a day to plan an assault on an island fortress in Helsinki, where he would be facing a Finn, two former special forces operatives, and a horde of Kaiser's faceless thugs.

But thanks to Blokhin and his team of hackers, Volkov felt confident that he could pull it off. Not only could they erase his presence with their digital tricks, but they could also give him something that the other side didn't have: a squadron of remotely piloted drones.

The idea had come to Blokhin shortly after seeing the name "Suomenlinna" in the digital text that he had decrypted. He had remembered reading an article about a test that the Finnish postal service had conducted in 2015 where they had used drones to deliver packages of varying shapes and sizes between Helsinki and the island fortress, and he felt they could do something similar.

Having served as a test pilot for Volkov during the past year while working out the networking kinks, Blokhin knew that his boss owned several drones for aerial surveillance, and he suggested that this might be a good time to use them.

Volkov heartily agreed and added them to the rest of the equipment that he would be exporting from Russia via the Baltic Sea. He had no idea what the other side would be bringing, but he planned to exceed them in every way.

He would bring more men.

He would bring more weapons.

And he would bring down his opponent.

In his mind, this would be his best victory yet.

CHAPTER 55

Payne's jet landed in Helsinki in the early afternoon, then it taxied to a private hangar. Jarkko had made all of the arrangements in advance and directed the pilot where to go.

Both Payne and Jones sensed this wasn't the first time that Jarkko had used these facilities, a fact that Jarkko confirmed when he let it slip that it normally housed his plane.

Jones blinked a few times. "You have a plane?"

Jarkko nodded. "Of course Jarkko have plane. How else would Jarkko fly to yacht?"

"By buying a ticket."

Jarkko grimaced at the thought of all the restrictions on commercial flights. "That is no good for Jarkko. Jarkko hates tiny bottles. Jarkko prefers big ones filled with vodka, so Jarkko buys plane instead. In long run, Jarkko saves money."

Payne followed his logic. "The man has a point."

Jones thought back to when they had first met Jarkko. At the time, they had assumed he was a humble fisherman, who would help them get into Russia for a few thousand dollars. Little did they know that Kaiser had entrusted their safety to one of his most important smugglers in Eastern Europe. "Dammit, Jon. Why did I waste so much time as a detective? I could have been making the big bucks with Jarkko all along."

Jarkko shook his head. "Jarkko does not need partner. Jarkko needs assistant. Does David remember how Jarkko likes his coffee?"

Jones grinned, recalling the nasty concoction that Jarkko had nicknamed *Kafka* and had forced them to drink during their first introduction. "No water, just vodka."

Jarkko laughed and put Jones in a friendly headlock. "David remembers! If David keeps this up, he won't be homeless for long!"

As the pilot parked the plane and activated the automatic door, Payne smiled at the scene. He knew things would get more serious as their battle approached, but for now, they were just good friends horsing around for possibly the last time. "I hope that means what I think it means: you want to adopt DJ! You can't believe how long I've waited for this day to come! And with me out of work, the timing is perfect!"

Jones reached out for Payne and pretended to wail. "No Mommy! Don't let Uncle Jarkko take me! Bad touch! Bad touch!"

Jarkko laughed and rubbed the top of Jones's head. "Jarkko has always wanted bambino. Jarkko will name him Työtön. That is Finnish word for 'unemployed'."

Payne was about to follow Jarkko's joke with one of his own when an outsider entered the plane through the open hatch. Payne instinctively reached for his holstered gun and was ready to shoot the interloper if necessary, until he realized who the visitor was.

Dressed in his usual attire, Kaiser was wearing dark blue jeans, a faded T-shirt, and a brown leather jacket. In his late-fifties with a medium build and slicked-back gray hair, he wasn't the type of man who would stand out in a crowd, except for two noticeable things: he wore a black patch over his left eye and walked with a severe limp.

The injuries had occurred in the woods near Garmisch-Partenkirchen, Germany, while helping Payne and Jones on one of their adventures. An enemy combatant had tried to kill Kaiser with a Remington 750, a heavy-duty rifle frequently used for large game like hogs and bears. Although the gunman had missed Kaiser's head by a few inches, the bullet had struck the boulder that Kaiser had been hiding behind. The resulting shards had erupted into Kaiser's face, tearing through the soft flesh of his cheek and causing significant damage to his left eye.

Forced to flee the gunman on foot, Kaiser had sprinted through the woods toward an underground bunker that they had been protecting. Under heavy fire, he had leapt through the open hole in order to escape his pursuer, but Kaiser had landed awkwardly, rupturing his patellar tendon and tearing every major ligament in his left knee with a sickening snap.

And yet, his "snap" had paled in comparison to the one that followed. When the gunman made it to the bunker, he had peered through the open hole and spotted an unconscious Kaiser. He had raised his rifle to finish the job, but before he could, Payne had grabbed him from behind. Needing to kill the man in silence,

Payne had twisted the man's head with so much force that the vertebrae in his neck had popped like corn in a microwave. After that, Payne had tended to Kaiser's multiple wounds until they were able to get him off the mountain.

"I see nothing has changed," Kaiser announced with a smile. "Jarkko and DJ are still acting like assholes."

Jarkko heard Kaiser's voice and turned to greet his friend. Unfortunately for Jones, Jarkko forgot to release him from the headlock before he made the turn, and the resulting torque slammed Jones into one of the plane's reclining chairs.

Jarkko quickly let go. "Sorry, Työtön. Daddy didn't mean it."

Jones rubbed his side. "Tell that to my broken ribs."

Kaiser chimed in. "Trust me, it could've been worse."

Jones winced, oblivious. "Oh, yeah. How do you figure?"

Kaiser held up his cane and pointed to his eye patch.

Jarkko laughed. "Kaiser is right! Next time Jarkko aim for face!"

The four of them quickly exchanged pleasantries inside the plane, briefly catching up on old times before focusing on the matter at hand. Kaiser filled them in on the advanced reconnaissance that his team had done and let them know what equipment he had brought to help them achieve their goals, including a few special items from Payne Industries. He also let them know that every surveillance camera in the facility had been disconnected to prevent Volkov's hackers from getting a sneak peak at their strategy.

Payne and Jones were quite appreciative of his groundwork, but they also realized that he had limited experience in the field. For this to work as smoothly as possible, they knew they were going to have to take the lead.

They just hoped that Kaiser agreed.

Payne spoke up. "I know that we just rolled into town, and you've been here scouting things for a while. But if it's okay with you, we had a few ideas on how this should go down."

Kaiser said nothing at first. He just stared at him with his one good eye.

Like an angry Cyclops, who was capable of violence at any time.

A few seconds passed before a smile appeared on Kaiser's face. "Well, thank God for that! I was a fucking supply sergeant, not a decorated war hero. My job was to get equipment to the right place, then I sat back and watched you bullet catchers do the dirty work. You saw what happened the last time I was in the muck. You killed the bad guys, and I left on a stretcher."

Payne laughed, relieved. "I wasn't sure you remembered that. You were unconscious and leaking oil at the time."

"Trust me," Kaiser assured him. "I remember my debts, and I owe you big time for saving my life. That's why I was so excited to get your call. It's finally my chance to save yours."

Jones smiled. "And eliminate one of your biggest competitors."

Kaiser grinned. "That's just an added bonus."

CHAPTER 56

Payne, Jones, Jarkko, and Kaiser left the plane and walked across the private hangar to a giant whiteboard where a few of Kaiser's top men had gathered. Kaiser had prepped a lot of briefing rooms in his day, so he had everything that they needed, including a giant map of Suomenlinna and enough food to satisfy everyone's appetite, including Payne's.

In Finnish, *Suomen* means "Finland" and *linna* means "castle", but there was never an actual castle on this island complex. Built as a bastion fortress by the Swedes in 1748, Suomenlinna had expanded over the decades. In the early years, it had been tasked with defending Helsinki, but after the Finnish Civil War in 1918, the purpose of the military base had started to evolve.

First, a prison camp was built on one of the islands. Then in 1973, the complex was turned over to a civilian administration known as the Governing Body of Suomenlinna, and the presence of the military was drastically scaled back. Although a minimum-security penal colony still remains, Suomenlinna is one of the most popular tourist destinations in all of Finland. Several museums exist on the islands, as well as the last surviving Finnish submarine, *Vesikko*.

During his advance research, Payne had learned that Finland was banned from operating submarines after World War II because of the 1947 Paris Peace Treaty. As one of five subs to serve the Finnish Navy, the *Vesikko* had been kept in storage—while the others were sold and scrapped—until she could be turned into a museum ship. He hoped to tour the small vessel once this confrontation was over, but for the time being, he managed to stay on task.

As usual, Jones was the one in charge of tactics, a rarity in most military units since that duty normally fell to the lead officer. But Payne had never played by the rules. He had always believed it was the team leader's job to maximize the strengths of his squad, and he had recognized Jones's ability quite early on and had never regretted it. Despite his boyish energy and teenage sense of humor, Jones was a gray-bearded wizard when it came to strategy.

In this field alone, *he* was the oracle.

Able to see things before they even happened.

Jones introduced himself to Kaiser's men, who sat on folding chairs in front of the whiteboard. Jarkko and Kaiser grabbed seats in the front row, but Payne remained standing in the back of the room. He would keep an eye on things from there while Jones ran the briefing.

In order to get the room's attention, Jones amped up his personality to a whole new level. Over the years, he had found that was the quickest way to take charge of alpha males who were getting ready to put their lives on the line for a common cause.

"First things first," Jones said to the group. "Tell me about the local cops. As a black man carrying a gun, that's always number one on my list."

Jarkko laughed. "Don't worry, my friend. Jarkko has taken care of everything. The Finnish Navy sometimes conducts war games around the islands. The local police are expecting drills this evening, so they will not be alarmed by gunfire."

"Excellent!" Jones said with a grin. "Then let's get to it."

Jones pointed to the map and did his best to pronounce the names. "Suomenlinna is made up of six islands. Starting in the northwest and moving toward the southeast, there is Särkää, Länsi-Mustasaari, Pikku-Mustasaari, Iso-Mustasaari, Susisaari, and Kustaanmiekka."

He glanced at Jarkko. "How'd I do?"

Jarkko grinned. "You fucked up every one."

Jones nodded and admitted defeat. "Just like I knew I would. And I don't like to fuck up, so we're changing things right now. From this point forward, these are the new names of the islands: Six, Five, Four, Three, Two, and One."

To emphasize his point, he picked up a black magic marker and wrote the matching numeral on top of each island, following the same order he had announced to the group. "So no more of these Hakuna-Matata, Kumbaya, Pikachu-sounding names. When my team kills, we kill in English. Do I make myself clear?"

"Yes, sir," the group said in unison.

Jones pointed to Island 6 in the northwest corner of the map. It was the only island that wasn't connected to the other five. "What's special about this island? As far as I can tell, absolutely nothing! So let's ignore it completely, like women do with Jarkko."

Jarkko grinned. "It's true. They do—until they see Jarkko's yacht! Then they can't wait to play with Little Jarkko. Sometimes he gets excited and spits up on them!"

The group laughed, while Jones put a black "X" over Island 6.

"Moving on," Jones growled to get the room to settle down. He was in his element, completely in control of the team. He had done hundreds of briefings like this and had forgotten how much he enjoyed it. "Islands Five and Four. They sit to the northwest and are connected by small bridges. I highly doubt that Volkov and his men are going to land way over there. If they do, they'll have to hike a few klicks through the civilian part of Suomenlinna before they get anywhere near us, so I'm gonna cross them out of existence as well."

With one giant "X", he eliminated Island 5 and Island 4.

Jones put the cap back on the marker and then used it to tap on Island 3. It was the large island to the northeast. "According to Jarkko, the public ferry comes to the main quay on the north side of this island. Service will stop long before our scheduled meeting, so we fully expect all of the tourists and most of the employees to be gone before Volkov arrives. However, there's always a chance that Volkov tries to slip some of his men onto the island for advance reconnaissance. With that in mind, we need patrols—"

He pointed to specific locations on the map. "Here, here, and here."

Kaiser nodded from the front row. "I'll see to it."

"Good," Jones said as he glanced at Kaiser. "Is the comm gear working?"

"My patrols are using it as we speak, so we're good to go."

"How well do you know these men?"

"I handpicked them myself."

"Glad to hear it," Jones said as he turned back toward the map and drew a circle in the center of Island 3. "Who's your best long-distance shooter?"

A man in the second row raised his hand. "That would be me."

Jones glanced back at him. "What's your name?"

"Archer."

"Like the cartoon?"

Archer shook his head. "Like a bowman."

Jones nodded. "Good answer, because the cartoon Archer is a drunk douchebag. Are you either of those things?"

"No, sir."

"How's your eyesight?"

"Pretty fucking good."

"Prove it. What did I circle on the map?"

Archer didn't even need to look. "The church."

Jones smiled. "Which means you're a sober bowman who did his homework. Nice to meet you, Archer. I'm glad you're on my team. Why did I circle the church?"

"It was built on top of a hill. From up there, you can see everything."

"Just like God Himself!" Jones said in the voice of a preacher. "And he who hath the high ground always winneth the war! So that's where I want you with a sniper rifle: in the second-floor window, facing southeast. Make sure you bring a guard or two in case Volkov goes for the church. I don't want you worried about your six. I want you focused on your twelve. Understood?"

Archer nodded. "Yes, sir."

Jones glanced back at the map. He pointed to Island 2. "This is where things get tricky. There's a single bridge connecting Island Three and Island Two. In wartime, I would blow the fucking thing to bits to prevent a rear assault. But Jarkko claims we can't do that here. I highly doubt that Volkov is going to land on Three and hike it across the bridge, but the guy is a fucking lunatic, so who knows what the hell he's thinking? With that in mind, we need to position a heavy gun on the north edge of Two, right next to the bridge. If anyone tries to cross from Three, we need to light their asses up. Kaiser, do you have someone who can handle that?"

Kaiser nodded. "Consider it done."

"Good," Jones said as he shifted his focus back to the map. "As you've probably guessed by now, our goal is to funnel all of the action to the south. It's away from the prison and the civilian population in the upper islands—although we've been assured that those numbers will be kept to a minimum. Jarkko has talked to local personnel and warned them of the coming storm. In fact, he paid them good money to make sure that they had somewhere else to be during this skirmish. I hope to hell they remember, because Island Two and Island One will get hit."

With his magic marker, Jones drew a giant circle around the bottom two islands. Although they had different names, they were actually connected in the middle by a narrow land bridge. On each side of the grassy isthmus, there was a shallow inlet where boats could dock, and overlooking each inlet was a well-worn path that ran between Islands 2 and 1.

Jones tapped on the two inlets with his marker. "If I had to guess, I'd say Volkov is currently hiding on one of the islands to the east. When it's time, he'll send men here or here. But *not* men he likes. Certainly not friends or relatives—*unless* he has a cousin that he really hates. Why? Because we'll control the high ground above the inlets, and we'll slaughter anyone who tries to dock. And yet, I get the sense that he'll try to push through in order to draw our attention. I figure, if Volkov is coming to the party, he'll be more than willing to sacrifice some pawns before his arrival. I also get the sense that he'll search for the path of least resistance when he gets here, which is exactly what we want."

"Sir?" Archer said, confused by the comment.

Jones grinned. "We're going to open the front door and let him march right in."

CHAPTER 57

After the mission briefing, the group split up and headed in different directions. For this charade to work, they needed to make it look like an actual transaction was taking place on Suomenlinna. That meant they had to arrive at the island complex in different boats at different times in case Volkov's men were monitoring things from afar.

Dressed in green camouflage, Payne, Jones, and Jarkko left the airport in a bulletproof SUV with heavily tinted windows. With most of their preparations focused on the islands, Payne was concerned that Volkov might stage an attack before they even reached the water. Thankfully, this was where Jarkko's local contacts came in handy. He had them positioned throughout the region, keeping an eye out for anything suspicious along the route from the airport to the city.

Helsinki sits on the northern shore of the Gulf of Finland, which is the eastern arm of the Baltic Sea. Approximately two hundred miles from Russia, the capital city is flanked by thousands of small islands that protect its natural harbor. Sprawling for blocks along the scenic waterfront is the world-famous Kauppatori Market. It comes alive with tourists during the warmer months, attracting a wide variety of vendors who sell everything from fresh fruits and grilled salmon to fancy jewelry and animal pelts.

As the SUV headed behind the marketplace, memories of their last visit came flooding back. This was where Payne and Jones had met Jarkko for the first time. The three of them briefly reminisced about their initial encounter while they kept an eye on the road ahead. At this time of day, most of the vendors were packing up their brightly colored stalls and loading them into trucks. The sun would stay up for a few more hours, but the workers were calling it a night.

A few blocks later, Jarkko's driver pulled up to the gate of a private marina and punched in the appropriate code. The mechanical arm lifted, and he drove the SUV into a small parking lot next to the water. Payne and Jones climbed out of the back seat and surveyed their immediate surroundings. As they did, their attention was drawn toward the large building behind them.

On a hill to their west was Uspenski Cathedral, a spectacular red-bricked church with thirteen green-and-gold onion domes, representing Christ and the twelve apostles. Modeled after a sixteenth-century church in Moscow, its bricks came from the Bomarsund fortress in Aland, Finland, which had been destroyed during the Crimean War in 1854. Regardless of its beauty, the largest Russian Orthodox church in western Europe somehow filled them with dread, as if Volkov himself was peering down at them.

Despite their confidence, they were suddenly unnerved.

It was a feeling they weren't used to.

Although Volkov wasn't at the cathedral, one of his goons was. He was posing as a tourist and pretending to take pictures of the church's central dome and monolithic pillars.

When the tinted SUV drove past on the road below, he shifted his focus to the vehicle and snapped several pictures with his telephoto lens. He took several more when the three passengers exited the vehicle and walked toward a speedboat in the marina.

Using the camera's zoom, he inspected the faces of the men and compared them to the photos on his phone that he had been sent that morning.

They were a definite match.

The Finn and the Americans were in town.

And they were heading toward Suomenlinna.

He quickly sent a message to Volkov, who forwarded the news to his other goons. They were patiently waiting to make their move but wouldn't do it until Kaiser arrived.

Once he did, they would launch their assault.

Unable to turn off the security cameras at a major airport, Kaiser's men smuggled him from the briefing room in the private hangar to a terminal on the other side of the facility. That way if Volkov's men were monitoring the airfield, it would appear that he didn't come in contact with Payne and Jones prior to their meeting at Suomenlinna.

To continue the ruse, he also took a different route into Helsinki and launched his boat from a different marina. Instead of departing from a marina near the cathedral, his driver took him to the West Harbour on the opposite side of the city. His voyage to the island complex would be slightly longer, but that was all a part of their plan. His friends wanted to get there first to make sure everything was in place for his arrival.

For this to work, their timing needed to be precise.

Jarkko parked his speedboat in the guest marina on the north side of Island 2, where he was met by two burly men with rifles who worked in the nearby Suomenlinna Dry Dock. The facility was massive and occupied the northern third of the island, but thanks to a narrow channel that separated it from the southern part of the isle, it would be kept out of harm's way.

Over the years, Jarkko had brought his boats to the dry dock for repairs and had stored them there during the cold winter months when the Gulf of Finland was clogged with ice. On several occasions, he had also utilized the workers' expertise to hide certain contraband in the gaps below his decks, so he was more than just friendly with the staff.

They were on his payroll.

In Finnish, these men assured him that they had spread word amongst the civilian population on the island about the upcoming battle and everyone had departed on the earlier ferries. The men had also flipped the circuit breakers for Island 1 and 2, which knocked out all of the security cameras in the warzone. Jarkko thanked them for their efforts by slipping each of them an envelope stuffed with cash before they headed back to guard the marina.

No one would be docking there on their watch.

Payne glanced at Jarkko. "We good?"

Jarkko nodded. "No people. No power."

Jones smiled. "Glad to hear it."

The trio hustled past the shipyard on their right toward the lone bridge to Island 3. As promised, Kaiser had positioned a man with an assault rifle on the southern side of the channel. Payne chatted with him briefly to make sure he understood his importance to the master plan. The guard seemed nervous, but that was perfectly normal before a major battle.

Thanks to the fortified bastions along the water, there were limited places to dock on Island 1 and 2. Unfortunately, there were plenty of docks on Island 3, 4, and 5. But as long as Volkov's men couldn't cross this bridge, the trio wouldn't need to worry about a rear assault.

Unless, of course, the Russians decided to swim for it.

If they did that, then all bets were off.

But Payne and Jones doubted they would.

They were facing henchmen, not frogmen.

Based on experience, they knew goons tried to stay dry.

Because of his limp, Kaiser ordered his boat to drop him off at the narrow isthmus between Island 1 and 2. It was as close to the rendezvous point as possible. From the western inlet, he had a short walk up the bank to a well-worn path that led to the center of the southernmost island.

That's where the fake exchange was supposed to take place.

When he reached the top of the knoll, Kaiser noted that his guards were no longer patrolling the western flank near the massive cannons from the abandoned fort. Instead, his men had concealed themselves in the trees and foliage scattered across the verdant isle. Having traveled the world, Kaiser noticed the similarities to the rolling hills of Scotland. As the wind whipped in from the sea, the overgrown grasses danced in spite of the coming war.

If not for the gun in his hand, he would have stopped to admire the beauty.

Positioned in the center of the island, Payne and Jones smiled when they saw Kaiser crest the hill. Ever since they had left his side at the airport, they had been concerned for his safety.

Obviously Kaiser knew his men better than they did, but Payne and Jones realized that loyalty only went so far. For the right price, they knew anything could be bought, and they were worried that this would be the perfect time for a guard to go shopping for a better deal.

Now that Kaiser was here, they could keep an eye on him.

Unfortunately, so could the traitor.

CHAPTER 58

Payne and Jones heard the drones before they could see them.

It started as a soft hum, carried across the island by the steady breeze, but as the machines got closer to shore, the noise transformed into something menacing, as if a swarm of killer bees had decided to attack Finland.

Jarkko glanced toward the sky. "What is that?"

Jones cursed as he searched the horizon. "Drones."

Payne clutched his assault rifle. "I don't remember drones in your briefing."

Jones kept searching. "Really? Because I covered *every* contingency in great detail. Maybe you couldn't hear me from the back of the room."

"Yeah, that must be it."

Jarkko looked at Jones. "Jarkko don't remember this. What is plan for drones?"

"Good question," Kaiser said as he finally reached the others. He was flanked by two muscular bodyguards. One was carrying a briefcase, just to complete the ruse.

"Easy," Jones said. "If you see a drone, shoot it."

Because of the swirling wind, it was tough to locate the direction of the sound. They kept searching from their position in the center of Island 1, but their vision was obscured by the rolling hills and interior defense walls that surrounded them. Payne ran from the path and climbed onto a wall to their east. Like an abandoned temple forgotten by time, the cut stone was covered with a thick layer of moss.

Payne touched his earpiece. "Archer, can you hear me?"

Archer replied from his sniper post in the church on Island 3. "Barely. I'm getting all kinds of interference. What about you?"

Payne answered. "That isn't interference. Those are drones."

"Drones? From where?"

Payne grimaced as he turned in a circle. "We were kind of hoping *you* could tell *us* that."

"Oh," Archer blurted. Since the church was built on top of a steep hill, he had the best vantage point of Islands 1 and 2. If he couldn't see the drones, then they were most likely coming in behind the church from the north. "I can hear the fuckers, but I can't—"

A loud roar filled Payne's comm, temporarily garbling his communication with the sniper. When it returned, Archer was in the middle of shouting a warning.

"—buzzed right past me! They're coming in low and hot!"

"From which direction?" Payne demanded.

"They flew past the shipyard and over the bridge to Island Three!"

A moment later, Payne could see them to the northeast.

Known as *octocopters* because of their eight fully functional propellers, these unmanned aerial vehicles had greater uplift, power, and acceleration than the smaller *quadcopters* and *hexacopters* that were cheaper and more commonly used by the public. The octocopters were also much louder. Not only could they reach dizzying heights, but they were incredibly agile and could fly through strong wind, which was crucial around Suomenlinna.

Unfortunately for Blokhin, he had neglected to factor in one crucial thing when he had suggested their use on this particular mission. Due to the limited range of consumer drones, Blokhin and his team of hackers had been forced to leave the comfort of their warehouse in Moscow for a boat in the Gulf of Finland where they would control the crafts with touchscreens.

Four of the drones were being used for aerial surveillance.

But the fifth one had been equipped with a special surprise.

Payne spotted the drones as they rounded the corner and skimmed the water near the isthmus between Islands 1 and 2. He raised his rifle and was prepared to shoot, but before he could, the flock scattered and zigzagged across the sky in multiple directions.

One headed north. One headed south.

Another soared across the island to the west.

A fourth one climbed vertically and remained in the east.

Payne focused his aim on that one, since it was closest to his position on the stone wall, but it was like trying to track a hummingbird in a hurricane. The wind was swirling, and the drone was darting back and forth, as if it knew it was being hunted.

Payne remained patient, waiting for the perfect moment to pull his trigger—when his attention drifted to something that wasn't there. He had counted five drones when they had first appeared, but now he could only account for four.

He glanced behind him and saw a group of men standing in the center of the island where their "transaction" was supposed to occur. Jones was with Jarkko. And Kaiser was there with two of his bodyguards. All clustered in one place.

In a flash, Payne knew what was about to happen.

"Move!" he shouted as he jumped off the wall. "Get away from there!"

With a rifle in his grasp, Jones had been tracking the drone to his west when he heard a shout from behind. Due to the loud buzzing of the propellers, he couldn't make out the words. He turned around and saw his best friend sprinting toward them from the east. He was frantically waving his arms for them to move.

That's when it clicked for Jones, too.

With no time for words, he grabbed Jarkko by the arm and pulled him toward the west as the fifth drone plummeted toward earth. Confused by the shouting, Kaiser's bodyguards assumed the threat was coming from somewhere on the island itself, so they shifted their focus to the surrounding terrain.

Meanwhile, Payne kept running toward the target.

Kaiser realized what was about to happen a split-second before impact. He wasn't sure why, but he knew he was about to get run over by a muscular locomotive that was coming at him full steam. So he let his body go limp to absorb the impact.

Payne buried his shoulder into Kaiser's gut like a linebacker sacking a quarterback, but instead of tackling him to the ground, Payne arched his back and kept his knees pumping as he scooped the lifeless man off the ground and kept on running.

A second later, the kamikaze drone came crashing down.

Armed with an explosive payload, the device erupted on impact, sending shrapnel in every direction and creating a massive fireball that could be seen by the neighboring islands.

Having piloted the killer drone himself, Volkov grinned as he tossed the controller to the ground. Volkov would have preferred to slit Kaiser's throat with a knife, but he still got plenty of satisfaction watching him and his men get blown to bits on the tiny screen—even if that meant he had destroyed a potentially key piece of evidence to finding the treasure in the process.

In his mind, a long-distance kill was still a kill.

And all of his goons had watched him do it.

That was how to earn respect in Russia.

By getting your hands dirty.

Volkov and nearly two-dozen henchmen had done all of their prep work on the far side of Vallisaari, a large island just to the east of Suomenlinna. But now that Volkov had landed the first strike, it was time to unleash the next wave of his attack.

With a nod of his head, four men started the engines on their rigid-hulled inflatable boats. Made of flexible tubes, the watercrafts were lightweight but high-performance and could hold up to six men each. Filled to capacity with armed Russians, three of them took off for the island complex, while the fourth one waited for Volkov.

Once he climbed aboard, they headed across the water as well.

Payne felt the explosion before he saw the damage.

The force of the blast threw him violently to the ground in a tangle of body parts, some of which weren't his. Temporarily disoriented from the concussive sound, Payne sat dazed in the grass as he tried to make sense of what he was seeing.

Two bodyguards were engulfed in flames. They screamed in agony as their skin bubbled off before they finally gave in to the pain. One after the other, they fell to the earth like trees in a forest fire, amidst the rubble of the device that had fallen from the sky.

Payne blinked. Then he blinked again.

Then he heard his name.

Not once. But twice.

And it came from underneath him.

So Payne rolled to his side to see who it was.

Kaiser was staring up at him with his one good eye.

He was just as dazed as Payne.

But he definitely wasn't dead.

"Jon!" Jones shouted as he staggered over to his friend. He had been farther from the impact than Payne but was still hearing bells. "Can you hear me?"

Payne opened and closed his jaw. "That depends. Are you humming?"

Jones dropped to one knee. "No."

Payne shook his head. "Then I can't hear you."

"Good. I'm deaf, too."

Payne looked over at Kaiser, who was still trying to process what had happened. He just sat there staring at his dead men as Jarkko tended to him. "Is he okay?"

Jarkko nodded. "Dazed, but fine."

Jones glanced over. "Please don't take this the wrong way, but Finland sucks."

Jarkko shook his head. "*This* is not Finland. *This* is Russia. That is why Jarkko hate them so much. They come to Jarkko's country and take what they want—*hurt* who they want. They have been doing this for years. And Jarkko is fed up. It is time to make them stop."

Payne leaned over and grabbed his rifle. "Fuck it. I have nothing better to do."

Jones nodded. "Me, neither."

"Good," Jarkko growled. "Then let's kill those commie bastards."

CHAPTER 59

With many cannons from the old fortress still mounted along the outer flanks of Island 1, there were several tunnels to service them. Cut through the exterior defense walls to the south were multiple stone archways that allowed lookouts to watch for invaders from the sea. The passageway that connected the arches ran along the southern shore, far from the combat zone in the middle of the island.

In Jones's mind, that was the best place to stash Kaiser.

Since his personal bodyguards were dead and he was hobbling on one good leg, Jones directed him there with two of his men, who could keep an eye on him during the battle.

No pun intended.

As Kaiser limped for cover, Payne, Jones, and Jarkko focused on the remaining aircrafts. Based on the drones' positioning—one to the north, south, east, and west—it seemed that their purpose was surveillance, not assault. That made sense, given Volkov's proclivity for cameras and video feeds. Unfortunately, these octocopters were powerful enough to soar well above the surface of the island, making them tough to shoot down in the gusty wind.

Having used drones for his detective work, Jones had a pretty good sense of their limitations. With that in mind, he set off to solve their drone problem, just as Payne received word from their sniper about the Russians.

"We have incoming," Archer said from the church.

Payne put his hand over his ear. "More drones?"

"Boats. Three of them. Filled with six gunmen each."

Jarkko groaned. "Do you *ever* have good news?"

Archer smiled. "Just calling them as I see them."

As Jones jogged behind a bastion that cut across the center of the island, he interrupted their chat with a question of his own. "Where are the boats coming from?"

Archer answered. "The big island to the east."

Jones laughed. "Nailed it."

Payne thought back to the briefing. Although Jones had neglected to factor in the drones, he *had* predicted where Volkov would launch his assault from and where they would land, and he had deployed Kaiser's men accordingly. "About time you got something right."

Jones kept on jogging. "What's that supposed to mean?"

"At no point did you say *Sputnik* was going to crash into the center of Island One."

"Yes, I did," Jones claimed. "That must've been when you were chowing down on Kaiser's spread. Wow, that sounded way more sexual than I intended."

Payne fought the urge to laugh over an open comm. They needed the others to stay sharp as Volkov's henchmen approached. "Archer, where are the boats headed?"

"One to the south. One to the eastern docks. And one to Island Three."

Jones slammed on his brakes. The boat to the south made perfect sense. It would head around the fortified walls of the southern tip and try to make land on the western side of the isthmus where Kaiser had landed earlier. Jones had sensed that would happen and had stashed plenty of men there to handle the issue. Wearing green camouflage, they were concealed in the tall weeds of the higher ground and would spring out at the appropriate time.

The boat heading to the eastern docks made sense as well. It was the shortest route from Vallisaari, the island to the east, and was just south of the narrow isthmus. Jones had planned for a boat to make land on the eastern shore, and the docks were a likely choice. That's why he had positioned men in the trees between the docks and the isthmus to the north. No matter which of those options was selected by the Russians, Jones had men to cover it.

But the boat going to Island Three didn't make sense at all.

If the northern drone's feed was working, Volkov would see that the bridge between Island 2 and 3 was being guarded by a heavy gun. Although Jones knew that Volkov would gladly sacrifice some men, it didn't make sense to lose them there.

Unless...

Jones thought back to the initial drone attack. The octocopters had flown down the narrow channel between Island 2 and 3, yet the man protecting the bridge didn't call in their approach or fire upon the aircraft as they flew right past him. Either the man had fallen asleep, or Volkov had managed to take him out—whether by blade or by bribe.

"Archer," Jones said over the comm. "I need eyes on the bridge. Is it still covered?"

"Hold on." Archer used the scope on his sniper rifle to check it out. A few seconds later, he confirmed what Jones had suspected. "That's a negative. That post has been deserted."

Jones cursed several times before Payne interrupted his flow.

"Don't worry," Payne assured him. "I got the bridge. You stay on the drones."

Jones nodded. "What about the—"

"I'll handle it. Meanwhile, switching to channel ten."

The beauty of this particular communication system was the ability to password protect certain channels. Since one of Kaiser's men had turned on them, they couldn't continue to broadcast on an open line without being compromised, so the coded channel allowed them to maintain communication. Only the people at the initial briefing had access to channel ten, and that did not include the guard who had abandoned his post at the bridge.

"Checking ten," Payne announced on the new channel. "Sound off."

Jones, Jarkko, Kaiser, Archer, and a few others checked in.

"Good," Jones said once they were done. "Enough with the pleasantries. Kaiser, who the fuck was guarding the bridge?"

Kaiser answered from the tunnel. "His name is Jim Harrison. Been with me for a while. A fuckin' American, if you can believe it. Hard to believe he would sell me out to a Russky."

Payne remembered him clearly. Shaved head, thick build, no neck. He had chatted with him briefly as they had passed his station after leaving the dry dock. Payne had sensed Harrison was nervous, but he had chalked it up to pre-battle jitters. Now he knew it had been more than that. "Loyalty only goes so far. Hopefully, he's the only one."

Kaiser groaned. "Should I let the others know?"

Payne nodded. "Might as well, but I get the sense he'll be hiding. He probably crossed the bridge and headed to Island Three."

"Should I send men after him?"

"No," Payne ordered. "Stick to the plan. We all have jobs to do, and we need to do them. Jarkko and I are on the bridge. DJ, you got the drones. And Kaiser, you stay hidden."

"What about me?" Archer asked.

"Do you still have your rifle?"

"Yes, sir."

"Then start using it."

Despite the explosion in the center of the island, no shots had been fired until the Russians tried to make land on the eastern shore. As soon as the first henchman jumped out of the boat to tie its line to the dock, Archer followed his orders.

A split-second later, the Russian's head exploded in a puff of pink mist.

Since the sniper's shot had come from the north, the five remaining Russians scrambled onto the dock and then sprinted toward the cover of the nearby trees, but all that did was make it easier on Kaiser's men, who had been positioned perfectly by Jones.

Dressed in green camouflage, they blended in with the leaves that surrounded them. From a distance, it seemed like the trees themselves had issued the death sentence. Before the thugs even knew what was happening, they were gunned down in a torrent of bullets.

In the blink of an eye, a quarter of Volkov's goons were dead.

From his boat in the Gulf of Finland, Blokhin cursed in Russian while watching the events unfold on his screen. He was controlling the eastern drone but had failed to spot Kaiser's men hidden in the trees, and that had led to the death of his comrades.

If the hacker had been given more time, he probably could have figured out a way to mount an infrared camera on the drone, which might have picked up the heat signatures of the enemy gunmen, but there was nothing he could do about it now.

Instead, he needed to shift his focus to Volkov, whose boat was a minute behind the initial three and was planning to make shore on the southeastern tip of the island. In order to prevent another grievous mistake, Blokhin ordered the driver of his boat to take them around the northern side of Vallisaari, where he could keep on eye on Volkov from above and from the water.

As a man of science, Blokhin believed in the power of information. As far as he was concerned: the more data, the better.

Blokhin turned his camera toward the south to make sure that the area was clear for his boss's arrival. While scanning the twisty paths that weaved throughout this part of the island, Blokhin noticed a man limping past an internal defense wall. When he zoomed in closer, he instantly recognized the figure.

"Shit!" Blokhin said in Russian. He immediately pushed the button on his headset in order to notify Volkov. "Sir, I have bad news. Kaiser is still alive."

Volkov seethed with anger. "How is that possible?"

"I'm not sure, sir. But I'm watching him as we speak."

If Volkov had been alone, he would have lashed out in rage, but sitting on a boat with five of his best henchmen, he realized he needed to keep his composure. So he took a deep breath and tried to spin the report to his advantage. "Good! I'm glad to hear it! After all of these years, I won't be fully satisfied with Kaiser's death unless I do it with my bare hands!"

Payne was a large man, but he was pretty light on his feet.

In a former life, he had been a star athlete at the Naval Academy, playing both football and basketball at a very high level. Thanks to his impeccable conditioning, he could still run faster than most people half of his age, and that was apparent as he sprinted across the isthmus to Island 2 and continued his charge toward Island 3.

Unfortunately, his running partner was not blessed with the same set of skills. Fueled by a steady diet of greasy foods and vodka, Jarkko struggled to keep up with his friend until he temporarily gave up and left the path to throw up behind a small cluster of houses on Island 2. While gagging but never puking, Jarkko spotted something in one of the driveways that would help his cause immensely: an electric golf cart.

Though not a religious man, Jarkko said a short prayer of thanks when he spotted the key in the ignition. He climbed in, started it up, and then sped toward his friend, who was sprinting toward the distant bridge.

With his ears still ringing from the blast, Payne heard the motorized hum behind him and assumed it was another drone. He was almost ready to turn and fire at the approaching craft when he heard the unmistakable sound of a horn. Just to be safe, Payne dashed from the path into the nearby trees until he could identify the source of the sound.

Much to his surprise, the cart skidded to a stop in front of him. Jarkko grinned. "Mind if Jarkko play through?"

Payne emerged from the trees. "Where in the hell did—you know what? It doesn't matter. You can tell me on the way."

Jarkko slid over to the passenger seat. "Jon better drive. Jarkko gonna be sick."

Payne laughed as he hopped in and pressed the accelerator.

The northern drone hovered high above Island 2. With its rotating camera, it had a clear view of the entire island as well as the northern section of Island 1.

The drone pilot, who was on the same boat as Blokhin and the other hackers, zoomed in on the golf cart as it headed toward the unmanned bridge. Quickly calculating the distance in his head, he realized that the cart would get there before the second boat could dock on Island 3 and get its passengers across the bridge.

"Boat two," he said into his radio. "Abort your approach."

The captain of the speeding boat slowed it to a crawl. "Why?"

"The Finn and the American are nearly at the bridge."

The captain cursed. He had fully expected the desertion of Kaiser's guard to give him and his men a clear passage into the battle zone. "Give me an alternative."

The drone pilot scanned the northern edge of Island 2.

Although it was lined with exterior defense walls, there was a small section that had been cleared for a tourist attraction. He had no idea if Kaiser's men were waiting in the trees, but even if they were, it appeared the boat could safely put to shore behind a relic from Finland's past. "Head toward the submarine."

CHAPTER 60

Payne didn't want to be accidentally shot by his sniper, so he called in the information about his vehicle. "Just a heads-up. Jarkko and I are headed toward the bridge on a golf cart."

Archer laughed. "Trying to squeeze in nine before the Russians arrive?"

Payne grinned. "Something like that."

Over the radio, Jones pretended to be annoyed. "You white dudes are all the same. Treating this world as your personal playground. You should be ashamed of yourselves."

"Relax, man. You're welcome to join us."

"Yes," Jarkko added. "We need a good caddy."

"Screw you," Jones said with a laugh. "I'm kind of busy at the moment. I'm trying to protect your lives with an act of heroism."

"By shooting unarmed drones?" Payne asked.

"I actually had something bigger in mind."

"Us, too," Payne bragged. "At least, that's what I'm planning. I think Jarkko needs a nap."

Jarkko groaned. "Jarkko wanted revenge. Now Jarkko wants drink. Where is clubhouse?"

Archer cleared his throat. "Sorry to be the bearer of bad news, but I might need to cancel your plans. The Russians just changed course. They're turning toward Island Two."

Payne slammed on the brakes. "Fucking drones! They probably spotted our cart. Where are they headed now?"

"Toward the submarine," Archer replied.

Jones chimed in. "We have a few men guarding the eastern side of isthmus. They're half a klick from the sub. I can send them over."

Payne pushed the accelerator to the floor and turned sharply to his right, much to Jarkko's chagrin. "I'll beat them there, but do it anyway. Just in case Jarkko starts to puke."

The third Russian boat cleared the southern tip of Island 1 and turned north. It headed past the exterior defensive walls that lined the western ridge of the island and the massive cannons that pointed toward a distant enemy that hadn't crossed the horizon in years.

In the glory days of the fortress, Finnish soldiers would have manned those cannons, and the boat would have been sunk before it even approached the shore. But in this digital age, a consumer drone hovered high above the western flank, making sure that the boat was clear to approach the inlet of the western side of the isthmus between Island 1 and 2.

If Blokhin had been forthright and had shared his earlier blunder with his fellow pilots, they would have known what to look for on their control screens, but since he had chosen to conceal the information in order to protect his own ass, the pilot of the western drone made the same mistake as his team leader.

He guided the boat to a slaughter.

Kaiser's men hid patiently in the thick trees on the higher ground. They waited until the rigid-hulled inflatable boat was dragged ashore by the Russians, who then turned and headed up the same ridge that Kaiser had climbed earlier.

And then his men opened fire from the trees.

One after another, the henchmen were mowed down in a torrent of copper and lead. As they died, they rolled back down the hill toward the rocky shore where they bled into the inlet like seals in an Inuit village. When the massacre was over, the shallow water had turned red, and six more goons were dead.

During his advance planning, Volkov had studied the southernmost island of Suomenlinna like a chessboard. He realized it was well protected by bastions on three sides, and he knew the fourth side—the isthmus to the north—would undoubtedly be guarded.

And yet, Volkov had sent two boats there anyway.

To achieve victory, he knew he had to sacrifice some pawns.

His goal all along was to draw the attention of Kaiser's men to the north while he headed to the large quay to the south. In his mind, it was the only suitable place for him to make an entrance, since it had literally been built for royalty.

Known as the King's Gate, it was the iconic symbol of Suomenlinna and the main entrance to the fortress. Built on the site where the ship carrying King Adolf Frederick of Sweden had been anchored while he inspected the construction of the complex in 1752, the two-story gate was made with rustic masonry and framed with marble stones.

Two decades later, the gate had been transformed into a draw-bridge, and wide stairs built from Swedish limestone had led down toward the water. Unfortunately, cannon fire during the Crimean War had destroyed the original quay and many of the steps in the nineteenth century, but the King's Gate had been refurbished multiple times over the years, most recently for Suomenlinna's 250th anniversary in 1998.

And the end result was quite impressive.

Particularly when approaching it by sea.

Impeccably dressed in a blue suit, Volkov felt like George Washington crossing the Delaware as he made his way toward the fortress, but unlike the courageous American general, Volkov remained seated in the back of his boat, hidden behind his men in case someone opened fire as they drew near.

"Are we clear?" Volkov asked on his comm.

Blokhin monitored his approach from above. As far as he could tell, the southeastern flank was wide open. "All clear, sir. Kaiser's men are headed toward the submarine."

"And where is Kaiser?"

"He is hiding in the tunnel to your south."

Prior to his mission briefing, Jones had asked to see a full inventory list in order to make sure that all of the equipment that he had requested had made it to Helsinki.

While going over their supplies, Jones's eyes had practically popped out of his head when he had spotted one item in particular. He had instantly asked about its presence on Suomenlinna, and Kaiser had said it had been his job as a supply sergeant to know what the troops might need to complete their duties even before they realized it themselves.

Jones had laughed it off at the time. He didn't think there was any chance in hell that he would be tempted to remove the item from its crate unless Volkov attempted a hostile insertion with a heavily armored helicopter, but lo and behold, it was the first thing Jones had thought of when the drones had made their appearance.

From personal experience, he knew that it was difficult to control drones in windy conditions without line of sight, so he reasoned that Volkov's mission control would be located on a boat in the Gulf of Finland where they could keep an eye on things. And since he had accurately predicted that Volkov's men would be based in Vallisaari, Jones felt there was a damn good chance that the boat would be floating in the water to the east of Suomenlinna.

Hiding in the trees between the isthmus to the north and the King's Gate to the south, Jones used field binoculars to spot the motorboat just across the channel between the islands. He watched for a moment, just to make sure the men onboard were actually controlling the drones. Once he was certain of their involvement, he reached down and picked up his weapon.

Nicknamed the *Vampir*, the RPG-29 was a Soviet rocket-propelled grenade (RPG) launcher. Adopted by the Soviet Army in 1989, it was the last RPG to be used by the Soviet military before the fall of the Soviet Union in 1991. Over the years, it had been phased out by more modern rocket-propelled weapons, but it was easy to find on the black market in Eastern Europe. And in spite of its age, it was still incredibly lethal.

Particularly in the hands of an experienced soldier.

Jones placed the tube-style, breech-loading, anti-tank rocket system on his shoulder, and then lined up the boat with the optical sight on top of the launch tube. Underneath was a shoulder brace for proper positioning, along with a pistol-grip trigger mechanism.

Prior to launch, Jones stepped out of the trees and steadied his breath as he studied the movement of the sea. The craft bobbed ever so slightly in the water near the northern tip of Vallisaari. If it had been farther out in the water, it would have been a much more difficult shot, but from this distance, Jones knew that the drones were about to be grounded for good.

Blokhin was focused on Volkov's boat as it made its way toward the King's Gate, but out of the corner of his eye, the hacker noticed a bright flash of light. He turned his head to the north and followed the loud roar as the sound drew closer.

Loaded with a TBG-29V thermobaric anti-personnel round, the Vampir had ignited the rocket before the projectile had even left the barrel, sending a massive discharge out of the rear of the weapon—which is why Jones had left the tree line. The missile instantly deployed eight fins as it left the launcher, which stabilized the rocket during its flight toward the boat.

"Fuck me," Blokhin said in Russian.

A second later, he and his hacker friends were punished for the past several years of their lives, time spent covering up hundreds of murders and thousands of crimes for Volkov and his comrades. And in an ironic twist, the hackers' deaths would never be reported—just like many of the crimes they had concealed—because the impact of the missile was so catastrophic that there would be no remains left to identify.

Jones felt the shockwave across the channel as the boat erupted in flames and debris. Unlike a conventional condensed explosive, the thermobaric round used the surrounding air to generate a high-temperature explosion, making the blast much more devastating.

Despite the show in front of him, Jones shifted his focus to the air above. He scanned the surrounding sky until his gaze latched onto the eastern drone as it plummeted from the sky and fell harmlessly into the cold water of the Gulf of Finland.

Behind him, the other three drones dropped as well.

Clearing the heavens of aerial surveillance.

And extinguishing Volkov's main advantage.

CHAPTER 61

Payne heard the blast while driving to the submarine. From his position on Island 2, he had no idea what had exploded until Jones called it in.

"Sorry about the noise," Jones said as he dashed back into the trees. "But I just took out mission control with a rocket launcher."

For the briefest of moments, Payne had been concerned that Volkov had brought out the heavy artillery to breech Suomenlinna. He was relieved to find out that it was his friend doing the damage. "You bastard! I wanted to use the RPG."

"I have to admit: it felt like old times."

"Speaking of time, shouldn't you be headed to the King's Gate?"

"Damn!" Jones said as he kept on running. He needed to be in position for Volkov's arrival. "Can't a brother have a moment to relish his victory? I just took out five Russians, four drones, and one boat in a single shot! I'd like to see you top that."

"Yeah, well, I'm getting ready to attack a submarine on a golf cart!"

Jones grinned. "Good luck with that."

"I'll be fine. I have Jarkko to help."

Jarkko groaned. "Jarkko no help. Jarkko stay in cart."

Payne laughed at his out-of-shape friend. "No worries. You won't like what I have in mind anyway."

Measuring 134 feet in length and 26 feet in height, the Finnish sub *Vesikko* sat on concrete blocks at the bottom of a hill on the edge of the water. Out of service since 1946, the submarine was about to see its first action in decades.

Shortly after the explosion near Vallisaari, the Russian boat reached the rocky shore, just north of the isthmus between Island 1 and 2. Using the submarine as a shield, the six henchmen crouched behind the vessel as they figured out their next move. No longer able to rely on the drones above, they had to decide how to proceed on their own. Unfortunately, these goons were better at following orders than making decisions.

Temporarily hidden by the *Vesikko*, a gunman named Alexei leaned back and admired the sub's color scheme. The bottom half of the vessel was coated red, while the top half was painted black and white. To gauge how thick the metal was, he knocked on the outer hull. He grinned like a child when it made a hollow clanging sound.

Alexei whispered in Russian to the goon on his left. "Does the sub still work?"

The goon glared back. "How the fuck should I know?"

Alexei shook his head in disappointment. "Damn, Vasily. There's no need to be rude."

Vasily snapped at him. "Unless you know how to pilot a Finnish sub, I don't see how your question could possibly be relevant."

Alexei sighed. "If the sub still works, perhaps it is filled with fuel. If the fuel is shot, perhaps the sub explodes. I don't know about you, but I think *that* is relevant."

Vasily grunted. "You make a good point. Hey, Dmitry!"

Dmitry glanced at him. "Shhh!"

Vasily shook his head. "Alexei has an important question."

Alexei spoke up. "If submarine fuel is shot, will it explode?"

Dmitry stared at Alexei. "Why? Is it leaking fuel?"

"I don't believe so. I meant the fuel *inside* the submarine."

Dmitry groaned at the stupidity of his team. Now he knew why his cousin had wanted to leave Volkov's empire to become a plumber. "The submarine is sitting on concrete blocks on dry land. There is no fuel inside the submarine. It is a museum ship. Not a vessel of war. For the time being, we are perfectly safe. Now shut the hell up before you give us away!"

Unfortunately for Vladimir and the rest of his crew, Payne already knew their position. And thanks to his advance research on the sub, he knew exactly how to exploit the situation.

Payne entered the water right around the corner from the *Vesikko*, where the thick trees hugged the shore. From there, he eased into waist-deep water and sank into a crouch while keeping his head and weapon above the waterline as he slowly crept toward the sub.

Although his rifle would probably function while wet, he preferred to keep it dry since he wasn't certain about its upkeep. He knew dry-gun lubricants and modern gun paints typically repelled water, but he had always been meticulous with his weapons prior to waterborne operations and wasn't willing to risk his life on someone else's maintenance.

In his former career, he had conducted hundreds of missions against all kind of enemy vehicles: boats, planes, tanks, helicopters, jeeps, Humvees, horses, camels, and even a train. But in all of his years of service, this was the first time he would ever fire at a submarine. If he'd had a military bucket list, this would have been on it—despite the weird circumstance.

Normally gunmen hid *inside* a vehicle instead of behind it.

And submarines were most effective when underwater.

But he wasn't going to point out their mistakes until it was too late.

"Now," Payne whispered into his comm.

Hidden in the trees on top of the hill that overlooked the submarine, Jarkko heard the command in his ear and grinned. Despite his nausea, he summoned all of his strength and courage to lean forward and hit the horn in the golf cart.

Then he did it again. And again. And again.

Honk! Honk! Honnnnnnk! Honnnnnnkkkk!

In the valley below, the Russians heard the honking and peered around the edge of the submarine to see if anyone was coming down the path toward them.

Vasily looked at Alexei. "Is that a car horn?"

Alexei shook his head. "It is too tinny for a car. It might be a goose."

"A goose? There is no way that was a goose!"

"Maybe not, but it wasn't a car, either!"

Frustrated by the incompetence of his coworkers, Dmitry

glanced back to tell them to shut up, but before he could, he saw a shadow emerge from the water.

Payne stood from his crouch and pulled the trigger on his assault rifle. He didn't feel agony or joy when he mowed down the Russians against the back of the submarine. He realized that these goons had been sent to kill him and his friends, and he was merely beating them to the punch.

Afterward, he didn't cry or gloat.

He merely called in the success of his mission.

Then he headed back to shore to help with Volkov.

Because of the thick trees near the submarine, Archer didn't have a clear view of Payne's assault. With nothing better to do, he scanned Island 3 in search of the traitor.

Upon leaving his post unattended, Harrison had crossed the bridge and headed to the rendezvous spot where the second Russian boat was supposed to make landfall. From there, he would have joined up with Volkov's goons before leading them back to Island 2 for an unexpected rear assault against Kaiser and his men.

But somehow that plan had gone to shit.

For some reason, the boat had docked near the submarine, across the channel from where he had been waiting. Reluctant to swim through the cold water of Artillery Bay, Harrison had decided his best bet was to get back across the bridge to meet up with the men from the second boat. Otherwise, he sensed that Volkov wouldn't honor their deal and pay him the money that he desperately needed.

As he approached the northern edge of the bridge, Harrison carefully checked his surroundings to make sure that Kaiser hadn't filled his post with another man. He peered across the channel to his south and searched the trees to make sure no one was hiding. Confident that he was alone, he started his journey across the span.

Harrison was halfway across when Archer pulled his trigger.

A moment later, the traitor's head had an extra hole.

CHAPTER 62

Despite his tremendous ego, Volkov was an intelligent man, and he knew his odds of success had plummeted when his drones had fallen from the sky. That setback had been magnified when he had lost contact with his men from the second boat amidst a torrent of gunfire to the north.

As his boat reached the quay in front of the King's Gate, Volkov did the math in his head. He had started with a team of thirty men, if he included the traitor. There were five men on his boat, but everyone else on his squad was likely dead. And as far as he knew, his side hadn't managed to take out many of Kaiser's goons in the process.

Certainly no one of significance, or else his men would have called it in.

With that in mind, Volkov had a critical decision to make. He could press forward with his invasion in hopes of killing Kaiser in the southern tunnel, or he could turn tail and run. He knew if he chose option two, there would be major consequences. Word of his failure would spread amongst his organization, and he would lose significant face.

In Russia, that was nearly as bad as death itself.

No, Volkov couldn't be seen as a coward.

That would cause too much damage to his reputation.

So he decided to go with option three.

Volkov pointed toward the narrow stretch of grass between the quay and the main stairs that led to the decorative gate. "Head to the grass! We'll launch our assault from there!"

His henchmen jumped to attention and swiftly exited the boat. Volkov was the last one to leave, purposely lingering behind in order to complete his plan. With his men facing the gate and focused on the dangers looming inside, none of them noticed their leader.

Standing behind his guards, Volkov raised his rifle and pulled the trigger again and again until he had killed every last man, guaranteeing their silence and allowing him to spin the fallout from Suomenlinna in any way that he saw fit.

Then, as if nothing had happened, he got back into his boat and sped away.

Jones and several of Kaiser's men were positioned in the trees on the other side of the King's Gate when they heard the gunfire. Confused by the commotion, Jones got on his comm.

"Archer," he said, "can you see the gate from the church?"

"That's a negative, sir. My angle is bad. But I can see the boat."

"What boat?" Jones demanded.

"The one leaving the quay."

"You mean *Volkov's* boat?"

"Yes, sir. It appears to be Volkov. He's wearing a blue suit and piloting the craft."

Jones cursed. The noise suddenly made sense. "Is he alone?"

"Yes, sir."

Jones left his hiding place and sprinted down the hill toward the backside of the King's Gate. If Jones's intuition was correct, Volkov had just repeated his pattern from Malta. He had killed his own men in order to conceal his defeat. "Keep an eye on him."

"Yes, sir."

"Jon!" Jones said as he slowed to a halt behind the internal defense wall. "Volkov just bailed on our welcome party. I think he repeated his methods from Malta. I'm going to confirm now."

Soaking wet and out of breath, Payne had just started his drive with Jarkko to the King's Gate. Assuming that Jones was correct, Payne turned the golf cart to his right and headed toward the Suomenlinna Dry Dock where they had left their boat in the marina.

Thankfully, it was very close to the submarine.

They could reach it in less than a minute.

"Waiting on confirmation," Payne said on the comm. Then he

turned to Jarkko and whispered, "Call your guys at the marina. Have them untie your boat and start it up for us."

Jarkko nodded and did as he was told.

Jones peeked his head around the corner and stared through the open gate. On the far side of the decorative wall on the grass below the steps were several dead henchmen. They were sprawled facedown, obviously shot from behind.

"Good Lord," Jones said as he charged toward them with his rifle raised. "There are five men down near the steps. The sick fucker just mowed them down."

"Five confirmed dead?" Payne asked

Jones stopped when he reached the bodies. He took a few seconds to inspect them before he made the announcement. "Five confirmed."

"Hang tight. We just reached Jarkko's boat. We can be there in less than five."

Jones glanced across the water to the east. As he did, he saw Volkov's inflatable boat pass the northwest corner of Vallisaari. "It looks like he's heading to their base of operation. If he has a chopper over there, we won't get to him in time."

Payne couldn't help himself. He had to tease his friend. "You just *had* to use the RPG for the drones. Outstanding planning on your part."

Jones grabbed a comm from one of the dead goons and held it up to his ear. Nothing was currently being broadcast. "Don't blame me. Blame Kaiser. The Vampir is reusable. If he had ordered multiple rockets, we wouldn't be in this situation."

Assuming it was safe to come out, Kaiser limped toward the quay. "Whoa! Whoa! Whoa! You laughed when you saw I brought *one*. Now you're blaming me for not bringing *more*?"

Jones laughed. "Didn't you say it was the job of the supply sergeant to know the needs of his personnel before they did? Well, how hard is it to count to two?"

Jarkko's men had his boat ready to go. Payne hopped in first but let Jarkko get behind the wheel. It was his boat to captain, and he knew these waters better than anyone. Without delay, the boat rocketed forward despite being in a no-wake zone.

"Kaiser," Payne said over the roar of the engine. "He makes a good point. Aren't you supposed to be a mathematical genius—someone who can juggle multiple numbers in your head at one time to calculate prices and shipping rates—yet you can't even count to two?"

Kaiser laughed over the comm. "I can definitely count to two, because I'm listening to *two* assholes right now."

Payne smiled. "One of whom saved your life. So watch your tone, mister!"

"You're right. My bad. I meant to call you a 'heroic asshole'."

Payne nodded in appreciation. "That's more like it!"

"So," Jones said as he stared across the water, "are you planning to join us for the hunt, or are you going to stay hidden in your cave like a scared troll?"

Kaiser finally reached the gate. "Turn around and see for yourself."

Jones looked back and smiled. "Glad you could make it. Just waiting on Uber."

Jarkko grinned as his boat raced past the isthmus. "Two minutes out."

Payne glanced into the cove and realized it was littered with bodies. "Hey Kaiser, we need to start clean up before it gets too dark. Have your men tend to their mess, and send someone down to the submarine. I don't have time to tend to mine."

Unfortunately for Volkov, he didn't have a chopper waiting on Vallisaari.

In fact, he didn't have an escape plan at all.

He had been so confident in his men and his drones that he hadn't bothered to prepare for failure. Of course, that was a common flaw in the egotistical. They were so used to having things go their way that they were unable to handle defeat. And since Volkov had built his empire on fear, he had no one to bail him out when he needed it the most.

No friends. No family. No one.

All he had was himself.

And that wasn't good enough.

Jarkko picked up Jones and Kaiser at the quay in front of the King's Gate before they raced across the channel toward Vallisaari. Although Payne was riding shotgun, his weapon of choice was an assault rifle. He held it against his chest as they charged forward.

Despite the late hour, the sun was still setting in the western sky, giving them all the light they needed to follow Volkov's wake. With no other boat traffic around, they didn't need any drones or fancy gadgets to track the Russian. The trail of churned water was as visible as bloody footprints in a fresh patch of snow.

"There he is," Jarkko announced to the others.

But his words weren't necessary.

Their weapons were already raised.

Ivan Volkov had always lived for the hunt. To him, there was nothing more satisfying than seeing the pure, animalistic fear of his prey when he finally closed in for the kill.

The way their lips quivered.

The way their legs trembled.

The way their eyes begged for mercy.

That had brought him more joy than anything else in the world.

But now the roles were reversed.

Now *he* was the hunted. The man who was running.

And he refused to be the source of someone else's happiness.

When he heard the roar of the engine, Volkov glanced over his shoulder and knew his time on earth was nearly done. With the

Finn at the helm and the Americans on board, he realized there was no escape from their wrath. He could have turned and fired on them in order to buy a few seconds more, but he didn't want to give them the satisfaction of the kill.

So he did what he had always planned to do when the enemy was at his door.

He put his gun to his head, smiled defiantly, and pulled the trigger.

Jarkko stopped his boat next to the dinghy for final confirmation.

Ivan Volkov was definitely dead.

A piece of his skull was missing, and so was a chunk of his brain.

Blood pooled in the bottom of the boat around his limp corpse.

Payne and Jones watched as Kaiser snapped a few pictures of the body to preserve the moment, but he did so without glee. Not because he didn't get a chance to kill Volkov himself, but because he knew someday he might be the one leaking brains.

Until then, he would make the most of his time on earth.

Doing the things he loved while surrounded by friends.

After all, that's what life was for.

Chapter 63

Sunday, June 17
Küsendorf, Switzerland

Marissa and Ulster had tried to distract themselves with work upon their arrival at the Ulster Archives on Saturday, but they had been far too worried about their friends' safety to accomplish much of anything in the way of research.

Having agreed to keep the discovery of the tunnel system in Malta from the rest of Ulster's staff, Marissa had spent most of the day uploading their pictures and videos to Ulster's office computer, while checking her phone every five minutes for an update from Payne.

Still, that was much more than Ulster had accomplished.

In times of crisis, he often found himself in the kitchen. First he would glance through his shelves of cookbooks until he had spotted a tasty treat that he was capable of creating, and then he would make a mess while trying to bake something that resembled the picture next to the recipe. In the end, his personal chef would always help him salvage the final product before Ulster carried the treats from room to room like a proud father showing off his newborn.

Except in this case, Ulster urged people to eat his creation.

Thankfully, the call they had been waiting for had come just before midnight, and Payne had told them that everything had gone as planned. Although he didn't provide many specifics, he had assured them that he, Jones, and Jarkko were unharmed and Volkov would be out of their lives forever. That had set off a lively celebration between Marissa and Ulster, which had resulted in the opening of a bottle of vintage champagne and the devouring of Ulster's remaining cream-cheese brownies.

Despite their late-night merriment, they had agreed to meet

for an early breakfast, followed by a long day of research in the archives. Both of them followed through with their promise, and they were well fed and ready to work before nine.

Unable to talk about the tunnels during their meal, they waited until they were in the privacy of the conference room in the lower level of the Archives to discuss their plan of attack.

"Where are you going to start?" Marissa asked as she logged into Ulster's private network with one of the laptop computers that he kept in the room. It would allow her to access all of the pictures and videos that she had uploaded to his office system.

Ulster answered her question with one of his own. "It's not *where* I'm going to start—it's *when*. Ever since we came across that wall at the bottom of the ramp in Cassar's tunnel system, I have been thinking about the date on the cornerstone: June 1798. As you are well aware, that date is quite significant in the history of Malta because it marks the arrival of Napoleon in Valletta. But what else does that date represent?"

Marissa glanced at him across the wooden table. "The date that Hompesch left Malta."

"Exactly," he said with a grin. "And if our theory is correct— that Hompesch loaded up the Maltese treasure before Napoleon arrived—then it stands to reason that he would check on its status after he departed Valletta. So my goal is to track Hompesch's move- ment after he left the island and before he landed in Trieste, Italy."

"And how are you going to do that?"

Ulster sighed. "I have no bloody idea."

Marissa laughed. "Well, I'm here if you need me."

He leaned back in his chair. "And what about you, my dear? What thread of history will you be tugging on today in order to unravel this mystery that we face?"

She motioned toward the door. "Although I *treasure*—pardon the pun—the vast amount of resources that are at my disposal in the archives, my initial focus will be on the images that we cap- tured in the tunnel itself. Two things dawned on me late last night while I was struggling to fall asleep. One, I should never eat mul- tiple cream-cheese brownies after midnight, no matter how tasty they are. And two, unless I'm mistaken, we overlooked one major thing while stumbling around in the dark of the tunnel system. Care to guess what it was?"

Ulster rubbed his hands together with anticipation. "A mystery *inside* our mystery. How absolutely delicious! I will most definitely hazard a guess!"

Marissa smiled at her mentor. "Somehow I knew that you would."

"Truth be told," he said with a twinkle in his eye, "there is so much to unpack in your brief-yet-brilliant monologue, I'm not even sure where to begin. Actually, I take that back. I know exactly where to start. Never—and I do mean *never*—apologize to me for a good pun. You know how much I enjoy wordplay!"

She laughed. "Point taken."

"Secondly, thank you for such kind words about my brownies. I slaved all day making those magical morsels, so I am glad you appreciated them on the way down. Like you, I started to regret my lack of restraint at some point during the night when those chocolate demons congealed together in my colon like the stone and mortar that sealed the tunnel near Marsamxett Harbour, and yet I get the sense that I will make that same mistake again in the near future. Perhaps not with a viscous substance like cream cheese, but certainly with another culinary delight that I whip up in a time of distress."

"Some people drink. You like to bake. There's nothing wrong with that."

"Actually," he said as he patted his stomach, "I like to do both, and I think that will eventually lead to my downfall. Or, at the very least, a larger belt."

She smiled at him. "Don't ask me why, but I get the sense that you're stalling."

Confusion filled his face. "Stalling?"

"You know, my mystery inside a mystery?"

"Good heavens! It seems I've done it again! I don't know what is wrong with me lately, but as soon as I start talking about desserts, my mind tends to wonder. Speaking of which, did you know that the word 'dessert' comes from the French word *desservir*, meaning 'to clear the table'. I don't know about you, but when dessert is on the way, I certainly push things aside in order to make room for it!"

"Petr," she said with a laugh. "You're doing it—"

Ulster cut her off. "I swear, my dear, that one was intentional. I figured my use of a French term would actually serve as a backdoor to your original puzzle, since Hompesch was hiding the Maltese treasure from the French. Anyway, while replaying your words in my mind—which I was able to do while droning on about desserts—I realized that you pointed toward the door at the start of your monologue. Whether your signal was intentional or not, I do believe that is the one major thing we overlooked while examining the tunnel system. It was lacking a door."

Marissa grinned in amazement. She had no idea how Ulster had picked up on the scent so quickly or how he had managed to use a mid-sixteenth century French word to get there, but somehow, in a matter of seconds, he had figured out the issue that had kept her awake.

"Exactly," she said as she carried the laptop to his side of the table. "We were so focused on the limestone tunnels and the two stone walls that we failed to look for a way in. If we assume the dates on the two cornerstones are correct, the southern wall was built in January 1798 in order to close the tunnel system off from the other auberges. That would allow Hompesch and the German knights to work in private. And the northern wall was built near the harbor in June 1798 to seal off the tunnel system for good. But if that is true, how did the knights access the tunnel in the five months in between? I didn't see any sealed passageways in the ceiling of the tunnel, and I find it hard to believe that the knights walked up that long spiraling ramp each and every time they wanted to do their mystery work in the tunnel. That doesn't make any sense at all."

Ulster rubbed his chin in thought. "Unless…"

"Unless what?" she demanded.

He continued to think. "What if the wall was *actually* a wall?"

She stared at her mentor and sighed. "Petr, I think it's time to set some ground rules here. Desserts are one thing—at least I enjoy those—but if you drift off on a philosophical tangent and start to talk about Kierkegaard's theories on existence, I swear to Jarkko, I'm going to work in another room. It is far too early in the morning to deal with theoretical rhetoric."

Ulster laughed. "No, my dear, you completely misunderstood my question! I meant it quite literally! What if the wall *wasn't* a barricade of some kind? What if it was the side of a room?"

She blinked a few times. "A room?"

"Yes!" he blurted much louder than he had intended. "When we came across the southern wall, we naturally assumed it had been built to seal off the tunnel from the rest of the system in order to give the German knights privacy. But what if that theory is partially incorrect? What if *our* wall—the one built in January of 1798—was the *second* wall that Hompesch had built in the tunnel system? What if the wall he had built to give them privacy was actually farther south into the system? That would mean the space in between the wall we inspected and the one even farther into the system would be…"

"A room!" she exclaimed.

Ulster grinned, glad that she had eventually caught on. Normally he liked for his students to figure things out on their own, but in major moments like these, it was tough for him to stifle his personal enthusiasm. "Think about it, my dear. If Hompesch secretly moved the Maltese treasure through the tunnel system after his predecessor's death like we assume he did, he would have needed some place to store it."

She nodded with excitement. "And why waste the time and energy to carve a vault out of the limestone underneath their auberge when all they needed to do was build a wall to cut themselves off from the rest of the tunnels? That would have given them all the privacy and protection they needed—especially if Hompesch used his men to guard the harbor door."

"Exactly!" he said as he sorted through the possibilities in his mind. "Obviously the original barrier would be a solid wall to protect the treasure, but it stands to reason the wall that we inspected would most likely have a way in. After all, someone would be coming to move the treasure eventually. Only we didn't know to look for a point of entry."

"Wait!" she said as she pointed at the computer. "You don't think…"

"Actually, my dear, I *do* think."

"Wait, wait, wait!" she said on the verge of freaking out. "You actually think there's a chance that the treasure is still sitting in *our* tunnel on the other side of *that* wall."

Ulster leaned back and smiled. "Who cares what *I* think? Based on the excitement in your voice, I'd much rather hear what *you* think."

"Okay!" she said as she leapt from her chair and started to pace the room as she tried to connect the dots in her head. If this had been a week earlier, she would have been unwilling to put her name on a theory that involved so much speculation, but ever since they had discovered a secret tunnel system underneath the streets that she had walked on many times before, she had started to view history in a whole new way.

Suddenly it was a living, breathing thing that could morph in the blink of an eye.

And she was at the forefront of change.

"Pictures!" she blurted as she rushed back to the table to search through the files she had uploaded the day before. "If our wall is the northern edge of a room—one that would eventually be opened by Hompesch or his men when it was time to ship the treasure from Malta—then you're right: there's no way that the wall is solid. Maybe some of it was solid for structural integrity, but it stands to reason that the very center of the wall would be made of a different substance. Perhaps a different kind of brick, or even a different type of mortar."

Ulster pointed at the screen. "I know I took several photos of the wall with my phone. Did you get them onto my computer?"

She nodded as she continued to scroll. "That's what I'm looking for now. I know they're in here somewhere, but there were so many files that it will—"

"There!" Ulster shouted. "That one! Go back to that one!"

She stopped and scrolled back to reveal a photo of the upper wall. She had taken it herself after she had finished filming the entire vault with the video camera.

"Can you enlarge it?" he demanded.

She clicked a few buttons and started to zoom in. "Which part do you want to—"

"To the left and down. A little more. There! Do you see it?"

The center section of the upper wall filled the entire screen. The image was zoomed in far enough that she could see individual stones and the substance in between. Having just mentioned mortar a moment earlier, her gaze was naturally drawn to it. She leaned in close, looking for anything that looked suspicious in the ancient cement.

She was getting ready to ask her mentor for a clue when she spotted an enigma on the left side of the screen. On one of the stones, there appeared to be a chiseled mark that she had seen thousands of times in Malta. She quickly tapped the arrow key until the image shifted over ever so slightly, and then she zoomed in a little more until the symbol filled the screen.

It was a cross.

A Maltese cross.

Carved right into the stone.

Associated with the Order of Saint John since the sixteenth century, the eight-pointed cross was formed by four V-shapes, each joining the others at its vertex while the two tips spread outward in a symmetrical fashion. The eight points of the four arms represented the eight original langues of the Knights Hospitallers while also symbolizing the eight obligations of the knights: to live in truth; to have faith; to repent of one's sins; to be humble; to love justice; to be merciful; to be sincere and wholehearted; and to endure persecution.

Marissa had memorized the list a long time ago, but upon seeing the symbol in the stone, the last obligation of the knights suddenly took on a whole different meaning.

After surrendering to the French, Grand Master Hompesch had been despised by most of the knights and had been ridiculed far and wide for his inactivity during the invasion, but he had never defended himself or said a word about his secret plans or the location of the Maltese treasure because he didn't think that was in the best interest of the Order.

Instead, he had endured the persecution as he patiently waited for the opportunity to move his treasure to the new home of the organization that he loved so dear.

An opportunity that never came.

CHAPTER 64

Payne, Jones, and Jarkko had planned to fly from Finland to Switzerland in order to help Marissa and Ulster with additional research at the Archives—or at the very least, to enjoy the mountain scenery and the use of Ulster's personal chef while the historians did most of the work. But all of that had changed when Payne received a giddy phone call from Ulster, who claimed to have found conclusive evidence of the treasure's location in Valletta.

Eager to reveal the information to his friends but unwilling to ruin the surprise over the phone, Ulster had purchased two plane tickets from Zurich to Malta to get to the tunnel system as soon as possible. That allowed the Payne Industries jet to fly directly from Helsinki instead of having to pick up Ulster and Marissa in Switzerland.

With a few hours to kill in Valletta before the guys arrived, Marissa finally had a chance to pick up her car and visit her apartment. Although she had appreciated Payne's generosity, she hadn't worn any of her own clothes since their initial meeting at the library. She had loved the excitement of the last week, but she also had missed her daily routine.

Dying to shower in her own bathroom, she spent nearly thirty minutes in the hot water, trying to wash away all of the stress that had been building since the shootout. While tending to the wound on her leg, she realized that the most nerve-racking part of the past week hadn't been when her life was in danger, but rather when she was awaiting word about Payne's safety.

Somehow, during the past five days she had fallen for him hard.

Or, at the very least, the idea of him.

She had always admired him from a distance, and when she combined that adoration with the excitement and adrenaline of their time together, it was the perfect formula to get swept away. And yet, as a levelheaded academic, she also knew that the two of them hadn't spent much time alone or had a lengthy conversation that didn't end in an argument, so she wasn't quite ready to start planning a wedding. But she was more than willing to go on a date.

And for her, that was the equivalent of a miracle.

Of course, her social life would have to wait while her professional life took priority. After putting on her lucky T-shirt and a favorite pair of shorts, she drove Ulster to a parking lot near St. Paul's Co-Cathedral before they walked the streets for nearly an hour while trying to figure out how much of Cassar's tunnel system still remained. In the end, they realized they wouldn't know for sure until they went back underground to look for themselves.

Just after dark, a black panel van—borrowed from Galea—pulled into the parking lot, and Payne, Jones, and Jarkko hopped out. Marissa and Ulster greeted them like conquering heroes, pretending to bow down in their presence. Hugs were exchanged and laughs were shared as the two groups were reunited. Both sides wanted to know what the others had been up to in their time apart, but they quickly agreed to hold off on the details for a more appropriate time.

For now, everyone's focus was on the treasure.

Since their last journey had been such a success, they decided to enter through the manhole cover in the same order as before. Payne went first, followed by Jarkko, Ulster, Marissa, and then Jones. This time around, they weren't dressed in black outfits or carrying nearly as much equipment—the bulk of which remained in the van. Instead, they brought lights to guide their way, a video camera to film their progress, and Payne's magic wand to open the door.

That is, if there was a door.

If not, this would be a wasted trip.

As they walked down the utility tunnel, they were relieved to see their sheets of plastic still hanging over the passageway that they had dug through the wall. Over the past several hours, Ulster's biggest concern wasn't about his research—he was confident that he was correct about his findings—it was about the sanctity of the site. Once he inspected the materials that sealed their hole and realized they were still intact, he breathed a huge sigh of relief.

"Marissa," Ulster said, "it was your photograph of the wall that led us back here, so I think you should be the one to break the seal."

Marissa smiled as Jones filmed her big moment. "It would be my honor."

She carefully peeled the tape on the right side of the hole and pulled back the plastic before she turned to face the group. "Before we go in, I just wanted to take a moment to say thanks to all of you. Despite a rocky start, this has been the best week of my life."

Jarkko grimaced. "What rocky start?"

"You know, the shootout at the library?"

"Heck," Jones cracked, "that was one of my highlights. Sometimes when I close my eyes, I can still feel the air on my face as I do my flip through the air. Truth be told, I'm still kinda pissed that no one filmed it. Speaking of which, take this damn camera. Last time, you missed me going through the wall. I don't want you to repeat your rookie mistake."

Marissa laughed. "Oh, so now I'm a rookie?"

Jones handed her the device. "Look around you, girl. All of us are experienced treasure hunters. I don't remember any major discoveries on your résumé."

"Maybe not," Ulster said in her defense. "But that's about to change."

Jones grinned. "Uh-oh! Petr's getting cocky. That's always a good sign."

"Speaking of signs," Payne said as he held back the plastic so Jones could climb through. "You still haven't told us what you two spotted in Marissa's photograph that brought us back. I'm assuming it's something big."

Ulster shook his head. "Actually, it's rather small, but that's all I'm going to say until we're standing in front of the wall. I've waited this long. I'm certainly not going to spoil it now."

Riding their wave of good luck, they entered the ancient tunnel system in the exact same order as the previous time. Jones went first, followed by Ulster, Marissa, Jarkko, and then Payne, who had an extreme case of déjà vu when he climbed through the wall.

After setting down his equipment, his gaze immediately went to the twisted web of roots that hung from the limestone ceiling. The trees' journey through the stone had taken centuries, slowly but surely pushing their way though the darkness until they had finally broken through.

In many ways, it paralleled his team's appearance in the tunnel.

Only they still had some digging to do.

Payne turned to his right and walked toward the stone wall where Marissa and Ulster were whispering to each other in the gloom. Upon his approach, they turned and faced him as he joined Jones and

Jarkko in front of the wall. To preserve the big moment, Jones worked the camera while Jarkko shined his flashlight on the historians.

Ulster glanced at his former student and gave her a slight nudge with his elbow. "Go on, my dear. Let them know why we're here."

She smiled at the others, completely confident in their findings. "On our previous trip, we were so overwhelmed by the grand scope of our discovery that we failed to appreciate the finer details of the site. It wasn't until Petr and I returned to the Archives to view our videos and photographs that we noticed something on the wall."

She turned and shined a green laser pointer at a single stone. It was approximately eight feet above the floor and a few feet left of center on the wall. "David, please zoom in on this brick and let me know what you see."

Jones did as he was told and spotted a symbol. "It's a Maltese cross."

Payne and Jarkko glanced at the camera screen and nodded in agreement.

"By itself," she explained to the group, "this wouldn't have been much of a discovery. After all, this symbol has been a part of the fabric of Malta for centuries. But then we spotted another one, just below it."

She shifted her laser pointer down a few feet, and Jones followed it with the camera. Payne and Jarkko stared at the screen as Jones zoomed in on the second symbol.

"Once again," she said as she moved away from the wall, "not a big deal. I'm sure if we walked through the streets of Valletta, we would see this symbol on several buildings. And flags. And T-shirts. Honestly, if we went outside right now, I bet we could find fifty of them in less than an hour."

"Okay," Jones said. "What's your point?"

She smiled at him, glad that he had taken the bait. "When Petr and I examined the wall, do you know how many crosses we found?"

Jarkko guessed. "Nine hundred and fifty-two."

She shook her head. "We found eight."

He shrugged. "Jarkko was close."

She continued. "Do you know how many points there are on a Maltese cross?"

Jones counted on the screen. "Eight."

"And do you know how many basic obligations the Knights of

Malta had?"

Jones smiled. "I'll go with eight."

She nodded. "That is correct."

Payne chimed in. "Eight crosses. Eight points. Eight obligations. The math makes sense, but I'm still not sure where it leads us."

"Then it's a good thing we're here," she said as she gently pushed the three guys to the left side of the tunnel. "Petr, come join me so I can show them what we found."

Ulster had a huge grin on his face as he moved away from the wall. "About a year ago, I was given this gizmo by a visiting scholar, but I could never quite make it work. Thankfully, Marissa figured it out in a snap. You know me, I don't even know how to set my digital clock. If not for Winston, it would still be stuck on a blinking twelve."

Marissa pulled out a small machine from her bag that was capable of projecting digital shapes. She set the device on the floor a short distance from the wall. "While examining the eight points, Petr and I realized that they weren't randomly spread across the stones. Instead, they formed a shape. A very specific shape. And all we had to do was connect the dots."

With a flip of the switch, the gloom of the tunnel was suddenly filled with red light. Projected from the tiny device, the laser light formed a large rectangular door on the wall—complete with a small circle to approximate a doorknob.

"I'll be damned," Payne said as he walked toward the wall to inspect the eight Maltese crosses that provided the pattern for the rectangle.

Marissa moved the device just a bit on the floor so the digital shape would line up perfectly with the symbols on the wall. "Obviously we added the tiny doorknob just for fun. That's not actually in the stone, but I thought it would help you visualize things better."

Jarkko hugged her from behind. "Jarkko love doorknob! Jarkko can't wait to open door!"

She patted the arm around her neck. "Jon, what do you think?"

Payne looked at her and grinned. "I'm with Jarkko. Let's open the damn door."

Wasting no time, Payne hustled back to the passageway and returned with his equipment. Realizing that the laser projector would be useless with workers blocking the beam, Marissa used a piece of chalk to carefully draw the rectangle on the wall. Unable to reach the top of the door, she handed the chalk to Payne, who finished the job as Jones filmed everything.

Before he powered on the sonic baton, Payne and Marissa put on work gloves and safety goggles—just to make sure neither of them ended up like Kaiser. Although the group had recently seen the device in action, they were still amazed by its precision and speed. The wall practically flaked away as Payne followed the chalk line along the left edge.

After a few minutes, they realized it wasn't just the device.

It was the mortar itself.

As Marissa vacuumed up the residue, the center portion of the wall started to crumble. One brick fell, and then another. Then a third practically leapt from the wall.

Realizing what was happening, Payne handed the magic wand to Ulster for safekeeping and called Jarkko over to assist. Two days earlier, he had used his strength to carry and stack thick chunks of limestone in the utility tunnel in order to keep their work site clean, but now he was going to do something a lot more fun: he was going to help Payne break down the door.

With his bare hands, Jarkko ripped a stone from the wall and was prepared to launch it against the side of the tunnel just to see if he could make it explode into dust, but before he could hurl the object, Payne grabbed his arm from behind.

"Whoa, big fella!" Payne said in a calming voice. "Settle down! We're in an ancient tunnel. The last thing we need is for you to hulk out down here."

Jones groaned from behind the camera. "Don't go using my line! I said the same thing to you, like, ten days ago—or whenever the hell we were down here last. I swear, I don't even know what month it is anymore."

Payne laughed. "The mind is always the first thing to go."

Ulster nodded. "It certainly is."

"Good," Jarkko said. "Then my willy will continue to work for a while."

Behind them in the tunnel, Marissa rolled her eyes. "Come on, guys! Keep your focus! We're *this* close to making history. You can talk about your willies later."

"Actually," Payne said as he glanced back at her. "I think there's a big enough gap for us to get a sneak peek at the room right now.

That is, if you're interested."

"Of course, I'm interested!" she said as she tried to squeeze in, but the workspace was already too crowded with bodies. "But you guys are too big."

Jarkko grinned. "Jarkko thought we were supposed to talk about our willies later?"

Marissa and Ulster couldn't help but smile.

Meanwhile, Payne looked at Jones. "You know, this might work better with the camera. That thing has a light, doesn't it? Why don't you turn that sucker on and hold it up to the opening? That way we can all look at the screen at the exact same time."

Payne glanced at Ulster. "Unless that offends you in some way."

Ulster laughed at the thought. "I'm sure Howard Carter is spinning in his grave right now, but if he had used a video camera when he cracked open Tutankhamun's tomb in 1922, perhaps he wouldn't have been cursed afterward."

Jarkko took a step back. "Ghost?"

Marissa put a reassuring hand on his shoulder. "No ghost."

Jarkko breathed a sigh of relief. "Okay. Jarkko ready."

"I'm ready, too," Jones complained, "but this plan won't work unless you move out of the way to let me in. Truth be told, I'm not even sure why I'm working the camera. I'm too damn pretty to be on this side of the lens."

Marissa smiled. "I'll gladly take over from here."

Jones playfully pushed right past her. "Not a chance, rookie. We know what happened the last time you were supposed to film. I did something cool, and you missed it completely."

"No problem," she said as she linked one arm with Payne's and the other with Ulster's as a sign of unity. "I'm happy to let you do your thing. I'll just stand back here and watch."

Jarkko was so nervous he was almost afraid to look. With one eye closed and the other one squinting, he stood behind Marissa while resting his chin on her shoulder.

Jones put the camera near the gap in the wall and got ready to turn on the light. "Okay, everybody, let's do this as a team. On my mark, let's count down from three. Are you ready? Does everyone know their numbers? You do? Good! Then here we go…."

In unison, the group counted aloud.

"Three…two…one…!"

Epilogue

Cameras flashed when Payne and Jones exited the black sedan and waved to the crowd.

A lot had changed since their initial trip into the utility tunnel near St. Paul's Co-Cathedral. Instead of sneaking through the darkness to avoid the police, they were now being escorted through the cheering masses by some of the same officers who had questioned them about the shooting at the National Library of Malta.

No longer persons of interest, they were now national celebrities.

Jones high-fived the people that he passed. "I could get use to this shit."

Payne paused to have his photo taken. "You mean being liked by white people?"

Jones laughed. "I meant having a police escort, but yours works, too."

Payne glanced back and realized that Galea had been swallowed by the boisterous throng that had gathered to get a glimpse of the treasure. Packed into the narrow streets of Valletta, the collection of locals and tourists alike had started to arrive on Monday evening when word of the discovery had leaked and spread around the globe.

Thankfully, Payne and his friends had been prepared.

After opening the wooden crates and documenting the assembled riches in the hidden room, the team had notified the Maltese government about their find. With the Ulster Archives taking the lead, Ulster had flown in his staff to coordinate the logistical nightmare of preserving, cataloging, and eventually displaying the treasure, while also asking Marissa to handpick a few regional historians to join the team. Not only would their expertise be invaluable, but it

350

would generate goodwill amongst the locals.

With a grin on his face, Payne went back and grabbed their driver. Appreciative of Galea's work, he made an announcement to the crowd. "This is Mark Galea. His local knowledge was crucial during our search for the treasure. You should be taking his picture, too. And if you need a local guide, he's the best one in town."

Galea beamed as people shook his hand and asked for his business card. "You didn't have to say that," he whispered to Payne. "I'm glad you did, but it wasn't necessary."

"Of course, it was. And I meant every word."

Payne was about to say more, but he felt the vibration of his phone before he had the chance. He pulled the device from his pocket and glanced at the screen. "Hey Mark, I need to take this. I'll see you downstairs in a few minutes. Just follow DJ. He'll get you into the site."

"Sure thing," Galea said as he hustled after Jones for access to the treasure.

Payne answered the call. "Mister Dial."

Dial laughed in his office at Interpol. "Mister Payne."

"Hang on," Payne said before he turned up the volume on his phone. "Can you hear me okay? It's kind of crazy here."

"I know. I'm currently watching you on my computer screen."

"That's kind of creepy, Nick. Please tell me you're wearing pants."

"I am, but you're definitely not."

"Excuse me?"

"Wait!" Dial said with a laugh. "I didn't mean it like *that*. I meant, you're being broadcast around the globe from Malta in your cargo shorts. You're *such* an American."

Payne smiled. "I've been called worse."

"Listen," Dial said, "I know you're busy, but I just wanted to thank you again for giving me the heads up on Volkov. As you can imagine, the Finnish authorities were overjoyed when they learned of his demise. His organization has been causing them problems for years, so they're more than willing to let your role at the fortress slide."

On his flight to Helsinki, Payne had called Dial to let him know that he would be meeting with an antiquities dealer on Suomenlinna and feared that Volkov might try to intervene. Without giving up Kaiser's name or any specifics about their plan, he had assured

Dial that he and Jones would be safe and any effort by Volkov would be thwarted. Dial had made Payne promise that he wouldn't be the aggressor, and Payne had kept his word. He hadn't fired his weapon until after the kamikaze drone had killed two of Kaiser's men.

"What role is that?" Payne demanded. "Everything was self-defense."

Dial laughed. "Once again, you keep forgetting about international gun laws. I really need to send you a pamphlet or something, because it's just not sinking in."

Payne smiled. "Please do that, but you should probably send it here to Malta. I plan on sticking around for a while."

"That's right! You don't have a job to worry about. I wish I could say the same."

"Actually," Payne said, "I've been giving your situation some thought."

"Which situation is that?"

"You know, the one where you hate your fucking job?"

Dial chuckled. "Oh, *that* situation. What about it?"

"Correct me if I'm wrong, but weren't you the one who built the homicide division at Interpol? I mean, you're literally the guy who came up with the basic framework of the department, the chain of command, and so on. Right?"

"Yeah."

"And the head of Interpol doesn't want you leaving your desk because he feels a division head shouldn't be involved in fieldwork because he views your post as a supervisor position?"

"What are you getting at?"

Payne smiled. "If you have the power to invent a new job in your department, why don't you create one that you actually like? Call it, Chief Investigator or some shit like that. Then instead of taking applications to fill the post, leave your job as division head and take the position yourself. That way you get to do what you actually want to do—which is investigative work—and you can stop doing all of the political bullshit that you hate."

Dial pondered the suggestion. "Wow."

Payne paused, unsure. "Good wow or bad wow?"

"*Great* wow," Dial said as he thought things through. "Obviously I'd need to make sure that my replacement is someone I can live with—"

"Meaning *not* your assistant Henri."

"Precisely! But, yeah, holy shit! That's exactly the type of gig that I'm looking for."

"Then you should go for it, Nick. No job is worth your current level of misery. Take my advice, and escape while you can."

Dressed in the same rumpled sport coat that he always wore, Boris Artamonov left the State Hermitage Museum in Saint Petersburg after his volunteer shift had ended and strolled along the Neva River. After spending the day amongst the artifacts that he loved so much, the former curator always liked to take the scenic route to his apartment.

Like many older Russians, he avoided modern technology whenever he could, so he knew nothing about the discovery in Malta and wouldn't find out about it for weeks.

But that didn't mean he was clueless about the treasure.

In fact, he knew exactly where it had been hidden.

Only he had kept its location to himself.

During his long and colorful life, Artamonov had faced count-less bullies in the former Soviet Union and had plenty of experi-ence in handling them. So when Volkov's men had stormed into his place of work—the building he loved more than any in the world—and had strong-armed him into the waiting limousine, the crafty old man knew exactly how to play it.

He would pretend to be helpful while doing the opposite.

Just like he had done with the dreaded KGB.

Although Volkov had kept his word and had provided both dinner and dessert for their tutorial, Artamonov knew that Volkov was an evil man who had no appreciation for history. That was obvious as the old man had tried to explain the significance of the ancient collection that Volkov had carelessly scattered across the floor. Dozens of museum-worthy documents had been trampled as Volkov paced back and forth while shouting insults at his employees.

During one particular tirade, Artamonov had used the distrac-tion to pocket a priceless letter that had been penned by Ferdinand von Hompesch, the former Grand Master of the Order of Saint

John. Written in German to one of his knights already stationed in Saint Petersburg, Hompesch explained that the French armada had arrived in the Mediterranean before he could safely move the treasure off the island. Unwilling to let it fall into the enemy's hands, he had sealed the tunnel near Marsamxett Harbour in order to prevent its discovery. Hompesch had volunteered to go back to Malta to recover the riches for the betterment of the Order, but he required men and ships from Paul the First in order to safely complete the journey.

As an expert in Russian history and a speaker of German, Artamonov realized the significance of the letter and knew that the Maltese treasure had never been found.

And thanks to his quick hands, it never would be.

At least not by Ivan Volkov.

When Artamonov got home from his walk along the river, the first thing he did was pull the letter out of his drawer. As a former curator, he realized that the document should be displayed in the museum that he loved so much, but he wasn't ready to part with it just yet.

After spending so much of his life taking care of artifacts for the enjoyment of others, he had decided to hold onto this one for a little while longer. Not only to keep it away from the likes of Volkov, but because he liked having something precious to come home to.

At this point of his elderly life, the past was all he had.

Payne spotted Galea near the stone wall, as the driver peered through the missing door in order to get a glimpse of the treasure inside the makeshift chamber.

The bricks and mortar that Payne had chipped away with the sonic baton had been moved elsewhere to make room for all of the people and equipment that filled the space. Despite the apparent chaos, everyone had a purpose as they buzzed around the site like a colony of worker bees, all of whom were trying to please the queen.

Or in this case, *king*.

Ulster's voice could be heard out in the tunnel. "Outstanding work, everyone! If you keep this up, I promise to whip up a batch of my cream-cheese brownies. That's what Marissa and I nibbled on while celebrating our big discovery. Speaking of big discoveries, let me tell you about this restaurant that I recently visited in Birgu. They make the most delicious soup I have ever tasted. My good friend Jarkko took me there, and let me tell you, it was heaven on a spoon."

"Mark," Payne said as he approached the driver. "Did DJ show you the site?"

Galea turned around and smiled. "Let me see if I got this straight. When I picked you up at the airport, you had no luggage. Then when I picked you up at the mall, you suddenly had luggage. Then when I picked you up at the hotel, you had trash bags filled with fancy rubbish. Then when I picked you up at the marina, you had absolutely nothing, but *I* had a van filled with mysterious wooden crates. And now when I come to see you at work, you have an entire tunnel filled with ancient riches dating back to the time of the Crusades?"

Payne nodded. "Yep. That sums it up."

Galea shook his head. "I hate to be the bearer of bad news, but there's no way in hell that your knickknacks are going to fit in my trunk."

Jones heard the comment and turned around. "What if you fold down the backseat?"

Galea laughed. "Not even if I *remove* the backseat."

Jarkko saw the group and rushed over. "Mark is selling backseat? Jarkko will buy!"

Galea smiled. "Why in the world do you need a backseat?"

"Russian scum stabbed seats in yacht with knife. What is price?"

"Jarkko," Galea said, "it was a joke. I'm not selling my seat."

"Mark is playing hard to get. Jarkko respects that. But Jarkko has deal that Mark will like." Jarkko unbuttoned his puffy shirt and revealed a priceless artifact around his neck. "For your backseat, Jarkko will give you gold crucifix from Holy Roman Empire."

"Jesus!" Jones shouted in astonishment.

"Yes," Jarkko said. "That is Him on cross. Pretty good deal, right?"

Payne growled at his mischievous friend. "Jarkko! How many times do I have to tell you that you can't touch the treasure?"

Jarkko pouted. "But Jarkko open door, so this is Jarkko's treasure."

Payne shook his head. "DJ, please deal with Jarkko."

Jones grabbed the Finn's arm and dragged him toward the treasure room. As he did, he whispered to his friend. "That was awesome! You should do the same thing to Marissa. I bet she totally freaks out and loses her mind."

Payne rolled his eyes as they walked away.

Galea glanced at him. "Speaking of which, who actually owns the treasure?"

Payne shrugged. "Truth be told, we're still trying to sort through the details. Obviously, with a major find like this, everyone is going to want a piece—whether that be the Maltese government, the country of origin of individual artifacts, even Jarkko himself. In the end, we'll do our best to make sure we honor the Knights of Malta for protecting this hoard. If not for Hompesch and his men, it would have been taken by Napoleon for sure."

"You know, the modern version of the Order does a lot of charity work here in Malta. Perhaps you can funnel some money their way?"

Payne nodded. "Trust me, they're high on the list."

"Good," Galea said, "then my job here is done."

Payne looked at him funny. "Wait. What?"

Galea smiled and pulled out a second business card. Unlike the one he had used for work, this one identified him as a member of the Sovereign Military Order of Malta, which was the modern-day iteration of the Knights Hospitallers. "I rarely discuss this part of my life with clients, but I figured I'd make an exception in your case. Our organization does incredible work around the globe. Once you figure things out, give me a call and I'll make sure I put you in touch with the right people. Your discovery could do a lot of good."

Payne shook his hand. "You mean *our* discovery."

Galea furrowed his brow. "How's that?"

"You helped us transport tools and equipment. You watched over us as we crept under your city streets. You even helped cover our tracks. The Knights of Malta were sworn to protect this island, and you must've had your suspicions that we were up to something. You could have put a stop to it anytime. But you didn't. That makes you a part of this."

Galea smiled. "The second obligation."

Payne grimaced, confused.

"To have faith," Galea explained. "I had faith that your intentions were honorable."

Galea turned to walk away, but then he stopped. "You're a good man, Jonathon Payne. I'm glad you were the one who found the Knights' treasure."

Payne waved goodbye and turned to enter the treasure room. But before he reached the missing door, Marissa came charging out.

"You have to do something about Jarkko!" she said in exasperation.

Payne groaned. "What did he do now?"

"He found a cache of ancient swords, and he challenged David to a duel."

Payne laughed. "My money's on DJ. He'll definitely use his gun."

Marissa smiled. "I think you're missing the point. Jarkko with a sword in a narrow tunnel filled with people is not a good idea."

"Good one! Tell that pun to Petr. He'll enjoy it."

"What pun?" she asked, confused.

"You were talking about a sword, and said I'm 'missing the point'."

"Oh," she said with a laugh. "Completely unintentional. Actually, I shouldn't have said that. Petr told me to never apologize for a good pun."

"Good advice," Payne said with a smile. "Speaking of Petr, has he had *any* sleep since you arrived from Switzerland?"

"Maybe an hour or two. Honestly, I have no idea how he does it. I'm ready to drop from exhaustion, but he's running around in there like a cartoon mouse."

"He's definitely animated, I'll grant you that."

She laughed. "I caught that one."

"So," Payne asked, "how do things work around here? Are you on a set schedule? Or can you come and go as you please?"

"Things are pretty flexible. Why?"

Payne shrugged. "Since you're so tired, I thought maybe you could use a good meal to recharge your batteries."

"Yes," she said with a smile. "That sounds wonderful. What about you?"

He nodded. "I could eat."

"Great! I know this fabulous place that looks out over the harbor. Does that work for you?"

He looked at her. "Do they serve food?"

She nodded. "Yep."

"Will you be joining me?"

"Definitely."

Payne smiled. "Sounds perfect, but before we go, there's something I need to do."

"What's that?" she wondered.

"I have to return the albino tiger."

Author's Note

Many of my longtime readers are aware of my connection to Malta, but for those of you who are new to my novels, let me take a moment to explain how I fell in love with this amazing country in the middle of the Mediterranean Sea.

My first international bestseller was a religious thriller called *Sign of the Cross*. Although it was the second book in the Payne & Jones series, it was the novel that allowed me to quit teaching to become a full-time writer. Back then, social media was in its infancy, but I encouraged readers to contact me via email through my website.

As a new author, I loved keeping track of where my fan mail came from. At first, it was strictly from North America, but once the British version of the book was released, I started to get mail from overseas: England, Ireland, Northern Ireland, Scotland, and Wales. After years of grinding, and rejections, and wondering if my books would be published in the United States, much less anywhere else, it's impossible to describe how exciting it was to hear from readers across the Atlantic.

As surreal as it was to have fans in the United Kingdom, at least I could figure out how they had heard of me. Penguin UK was based in London, and there had been a huge promotional campaign for the book, which ended up debuting on the *Sunday Times* bestseller's list. So fan mail from that part of the world made sense to me on some level. But what didn't make sense at all was the letter I received from Malta.

For one reason or another, that completely blew my mind.

Obviously I had heard of Malta, but I knew very little about the country. So little, in fact, that I couldn't comprehend how a copy of my book had ended up in the middle of the Mediterranean. Although my agents had sold the foreign rights to *Sign of the Cross* to publishers around the globe, I knew I didn't have a publisher in Malta, so I wrote back to the reader (Robbie Govus) with more questions for him than he had for me.

Truth be told, I felt like Payne and Jones trying to solve a mystery.

Eventually I learned that Malta was part of the British book distribution channel, and the reader had purchased a UK paperback from a store in Malta. And yet, all I can remember thinking was that my novel had somehow made it to the middle of the Mediterranean. As a neophyte author, I thought that was the coolest thing in the world!

By then, I had already finished writing *Sword of God* and was starting to work on *The Lost Throne*. Just for fun, I decided to mention Malta in the book—not only as an inside joke for me, but also as a reward for the fan. I figured, he had given me a huge thrill by writing to me, so I would do the same for him by mentioning his homeland in my book. Unwilling to mess with a good thing, I did it again in *The Prophecy* and have continued the tradition ever since, always finding a way to mention Malta in my novels.

Honestly, I didn't think that anyone else would even notice. Like most authors, I fill my books with inside jokes that are meant for a select few, and I figured that's what this would be—merely an Easter egg for a loyal fan. But everything changed when I received an email from a Maltese journalist named Stephen Calleja.

After spotting the reference to Malta in *The Lost Throne*, he reached out to me to find out if I had a personal connection to his country. Unbeknownst to me, his homeland tended to be excluded in maps of Europe that were used by authors in my genre, so he was beyond thrilled to see Malta actually mentioned in the story itself. Once I explained the reason why, he wrote an article for his newspaper that detailed my interaction with the fan from Malta and my decision to include Malta in future books.

Obviously this was very well received in Malta, a place filled with tremendous pride for its unique history and culture. So much so, that the Malta Tourism Authority invited me to Valletta in 2015 to thank me for spreading the word about their country by showing me (and two of my author friends, Graham Brown and Boyd Morrison) the best that Malta had to offer. Not only did the MTA invite us to the Mediterranean, but we were given private access to several of Malta's most important documents and historical sites. Needless to say, we were blown away by their hospitality and have viewed Malta as our home away from home since that once-in-a-lifetime adventure.

Much of that trip was portrayed in the details of this story—including the author book event that was described in Chapter 8. I vaguely remember seeing Payne and Jones walk past on their way to Cinnabon, but I was so distracted by the two beautiful women (Anna Gauci and Randi Morrison), the Maltese journalist (Stephen Calleja), and the large crowd of local readers that I was unable to warn the duo about the troubles that lay ahead.

And it's a good thing, too, or else this book wouldn't exist.

GAG REEL

I'm trying something completely new here, and I think it's going to be awesome. But a word of warning: do __not__ read this section before you've finished the book. There are major spoilers ahead—and hopefully plenty of laughs.

Payne glanced at the carnage in the library. From where he was standing, he could see multiple bodies, plenty of blood, and several bullet holes. Plus, for some strange reason, Jarkko was now sitting on the floor behind one of the dead gunmen.

"Hello," Jarkko said in a thick Russian accent as he worked the goon's arms like a creepy puppeteer. "My name is Sergei, and Sergei is looking for love. Sergei likes long walks in snow, hats made of fur, and shirtless dictators who ride horses."

Jones tried not to laugh, but he couldn't help himself.

"Perfect match for Sergei is big-boned woman who can cook cabbage and get bloodstains from T-shirts. And sewing would help, since Sergei has hole in chest."

Petr Ulster took off his glasses and rubbed his tired eyes.

He had been hard at work in the Forbidden Room of the Ulster Archives for several hours and finally needed a break. He stood from the elaborately carved desk and stretched his aching back. He was tempted to head upstairs to the kitchen for a late-night snack but realized that wasn't what he craved at that particular moment.

Instead, he waddled to the bulletproof security door and opened it slightly. He peeked his head into the hallway and looked around. When he was confident that he was alone, he closed the door and turned to the touchscreen that was mounted nearby. He punched in his special code and waited for the boring numerical keypad to morph into his secret menu.

Once it did, he hit the neon button labeled HEAVY P.

The lights instantly dimmed, and a disco ball descended from the ceiling.

A moment later, Latin dance music filled the room.

Ulster was quickly swept up in the erotic rhythm.

One, two, step, thrust! One, two, step, thrust!

Sweat glistened on his forehead as he shook and shimmied to the beat.

Despite his size, he moved with incredible grace, as if he was put on earth to do more than study history. He was also put here to dance, dance, dance!

"Good morning," Jones said as he entered the classroom. He walked directly to the whiteboard at the front of the room and picked up a black marker. Before he turned and faced the class, he wrote his name and ENGLISH 101 in giant letters on the white surface. "For those of you who don't know me, my name is Professor Jones, and this is English One-Oh-One."

Jarkko sat alone in the front row of desks. He was armed with a notebook, a freshly sharpened pencil, and a bunch of magic markers. He glanced around the empty classroom on the University of Malta campus and wondered why he had been summoned there at the crack of dawn and who else Jones was talking to, so he immediately raised his hand.

"Come on!" Jones snapped. "How can you possibly have a question already?"

"Because you are bad teacher."

Jones growled and instinctively reached for his gun, but thankfully Payne had confiscated his firearm the night before. That was when he had talked Jones into this scholastic intervention. "Come on, man. It's too early for your bullshit."

"No bullshit. Serious question."

"Fine. Go ahead."

"Why is Jarkko here? Jarkko speaks good English."

"Because of first-person pronouns."

"What are those?"

Jones nodded. "My point exactly."

Jarkko stared at Jones, and Jones stared right back. Neither man willing to blink. This went on for nearly a minute before Jarkko finally caved. "Ugh! School sucks! Jarkko wants to go to beach and see beautiful women with almost no clothes. Doesn't that sound good to David?"

"That sounds great to David, but...dammit! Now you've got me doing it!"

"Doing what?"

Jones took a deep breath to regain his composure. "Seriously, dude, this is basic stuff. All you need to do is pay attention, and we can be at the beach before the clothes come off and the boobies come out. Okay?"

"Okay!"

"Just repeat after me: *I went to the store.*"

"David went to the store."

"No, Jarkko. Listen carefully: *I went to the store.*"

"Which store?"

"It doesn't matter!"

"Of course, it matters! If Jarkko needs vodka, Jarkko doesn't go to bakery. That would be stupid. Wait. Are you calling Jarkko stupid?"

"No!" Jones assured him. "I'm not calling Jarkko stupid. Dammit! David did it again!"

While working at his desk in Germany, Kaiser heard a knock on his office door.

"Come in," Kaiser said as he glanced up from his keyboard.

"Sorry to disturb you," his assistant said as she hustled into the room. "This package just arrived via courier. It's stamped *urgent.*"

Kaiser stood up, intrigued. "Who's it from?"

"I'm not sure, but it came from Finland."

"Finland?" Kaiser said as he grabbed the package. The box was small and wrapped in plain brown paper. He glanced at the label and instantly recognized the handwriting. "Thanks, Heidi. That will be all."

His assistant nodded and left the room, closing the door behind her.

Kaiser felt like a child on Christmas morning as he ripped the paper off the package, revealing a white box and a simple card taped to the top that read:

TO THE MAN WHO HAS <u>ALMOST</u> EVERYTHING,
HERE'S A TOKEN FROM OUR RECENT ADVENTURE!

YOUR PAL,
JARKKO

Kaiser put the card aside and picked up the small box. Much to his surprise, it was cold to the touch. Without delay, he lifted the lid and was shocked by the sight. Nestled in cold packs was a single object staring back at him.

Literally staring.

Inside the box was Volkov's left eye.

Winston walked stiffly into the kitchen to check on his master's dinner. As he did, he saw a bright flash of light on one of the video screens. Worried about a possible security breach, he hustled to the bank of monitors and focused on the center screen.

And that's when he saw it.

Wearing suspenders over an unbuttoned shirt, Ulster was still bumping and grinding to the Latin beat, completely lost in the rhythm.

One, two, step, thrust! One, two, step, thrust!

Winston sighed and turned off the monitor before anyone else could see.

Jones growled in frustration as he retreated to the whiteboard in the college classroom. Since he couldn't get through to Jarkko verbally, he opted to take a different approach. He planned to write a few sentences on the board, which Jarkko could read aloud.

To make room for his grammar lesson, Jones first had to erase his name and the subject of the class. He grabbed the dry eraser from the metal tray and tried to erase the giant letters, but for some reason, they stayed put. He pushed harder and harder until he literally strained from the effort, but the damn letters wouldn't come off.

"What the fuck?" Jones mumbled under his breath.

"What is wrong?" Jarkko asked from his seat.

"The damn marker won't erase."

"Which marker?"

"The black marker."

"Oh," Jarkko said. "That's David's marker."

Jones raised an eyebrow. "What do you mean it's 'David's marker'?"

"Jonathon tells Jarkko that David is secret racist and will only use black marker on whiteboard, so Jarkko gets here early and replaces other markers with special black marker from Jonathon."

"Nooo!" Jones shouted.

"Yessss!" Jarkko replied. To prove his point, he held up a rainbow of dry-erase markers from his seat in the front row. "Jarkko did good, no?"

Jones groaned and looked closer at his marker. As he suspected, it was a permanent marker that wouldn't be coming off the whiteboard anytime soon.

Suddenly, everything made sense.

The grammar lesson. The college campus. The confiscated weapon.

Jones was the victim of a practical joke.

One in which he had unwittingly vandalized a classroom with his own name.

"Shit!" Jones said as he hustled toward the door. "Class dismissed."

Josh McNutt charged into the void and was confused by his surroundings. He quickly raised his rifle, ready to open fire. "Where the hell am I? Where'd everybody go?"

Jack Cobb rolled his eyes as he stepped across the threshold and grabbed his friend. "Josh, you're such an idiot. You're in the wrong series."

"Oh!" McNutt said as they headed back to *The Hunters*. "That explains it."

Winston glanced up and down the hallway to make sure he was alone before he punched in the security code to the Forbidden Room. The door popped open, and he stepped inside the chamber where Ulster was now twerking, totally oblivious to Winston's presence.

"Sir," Winston called out while closing the door behind him. "Sir!"

Ulster heard his butler's voice and instantly froze in place. Before turning around, he asked, "How long have you been standing there?"

"Long enough," Winston said as he walked over to the touch-screen and turned off the music. "What have I told you about that song?"

Ulster lowered his head in shame. "The lambada is the forbidden dance."

"Exactly!" Winston said as he rolled up his sleeves. "Besides, I prefer the Bee Gees."

With a touch of a button, disco music filled the room, and the surprisingly agile butler started to wiggle and gyrate, much to the amusement of his employer.

Inside the war room at the Pentagon, the President of the United States tried to gain control of the meeting as admirals, generals, and administrators of varying ranks shouted at each other across the long table. Tension was at an all-time high, as the weeklong crisis in the Far East turned uglier by the minute.

"The nuclear option has to be available!"

"Not unless he fires first!"

"Send in the Pacific fleet!"

"Not without air support!"

With the fate of the world hanging in the balance, the main door swung open, and in walked Randy Raskin. Wearing noise-cancelling headphones, his fuzzy blue bathrobe, and slippers in the shape of panther heads, he whistled a tune as he trudged across the carpeted floor toward the mini-fridge in the corner. He opened it up and was appalled by the sight.

Suddenly angry, Raskin slammed the refrigerator door shut.

Silence filled the room as everyone focused on the elite hacker.

Raskin ripped off his headphones. "*Who* drank my Mountain Dew?"

No one dared to move, not with the alpha male in the room.

As his indignation grew to rage, Raskin picked up a chair and hurled it against the wall. "Come clean now, or I swear to God that your porn habits, your extra-marital emails, and every other cyber secret you've been keeping will be sent to every journalist in the country by midnight. You know I can do it, so I'll ask again: *who the fuck drank my Mountain Dew?*"

A two-star general timidly raised his hand. "Sorry, sir. That was me."

Raskin strode over to him and slapped him across the face. "That is completely unacceptable! Take off your stars, and get the fuck out!"

The general started to argue, but before he could utter a word in his defense, he felt the cold judgment of his peers as they stared at him in disgust. He turned to the Commander in Chief, hoping for a last-second reprieve, but it would not be granted.

The president stood and pointed at the door. "You heard the man. Get the fuck out!"

Manley Borg—Malta's most famous porn star—took his spoon and dipped it into the steaming bowl of chowder as Jarkko watched from across the table. Gathered around them was the entire kitchen staff from the restaurant in Birgu, all of them waiting for the final verdict.

Borg closed his eyes as he tasted the creamy substance, before he slowly and seductively licked the utensil clean. Then, with a satisfied grin on his face, he opened his eyes and focused his gaze on the anxious Finn.

"Well?" Jarkko demanded.

Borg nodded. "You're right. This soup *is* better than a blowjob."

Ulster sat next to Jarkko on the vinyl bench and gently patted his knee. He could tell from the look on the fisherman's face that he was unsure about this course of action.

"I know you're scared," Ulster said in a calming tone, "but I promise you'll be fine."

Jarkko took a deep breath. "Jarkko is used to being on other end of equation."

Ulster nodded at the irony. "I realize that, but drastic times require drastic measures."

"Okay," he said in acceptance. "Jarkko is ready. Now what?"

Ulster smiled. "Just put them in and wait to be kissed by a hundred lips."

Jarkko squirmed as he dunked his bare feet in the lukewarm vat of water at the fish salon, a popular spa in Malta. Within seconds, dozens of red garra—a variety of toothless carp often called *nibble fish*—started eating the dead skin from Jarkko's toes. After seeing his friend's nasty feet aboard the yacht, Ulster had insisted on a pedicure of some kind, and this was the only joint in St. Julian's that was willing to accommodate their special needs.

"It tickles," Jarkko said with delight. "It actually tickles!"

"Glad to hear it," Ulster said as he signaled to the spa attendant. "Unfortunately, the *Garra rufa* is just the warm-up. For feet that look like yours, sometimes a larger species is needed to get the job done, which is why I had these flown in from South America."

Without saying a word, the attendant dumped in a bucket of much larger fish before hustling away from the carnage that was about to occur.

Ulster leaned closer to examine the impending scene. "Say hello to *Serrasalmus rhombeus*. Or as they're more commonly known to anglers, the black piranha."

Before he could object, Jarkko felt a nibble. Then a bite. Then a wave of agony as the water turned red from the most aggressive pedicure in history.

"Excellent!" Ulster said as Jarkko screamed in pain. "I can see bone!"

Jones ran back into the Maltese classroom, armed with his permanent marker. Instead of completely crossing out his own name, he made a quick alteration to PROFESSOR JONES.

Thirty seconds later, it read:

PROFESSOR JONES:
BEST. TEACHER. EVER.

SEND ME THE BILL,
JONATHON PAYNE

Then Jones turned out the lights and dashed out of the room.

ABOUT THE AUTHOR

Chris Kuzneski is the international bestselling author of twelve novels, including his latest, *The Malta Escape*. His books have been translated into more than twenty languages and have sold millions of copies worldwide. Chris is the first (and only) adventure writer to win an ITW Thriller Award. Although he grew up in western Pennsylvania, he currently lives on the Gulf Coast of Florida where he will probably die alone because he spends way too much time watching movies and sports.

CONNECT WITH CHRIS

E-mail: chris@chriskuzneski.com

Facebook: www.facebook.com/chriskuzneski.books

Twitter: www.twitter.com/chriskuzneski

Website: www.chriskuzneski.com

CPSIA information can be obtained
at www.ICGtesting.com
Printed in the USA
LVHW031220060119
602927LV00005B/700/P